She was the tou... *legendary son. From the beginning, the sparks began to fly.*

Matt captured Sam's face and bent toward her. For an instant she heard the cheers of his buddies, but then the man's mouth covered hers.

Shameful seconds passed. Suddenly she felt his tongue take a turn to the erotic, and hers followed right along. With a forceful push, she broke away and glared up at him. He had tricked her into running to his aid!

"It seems you've never heard the story of the boy who cried wolf," she said. "Perhaps the doctor won't be so quick to run to your side next time."

"It was worth the risk," he replied with a grin.

Forcing an amicable look to her face, she started to turn. "Oh," she added. "I nearly forgot this."

Without warning she struck a swift, stinging slap across his cheek. The other men dissolved in laughter as Matt Tyler's insolent smile drained away.

"Have a nice night," Sam tossed back, and felt his amber eyes following every step as she walked away.

SUSPICION OF INNOCENCE

by Barbara Parker

This riveting, high-tension legal thriller written by a former prosecutor draws you into hot and dangerous Miami, where Gail Connor is suddenly caught in the closing jaws of the legal system and is about to discover the other side of the law. . . .

Available now from **SIGNET**

RIVERBEND

Marcia Martin

AN ONYX BOOK

ONYX
Published by the Penguin Group
Penguin Books USA Inc., 375 Hudson Street,
New York, New York 10014, U.S.A.
Penguin Books Ltd, 27 Wrights Lane,
London W8 5TZ, England
Penguin Books Australia Ltd, Ringwood,
Victoria, Australia
Penguin Books Canada Ltd, 10 Alcorn Avenue,
Toronto, Ontario, Canada M4V 3B2
Penguin Books (N.Z.) Ltd, 182–190 Wairau Road,
Auckland 10, New Zealand

Penguin Books Ltd, Registered Offices:
Harmondsworth, Middlesex, England

First published by Onyx, an imprint of Dutton Signet,
a division of Penguin Books USA Inc.

First Printing, December, 1994
10 9 8 7 6 5 4 3 2 1

PUBLISHER'S NOTE
This is a work of fiction. Names, characters, places, and incidents either are the product of the author's imagination or are used fictitiously, and any resemblance to actual persons, living or dead, events, or locales is entirely coincidental.

For my first audience,
my sisters Kerry and Sherry,
who taught me the joy of storytelling

Thanks and acknowledgment to

James F. Alderman, M.D.

Page Hudson, M.D.

Patrick McIntosh,
U.S. Fish & Wildlife Service

Jane Baker Pasquini

John A. Pasquini, M.D.

and
Chateau Elan Winery

I have set before you life and death; blessing and cursing; therefore choose life, that both thou and thy seed may live.

—Deuteronomy 30:19

Prologue

Riverbend, Georgia owed its existence to the powerful
Tyler family of Savannah. Among their ancestors numbered a signer of the Declaration of Independence, and
various statesmen; among their assets numbered land
holdings in several states, and an empire founded on the
shipping industry. Century-old ties along the Eastern
seaboard had seen them safely through the Civil War that
decimated many Southern fortunes.

It was in 1870 that Charles Tyler married a woman
from the wine country of France, and returned home
with a supply of cuttings as well as a bride. Purchasing
vast acreage along the Savannah River, he founded
Riverbend Vineyards, and a town was born.

By 1920, when Prohibition struck, the countryside
chateau was home to Charles' great-grandson Jonathan,
his wife, Mary, and their young son, John. As always, the
Tylers were the talk of Riverbend, as was their Haitian
nanny, Juda—a striking woman with caramel-colored skin
who'd mysteriously appeared in Riverbend shortly after
the birth of young John, and somehow managed to en-
trench herself in the household.

Servants talked pityingly of Mary, who was slight and
pale and had never recovered from a difficult childbirth.
They even forgave her habitual visits to the corn liquor

still. On the other hand, they whispered scathingly of
Juda, who was shameless not only in her lusting for Jonathan Tyler, but also in her open practice of voodoo. The
master, they said—who had traveled widely and was
somewhat of a philosopher—was tolerant of Juda's pagan
religion, and apparently unaware of her adulterous desires.

It was said that Juda was in league with the devil, and
that she had the "evil eye." None at the chateau would
dare to cross her—even when they became certain that
the Haitian witch was casting spells against poor Mary.
One morning, cow dung was found smeared on the mistress's bedroom door; one afternoon, the chamber maid
discovered the bones of a human hand carefully arranged
on the dresser. And then, on a stormy night in April
1922, the mistress, herself, found a slaughtered chicken
on her pillow.

The master was down below when frail, little Mary—
wearing no more than a nightdress and swaying on her
feet from too much moonshine—challenged the fearsome
Juda and ordered her out of the house. The entire household staff was watching as the master came out of the
study, and was obviously shocked when Juda raced down
the stairs and threw herself into his arms. Abruptly disengaging himself, Jonathan Tyler stepped back, and the
rest of the story made its way word by word into
Riverbend history.

"You cast me away, then?" Juda challenged.

"My duty is to my wife and my son," he answered.

"And what of your heart?" she railed.

"My heart has never belonged to any woman other
than my wife. I think it best you pack your things, Juda."

"To hell with my things!" Stalking to the doorway, Juda
drew it open and whirled. The stormy wind whipped at
her skirt and hair as she raised a fist. "And to hell with
you, Jonathan Tyler! You and your descendants. Your family will wither like worm-eaten grapes on the vine. As for
your wife"—she looked up the staircase where Mary
clung to the banister—"You are no more, missus," she

pronounced. "Even now you stand there as a shadow. By the next fullness of the moon you will do yourself in and be dead." Then, with a final glare for all within the house, Juda disappeared into the rainy darkness.

By the next morning the story had spread throughout Riverbend. Six days later, when Mary Tyler hanged herself in the wine cellars, the gossip reached a fevered pitch. No one had the nerve, however, to openly condemn a Tyler for committing a cardinal sin, or to object when she was buried in hallowed ground—alongside devout Christians—in the cemetery of Riverbend Baptist Church.

It was public knowledge that Juda moved into an outlying farmhouse, where she lived in notoriety with a sharecropper who'd been sweet on her since she arrived. Everyone steered clear of her, including Jonathan Tyler who—after padlocking the wine cellars—packed up his son, returned to the family home in Savannah, and never set foot in Riverbend again.

When Prohibition was repealed in 1933, the question rose as to whether or not the Tylers would reopen the vineyards. They didn't. Although caretakers were paid to keep up the house, the winery remained closed, and the acres of grapevines grew wild.

Years passed, generations came and went, and the people of Riverbend continued to take interest in tracking the hard luck of the town's founding family. Although their fortune flourished, their numbers dwindled. There were "freak accidents," "tragic illnesses," and each time news of death reached Riverbend, old-timers repeated the story of the night the Tylers were cursed.

From time to time, some family member or another made the trip from Savannah to visit the old chateau. But they never stayed long. And even those visits came to a halt as the clan diminished.

Finally, it was told, there were but three Tylers left.

And then suddenly, after a plane crash in the Appalachians, there was only one . . . the one who came back.

Chapter One

In the filtered light of shaded windows her suntanned body appeared brown as toast, her breasts pale and luminous . . . like scoops of cream topped with cherries. He gathered one in his mouth, and the taste of perfumed flesh mingled with a lingering flavor of bourbon.

With a slow grind of his hips, he plunged deep. She arched, her legs clenching his waist. Another move of his hips and her spasms began.

Matt grabbed fistfuls of sheet, steadying himself as the familiar, swelling throb swept him from head to toe. When climax shook him, he would have called her name if he could have remembered it.

"God!" he exploded instead. As the shuddering subsided, he opened his eyes and looked down. She was smiling lazily up at him, her blond hair fanning across the pillow.

"*God* is right," she mumbled. "I've died and gone to heaven."

His thoughts spinning, Matt returned her smile and watched her eyelids close. A minute passed as he tried to pinpoint exactly who the hell she was and where the hell he was. Oh, yeah. The polo match. Charleston. He was in Charleston.

The sound of light snoring drew his attention back to the woman. She was out cold. No wonder. They'd been drinking since noon. He'd spotted her at the refreshment cabana before the match, and from the moment their eyes met, he'd known where it would lead.

Ellen. No ... Eileen! That was it. Eileen.

Carefully withdrawing, he pressed a kiss to her cheek, climbed out of bed, and gathered his clothes. He dressed in the next room where he could look out the patio door. The sun was low, a veil of shadow spreading across the grounds of the unfamiliar apartment complex. Pulling on his boots, Matt strode to the glass and peered across palm-trimmed lawns studded with flumes of pampas.

It was a time like many others—coming around after too much drink in an unknown place ... with an unknown woman.

A feeling of loneliness stole over him. Eileen was a nice enough woman. Pretty, too. But lately it felt like he'd stood and looked out too many unfamiliar windows, and the thought of striking up another affair seemed pretty pointless.

There was more than this. He knew it. He'd seen it in other men. Though his own so-called marriage was a fiasco, he knew a few happily paired-off guys who might complain to their chums about being "tethered," but always went serenely home to their wives. To hear them tell it, Matt Tyler lived every man's dream—answering to no one, footloose and free to go with any lady who caught his fancy.

Lately he'd been figuring it was the tethered ones who were lucky. They had things he'd never known, things that lasted—like a real home, real family, real love. What he had was an assortment of mistresses and an estranged wife he couldn't bear the thought of. As for love, there was only the soil of Riverbend.

Love. The word sounded in his mind with both the ring of a sneer and the whisper of longing. Riverbend

Vineyards was thriving, as was the freewheeling social
life he'd led for years. It should be enough. But it wasn't.
For all practical purposes, he'd been on his own for as
long as he could remember, and had been envied for that
freedom just as long. But he was turning forty in a couple
of months, and there was no denying that a curiosity
about "something more" had turned into a hunger the
past few years.

Maybe some people just weren't born the settling-
down kind, he theorized. Maybe for some people, such
things as love and family just weren't in the cards. . . .

The thought of his buddies yanked him back to reality.
Picturing their shocked faces if they caught wisecracking,
skirt-chasing Matt Tyler in the midst of such romanticiz-
ing, he turned from the patio door and rubbed at his
forehead. The effects of the bourbon were receding, his
head clear but for the pounding in his temples. With a
parting look into the silent bedroom, he took note of the
apartment number and drove to a florist shop he knew
that was open seven days a week.

Roses. Eileen was the type to like roses.

Having placed the order, Matt selected a calling card.
Thanks for a memorable afternoon, he wrote and, sealing it
inside the envelope, almost penned her name on the outside. On second thought he left the envelope blank, instructed the guy to deliver the flowers the next morning,
and turned onto the southwest highway leading home.

Maybe her name was *Ellen* after all.

St. Elizabeth's Hospital
Boston, Massachusetts

"We're losing him!"

In the cloistered operating room, the anesthesiologist's
voice rang like an alarm. Bracing the incision with one
gloved hand, Sam briskly extended the palm of the other.

"Clamp," she said, the command crisp and distinct despite the barrier of a surgeon's mask.

Within fleeting, life-or-death seconds her sure fingers averted the hemorrhage, stirring a murmur of appreciation from the surgically masked team of the O.R.

"Pulse is gaining," the anestheosiologist pronounced a moment later. Within a half hour the surgery was completed. Sam stepped back from the table.

"Would you like to finish up, Dr. Bennett?" she asked.

"It would be my honor, Dr. Kelly," he replied with a smile in his voice.

"Be well, Mr. Monahan," she murmured to the sedated patient, and walked into the washroom, her step heavy with the knowledge that this was the last time—for a long time, at least—that she would walk this path. For five years of training, and an additional two specializing in surgery, St. Elizabeth's had been home. And now she was leaving.

Stripping off the mask and gown, Sam moved to her locker and felt the dismal sensation grow heavier. She'd cleaned it out two weeks ago. All that remained were the jacket, shoes, and shoulder bag she would take with her. Sitting down on the bench, she pulled off worn sneakers, stuffed them in her bag, and slipped into the low-heeled pumps. She was straightening the cuffs of her jacket when the rest of the surgical team spilled into the locker room.

"Great job, Sam!" and "Well done, Doctor!" came the calls. "We're going to miss you, Sam," Will Bennett added, drawing her eye so that she was looking straight at him when he winked. "Y'all take care of yourself down yonder in Georgia, now, ya hear?"

Making a sour face, Sam stuck out her tongue and grinned, though—in truth—she'd never felt less like smiling. *Georgia.* The name drawled through her mind with syrupy sloth, sending chill-bumps scurrying along her arms. Tomorrow she was leaving Boston to live in Riverbend, Georgia, a tiny dot on the map smack in the middle of rural nowhere. She steeled herself against images of endless cornfields, rundown shacks, and tobacco-stained teeth.

When she'd applied for the government loan to begin

med school, the price of a year's service at a federal clinic
hadn't sounded like much. Now that the debt was due, the
phrase boomed like a cannon in her ears—*A YEAR!*

Her reverie was interrupted as John Thomason approached. Sam's fixed smile drooped, her gaze settling on
the twinkling eyes beneath the bushy white brows. In
the past two years John had been more than Chief of
Surgery, he'd been teacher, mentor, and friend.

"Thanks for giving your Sunday to Monahan," he said.

"There's no need for thanks," Sam replied. "I wanted
to be here. You know the feeling. After all, you're here,
too, aren't you?"

He smiled. "Couldn't miss the farewell performance of
my protegée, could I? You're flying out on Friday, right?"

She nodded. "The theory is I can use the long weekend to settle in, and have the clinic up and running
shortly after Labor Day. Of course, who knows? This is
the first time the National Health Service Corps has
placed anyone there."

"It should be quite a challenge. Don't forget to contact
Gary Brooks."

Sam smiled. When John heard where she was being
stationed, he called an old friend who was head of the orthopedic wing at Candler General in Savannah—the only
metropolitan area within a hundred miles of Riverbend.
Dr. Brooks had promised to line up a resident to cover
Sam's post over the Christmas holidays so that she could
come back to Boston.

"You couldn't have thought of a nicer going-away present," she said. "Knowing I can come home in a few
months almost makes the thought of leaving bearable."

"Good," John replied.

"I said *almost.*" Sam searched his smiling eyes. "I hate
the fact that I have to go, John."

"Likewise," he responded, his smile dying away. "I
crossed paths with Arch Reynolds last week. He took ill-
disguised glee in confiding that the Etheridge Center has
made you an offer."

Sam glanced away as the memory of Chad Etheridge

broke over her like a wave. "I didn't think it was worth mentioning," she said. "You know I'm coming back to Saint Elizabeth's."

"I would understand," John said, his voice low and quiet and for her ears only. "You're gifted, Sam. I've known it from the first time I saw you work. You can go as high as you want, cater to whatever clientele you want. For a superstar surgeon on the rise, the Etheridge Center is the place to be."

"My star can shine just fine from here."

He put a tender hand on her shoulder. "This will be my last effort to persuade you otherwise, and I make it only because I care about you. Don't you think I know why you're so deadset against anything tagged with the name, Etheridge?"

Of course, he knew. Everyone in Boston's medical community knew. Four years had passed since the affair splashed across the scandal sheets. Still, everyone remembered. Sometimes she felt the staff at St. Elizabeth's still thought of her as Chad's girl.

"What better way to get back at him than to use his facility as your own personal launch pad?" John added. "*If* you can get past your feelings."

"I *am* past my feelings," Sam returned. "Any feelings whatsoever. That's why I have no need to get back at anyone." He arched a doubtful brow. "It's the truth, John. I'm coming back to Saint Elizabeth's, and that's that."

Removing the hand from her shoulder, he gave her a sweet smile. "Well, then . . . I'll save your locker for you with pleasure."

"Thanks," Sam murmured. With a quick parting hug, she stepped around John, hurried out of surgery, and denied herself the bittersweetness of a backward look.

Mr. Monahan's surgery had taken longer than planned. By the time she left the hospital, the sun was going down. For six years her footsteps had turned methodically toward the modest apartment two blocks away. But that, too—like her locker—had been divested of anything pertaining to Samantha Kelly. There was the flash of an image of Chad smiling over his shoulder as she waved from the doorway ... Turning her back on the memory, Sam headed to the station and boarded the rail for Dorcester.

Still, Chad haunted her in a way she thought she'd crushed long ago. She told herself it was purely because he was part of all she was leaving behind. Sitting back, she watched the city flash past. For five more precious nights she would remain in the shelter of the family home where she—and seven brothers and sisters—had grown up. But on Friday night ... She didn't want to think about Friday night.

Getting off at the familiar stop, she walked the short distance to the stately old town house, and was shocked into speechlessness when Mother and Father ushered her into the parlor to a resounding chorus of *"Surprise!"*

Patrick and his wife, Kate, had come over from Brookline; James and his new bride, Helen, from Cambridge. Maureen, Bobby, Jerry, Erin, and Frances still lived in the old triple-decker. The entire Kelly brood had come together to wish her farewell. As Sam walked hesitantly forward, the lot of them converged on her, bestowing embraces that simultaneously filled her with warmth and fed a cold sense of dread.

A short while later she moved to a private corner, leaned back against the wall, and savored the scene as though she'd never again have the chance to see it. Beyond the windows overlooking the street, the sidewalk was bustling with neighbors taking the evening air and children playing a last round of hopscotch before being called in for the night. Inside, the cozy parlor was filled with familiar voices and laughter, and then the stirring notes of a Tchaikovsky overture as Mother was persuaded to the piano.

It was a time like many others. Sam could almost close her eyes and turn back the hands of the clock—almost pretend this was only one of countless birthday parties that had taken place in this parlor. Except this time the cake on the sideboard was inscribed with *Bon Voyage, Sam.* At the piano Father was standing behind the seat as usual, gazing over Mother's shoulder as she played. Sam must have seen him stand like that a thousand times. A lump gathered in her throat.

Growing up the eldest of eight children born to a bookshop owner and piano teacher, she may have had to do without the extravagances showered on some of her well-to-do schoolmates. But she'd always known she had something more important—a truly loving family, a truly happy home. And if there wasn't enough money for expensive trips and presents, there had always been enough for the ballet, the symphony, the theater. Mother and Father had stood firm on that—Boston was a "cultural oasis," and the Kellys were "Boston through and through."

Sam swallowed hard. There was no way to fathom how much she was going to miss them . . . how much she was going to miss *everything*—the hospital, the city, the aroma of fresh-baked rolls coming from Tony's Bakery down the street—

What did people eat in Georgia, anyway? Grits?

Glancing aside, she met her reflection in the mirror over the mantel. In the waning light, her auburn hair appeared dark and lifeless, her green eyes wide and startled, her normally pink cheeks pale as alabaster. God, she looked as scared as she felt.

Forcing a smile to her lips, Sam joined the group and did her best to ignore the sense of doom that trailed her from one minute to the next. But it was no good. She was going to *that place* in a few days, and there was no chasing the inevitability out of her mind. She almost wished she could walk out right now and be done with the pain of leaving.

She'd just finished cutting the cake when the doorbell rang. "I'll get it," Sam announced. Grabbing a napkin, she wiped frosting from her fingers as she walked out of the parlor.

"Yes?" she said, swinging the door wide . . . the expectant look freezing on her face.

"Hello, Sam." She hadn't heard that voice in four years. The sound of it jolted her.

"May I come in?" he added. "I brought you something."

Without waiting for permission, he stepped inside and held out a rather large package tied with a silver ribbon. Leaving the door purposely open, Sam held onto its edge and made no move to reach for the gift. Her hands were shaking, and she was determined he wouldn't see them. There he was, Chad Etheridge in all his perfect patrician fairness . . . suit perfectly tailored, hair perfectly styled, teeth perfectly straight and white as he smiled.

"Take it," he prodded. "I got this just for you."

"What is it? A peace offering?"

"Not a bad idea. Let's make peace. What do you say?"

"I say it's about four years too late for that."

His smile faded. "All right. If you won't open it, I will."

Tearing off the ribbon and paper, Chad produced a doctor's bag and thrust it into her hands. It was beautifully crafted of the finest black leather, and just below the handle was a brass plate engraved with the designation: *Samantha Kelly, M.D.*

"Big-city surgeons don't carry bags," he said. "But considering where you're going, I thought this might come in handy."

She looked up to meet the remembered eyes. Clear and blue, they appeared as sincere as ever—incapable, one would think, of concealing murky secrets. The noise of music and voices continued to stream from the parlor, but the sounds grew dim as Sam remembered.

She was beginning her third year of med school when Chad—grandson of the founder of the famed Etheridge Medical Center—appeared at St. Elizabeth's for a final year of specialized training. When they met, it was love at first sight. For seven months Chad virtually lived at her small off-campus apartment. Their plans, she'd thought, were solemn vows—to marry, to build a practice together, Etheridge and Etheridge. . . .

How quickly vows could be shattered—all in the time it took to open a door.

She'd thought nothing of the camera bug who snapped

their picture one rare night when they'd gone to dinner at one of Boston's popular spots. A week later she'd opened the apartment door to a barrage of flashing camera bulbs. Her horrified expression had appeared in newspaper after newspaper—along with an accounting of Chad Etheridge's med school romance ... Chad Etheridge of the Beacon Hill Etheridges ... Chad Etheridge, long-time fiancé of Miss Constance Wellington, an aristocratic beauty who claimed bloodlines as unimpeachable as his own.

"Do you like the bag?" he asked. "I commissioned it from Swaine Adeney on my last trip to London."

Sam barely heard as her thoughts whirled. Mere days after the scandal hit, the Society page headline announced that Chad and his fiancée had set a wedding date. Sam remembered him showing up at the apartment that night—words tumbling from his mouth in a rampant stream. She'd had no idea what he was saying. All she'd been able to hear was her own voice booming: "Get out!" The two words had been all she could muster, though she remembered repeating them over and over.

"How could I have been so stupid?" she mumbled.

"What?"

Sam looked up with new alertness. "How could I have failed to realize what was going on all those times you didn't take me to Beacon Hill?" His only reply was a knitting of sandy brows.

"The Halloween ball," she went on, gaining steam. "The New Year's dance, even your own birthday party. Each time your excuses sounded so plausible. The truth was you were keeping me a secret from the almighty Etheridges. The truth is you knew all along it would never work out for us."

"Maybe I wanted to pretend that it could."

"Maybe you shouldn't pretend with someone else's life!"

Chad offered a smile that looked more sheepish than anything else. "I see the years have done nothing to soften that sharp tongue of yours, *or* the Irish temper. That's okay. I used to find them both entirely stimulating. Still do."

Sam glared as she shook her head. "Go away, Chad."

His smile disappeared. "No."

"There's nothing to be said between us."

"That's not true. There's an apology to be said. I'm sorry, Sam. But I had no choice."

"That's not how I see it."

"The marriage was arranged by the families years ago."

"You should have told me."

"Then I'd have lost you," he replied quietly. "What did you expect me to do? Give up my inheritance instead?"

"If that's what it took."

After a moment's hesitation Chad gripped her by the shoulders and stared into her eyes. "I never spent a day without thinking of you, Sam. I followed your career, applauded your successes, took pride as you added feather after feather to your cap. You've worked hard, and you're on top. It isn't fair to ask you to waste a year. I brought you a going-away present, yes. But the truth is I hope you never use it. I don't want you to go to Georgia, Sam."

His touch had made her heart race. Doing her best to ignore it, Sam twisted out of his grasp.

"You don't want me to go? How can you show up after four years and say such a thing?"

"You know what those clinics are like—never enough equipment, never enough of anything. The kind of salary the government pays barely covers operating expenses, not to mention start-up costs. Do you really want to spend your first practicing year in the middle of nowhere under such conditions?"

"Whether I want to or not doesn't figure in," she returned. "I made a deal with the government. They gave a year's funding; I give a year's service. That's it."

"That doesn't have to be *it.*"

"No?"

"No. I've talked to a few people. Strings can be pulled, records mislaid. If you take a post at the Etheridge Center, you can come to work as early as next week. Or, like any sensible surgeon fresh out of training, maybe you'd prefer a nice, long vacation—"

"Vacation!" Sam interrupted. "You're talking like a madman."

"Maybe so. It's certainly true I'm mad about you."

"Get to the point, Chad."

His eyes bored into hers. "The point is that ever since I heard you were leaving Boston, I haven't been able to think of anything else. The point is I want us to be together."

Sam regarded him in doubting silence, a fearful hope slicing its way through her as a swell of voices rose from the parlor. Taking the medical bag from her hands, Chad dropped it heedlessly to the floor, drew her into the privacy of the darkened stoop, and gathered her up in a passionate kiss. The evening was cool, but Sam felt as though she were melting. When Chad finally tore his mouth from hers, he continued to hold her tightly.

"I've missed you," he mumbled against her hair. "All these years I kept up with you from afar. Plenty of guys came around, but you never dated anyone more than a few times, never became involved. I told myself it was because you missed me, too. Because no one could take my place. Was I right?"

"It's not that simple—"

"I don't want to dwell in the past," he broke in. "I want to talk about the future. Think of it, Sam. Things could be just as we planned—working together, being together. Maybe we could even get a place on the shore, the kind we used to dream about."

Pulling back, Sam peered at him. "Are you telling me you've left your wife?" The fire in Chad's eyes died, and as it did Sam pushed out of his arms, the old hurt banging at her chest with new life.

"I can't do that," he answered finally.

"I see. So, what you're suggesting is keeping me a secret all over again."

He glanced aside before meeting her eyes once more. "What's more important, Sam? Being my wife, or being the woman I love? I'm offering you everything I have to give," he concluded in a tone of great earnestness.

"I'm sure you are. Unfortunately, that's never been enough." Even in the gathering darkness Sam discerned the look of anger that swept to his face.

"I'm offering you a way out of Georgia," he returned evenly. "A way to flash onto the Boston medical scene like a comet. You can't deny it's what you want. To be the best in Boston—that was always your goal."

"Yes, but not at the cost of every shred of honor I have. Tamper with federal records? Live in the shadows as your mistress? It may sound like a good deal to you, but not to me."

"I imagine a month in the godforsaken wilderness will change your point of view," Chad snapped. "My card is in the medical bag. I'll be waiting for your call."

A few quick steps and Sam was back inside; a single swing and the door slammed in his handsome face; a swift kick, and the expensive leather bag sailed half the distance to the parlor.

Following its flight, her vision lit on her mother, who was standing quietly nearby. It was then that Sam noticed her eyes were brimming with tears. Blinking them back, she brought a masking smile to her face.

"Hello, Mother," she said brightly. "How long have you been standing there?"

"Long enough to see Chad Etheridge spirit you out the door."

"Yes, well . . ." Despite her best efforts, Sam's smiling lips began to tremble. "Leopards don't change their spots, I suppose."

Her mother shook her head. "My poor, strong Sam," she said tenderly. "You don't have to be strong *all* the time, you know."

When she opened her arms, Sam stepped inside them and wept—her streaming tears laden with all the sorrow of what was past, and all the dread of what lay just ahead.

Chapter Two

Friday, September 3

Thanks to the influence of Tyler forefathers, the state highway took a turn north of town—respectfully skirting the vineyards, house, and grounds for a good two miles before resuming a northwesterly path paralleling the Savannah River.

Until last spring the fork that led into Riverbend Vineyards had been a dirt road, one that had borne the ruts of ancient wagon wheels as well as modern tractors. Now, swelling off the highway in a graceful curve, newly paved asphalt streaked through the green fields like a black snake. And at the trellised arch, which had presided over the entrance for more than a century, a new sign was going up.

With George planted on a ladder at one end, and Drew at the other, Matt backed away and took a critical look. A dozen feet of fresh-painted billboard carted all the way from Savannah, the sign announced RIVERBEND VINEYARDS in tall red letters against a white background bordered with a green length of trailing grapevine.

Planting his hands on his hips, Matt drew a long breath of satisfaction. That was more like it. Now, the place looked like what it was—the most up-and-coming vineyards in the entire Southeast.

His memory flashed on the time over a decade ago when he and Drew and George had joined forces. The vines had been a wild thatch of untended growth; the winery hopelessly outdated and broken down. Everyone had said they were crazy. The odds had only sharpened Matt's resolve, and he sensed it had been the same for his partners. All three of them had needed something.

Like himself, his college football buddy, Drew Pierce, had never gotten his feet on the ground after leaving school. George Waters, a local man twenty years their senior, had always hungered for the opportunity to do more than scrape a living for a family of six from a little farm.

Together, it seemed, they had what it took—Drew, a quick adeptness at anything he put his hand to, from carpentry to dealing with clients, just like when he was quarterbacking at Georgia. From George had come a steady patience and uncanny understanding of the soil that was almost mystical. As for Matt, he guessed the only way to label what he had supplied was to call it *drive*—the nonstop, head-on, whatever-it-takes kind. And of course, he'd provided the land itself.

His gaze swept beyond the sign to the rolling, leafy acres that were Riverbend. He'd given her days of blistering his back while he made sure she had water, nights of choking rain and mud-filled boots as he sandbagged her banks against flash flood. And look what she'd given back. God, he was proud.

"Hey, big brother!" Drew yelled. "Do we have to stay perched up here all day? It's hot as blue blazes!"

Matt's eyes focused on Drew who, like himself, wore a hat but no shirt beneath the high sun. George, on the other hand, who was black as the ace of spades, was clothed against sunburn in his usual long-sleeved cotton workshirt and dungarees.

"Just a couple more minutes, okay, boys?" Matt called.

"To hell with that!" Drew erupted. "I'm not staying up here like a damn chicken on a spit!"

Matt laughed. "Come on down! It looks great!" Once again he directed a sweeping look across the face of the vineyards. "Just great," he repeated as Drew and George joined him.

The three of them stood there for a quiet moment, appreciating the sight, thinking their own thoughts . . . until Drew snatched off his hat and released a war whoop.

"Who'd have believed it ten years ago, huh?" he challenged.

"Hell, who'd have believed it *five* years ago?" Matt returned with a chuckle.

"Hell, my accountant wouldn't have believed it *one* year ago," George commented with a rolling laugh.

"I say we take the rest of the day off," Drew suggested.

"You're *always* saying that," George said on a teasing note. "This time I agree with you, though. The fields are in good shape, the hands lined up, a long weekend on the rise."

"Come on, Matt," Drew urged. "What do you say? Let's get cleaned up, go into town, and buy each other a Labor Day celebration."

Matt's smile drooped as he remembered the chore he'd avoided for three days. Lucy. He had to call Lucy. If he didn't, she might show up in Riverbend with an entourage of attorneys.

"You two go ahead," he said. "Maybe I'll see you later."

As Drew and George loaded ladders in the truck and drove off toward the winery, Matt took his time retrieving his shirt and walking over to his Jeep. Like the truck and all other company vehicles, the Jeep was a fresh-painted white, its door emblazoned with the red and green of the vineyards logo. Once again his spirits swelled, lifting him as in a sunny bubble from the dark depths toward which the mere thought of Lucy dragged him.

Leaning against the cab, Matt scanned his lands once

more. Critics had said he was mad to pay such wages to common hands. But the result showed. He had close to three hundred happy employees now, counting the pickers that would come on line in another week. The crop was thriving, the winery humming, and the orders filled in the past month outstripped the first five years put together.

With a last glance at the new sign, Matt climbed into the Jeep and moved off at a reverent pace toward the buildings on the distant hill. It was a moment of victory. He savored it as he looked across the acres and breathed in the scent of the fields. For it was only a moment. Harvest lay ahead.

She'd been told a vehicle had been reserved for her use, and would be waiting at Savannah International Airport. What Sam found was a rustic white van with a fair share of dents, a broken radio, and the word AMBULANCE painted in fading letters on both sides. Still, it started up without complaint and had a full tank.

As the engine warmed, she reviewed the map she'd been carrying for days. Not that there was much to review. There was only one sensible course to Riverbend, which lay fifty miles northwest where the Savannah River took a curve. Sam checked her watch. Four o'clock. It would be after five by the time she got there.

Donning dark glasses against the bright afternoon sun, she shifted into gear, drove away from the airport, and swiftly left behind the civilized outskirts of Savannah. The country highway took her into a scene more intense than what she'd imagined. No cars. No people. Just empty fields stretching away from the road on both sides as far as the eye could see, the sunlight blazing from a pale sky to parch weeds that drooped without a flutter in motionless air.

Every now and then she passed a lonely thicket of trees, a dilapidated fruit stand, a stone chimney presiding over the crumbled remains of a house. The occasional barn that continued to stand typically displayed a side wall painted with a weathered advertisement from days long gone—an hour-glass bottle hawking Coca-Cola for ten cents ... an imp wearing a cap labeled "Speedy" offering a sparkling glass of antacid.

There was a feeling of utter desolation, and the spine-tingling sensation that this went on without end, the heat sealing it all around her in a shimmering vacuum of silence.

Both windows were down, but they delivered only hot wind. Having discarded her jacket, Sam was dressed in a light cotton blouse and slacks. Still, perspiration gathered on her lip and trickled down her back. She longed to pull over and pin her hair off her neck, but didn't dare risk stopping the van. What if the damn thing stalled, and she got stuck in the twilight zone forever?

Brushing the bangs from her brow with the back of a hand, she drove doggedly on. The sooner she reached her destination, the better. Riverbend had to be better than this.

She hadn't thought she'd be sorry to reach the end of the silent brown fields, but she was. Replacing them with unsettling abruptness was swampland—the trees gray and oppressive, the water covered with slime, the cries of unseen birds more lonely than silence. It seemed as though she traveled leagues, though it must have been only several miles before the vista opened up to reveal the Savannah River—broad and shining and flowing lazily through the landscape as it must have done since the beginning of time.

Passing a "Reduce Speed" sign, Sam rounded a curve and came upon the town. Heralded at the south end by a sprawling place labeled CARTER LUMBER, Riverbend was, at a glance, a picture-book rendition of a sleepy, Southern town. Though the primary streets were paved, there were side lanes of cobblestones, the lot of them lined with live oak dripping veils of Spanish moss that looked as though they hadn't been disturbed since the Civil War.

Along the main road, tall, old houses with columned

porches were interspersed among quaint buildings—
Town Hall and Jail, Pettigrew's Mercantile, Simon's Pro-
duce, Riverbend Bank, an inn with a sign announcing
Rae's Place. . . .

There was no doubt the place was picturesque, but as
Sam continued slowly down the main street, she was
struck as much by its emptiness as its antiquated charm.
Five-thirty in the afternoon, the beginning of a holiday
weekend, and not a soul to be seen? *Weird,* she thought,
a feeling of eeriness prickling down her spine and along
her limbs. It was as though she'd escaped the twilight
zone of deserted countryside only to enter an enchanted,
abandoned village.

Toward the end of the street, a white church with a
steeple overlooked an old cemetery fenced with black
iron, and populated with the stone markers and monu-
ments of "raised graves" that were typical in a low-
country region. She'd been to New Orleans once, and it
had similar cemeteries. In fact, there was a sort of New
Orleans, wrought-iron and Spanish-moss flavor about the
whole of Riverbend. Only New Orleans had people. Sam
had yet to see a single person in Riverbend, although she
had the creepy sensation of being watched by invisible
eyes.

Finally, beyond the church—and planted prominently
in the middle of the street so that the road branched
around it—a pretty town square remained miraculously
green in the heat, its oak-shaded lawns featuring a gazebo as well as benches and picnic tables. Beyond the
commons, the town came to an end, and the street became, once more, the highway.

Circling around the square, Sam headed back the way
she'd come. The house she sought had a Main Street address, and this was undoubtedly the most "main street"
in town. As the first corps doctor assigned to Riverbend,
she was to set up the clinic in the Main Street residence
of the late Dr. Daly, who had served the community for
forty years. Her heart sank when she spotted the sprawling, two-story house with boarded windows.

Pulling over directly across from the inn she'd noted earlier, Sam peered with dismay through the van window. The fence was down, the yard overgrown, and though it once must have been a grand structure with an elegant six-column verandah, the house now sagged at every seam.

Turning off the engine, she made herself walk briskly along the weeded path and up the brick steps. The key she'd been sent turned with creaking complaint in the lock. Taking a deep breath, she pushed open the door.

Her first impression was that everything was covered with sheets. Those surfaces left uncovered, including the floor, were blanketed with dust, and a smell of must hung in the air. As she moved inside, the sound of her steps rang against absolute quiet.

Instinct must have led her into the room on the right, which she immediately recognized as the site of Daly's practice. Pulling the sheets from two fixtures that seemed to divide the room in halves, Sam uncovered black-leather-topped examining tables with porcelain bases and sheets of white paper rolled across their surfaces. There was also a sink, a desk finished with outdated lab equipment, shelves devoid of anything but a few useless items like glass hypodermics, and a supply closet whose major asset was an X-ray machine that looked as though it belonged in a museum.

No oxygen. No EKG or IV setup. No defibrillator, or autoclave, or lifesaving "crash cart" for victims of cardiac arrest, shock, or seizure. Not to mention the lack of linens, bandages, drugs, vaccines, antibiotics. . . .

She had the number of a medical supply company in Savannah. Sam only hoped they were well stocked and quick on delivery; right now the only conceivable tools at her disposal were in the black bag Chad had given her. He was right. The salary paid by the corps wouldn't come close to covering the start-up expenses that were about to come out of her pocket.

Taking brisk strides out of the room, Sam made a tour of the house, snatching sheets off sofas and chairs and tables as she went. In addition to the examining rooms, the downstairs floor offered a parlor/waiting room, kitchen, and half bath. The upstairs had three bedrooms—only one of which had a bed—and a full bath. One of the other two bedrooms was crammed with spare furniture and boxes. The third, obviously Daly's office, was monopolized by a huge desk stacked with files but for a small square of surface where he must have done his writing. Faded photographs lined the walls. Books and memorabilia bulged from built-in shelves to fill chairs and corners.

Sam moved to the head of the staircase and peered dismally down the elegant, dust-ridden banister. Furnished with the faded opulence of years gone by, the late Dr. Daly's house was big and rambling and filthy. She'd known he passed away several years ago; she hadn't realized no one would have set foot in the place since. It looked as though no one had put a mop to it in twenty years.

Going back downstairs, she entered the kitchen and turned the faucet to behold a sputtering, rust-ridden stream. After a minute or so, the water ran clear. But it did nothing to lift her spirits. So, the water worked. Thank you very much. Jerking the knob back to its resting place, she walked into the neighboring room and flipped a switch. A glow of light appeared under a sheet in the far corner. Electricity, too. How gratifying.

Spotting an antiquated phone on a side table, Sam stepped over and lifted the receiver. Nothing. It didn't matter that she suddenly recalled having been notified that there would be no service until the day after Labor Day. The silent phone was all that was needed to trigger cataclysms of rage and despair.

Slamming down the receiver, she swept the room with a scathing look. Damn! Damn! Damn! Loneliness coiled around her, tightening like a dreadful snake as she pictured home and family and everything familiar that had suddenly ceased being her reality. *This* was reality. *This* . . . mess.

She stood there a moment more, feeling angry and hopeless—until an image of her mother dawned. *The job won't get any easier as you stand there and look at it,* she always said. Even so, Sam thought belligerently, she absolutely was *not* spending the night in this boarded-up tomb. The shock of seeing it was enough for one day. Tomorrow would have to be soon enough to begin the massive task of putting things right.

She walked out on the porch and cast a look at the inn across the street. Shaded by live oak and graced by white columns, the two-story, old-brick structure also featured saloon doors and a boardwalk out front. A curious blend of Old West and Old South, Rae's Place had definite charm. Sam prayed it had a vacancy as well. Returning to the van, she'd just opened the back when the sound of a scream made her look up with a start.

A short distance up the street, a woman fell to her knees beside a small form lying in the road. Grabbing her medical bag, Sam hurried in their direction. By the time she arrived, a half-dozen people had spilled out of seclusion and were gathering about the woman, who was wailing hysterically.

"Let me through, please," Sam said, shouldering her way among the onlookers. "I'm a doctor. Please let me through."

The small form was a boy about two years old. His limbs were rigid, eyes rolled back. Pushing past the mother, Sam bent to him. His face was bright red and burning hot. Febrile convulsion. Using both hands, she pried his jaws open. She knew that contrary to the old myth, a tongue couldn't be swallowed. But it could surely block a windpipe. As she pinned the child's tongue with two fingers, his teeth clamped down with unbelievable force below her knuckles.

"Where's the nearest bathtub?" Sam demanded.

Seconds of silence passed and she looked away from the boy for the first time, her gaze scanning the curious faces above her.

"I've got to bring down this child's fever, and I need a bathtub full of tepid water."

A buxom, dark-haired woman in a ruffled blouse and denim skirt stepped forward. "My place," she said. "Follow me."

Scooping up the boy, Sam started up the road at a brisk pace. The boy's mother trotted along beside her, tears streaming down her face, sobbing questions pouring from her mouth.

"He'll be all right," Sam said without slowing. "This looks worse than it actually is. Has he ever had a convulsion before?"

"This?" the woman shrilled. "No! Never!"

"Don't worry. He'll be fine once the fever breaks."

The brunette led them into the inn. But for noting that they hurried through a spacious room with a bar and checker-clothed tables, Sam paid scant attention to her surroundings as she followed the woman up a staircase and along a hall lined with doors. When they reached a bathroom, Sam didn't wait for the tub to fill. As the brunette started the water, she stepped in, shoes and all, and sat down with the boy.

Cradling him with her body, she ladled the rising water over his chest, along his arms and legs, carefully over his face, and was dimly aware that her dark-haired hostess and the child's mother stood at the tub's edge, looking on in stunned silence. As the water level closed over the boy's belly, Sam felt his rigid muscles begin to relax. Finally the teeth embedded in her fingers loosened. Once the fever broke, it was mere moments before he was looking up at her with big brown eyes.

"You're all right," Sam said with a smile. "You're fine now."

His eyes filled with tears, nonetheless. "Mama!" he cried.

"I'm here, Jason!" his mother responded, kneeling anxiously by the tub and reaching for him.

Still smiling, Sam looked up at the brunette. "How about a towel for this boy?"

* * *

Producing fresh towels from the linen closet, Rae settled Hannah Mathers atop the commode seat with her boy on her lap. The new doctor, soaking wet from the neck down, continued to sit in the tub—washing her hands under the flowing faucet as she talked to a wide-eyed Hannah about fever-induced convulsions.

"I know it looks scary," she said. "But it's not as frightening when you realize what you're dealing with. A convulsion can result when body temperature takes a sudden, swift rise. Keep Jason's fever down, and he'll be fine. Dress him in cool clothes, and if he seems to be getting warm, give him a sponge bath. Also, I have some medicine I'd like you to give him every four hours."

Turning off the water, the doctor reached for the black bag by the tub. It was then that Rae saw the bloody gashes across her fingers where the boy's teeth had lodged. Swiftly wrapping a strip of gauze about the injury, she seemed to pay it no mind as she went about the business of searching out a vial from her bag and extracting a small amount of red liquid. Holding the dropper up to the light, she checked the amount and leaned toward the child.

"You'll like this, Jason," she said. "It tastes like cherries."

There was a definite Yankee clip to the way she talked, but there was something in her voice that calmed and soothed. If she said everything would be okay, a person believed that it would be. Rae wasn't surprised when the child took the medicine without hesitation and then shyly smiled at the new doctor.

"You can take him home now, Hannah," she said. "If you have trouble keeping the fever down, bring him to see me. Otherwise, give him a teaspoon of the medicine every four hours for the next three days, okay?"

As Hannah stood, clutching both her son and the precious vial, the doctor stood as well.

"What do I owe you?" Hannah asked timidly.

"This one's on me. My first case in Riverbend."

Hannah extended a hand. The doctor offered her own and was obviously surprised when Hannah lifted it to her lips and pressed a reverent kiss on its back.

"Bless you, ma'am," Hannah murmured.

Stepping aside as mother and son departed, Rae looked back to the tub. The doctor continued to stand within it, dripping wet and bedraggled, but with a kind of glow lighting up her face. It was then that Rae noticed she was beautiful—a mite skinny some would say, but pretty as a picture with a peaches-and-cream complexion and bright green eyes.

"Thanks for the use of your tub," she said.

Stepping over with a smile, Rae offered a towel. "I'm Rae Washburn, and you're in Rae's Place—motel, restaurant, saloon, and the only place in town that stays open till midnight."

"I'll keep that in mind," she replied in friendly fashion. "I'm Samantha Kelly. Most people call me Sam."

With a swipe at her face, she ran the towel over her damp hair. That was beautiful, too, Rae decided. Waving to her shoulders, it was about the length of Rae's own, but the most striking color, a deep glossy auburn that caught the light.

"You come all the way down from Boston today?" When she nodded, Rae added, "Flew into Savannah, and then drove out here in that beat-up-looking van?"

She laughed. "I know. It's horrid, isn't it? But unfortunately, it's all I've got. By the way, I'd get out of your tub, but I'm afraid I'd make a terrible puddle on your floor."

Rae gave her an assessing look. "I think I can find you something dry to put on." Catching the woman's quick look of doubt at her ample bosom, Rae chuckled as she went out the door. "Don't worry, honey," she tossed over her shoulder. "I wasn't always built like this."

Walking down the hall to the master suite, Rae thumbed to the back of her armoire. As soon as she looked at the silk dressing gown she hadn't been able to fit into for years, she knew it would be right. Delivering it to the new doctor, she waited outside the guest bath door, and found herself retracing the scene from the street—the stricken boy, Hannah's frightened eyes, Sam Kelly's sure-handed ministrations. . . .

"That was nice of you," Rae called around the doorjamb. "Helping Hannah Mathers that way. Not everybody around Riverbend is quick to lend Hannah a helping hand."

"Really? Why not?"

"Hannah fell in love with a black man and married him. It didn't matter that folks around here had known the both of them since they were born. When they got married, both sides turned their backs. Black and white. Then Big Jason died last spring. Hannah and the boy have had a hard time."

"That's a sad thing to hear," came the brisk reply. "One would wish such backward thinking was confined to the past."

Rae's brows lifted. If she thought *that* was backward, wait till she found out how folks around town reacted when they heard the new doctor was going to be a woman—and a Yankee at that.

"Did this come from the Orient?" she called.

"Yes," Rae answered, her thoughts shifting as she pictured the gold silk. Cut along narrow lines, the sleeveless sheath reached the ankle, but was slit on both sides to above the knee. Matt had said the color lit up her eyes, and the splits showed off her legs. But then that was more than a dozen years ago.

"A friend of mine brought me that from Japan," Rae added.

"A gentleman friend?"

"I guess you could have put it that way a long time ago." Rae grinned as she added, "Anyway, when you get a gander at Matt Tyler, I doubt *gentleman* will be the first word that comes to mind."

"Why is that?"

"Oh, he's tall as an oak, built just as solid, and generally goes without a shirt from May to November. Black hair to his shoulders, skin brown as the earth. He's got a reputation as a devil, particularly with the ladies, and I reckon he looks the part. You can't miss Matt Tyler."

Rae's grin vanished. No, the new doctor wouldn't miss Matt; but then neither would *he* miss *her*.

"Mind if I ask a personal question?" Rae said.

"Go ahead."

"How old are you?"

"Thirty," came the reply. With that slim-as-a-reed body of hers, Rae thought, she looked years younger.

"You married?" Rae questioned.

"No. How about you?"

"Nope. Not that I haven't checked out quite a few, but I never found the right one, I guess."

It was a lie. Rae had found her one true love at the age of eleven, when twelve-year-old Matt Tyler came for the first time to Riverbend. There had been a watering trough in front of the feed store back then, and Hal and Red Carter were taking turns dunking her. Each time she managed to swing a frustrated fist at one of them, they laughed all the louder. Finally they stopped, and when Rae pulled the wet hair out of her eyes, she saw why. A boy was walking toward them—a tall, beautiful boy with a frown on his face. Red taunted him, and got a punch in the nose for it. As the Carter boys took off running, Matt helped her out of the trough.

She remembered watching him ride away in the back of a long, black car, a gray-haired lady sitting beside him. Rae didn't have to ask who he was. As soon as the car disappeared beyond the square, the town erupted in gossip. He was Matt Tyler, the last of the Tylers; the gray-haired lady, his guardian, a spinster aunt on his mother's side. The talk was that the boy had been brought to view the property that was part of his inheritance.

A variety of Tyler stories circulated, but the most popular tale, by far, was that of Mary and Jonathan and the curse.

Like everyone else, Rae expected Matt and his guardian to clear out after a day or two. Then word spread that the boy had fallen in love with the old chateau and talked his aunt into spending the summer. The caretaker's wife, Nadine, became head of a household staff, and Riverbend once again had a Tyler in residence, albeit for only three months out of the year.

"This is very fine silk," the new doctor called. "Are you sure you want to lend it out?"

"I'm sure," Rae absently replied, her thoughts hovering in the past as images of Matt turned through her mind like memorized pages of a well-loved book.

She'd trailed him like a puppy summer after summer—her spirits plummeting in the fall when he returned to school in Savannah, skyrocketing when June rolled around. Over the course of teenhood they smoked their first cigarettes together, drank their first beers, and lost their virginity. Her heart broke when he went away to college, and the summer visits dwindled.

Shortly after he graduated, his aunt died, and Matt settled into the Savannah house. Rae kept hoping for the day he would come back to Riverbend. The black day arrived when he returned only to confide that Savannah socialite Lucy Beauregard was pregnant, and that he was getting married. It was then—when Rae was so obviously crushed—that Matt gave her the old Tyler Inn, and helped her set up the development of what was now Rae's Place.

The next news she'd heard was that his bride had miscarried in her seventh month. A year later the gossip made its way upriver from Savannah: Mr. and Mrs. Matt Tyler might share the grand, old home in the historic district, but they didn't share anything else. Another two years passed before they legally separated.

There had been a brief revival of Matt and Rae's teenhood romance at that point. That was when Matt traveled to the Orient and brought her the gold silk. Rae had been thrilled, although she knew he must have brought back other gifts for other women. It was during those dark years with Lucy that he acquired his reputation as a drinker, gambler, and womanizer.

When Matt announced he was moving to Riverbend

on a permanent basis, her hopes had soared. But as he threw all his time and energy into restoring the vineyards—and fended off her several attempts at seduction—it became painfully clear to Rae that he wanted their relationship to settle into friendship.

Twelve years had passed since then. She'd had plenty of affairs and even a few proposals, but her one and only love was Matt—who continued to play the field with willing ladies scattered across three states.

She'd often wondered what kind of woman it would take to conquer Matt Tyler's heart. Certainly his estranged wife never had. Now, as Rae pictured Dr. Samantha Kelly in the context of her wonderings, she felt a chill run up her spine.

Closing his eyes, Matt trained his voice to a reasoning level. "Lucy . . . the vineyards are part of a corporation formed years after we separated. I don't *own* it, I *work* for it. For God's sake, don't you have enough? You got the Savannah house and everything else you wanted."

"We both know why I got the Savannah house," she stated blandly. "Because you couldn't keep your hands off anything in a skirt."

Although he'd heard it for years, the cold tone of her voice chilled him all the same. Matt thought of the first time he met her, when her cool aloofness had seemed an alluring challenge. Having just returned from finishing school, twenty-year-old Lucy Beauregard was the toast of Savannah society. Having graduated from the University of Georgia, Matt, too, had recently returned, bringing Drew with him. Lucy's air of distance had attracted both of them as much as her blond beauty.

Drew took the first shot, and never made it to first base. Then Matt stepped in. It took months of courting to woo her to his bed. As fate would have it, one time was enough. When Lucy turned up pregnant, he married her. That was fifteen years ago; they'd been separated the past twelve.

"You do recall the circumstances, don't you, Matt?

Let's see, there was the cocktail waitress in Charleston, the stewardess in Atlanta, the exotic dancer—of all things—in Miami."

"Stop it, Lucy!"

"I can see that you *do* recall," she purred as Matt's temples began to throb.

Hell, yes, he'd had affairs! What else was a man supposed to do when his wife barred him from their bedroom? He'd stood by her for a year after the miscarriage—attributing her icy reserve to grief—until the truth sank in. Lucy wasn't grief stricken, she was frigid. Blaming him for what she called "the agony of pregnancy," she couldn't bear the sight of him, much less his touch. Still, each time Matt brought up the subject of divorce, she flatly refused to discuss it.

She'd made no objection when he started staying out nights and taking off on extended trips. Later he realized she'd only been biding her time. When Lucy attacked with her legions of lawyers, she had evidence of adultery spanning several years, including compromising photos of a half-dozen women, two of whom happened to be married. Unless Matt wanted all their names dragged through the mud, he could do nothing but accept Lucy's unconditional terms: possession of the Tyler family home, an extravagant monthly stipend, plus a fifty-percent share of annual net profits from Tyler holdings. The clincher was that if Matt tried to divorce her, she'd take him for everything.

"Enough reminiscing," she then said. "My attorneys are of the opinion that this corporate structure of yours is nothing more than a shelter designed to shut me out of my share of Riverbend. Your officers are a joke, Matt. Drew Pierce as vice-president? The only thing he's ever presided over is a football field. And then, of course, there's your treasurer, George Waters, a black country boy who never finished high school."

Yanking his hand away from his aching forehead, Matt glared down the hall. "When I moved here twelve years ago, Riverbend was nothing more than an old summer house. I couldn't have made it what it is today without Drew and George."

"We'll just have to wait and see what the judge says about that, won't we?"

"I'll fight you on this, Lucy."

"How tantalizing. We haven't had a good scrap in years."

Matt's shoulders slumped. "You're one of the wealthiest women in Savannah. You live in luxury, doing whatever you want, buying whatever you want. Why, Lucy? Why can't you leave me alone?"

"Because making you miserable is the joy of my life," came the flat reply. "My attorneys will be in touch with a court date."

Slamming down the receiver, Matt stalked into the dining room, poured himself a bourbon, and moved to the window. It was half-past six. Beyond the vineyards, the descending sun turned the distant strip of river to gold. He'd always loved Riverbend. As a kid, it had been for the fishing and hunting and running wild with locals who were so different from his prim-and-proper Savannah friends. Twelve years ago, it had seemed the one place left to him that Lucy hadn't spoiled.

He'd returned with the need to sink his teeth into something that mattered, to find the sense of purpose life had lost. Through years of struggling and building, he'd found that purpose in restoring Riverbend. But now that the vineyards were a success, Lucy wanted *them*, too.

Matt tossed down the contents of the shot glass and poured another. Drew was in town, and the Riverbend hands had gone home. Except for Nadine's absent humming drifting from the kitchen, the house was quiet. Too damn quiet. Disposing of the bourbon in the swift fashion of before, Matt headed for the Jeep in the drive.

He wanted jukebox music and laughter, the bustle of drinks being poured and cards being dealt. And maybe if he was lucky, the honky-tonk of Rae's Place would drown out the dismal echo of Lucy's voice.

Chapter Three

Sam peered down the front of herself with dismay. Rae Washburn, who had offered basically the shirt off her back, was undoubtedly one of the most gracious people she'd ever met. She couldn't possibly refuse the loan of the gold silk, even though it clung so that her nipples as well as her navel were outlined with alarming clarity, even though the skirt was split indecently to the thigh, even though as Sam looked in the mirror she decided the only place she would look truly at home was in the boudoir of a bordello.

Rae, apparently, deemed the garment an appropriate cover-up. In fact, Sam sensed the woman treasured the silk—a gift from an old beau—thus making her gesture all the more magnanimous.

"You about done in there?" Rae called.

"Just about."

"Well, come on out. I want to see how you look."

Sam gave her reflection a final once-over, her expression both anxious and surrendering. There was nothing she could do but accept Rae's kindness, and hope she could make it across the street to the van without arousing notice. As she bent to collect her things, the silk cupped her bare bottom, reminding Sam that she was nude beneath the shimmering fabric. She had no choice—if she left on her wet bra and panties, they'd only soak through.

Folding blouse and slacks atop the undergarments in the crook of her arm, Sam picked up soggy Italian leather flats with her left hand, her medical bag with her right. So, here she was . . . barefoot and nearly naked and preparing to sally forth into the redneck burrough that was to be home for the next year.

"Okay," Sam muttered under her breath. "You can handle it." Plastering a pleasant look on her face, she opened the door.

"I knew it," Rae greeted with a smile. "Fits you to a tee."

Sam smiled back, her gaze really registering Rae Washburn for the first time. Appearing to be in her late thirties, she had dark wavy hair, heavily lined brown eyes, and a voluptuous figure that made it hard to believe she'd ever worn the gold silk.

"Thank you for the loan, Rae." She waved a hand as though the matter were of no consequence. "I was wondering," Sam added. "Do you have any vacancies?"

"Sure!" she exclaimed. "Old man Tuttle lives at one end, and I live at the other. The four rooms in between are open."

"I was thinking that by the time I unload the van, it will be getting dark. And until I have a chance to make a few changes, the Daly house is not a place I want to spend the night."

"Pretty bad, huh?"

"Pretty bad," Sam affirmed.

Rae nodded. "Doc Daly and his wife never had any children. He left his property to the town, and when he passed on, the house was locked and boarded up. Four years is a long time for a place to go unlived in. There's a girl who sweeps up for me. Celie Johnson. Her ma died a few months back, and she could use a few bucks if you'd like somebody to help you clean up the place."

"Could she start tomorrow?" Sam asked so eagerly that she drew a laugh.

"Well, I know she works at the Ingram place on Saturday evenings," Rae replied. "But I reckon she could help you out most of the day. Want me to have her come round about nine?"

"That would be wonderful," Sam said, and as she stepped out of the bathroom doorway, became suddenly aware of the hum of voices drifting up the stairs from the floor below.

"Who's that?" she asked with a swift look down the hall.

"Word travels fast in a small town. I reckon some of the folks have come to get a look at the new doctor."

"How nice," Sam replied, her heart sinking.

"Since you're coming back, you wanna leave those wet things here?" Rae asked.

Sam clutched her bundle of clothes. They were her only hope of camouflaging the full frontal glory of the gold silk.

"No, no," she replied hurriedly. "I'll just ... put them with my other things." Her eyes cut nervously down the hall.

"Need some help unloading the van?" Rae asked. "I'm sure some of the menfolk downstairs would be happy to—"

"That's quite all right. I can manage. I ..." Drawing a deep breath, she concluded: "I suppose I should go ahead and get started." At that, Rae moved down the hall, and Sam reluctantly fell in beside her.

There was a burst of chatter and even a few whistles when she appeared at the head of the stairs. *Damn*, Sam thought. A scant half hour ago, the rustic dining room had been empty; now every checker-clothed table was surrounded. Her spirits dropped to her bare toes as she produced a smile for the crowd. There were dozens of them; to her despondent eyes it seemed there were hundreds, the men gawking, the women staring with arch-browed disapproval.

As Rae descended, Sam made herself follow smilingly down the steps. Where had they all come from? When she drove through town, there had been no one ... *No one!* When she reached the bottom, the crowd converged—the first to step forward, an attractive man some years her senior with brown hair and a beaming smile.

"I'm Drew Pierce," he said. "Welcome to town, ma'am. If you'll allow me the pleasure, I'll be happy to show you the sights—"

"What sights?" another man broke in. Approximately the same age and coloring as Drew Pierce, he was shorter and stouter and not nearly so handsome. Sweeping off a hat with a badge on the brim, he announced, "I'm Larry Edison, town constable and the law around these parts. Now, if there's anything you need, you just come right on over to the jail down the street."

"Thank you," Sam murmured, shrinking back a pace as the strangers pressed close.

"Hold on, everybody," Rae's voice boomed. "I'm sure the new doctor wants to meet y'all, but she just got here. She hasn't even had time to unpack. Give her a chance to settle in, huh? Come on, now. Clear a path. Let her through."

In the rippling fashion of a parting sea, the crowd opened a path to the doorway. Casting a quick look of thanks at Rae, Sam proceeded between the townspeople—nodding and smiling as she went, trying her best to file away the barrage of names thrown at her as she passed. Glancing ahead, she saw with relief that the block of light marking her exit was almost within reach.

"Folks who don't know nothin' ought to mind their own business."

The churlish voice was as coarse as the stranger's words. Despite the burgeoning instinct for flight, Sam halted and turned to confront a heavyset man with a thatch of orange hair and a cigar lodged in a corner of his mouth.

"Were you speaking to me, Mr. . . . ?"

"Carter. Red Carter," he supplied without hesitation.

"Let her alone, Red," Rae called.

Sam lifted a quieting hand. "It's all right, Rae. What was it you said, Mr. Carter?"

He folded his arms over a barrel-like chest, calling attention to the stains on his undershirt. "I said you'd do better to learn our ways before you start butting in where you don't belong." A chorus of surprise rose from the crowd.

"I wasn't aware I'd butted in at all," Sam replied. After a brief crescendo, the chorus stilled to a buzz of expectancy.

"That just goes to show you ain't got no idea which end's up around here," Red Carter pronounced.

Sam's grip tightened on the handle of her bag. "Perhaps you should fill me in."

He snatched the cigar out of his mouth. "Folks 'round here don't cotton to no Mathers—not Hannah, and not that little half-breed brat of hers. Folks 'round here know to leave the Mathers alone."

Revulsion swept over Sam in a chilling shower. "I'm sure you don't mean I shouldn't have helped that little boy," she said.

The man's narrow blue eyes turned to slits. "What if I do?"

"Then I'd have to say I pity you, Mr. Carter."

Turning on her heel, Sam marched along the aisle. The excited noise barely dented her consciousness now, although she knew that some people were laughing, a few scowling, and the majority whispering to one another with shocked expressions.

Perfect, Sam thought with the utmost sarcasm. She'd been in town barely an hour, and was already locking horns with the locals. If she'd tried to dream up the most awkward entrance she could have made to Riverbend, she couldn't have outdone this. As she neared the saloon doors, a gray-haired man stepped forward. Thumbs tucked in his suspenders, he wore a look of self-satisfaction.

"I'm Edwin Pettigrew," he announced. "Mayor of Riverbend."

"How do you do, Mayor," Sam acknowledged without slowing. A moment later she was pushing through the swinging doors and leaving the ogling crowd behind.

* * *

Matt was approaching Rae's Place when the saloon doors flew open and Rae emerged to turn and step into the street. She was wearing that gold thing he gave her years ago. Springing to action, Matt moved swiftly up behind her, caught her from the back, and lifted her off the ground. She sputtered with surprise, and he laughed.

"You're losing weight, Rae," he teased as he swung her around, her feet flying.

She squirmed. Matt shifted his hold, his arm lodging diagonally across her torso, his hand closing without design on one of her breasts. And then he instantly knew— this wasn't Rae.

Sam's arms were pinned, her legs thrashing the air. The bundle of clothes tumbled unnoticed to the ground as impressions tumbled across the startled surface of her mind—the dizziness of being lifted high above the earth, the breathlessness of being crushed in a grip of steel, the helplessness of being captured and held by the unknown . . . all laced with the aroma of bourbon.

When the assailant grabbed her breast, instinct took over. One second Sam was driving her heel as hard as she could into his shin, the next she was dropping through the air to land smack on her bottom. Spinning quickly around, she found herself staring at a pair of huge work boots.

Her stunned gaze started climbing. The jeans tucked in the tops of his boots went up and up and up some more . . . met at the band by a white shirt open to the waist, its fronts revealing the bronze V of a massive chest, its short sleeves snug around bulging biceps. The top of the spectacle was backlit by the fiery sky of sunset so that all she could determine was the dark lines of long hair and a cowboy hat. She had the sensation of kneeling at the feet of a giant. And then he was bending to her, extending a hand.

"You all right?" came a deep voice that seemed to rumble from the heavens.

Scooting away on her backside, Sam made no reply as she noticed her strewn clothing and began grabbing for it. When the stranger dropped to a squat and started to help, she scrambled to her feet, her slacks and blouse balled up in a single hand. He slowly straightened to his full shocking height.

"I beg your pardon, ma'am," he said, although he didn't look one bit sorry with a smile glowing from his shadowed face like the moon from a night sky.

He swept the hat from his head, and she clearly saw him for the first time—coal-black hair waving to his shoulders, squared-off jaw, sharp cheekbones, nose straight as an arrow. Beneath brows as dark as his hair, his eyes were contrastingly light, appearing more amber than brown in the sun-burnished setting of his face. She could picture war paint on the high planes of those cheeks.

"Didn't mean to be so familiar," he went on in a rolling Southern voice. "I thought you were someone else."

"So I gathered," she managed.

"I'm Matt Tyler."

"Sam Kelly." He nodded as if considering a weighty thought, his gaze dropping to her hand.

"Now that I take a good look at that bag of yours, I can see it for what it is."

Sam had forgotten she even had her bag. Now she realized her fingers were locked around the handle.

"I guess it means you're the new doc," he observed.

"That's right."

His gaze moved brazenly down her body before returning to her face. "You don't dress much like a doctor," he said. "*Or* a Sam."

The sound of chuckling issued from nearby. Sam looked around to see that people were spilling out of Rae's Place to watch. Her cheeks began to burn as her gaze snapped back to Matt Tyler.

"You'll find I normally dress more professionally than this," she announced in a businesslike tone. "There's been some excitement here today."

"I can see why," he returned in a sexy drawl that drew a round of laughter from the onlookers.

His smile broadening, he slipped her a wink, and it dawned on Sam that whatever she said, the man was going to capitalize on it with a suggestive comeback. He was enjoying this little performance—albeit at the expense of any hope she had for getting through the rest of her first day without further deterioration of her respectability.

"You might need these later," he added, and to Sam's horror, extended a hand to show her bra and panties dangling from his fingertips. This time the response from his audience rang with full-bodied guffaws.

God, she longed to slap him in the face with that wet underwear!

But despite her inclinations, Sam had enough sense to know that right here, right now, he was the cat and she the mouse; he the homeboy with the amused support of his friends, she the outsider standing alone in the street like a barefoot geisha. The best she could do for herself was make a dignified retreat.

"Thank you, Mr. Tyler," she said as she snatched her underthings out of the air. "And now if you'll excuse me, I have a great deal to do."

The Daly house was just across the street, but a walk had never seemed so long as Sam moved sedately toward the sanctuary of its splintering walls.

When the crowd—including Matt Tyler—went inside Rae's, she dashed out of the house to the van, grabbed as many bags as she could carry, and hurried back up the steps. Situating herself behind a street-facing window, she peeped through a crack in the boards as she peeled off the gold silk and replaced it with walking shorts and sleeveless shirt. The heat and mustiness of the old house were stifling, but although she longed for the comfortable privacy of a room at the inn, Sam made herself wait. She had no intention of crossing paths with Matt Tyler again, particularly in front of the audience at Rae's Place.

By a quarter-past seven the crowd had begun to thin, although *he* hadn't come out. She moved to the porch and sat behind one of its massive columns. Though the outdoors wasn't much cooler than the house, at least she escaped the cloying stench of must.

Another half hour passed before the tall figure she'd

been watching for emerged, the center of a group of five or six men. Amidst a round of farewells she heard references to the lot of them meeting at the square at midnight. Then, as the majority turned and walked down the street, Matt Tyler and a companion got in a white Jeep and drove off in the opposite direction.

When the vehicle disappeared from view, Sam shouldered her overnight bag and crossed the street. Rae was serving a couple of beers to the last two patrons at the bar when she walked in.

"I was beginning to think you'd changed your mind," she greeted.

"I got caught up in straightening a few things at the house," Sam lied, and handed over the gold silk. "Thanks again."

"Sure. I was thinking you might be pretty hungry about now."

"Starved. Is there anything I could take with me to the room? Suddenly, I feel dead tired."

The guest room was furnished with quaint, Southern charm—braided rugs scattered on a hardwood floor, colorful quilt folded at the foot of a four-poster bed. Flanking the door to the bath was an antique washstand. It was there that Rae deposited a tray laden with a chicken salad sandwich and tall glass of milk.

"Your place is lovely, Rae."

She smiled. "Thanks, but I can't take credit. I sort of inherited the place lock, stock, and barrel."

Setting down her bag, Sam moved to the washstand and picked up the sandwich. "What's happening at midnight? I heard some of the men talking about meeting at the square."

"Coon hunt."

Sam paused in the midst of taking a bite. "Coon hunt?" she repeated with a lift of her brows.

"It's kind of a Friday night tradition round these parts. The men set out about midnight with their trucks and hounds, find a spot, build themselves a campfire, and let the dogs go. Now those dogs—*they're* the ones that do the real huntin'. Soon as they tree a coon, they let loose with the damnedest howling you ever heard. All a man has to do is go over and shoot the coon right out of the tree."

"How interesting," Sam murmured, and took another hesitant bite.

"Ever eat coon?"

The chicken salad turned into a lump at the back of her throat. Swallowing hard, Sam shook her head.

"If you know how to fix 'em, they make pretty fine eating. Have to musk 'em, though—if you don't get rid of the musk glands, coon's the most awful, smelly mess in the world."

With a flickering smile, Sam returned the sandwich to its plate. "Sounds like I have a lot to learn about Riverbend. Maybe I'll take a walk in the morning. Are there any landmarks I should see?"

"The best I can think of is the pine knoll out past the square. There's a real pretty view of the river from there, but for the Lord's sake, don't go by way of Old River Road. It ain't nothin' but an oyster-shell levee, and after a good rain, moccasins have been known to swim clean across it. Not to mention the gators. Besides, it goes straight through Ezra's Swamp. Starting with old Ezra, people have been known to go in there and never come out."

"Thanks for the advice," Sam said, this time her smile unavoidably shaky.

"Sure," Rae cheerily returned. "Reckon I best go look after the gents downstairs. If you need anything, just holler."

When she left, Sam flopped across the bed. *Coons . . . moccasins . . . gators . . .* If she had to digest one more shocking image today, she was going to start howling like one of the local hounds.

Taking his evening constitutional along the streets of historic Savannah was Robert Larkin's favorite part of the day. He'd visited many a city in his lifetime, but to his way of thinking, none measured up to his hometown.

Built on a cluster of bluffs overlooking the river, Sa-

vannah dated back to 1733 when General James E.
Oglethorpe—a member of the British House of Lords—
chartered the Georgia Crown Colony in the name of
King George II, and founded the city of shaded streets
and graceful, public squares.

Though situated some miles inland from the Atlantic,
its location on the all-important river made Savannah a
thriving port from the beginning. Nautical relics from
colonial times could be found throughout the historic
section, as well as English antiques, Greek revival architecture, and an antebellum spirit of wrought iron, mag-
nolias, and Spanish moss.

Of course, the centuries hadn't passed without leaving
some marks. Colonial homes had become antique muse-
ums; and the old cotton-trading docks, a scene of riverfront
shops, inns, and restaurants. Parts of the city had zoomed
into the nineties; others had fallen into decrepitude. But
despite the ravages of time, and even the military occupa-
tions of the Revolutionary and Civil wars, here in the historic section—where Robert was lucky enough to have
been born and bred—Savannah survived with the gentility
of an era gone by. And he loved her for it.

Approaching an eighteenth-century homeplace fronted
with scaffolding, he noticed Anne Trent watering her gar-
dens.

"Restoration's coming along nicely, Anne!" he called.

"Thank you, Robert! But we've still a ways to go!"

Waving his walking cane in farewell, Robert proceeded
along his favored path to the river. Restoration was a constant occupation in the historic section. And the result
was carefully preserved antiquity—from collections of
Paul Revere pewterware, to architecture designed by the
historically acclaimed William Jay, to a system of Southern tradition that had been handed down as painstakingly
as the family silver. The "Savannah way" embodied a rev-
erence for social grace, heritage, and the finest in all
things. There might be a few bothersome idiosyncrasies
mixed in with the good, but like a passionate lover, Robert tended to forgive those flaws.

As the bells of St. John's Episcopal began chiming the hour of eight, he thought of the house not so far from his own, the historic site General William Tecumseh Sherman had occupied during the final stage of his campaign. It was said the Union general had suggested making ammunition from St. John's bells—whose ringing annoyed him at night—but that Lincoln had vetoed the idea.

Five ... six ... seven ... Robert tapped his cane with every chime. It had been forty years since he returned to Savannah, fresh out of law school. Since then, his practice had become a prestigious, complicated association; his children had grown up and moved; and his wife had passed away. It gave him feelings of peace and continuity to hear the bells of St. John's, and to breathe the air off the ancient river.

Arriving at his favorite lookout, he stepped to the edge of the bluff and propped his arms on the rail. His gaze turned familiarly across the way to the statue of *Florence,* the "waving girl," who was said to have greeted every ship that entered the port from 1887 to 1931. Sculpted by the famed Felix de Welcon, she overlooked the Savannah, waving and waiting year after year—as the legend went—for her merchant marine to come home."

"I knew I'd find you here. Hello, Uncle Bob."

Robert's peaceful expression vanished as he turned. When Lucy Beauregard Tyler, daughter of his late best friend, called him "Uncle," it meant she wanted something. And this time he knew what it was.

"The heat isn't so beastly here by the river, is it?" she added.

Dressed in a white dress and matching gloves, she positively glowed in the twilight, and didn't look as though she'd suffered one mite from the heat. In fact, she'd never seemed more like the Lucy of his mind's eye—fair hair pinned in place, pleasant smile pinned on her lips. Cool as the proverbial cucumber. Glancing beyond her shoulder, Robert spotted her car and driver a short distance away. Of course. Lucy never would have walked the few blocks from her own historic residence to the river.

"You've been admiring *Florence* again," she commented.

"I never tire of her. I suppose I'm a hopeless romantic."

Lucy tendered a coy smile. "I never thought of you as being a romantic, Uncle Bob. Hearts and roses? Estranged couples being reunited? Somehow, that hardly seems you."

Her reference to the many divorce cases he'd handled was meant to draw a laugh. The best Robert could do was a small smile.

"For heaven's sake," she lightly scolded. "Where's your sense of humor? Have you lost it along with my phone number?"

Robert's gaze fastened on the pretty blue eyes beneath the finely drawn brows. Sometimes he fancied Lucy the personification of Savannah—beautiful and indomitable, remarkable in all her Southern charm . . . and eccentricity.

"I didn't return your calls because I knew you'd only badger me," he said forthrightly. "I wish you'd accept what I told you weeks ago, Lucy. I've retired."

"*Partial* retirement, you said."

"*Partial* means I take only the cases I want to take."

"And you don't want to take mine?" she questioned, her brows arching high.

"No."

She lifted a gloved hand to her breast as though she might swoon. "But . . . I told Matt mere hours ago that you'd contact him with a court date."

"Then you spoke out of turn. I don't intend to be your weapon against him, Lucy. Not again."

"But, Uncle Bob—"

"No but's. Twelve years ago I got you the most lavish separation settlement in Savannah history. Why it's not enough for you is beyond me. And to tell you the truth, in recent years I've felt downright guilty about the way I treated Matt Tyler."

"But he wronged me!" Lucy exclaimed. "You know that he did!"

"I've had a number of years to think over the ways he

wronged you, Lucy. But it's become common knowledge that you were not entirely blame-free."

"What?! I *never* indulged in an affair! *Never!*"

"Not even with your own husband," Robert pointed out.

Hot spots of color flashed to her cheeks. To Robert's eyes, they made her look infinitely more lovely. For once, Lucy was beyond the limits of her own iron control, and seemed actually . . . human.

"I can't believe you're saying such things to me. If my father could hear you—"

"If your father could hear me, I'd like to think he'd say bravo. Someone who cares has to speak up and tell you the truth, Lucy. You have your charity work, and the women's league, and the symphony, and so on. But the only sign of real passion inside you is your hatred for Matt. It's a sad thing to see. Twelve years ago I never realized the sentence I was allowing you to impose on both yourself and your husband."

"That's right, *husband*," she said, her voice and manner once again tightly in rein. "*Adulterous* husband."

Robert spread his palms. "What did you expect him to do? Kneel forever at your feet like a peasant at a shrine? Receiving nothing but the crumb you might toss from time to time? I know some women crave that kind of adoration. Are you one of them?"

"What I am is a *lady*," she returned serenely.

"You'd do better to stop being a lady quite so much, and try to discover how to be a woman."

Once again, he managed to shatter her mask.

"I never dreamed I'd hear such things from you!" she exclaimed.

"Should have said them years ago," Robert blandly replied. "The whole thing seems so clear to me now. What you need, Lucy Beauregard Tyler, is to stop wasting your life on seeking to destroy a man, and start trying to find happiness with one."

"Preposterous!"

"There are any number of beaus who would file to

your door if you'd only give them a nod. Drew Pierce, for example."

"Drew?!" she shrilled, her voice still carrying an endearing note of surprise. "You must be joking!"

"No. He tries to hide it, but every time he's around you, well . . . even I can see the sparks."

"So, what you're proposing is that I have a rendezvous with my husband's *foreman*?!"

"Drew is a corporate officer, not a foreman. And I'm not proposing anything of the kind. What I'm suggesting is that you get on with your life. And to do that you must release the past. Let Matt go. Divorce him."

"Never," she hissed.

"Then I'm afraid I see nothing ahead but tragedy."

"Only for Matt," she replied shortly. "So, your answer is final, Uncle Bob? You won't help me?"

"Down a path of destruction? No. You can't win in this hearing, Lucy. No judge is going to give you more than you've got."

Quickly straightening her gloves, she tossed him a miffed look. "We'll see. I'm sure there are hordes of very persuasive attorneys who will be only too happy to accept my exorbitant retainer."

"I'm sure you're right," Robert replied solemnly. "People sometimes do things for the basest of reasons."

With no more reaction than a flash of her blue eyes, Lucy turned and walked away. From the corner of his vision, Robert watched as she was handed into the back of the silver Mercedes.

"God help them," he muttered, his frown relaxing as he looked to the west, and focused once more on the eternal patience and hope of *Florence*.

Chapter Four

Sam may have escaped the physical confines of the Daly house for a night, but she'd been unable to stave off its looming presence in her mind. Having dreamed of prisons and tombs, she'd tossed and turned through the night, and at first light gave up and climbed out of bed. Neither Rae nor old man Tuttle had stirred when she slipped down the stairs, unbolted the front door, and took care to lock it behind her.

The street, too, was still with early morning as she crossed to the Daly house and confirmed that it was, indeed, as awful as she recalled. Putting down her overnight bag, Sam walked out in the yard and took a long look at the place.

Somehow, though, things seemed better today. At least she could see the obvious starting point. Every downstairs window was boarded, as well as several on the second story. The first thing to do was strip the windows. Maybe she could borrow a ladder and hammer and crowbar from Rae. Hell, Sam thought with a flicker of good humor, maybe she could borrow a bulldozer.

Casting a look over her shoulder, she saw that Rae's Place remained quiet. And a couple of hours remained before Celie Johnson was due. Stuffing her hands in her pockets, Sam ambled off in the direction of the square.

Though the sun was still on the rise, it was hot and brilliant, and had melted away any lingering coolness from the night by the time she reached the greens. She walked across the shaded commons, and was considering taking a seat on a bench beneath an oak, when a convoy of pickups came barreling into town from the north.

Screeching to a halt near her chosen bench, the trucks stirred up a cloud of dust and a cacophony of noise as men began jumping down from flatbeds—some of them leading baying hounds, others holding up trophies of dead animals as they called to one another in triumphant voices.

Unconsciously gaping, Sam was unaware of Matt Tyler's presence among them, until the dust cleared and she spotted him moving in her direction. A boy of perhaps seven or eight came with him, his slight size making the man seem even more giantlike than she remembered. Today, the long black hair was tied back beneath the cowboy hat, and in lieu of a shirt, he wore a sleeveless hunter's vest in a camouflage pattern, the front of which was studded with tiny pockets loaded with bullets. One shoulder was slung with a rifle, the other with a weathered-looking leather pouch.

As he walked toward her, the fronts of the vest flapped open to display his extraordinary chest. No less impressive were the bare, sun-bronzed arms ... or the long, muscular legs filling out the faded jeans. He was an incredible figure of a man, and she was sure he knew it. The closer he came, the more his walk seemed to turn into a hip-rolling swagger. Sam folded her arms and returned his direct look. The mere sight of him put her in a confrontational mode. As he arrived, he flipped open the leather pouch and held it out for her to look.

"Care to sample a little local fare?" he asked. "These would dress out mighty nice."

Sam hid a cringe as she glanced at the limp, furry body of a raccoon. Or perhaps there were two. She didn't look long enough to be able to tell.

"No, thanks. I'm afraid I have no idea how to prepare such . . ."

"Delicacies?" he supplied with a taunting grin.

"I was thinking of carnage," she couldn't resist replying.

"Some of the folks around here eat on this carnage all winter long," he said, and planted a hand on the boy's shoulder. "Skeeter, here, bagged two coon dinners last night."

Sam's gaze swerved to the boy. Tow-haired and freckle-faced, he looked incredibly young and innocent—a child who should be handling nothing more sinister than a water pistol.

"Surely, you don't mean this boy was firing a gun."

"A 22-caliber rifle, and doing a damn fine job."

She looked back to the towering man. "You mean, you actually support the idea of a child handling a firearm?"

"Not handling, mastering. A boy needs to know how to shoot. Guns are a way of life around here."

"Guns are responsible for hundreds of deaths every year."

"Not in Riverbend," he retorted with one of his sly winks.

Her temper flaring, Sam eyed him as though she couldn't believe what she was seeing. With her attention focused squarely on Matt Tyler, she failed to notice that the other hunters were following the exchange with avid interest.

"What does that look mean?" Tyler asked.

"I don't think you want to know what it means."

"Sure, I do."

"All right, then, I'll tell you," Sam briskly replied. "A gun is a dangerous weapon in anyone's hands, especially those of a child. In my opinion, you're trying to defend the reprehensible with the lame excuse that things have always been that way."

"And in my opinion," he returned, "you're trying to fit Boston rules on the Georgia countryside. It won't work,

lady. You might as well try to lasso a mustang with a ball
of yarn and a couple of knitting needles."

At that remark the all-male onlookers crowed. Sam
paid them little heed as her ire mushroomed.

"You just don't like guns period," Matt Tyler added
with a fresh grin.

"No. I don't."

"I'll bet you're even pro-gun control."

"That's right," she answered. "Some of the best minds
in the nation are pro-gun control."

"I'll lay money a single day down here would change
a few of those best minds."

"It hasn't changed mine," Sam retorted.

"I beg your pardon," he replied with an exaggerated
look of apology. "I didn't realize you were including yourself in that distinguished group."

"Honestly!" Sam exploded, forgetting for the moment
that there was anyone within earshot but Matt Tyler. "I
have never encountered a more insulting, boorish,
narrow-minded—"

She broke off as a roar of laughter reminded her they
were not alone. With a parting glare for the grinning giant, she turned on her heel and stalked away—off the
green lawn of the square, onto a cobblestone lane that
led who-knew-where. It wasn't until the cobblestones
turned into crushed shell that she realized she'd taken
the turn out of town toward Old River Road, the levee
Rae had warned her about.

*After a good rain moccasins swim clean across it. Not
to mention the gators . . .*

Squaring her shoulders, Sam passed beyond the shelter of oak and entered the open sunshine blazing down
on the shell-covered strip of land. It hadn't rained, and
the sun shone from a cloudless sky. Anyway, she couldn't
turn around now—not when half the men of Riverbend
had just watched her march angrily away, and were probably still watching.

Cypress lined the narrowing isthmus, its banks scarcely
six feet above the swamp water stretching away on both

sides. Ezra's Swamp. As she stared across the immenseness of it, Sam's resolve was shaken. Looking ahead once more, she took heart as she spotted the roof of a house peaking beyond the cypress bordering the distant bank. There was solid ground on the other side. All she need do was traverse the oyster-shell bridge to reach it.

Sound seemed to die away as she moved into the swamp—the sunny silence unbroken but for the distant buzz of insects, an occasional *plunk*! in the glassy water that made her wonder what the hell had made the noise . . . and the crunch of her footsteps on the oyster shell, which in the face of such quiet seemed to announce her presence like the blare of a trumpet.

Keeping her eyes trained on the roofline beyond the cypress, she was nearly halfway across when part of the bank just ahead seemed to separate from itself and come to life. Sam froze as the thing crawled up on the road and looked her way. An alligator! As she stared in horror, its jaws opened to reveal a pink cavern lined with pointed teeth, and then it hissed like a gargantuan snake.

Although it seemed an eternity passed, it must have been mere seconds before she heard approaching footsteps, and then the quiet command: "Don't run."

Sam's eyes turned—they seemed the only part of her body capable of movement—and she beheld Matt Tyler taking aim with his rifle. *Run?* Hell, she couldn't even breathe. A deafening crack split the air . . . and then another! Sam had the sensation of bullets whizzing past her nose, sweeping her gaze back to the alligator as two bloody holes appeared between its eyes. The gaping mouth banged shut as it slumped to the ground.

"Is it . . . dead?" she whispered as the man stepped up beside her.

"If she wasn't, she'd be closing in on both of us by now. Usually, gators leave people alone. They're more interested in fish and small mammals. But there are occasions when a gator will attack—like when a bull establishes his territory, and somebody's unlucky enough to cross into it. Or like today, when somebody stumbles across a late nester. See that pile of brush and vegetation on the bank over there?"

Following the direction of his pointing finger, Sam dumbly nodded.

"If we were closer," he went on, "we'd be able to see the slide marks where she's been coming and going. Mama gators don't like *nobody* messing around their nests. She was on her way to attack. There was nothing to do but shoot her."

Matt Tyler continued talking. He said something about having to contact the constable, Larry Edison, so the gator could be tagged . . . something else about turning the carcass over to the state. Sam only heard bits and pieces as she replayed the horrifying moment when the thing bared its teeth and hissed.

"You mean," Sam finally mumbled, "it would have just walked over and . . ."

"Galloped over is more like it," Matt Tyler replied when she trailed off. "A gator can move pretty fast over a short distance. And once it drags you in the water, well . . ."

He didn't finish. He didn't have to. She'd viewed the scene in many a Tarzan movie. Clapping a hand over her mouth, Sam spun and buried her face in the rough fabric of his hunting vest.

"You see, gators don't have any natural enemies," he said, putting a light arm about her shoulders. "Consequently, they don't have any fear, either. When one gets riled up, there's no backing it down. And this one had its sights set on you."

As a shuddering tremor raced over her, Sam was only dimly aware of the warmth of the man's hand traveling down her back.

"Considering your views about guns, I hope I haven't offended you," he added in a lazy drawl. "There didn't seem to be time to ask your permission to shoot."

Piercing the shock of the moment, his amused tone brought Sam sharply to her senses. She pushed out of his embrace and looked up to find him grinning.

"I was about to thank you for rescuing me," she snapped.

"It was my honor."

"You needn't look so pleased about this."

"No, ma'am."

"Someone could have been hurt."

He chose that moment to shoulder his rifle. "Yes, ma'am," he agreed, his know-it-all grin spreading.

"Honestly!" Sam exclaimed. "You truly are the most infuriating person I've ever met!"

"Infuriating, too?" he said with lifting brows. "Let's see, that makes me infuriating, insulting, narrow-minded, and boorish. That's the one I like best. Boorish."

When he chuckled, Sam spun curtly around and began backtracking as fast as she could without breaking into a run. Even so, she couldn't outdistance the careless stride of the man's towering legs, and so was subjected to Matt Tyler's trailing, smiling silence all the way back to town.

Celie Johnson was a pretty, fifteen-year-old black girl with a dimpling smile that made her look younger—as did the cutoff overalls she was wearing, which hung with room to spare on her slight frame.

She was fascinated by the fact that Sam was a doctor, and as they spent the morning prying away rusty-nailed boards with tools borrowed from Rae, Sam found herself recounting story after story about school, and St. Elizabeth's, and Boston. Thinking of home, she found it impossible to believe she'd left it only yesterday.

The unveiling of the windows made a marked difference. But although fresh air helped to dispel the staleness within the house, the sunshine streaming into the rooms pointed at all the dirty jobs that cried to be done. Standing in the dust-ridden parlor, Sam and Celie looked with dismay toward the grimy kitchen.

"I believe it's time to buy some cleanser," Sam commented.

"Lots of it," Celie agreed.

They walked up the street to Simon's Produce, which

Sam discovered was a limiting label for all the establishment offered. In addition to fresh fruits and vegetables and provisions of every description—including an array of jars of pickled pigs' parts lining the counter—the store featured a soda fountain up front, and the local post office in back.

She met Tully and Clara Simon, a smiling middle-aged couple who treated Sam in the friendliest of manners, but undoubtedly peered at her as though she'd dropped from another planet. When she asked if they had any bagels, they looked as though their eyes might pop, and suggested corn bread mix instead.

She and Celie filled up four bags with necessities. As Sam was preparing to pay, she received a tug on her arm and turned to find Celie offering a wide-brimmed straw hat similar to the one she herself had put on when they left the house.

"It keeps the sun off," Celie explained. "But the straw lets it breathe. You ought to have one, Dr. Sam. For the scorchers."

And so Sam added the hat to her purchases, eliciting a bright smile from Celie as she plopped it on her head. On the way out of the store, Sam caught sight of herself in a full-length mirror. The sneakers, khaki shorts, and T-shirt were familiar. The face in the shadow of the hat brim was not—having suddenly transformed, it seemed, to the face of some rural stranger who wore straw hats. Still, when she stepped out of the air-conditioning and into the blistering sun, Sam couldn't deny she was glad of the shelter.

The walk back seemed longer than the trip over—maybe because Sam caught herself falling in with Celie's pace, a slow-moving amble she imagined to be the Southerner's response to a temperature climbing toward a hundred. As a physician, Sam couldn't help but note it as healthy. Such humid heat warranted a lazy gait.

After scouring a quick path through the kitchen, they made a lunch of ham sandwiches and Clara Simon's homemade potato salad, and sat down at the circa 1920s breakfast table in the kitchen. This time it was Sam who drew Celie out. The girl spoke of Rae, who she said had a heart of gold, the Simons, who bought everything locally from people's dairies and "truck patches," the Reverend Bishop and his wife, who ran the local church and school, and the Pettigrews, who had two sons at the university in Athens, the youngest still at church school.

"Is that where you go to school?" Sam asked at one point.

"Oh, no. I take the bus to the district school. That's where everybody else goes."

"Everybody else?"

"Except the townfolk," the girl answered as though that explained everything.

"But don't you live in town?" Sam questioned.

"Sure. But I ain't one of *them*."

Them—it turned out—were the children of the well-to-do folk in town. The *white*, well-to-do. The distinction Celie made without batting an eye stuck in Sam's craw, but she reminded herself that her duty was to be a doctor to these people, not a judge of their social mores. She and Celie were clearing off the table when the girl brought up the subject of Riverbend Vineyards.

"It's because of the Tylers that the town got born," she said. "And it's because of Mr. Matt that a lot of folks today don't go round hungry."

The image of a gloating giant leaped to Sam's mind. "What does he do," she said without thinking, "go out and shoot down a few raccoons for the good girls and boys?"

"Oh, no ma'am!" Celie exclaimed in all seriousness. "Now that he's brought the vineyards back, folks have got jobs and a little money and hope for what lies ahead."

"He'll always be a savage to me," Sam muttered under her breath.

"What was that, ma'am?"

"Nothing," Sam replied with a smile. "How about it, Celie? Are we ready to tackle this kitchen in earnest?"

Celie was not only a cheery companion, but also a

most efficient worker. By late afternoon when she prepared to leave, the kitchen was well on its way toward reclamation, and Sam had secured her services for every day until school started.

"See you after church tomorrow!" Celie called as she trotted down the steps.

Closing the door behind her, Sam cast a dejected look up the stairs toward the bathroom. She was hot and tired and didn't feel like touching another scrub brush for the rest of her life. Nonetheless, she began gathering her rags and pails.

If nothing else, Sam vowed as she climbed the stairs, she would feel safe in taking a shower before the night was through.

Rae flipped off the kitchen lights and strolled into the main hall. By habit, her gaze made the familiar round. Dominating the left half of the room, the cafe tables were in order, the chairs lined up against the wall and ready for the next morning. To the right, the antique bar that was the curving centerpiece of the room shone with a fresh coat of polish. Behind it rows of glasses glinted in the muted light; before it the felt-covered card tables were empty but for the one by the street-facing window.

The supper crowd was long gone, the saloon regulars narrowed to a familiar four: Matt, Drew, Larry, and Edwin. A popular tune was wailing from the jukebox, but otherwise the place was quiet.

This time of night was usually her favorite. It filled her with a kind of peacefulness, especially when Matt was in the place. But tonight Rae felt a worrisome tug at her heartstrings—why, she couldn't figure.

Bringing a smile to her lips, she delivered a fresh round of drinks and pulled up a chair. Larry was dealing, and there was a fair amount of money on the table ... And then she knew, when the upstairs lights came on across the street, and the men's interest swerved away from poker.

"I don't care what you say about new ways," Edwin grumbled. "She don't look old enough to be a doctor."

Drew leaned back in his chair and smiled. "She looks good, though. You have to admit that. I'll bet she feels good, too. How about it, Matt? From the looks of things yesterday, you got a little firsthand knowledge out there in the street. Does the lady feel as good as she looks?"

"I'd say so," Matt admitted with a slight grin.

"And the way she talks," Larry commented. "I never heard the like. Do you reckon all the ladies in Boston talk like that?"

"I've heard about Boston folk," Edwin responded. "Straitlaced and uppity. And that's exactly how she was— marching along with her nose in the air, brushing past with hardly a *how-do-ya-do*. She ain't ever gonna fit in here. Who'd go to a woman doctor, anyway?"

"I might," Drew answered. "It would give the idea of 'take a deep breath and cough' a whole new meaning."

"She ain't as young as she looks," Rae put in. "And she's tough. Make no mistake about it."

"Tough?" Drew repeated on a questioning note. "Her? Nah!"

"You're wrong, Drew," Rae insisted.

"What makes you think so?"

"*She* makes me think so. And I reckon I know better than most. After all, it was my roof she spent last night under."

"And what did you find out?" Drew pressed. "She's not married, is she?"

"No. And she's nobody's easy pickin's, either."

"That's right, Drew," Larry said with a laugh. "Yesterday, she faced down Red Carter. Today she stood up to the lot of us about gun control. Tell the story about the gator, Matt."

"You've already heard it ten times."

"But I like it," Larry objected. "When I got out there, that mama was lying on the levee, shot dead between the eyes, just like you said. Tell me again how the doctor lady sashayed up Old River Road like the Queen of England."

"Like I said," Matt rumbled, "you've already heard it."

"You sure you're not leaving out any juicy details, big brother?" Drew taunted.

As the other men broke into laughter, Matt propped his elbows on the table, studied the window across the street, and remembered yesterday—the litheness of her body as she squirmed in his arms, the rosy glow of her face when she turned and confirmed it wasn't Rae he was holding, but a stranger with the widest, greenest eyes he'd ever seen.

Kelly. The color of those eyes did her name proud.

Then, this morning she'd been wearing nothing more spectacular than a pair of those long walking shorts he didn't like, a T-shirt, and sneakers . . . and he hadn't been able to take his eyes off her behind all the way back to town. Her shadow passed across the lighted window, and a primitive pounding filled his veins.

"She's no match for a Southern boy," Drew was saying. "In fact, I think I feel a touch of the flu coming on, and I'm sure the cool touch of her hand on my brow would make me feel *much* better."

"You were a damn good quarterback at Georgia," Larry replied. "Particularly when you had Matt, here, blocking for you. But running a play on that little lady?" Larry shook his head. "I don't know, Drew. I say she'd throw you for a loss before you even got started."

"He's right," Edwin put in. "The woman's uppity. She wouldn't give a one of you bucks the time of day. I wager she'll stay locked away in that old tower over yonder, and hightail out of here fast as she can as soon as her year's up."

Matt slapped a twenty-dollar bill on the table. "Ten-to-one I can get her down out of her tower right now," he said. "And steal a kiss to boot."

There was a moment of surprised silence as the others turned to peer his way.

"No, Matt," Rae tried to interject. But she went unnoticed as the men leaned eagerly forward.

"Ten-to-one?" Drew repeated with a smile full of mischief. "I'll take that bet."

It had taken two hours to scrub the bath to the point that Sam felt comfortable in stripping off her clothes and stepping into the claw-footed tub—where she luxuriated under the jets of the shower until the water ran icy cold. After a light supper, she'd hand-washed the clothes she wore that day, and made up the bed with linens that smelled comfortingly of her mother's cedar chest.

Fishing her travel clock out of her shoulder bag, she set it on the bedside table. Ten o'clock—the shank of the evening, Father always said. Sam wondered what he'd say if he took a look at Riverbend, which except for Rae's Place, folded up its streets at dusk.

The sound of jukebox music wafted through the bedroom's street-facing window, joined by a chorus of crickets from the window overlooking the side yard of waist-high weeds.

There was no TV—the antiquated set downstairs delivered only a flopping image of snow. No radio—her transistor picked up only one station, which played a kind of wailing country sound she refused to listen to. The sense of isolation creeping through the old house was as suffocating as the heat.

Grabbing her notebook and pen, Sam sprawled across the bedspread. She'd turned on the precious fan she purchased from Simon's Produce. Even so, despite the fact that she'd opened every second-floor window, pinned up her damp hair, and was clad in nothing more than a T-shirt and underwear, she was burning up.

Air conditioner, she added to the growing list of necessary repairs, although she figured the ancient units interspersed among Dr. Daly's windows were beyond repair. Completing the notation, Sam propped the end of the pen between her lips and directed a sweeping gaze about the room.

Like the rest of the house, what once had been grand was now shrouded with age—the wallpaper of trailing roses faded to a dingy gray ... the antique chiffarobe and dresser covered with dust ... the Victorian lamps with dirt-streaked globes giving off a flickering glow reminiscent of gaslight. The only items in the room that looked as though they belonged in the present were the unopened bags standing by the door.

Refusing to unpack until she'd scoured the closet and dresser drawers, she'd removed the few things she found necessary for a night's stay and fed the fantasy that she was merely camping out. Rolling onto her back, Sam closed her eyes.

It will be all right, she told herself, but ... *God,* she wanted to feel cozy and clean, not grand and dirty! She wanted to hear the Kelly kids running up and down the stairs, not the stealthy rustle of what she hoped was only beetles. She wanted to walk out on the stoop and be enveloped by the vibrant city, trot down the block and pick up one of Tony's fresh-baked rolls ... Here, if she ventured so much as the length of three city blocks, she'd find herself mired in a swamp.

She lay there a minute more, longing for all she missed, until Chad's voice echoed in her memory: *A month in the godforsaken wilderness will change your point of view!*

A month? She had yet to make it through the second night. Rolling over, Sam turned to a fresh page of the writing pad.

Dear Mother, she began. *Things are great here—*

"Oh, my God! He's dead!"

Sam jumped as the exclamation boomed through the open window. Scrambling off the bed, she pulled aside the curtain and peered across the yard. Directly in front of the house, a man was lying in the street. Several others were milling around him.

"He's dead, I tell you!" one of them yelled.

Sam darted to the door, halting in midstride as she remembered what she was wearing—a flimsy pair of panties and a T-shirt that barely covered her bottom. She cast a quick look at her suitcase, considered taking a minute to pull out a pair of jeans. The shouting from the street escalated.

"Damn," Sam muttered and ran down the stairs and through the front yard. Passing swiftly through the gate, she hurried to the fallen man. It was Matt Tyler. Sam dropped to her knees beside him. Having changed from the hunter's vest of the morning, he was wearing an unbuttoned white shirt that was open to his navel. Nonetheless, she yanked his collar wide before pressing searching fingers to the side of his massive neck.

"What happened?" she demanded without looking at the men hovering about. Hastily scanning his face, she found no contusions. Just as she determined a strong steady pulse, the men surrounding her began to chuckle.

"I'd say he was lovestruck," one of them commented.

Glancing up, Sam began to get the idea that—

She looked swiftly back to Matt Tyler. His eyes were open, and he was smiling. She had no time to think any further as two huge hands captured her face, and she was pulled inexorably down. His shining eyes loomed, her hands flew to futile posts against the wall of his chest, and then his mouth was on hers—his lips parting, their pressure parting her own.

As the wetness of their mouths collided, Sam was stunned by an explosion of sensation. His tongue filled her, caressed her, its sure movements flavored with a taste of bourbon. His massive hands imprisoned her, directed her, turned her to receive a new, full-tongued exploration. She was aware of the smallness of her body against his, and the sense of being overwhelmed by sheer masculine power. A kind of reaction Sam had never known flared to life—something primally female that sent rays of heat through her insides like so many shooting stars. The shock of it was immobilizing . . . mesmerizing. . . .

Shameful seconds passed, and suddenly she realized just how long and involved the kiss was becoming. Suddenly she saw that somewhere along the line Matt Tyler's tongue had taken a turn to the erotic, and hers had followed right along.

Drawing a swift breath through flaring nostrils, Sam pushed with all her strength against the rock-hard warmth of his chest. And then it was over and he was lifting her away, fixing her with a devilish grin as he climbed to his feet and offered a hand.

Painfully aware of the snickering men standing around her, Sam accepted his hand and rose to her feet with as much dignity as she could muster. She couldn't stop herself from snatching away from his helping grasp as soon as she was on her feet, particularly when she looked up at him only to be awarded another of his flirting winks. Folding her arms, she summoned an amicable expression.

"It seems you've never heard the story of the boy who cried wolf," she said. "Perhaps the doctor won't be so quick to run to your aid next time." He directed an appreciative look to her bare legs before meeting her eyes once more.

"It was worth the risk," he replied, his grin flashing wide as his friends hooted. Keeping her pleasant demeanor carefully intact, Sam nodded and started to move away.

"Oh," she said, turning back with a mock look of thoughtfulness. "I nearly forgot this."

Without warning she struck a swift, stinging slap across his cheek. The other men dissolved in laughter as Matt Tyler's insolent smile drained.

"Have a nice night," Sam added and felt his amber eyes following every move as she turned her back and walked away.

Across the street Rae spun from the window and closed her eyes. But it did nothing to stop the recurrent image flashing behind her lids like a broken reel of film—the pretty woman poised above him . . . his hands pulling her down. . . .

"Matt," Rae uttered, the name escaping her lips in a hoarse whisper. Would the pain never end?

Chapter Five

Sunday, September 5

Shortly after Celie arrived at half-past noon, Sam answered the door to behold a quartet of middle-aged ladies bearing gifts. Although they varied in height and build, there was a uniformity about them. All wore silver-framed glasses, Sunday hats, summer dresses that reached well below the knee . . . and serene expressions of carefully nurtured piety.

"Welcome to Riverbend, my dear." A woman carrying a hefty plastic container stepped forward. "I'm Mayor Pettigrew's wife, Eloise."

With that, she swept past and was followed single-file into the parlor by the others. Lettie Campbell carried a basket of ham biscuits; Grace Whitehead, a platter of fried chicken; and the Reverend Bishop's wife, Sarah, a bundle of fabric that, at a glance, looked like velvet drapes the color of olives.

"Oh, hello, Celie," Eloise Pettigrew said, and tossed a glance in Sam's direction. "She's such good help, don't you agree? As was her mother before her." Preening as though she'd bestowed the ultimate compliment, the woman thrust the plastic bowl into Celie's hands. "There now. You go on and put that fruit salad straight in the icebox."

Instantly put off by the woman's manner, Sam took swift note of her hawkish nose, pointed chin, and beady eyes, and was reminded of a bird looking disapprovingly down its beak.

"Go on," she chirped. "Be quick about it."

With downcast eyes Celie turned to leave.

"Thank you, Celie," Sam made a point of saying, and received a swift glance from the mayor's wife, who was undoubtedly the leader of the flock that had descended on the parlor. As the others deposited their bundles here and there, Eloise turned in a slow circle and surveyed the room.

"I see you've got a long way to go with the house," she said. "Though I guess it will never look the way it did when poor Peg was alive. After she died, Dr. Daly simply let it go."

"He was a devoted husband," Sarah offered.

"And a good doctor," Grace reported.

"He brought all our children into the world," Lettie supplied.

"How many years have *you* been a doctor, my dear?"

Sam's gaze swerved at the sudden question. "Actually, Mrs. Pettigrew, I just finished my training." An ill-disguised look of alarm swept their faces. "Though, of course, I've been a practicing physician since I graduated from medical school."

"Indeed," Eloise said and tendered a patronizing smile that irritated Sam to no end. "There's a delicate matter I feel I must bring up, my dear. You see, after Dr. Daly died, we and several others here in town began seeing a doctor in Savannah. While it's wonderful that we now have our very own in Riverbend for emergencies and such, I hope you understand ... well ..." She trailed off with a light chuckle.

"I understand," Sam replied. "I wouldn't dream of interfering. Still, I'm here if you need me."

"How very dear of you," Eloise murmured.

"Not at all," Sam returned, and the two of them exchanged a smiling look that failed to temper the adversarial undercurrents flowing between them. Sometimes, people knew immediately when they liked each other. Sometimes, they knew when they didn't.

"Well!" Eloise then exclaimed with a clap of her hands. "Come along, girls. As you can see, Miss Kelly has much to do."

"Please," Sam said, grinding out another smile. "Call me Sam. And thank you so much for coming."

"Enjoy the biscuits," Lettie said.

"And the chicken," Grace chimed in.

"The drapes were in our schoolhouse for a number of years," Sara said. "But they've still got plenty of use in them. I thought you could put them up in the bedroom. You're a single woman, you know," she added with the arch of a brow. "You should be aware that things show through these old venetian blinds."

"Of course. You're very kind."

"It's the Christian way," Sarah replied, her eyes growing suddenly wide. "You *are* Christian, aren't you?"

"I come from an Irish Catholic family of ten, Mrs. Bishop."

"Catholic!" she cheeped. "Really? How interesting."

After that the ladies quickly departed, and Sam tried not to appear terribly eager in hurrying them along.

By late afternoon, she and Celie had completed the major tasks required in the parlor/waiting room. Every corner was divested of cobwebs; every fixture, polished. There was nothing to be done about the heat pouring in through the open windows, but at least the sunlight fell on gleaming surfaces. The same was true in the kitchen where they took a break, and made a snack of Lettie Campbell's ham biscuits. Sam was rinsing off the dishes when the doorbell rang. Celie went to answer it, and returned with a bouquet of sweet-smelling gardenia.

"Mr. Matt's in the parlor, and he brought you these," she announced with glee, and proceeded to put the flowers in a vase she procured from the cabinet.

"Mr. Matt?" Sam questioned. "Tyler?"

"Now, what other Mr. Matt would there be, girl? Why don't you comb your hair and pinken up those cheeks a little?"

Sam looked around in surprise. Suddenly, Celie sounded not at all like the teenager with whom she'd spent the past two days.

"Comb my hair?" she murmured. The memory of last night barreled into the present, and once again she saw Matt Tyler grinning down on her in the most obnoxious way.

"I should say not," Sam added briskly. Tossing her sponge at the sink, she wiped her palms across the seat of her shorts, and went to meet him.

He was wearing a white, short-sleeved shirt buttoned halfway up—which, she gathered, was as formal as he got—and khaki pants that form-fitted his muscular legs. Every time she saw him, his height and physique struck her as staggering. Earlier in the day when she and Celie swept the parlor floor, she'd thought the room spacious. Now, with Matt Tyler standing in the center of it, the chamber seemed small and low-ceilinged.

The cowboy hat he'd removed and held before him suggested a show of respect; the cocky look on his face, just the opposite.

"I hope you don't mind me dropping in unannounced," he said. "I would have called, but your phone isn't working."

"It won't be hooked up until after the holiday. What can I do for you, Mr. Tyler?"

"For starters, you can call me Matt. I think we've grown close enough for first names."

"Do you?" she said humorlessly.

Ignoring her cold look, he smiled. "I was hoping flowers might smooth your feathers a little, but it looks like you're still mad at me."

"Why should I be mad? Just because you seem to have made humiliating me your latest thrill?"

"You got me back." Still smiling, he felt of his jaw as

though it continued to smart from her slap. "I haven't been put in my place like that in a long time."

Helplessly seeing past blinders of anger, Sam noted the beauty of his smile . . . his face . . . and long, glorious hair that shone with the luster of black satin.

God, he was a magnificent specimen! She'd never felt such an impact of pure maleness. It was like a radiating aura impossible to ignore. A woman couldn't look at him without part of her mind drifting to the fact of how spectacular he was.

"Even though it *was* kind of like closing the barn door after the horse was long gone," he added.

Sam's dreamy thoughts came to a skidding halt. "What do you mean by *that*?"

"I think you know."

"I'm sure I don't."

"Uh-huh," he replied, his tone heavy with disbelief.

"Mr. Tyler—"

"Matt."

"All right then, Matt." Folding her arms, Sam tendered her most formidable glare of rejection. "Why don't we just go ahead and get this thing out in the open?"

He grinned in the sexiest of fashions. "What *thing* did you have in mind?"

"You see? There you go. Another double entendre."

"Another what?"

Sam returned his amused perusal with a starch look. *"Double entendre,"* she repeated patiently. "Leading remark, innuendo, flirtation . . . whatever you want to call it. Ever since you first grabbed me outside Rae's Place, you've regaled me with it. Then last night you delivered the *coup de grâce* with that little scene in the street."

"You saying you didn't like it?" he drawled.

"Of course I didn't like it. What could I like about your making me the butt of your jokes? What could I like about the offhand way in which you treat me?"

"I beg your pardon, ma'am, but there's nothing offhand about it."

"I beg to differ," Sam returned. "I'm going to have

enough trouble winning these people's respect as a doctor without your making such a show of treating me like a . . ."

"Woman?" he supplied when she hesitated.

"That's right," she confirmed. "I prefer that you see me as a doctor only."

His gaze traveled the length of her. "I believe I'd have to put on some mighty dark glasses to manage that."

Sam rubbed a hand across her brow as she fought down her temper. "I've worked many years to become a surgeon."

"A surgeon, is it?"

"That's right. And where I come from women demand the right to be treated as professionals."

"Where I come from women aren't afraid to be women."

Sam gave him a sharp look. "In Boston women are recognized for more than their sex."

"In Georgia they're appreciated for it."

"Honestly! Why must you insist on being so difficult?"

"You just read me that way. Actually, I'm as simple as pie. As basic as"—he flashed a new grin—"the birds and the bees."

"I know all about the birds and the bees," she snapped. "I'm a doctor, after all."

"And a woman," he reminded.

"I know all about that, too."

"Do you?" he questioned. "You look mighty young to have learned all there is to know about that."

"I'm nearly thirty-one, and the opposite sex has been making its presence known since I was eleven," she retorted. "That's twenty years' worth of experience."

"Hands-on experience?"

Stifling the impulse to smack him once again, Sam forced a bland smile. "Is there a point to this visit? Other than putting me in a rage, I mean?"

He laughed. "There's a point."

"Why don't you make it?"

"My housekeeper, Nadine, is having some trouble," he

replied, his look of mirth dying away. "Even though she'd be the last one to admit it, she just doesn't get around well anymore. Last night when I got home, she was sitting up, soaking her feet. Couldn't sleep, she said."

Caught offguard by Matt Tyler's first show of any behavior other than shameless flirting, Sam silently stared.

"I was thinking you might check her over," he added.

"Of course," Sam responded. "Normally, I'd ask her to come to the clinic, but as you can see, there *is* no clinic yet. I could drive out to see her."

He nodded. "She'll be gone tomorrow for the holiday. Maybe you could make it Tuesday."

"Tuesday afternoon, then," Sam agreed.

Within an instant the respectful, civilian-to-doctor air was gone, the blatant sultriness that was becoming a hallmark back in his voice and eyes.

"Good. Then you can take a look at my place."

"Where is it?" Sam questioned on a determinedly casual note.

"North of town. Take the road past the square, then the turnoff to Riverbend Vineyards. There's a sign."

"Okay," she replied lightly.

He stood there—big and impossibly handsome, and wearing a half smile that suggested he knew something she didn't.

"Was there something else?" Sam demanded.

The smile spread. "Now that you mention it, yeah. Why don't you let me take you to supper tonight? Savannah's only an hour away. If you like good seafood, you can't do better than a little place I know on the coast."

"I don't think so."

He took a slow pace forward. "Why not?"

Countering his move with a backward step, Sam cut her eyes to his. "Any number of reasons." Although he didn't move any closer, the intensity of his gaze made her feel like he had.

"Doesn't the fact that I slayed a dragon for you carry any weight?"

"I'm grateful for that, of course."

"But not enough to have dinner with me?"

"I consider a simple thank you enough. After all, I'm sure you would have done the same for anyone in my position."

Propping an arm on the mantel, he attained a sexy, hip-thrusting stance as he continued to study her. Sam could do nothing to prevent an uncomfortable heat from rising to her face.

"I'm trying to figure this out," he said finally. "I know you're not married."

"How do you know that?"

"Word gets around. Besides, you don't look married."

Sam arched a brow. "I'm sure I'm going to regret asking, but how do married women look?"

"Kinda full and satisfied," he replied with a raking look. "Not lean and hungry like you."

"I certainly am *not* hungry. Not for what you're offering."

He cracked a grin. "And what exactly do you think I'm offering?"

"I'm not naive," Sam returned. "I know a pass when I see one."

"I'll bet you do."

"So, I may as well tell you here and now that I'm not in the market for a fling."

"Fling," he repeated, his infernal grin deepening. "I think all I asked for was your company at supper."

The more irresistible he became, the more she felt the urge to resist—to throw his damnable attractiveness back at him and wipe the cocky look off his face.

"And I think I said, no thank you."

His grin did, in fact, fade. But his arrogance remained. "And I'm still trying to figure out why."

"Maybe I just don't like you," Sam offered.

His gaze searched her eyes. "Maybe you like me more than you want to admit."

For a few sputtering seconds Sam was struck speechless. It was long enough for him to start grinning again.

"You're the most arrogant man I've ever met," she said finally.

"Confident," he corrected. "I have complete confidence you feel the same attraction I do."

"I can't imagine what brought you to that conclusion."

"Last night brought me to that conclusion. You and I both know I wasn't the only one doing the kissing."

"You're mistaken," Sam snapped, her face suddenly on fire. "I was merely taken by surprise."

"Uh-huh," he returned in the same doubting way as before.

Moving staunchly around him, Sam strode to the door and opened it. "I don't intend to continue this. I'd like you to leave."

Without moving, he gave her a lazy once-over.

"Now," she added curtly. As he swaggered up to her, it was all she could do to look him straight in the eye. Her pulse was pounding, her blood racing, and worst of all, he knew it.

"Sorry if I shocked you," he drawled. "Most women appreciate a direct approach."

"It's impossible to generalize about women that way," she returned. "Every woman is different."

"*You* are different," he conceded. "I'll grant you that."

"But I will say," Sam continued briskly, "that your direct approach, as you call it, saves time. Now that this is behind us, maybe we can start again on the right foot."

"What foot would that be?"

"I'm the only doctor in this town, and you're its principal employer. It would be nice if we could be civil."

She steeled herself against reacting as he lifted a hand to her face. His knuckle traced her cheekbone to the hairline.

"You're got a dusting of freckles across your cheeks," he observed.

She backed away from his touch. "I'm aware of that." Grasping the edge of the door, she drew it wide. Finally he took a slow step toward the threshold.

"See you Tuesday, then."

"Tuesday?" To her own ears Sam's voice sounded irritatingly like that of a parrot.

"When you come to see Nadine."

"Yes. Of course."

His amber eyes narrowed on hers, and she did everything within her power to appear totally unaffected.

"You sure you won't change your mind about supper?" he asked. "This is one of my last free nights before harvest sets in. I'll be unavailable for a while."

"I'll try and bear up."

"Maybe you shouldn't try so hard," he suggested as he stepped out on the porch.

"Maybe you don't know me well enough to suggest what I should or shouldn't try," Sam retaliated.

"Maybe not yet, but I'm getting there. Oh, Doc ..." As he turned on the steps, the afternoon sun sparkled in his eyes and flashed across the surface of a white smile.

"Couldn't help noticing you feel a mite warm," he added. "Maybe you should check your temperature."

She closed the door in his face, but not before she heard the beginning of a rumbling chuckle on the other side. Spinning toward the kitchen, she was confronted with the sight of Celie, who was standing just inside the parlor and grinning from ear to ear.

"Don't ... say ... a word," Sam commanded, her expression as stern as her exaggerated enunciation.

Clapping a hand over her mouth, the girl did her best to stifle her giggles as she scampered from the room.

The lingering twilight finally succumbed to darkness around nine o'clock, when a sharp rap sounded on Sam's door and Rae walked forthrightly in.

"Is it too late for a neighborly visit?" she asked. "Things have slowed down across the street, and I thought I'd bring over this pitcher of iced tea."

They retired to the kitchen, where the sweet scent of gardenia wafted from the vase by the sink. Making herself at home, Rae directed Sam to a seat at the table,

poured tall glasses of the frosty tea, and put the pitcher
in the fridge.

"I had no idea anything could taste so good," Sam
murmured.

With a merry smile Rae fluttered her fingers in the air.
"What can I say? The hands are magic. By the way, how
are you and Celie getting on?"

"Famously," Sam replied. "I hate to think what it
would have been like around here without her. She's
coming back tomorrow and the next day. In fact, I was
thinking of offering her an after-school job."

"That would be great. Since Celie's ma passed on, it's
just her and her grandpa. The poor old man can't do a
thing but sit. He's been crippled up with rheumatism as
long as I can remember."

"Maybe I could prescribe something for him . . ."

And so the talk went on. The tea glasses were nearly
empty when Sam became aware of a lull in the conversation, and then the intense perusal of Rae's dark eyes.

"What?" Sam prompted with a smile.

"Mind if I ask you a question?"

"Not at all."

"Those gardenias over there . . . Matt brought them,
didn't he?"

Sam's smile faltered. "Yes."

"I thought so. He used to bring them to me from time
to time. Of course, that was more years ago than I care
to count."

Sam hesitated for a moment before saying, "Mind if I
ask *you* a question?"

"Shoot."

"You still care a great deal for him, don't you?"

Rae laughed, but the sound was brittle. Sam gazed at
her patiently, watching as the smile lines drooped and
the dark eyes turned away.

"Sure I do. I've loved him from the time I was eleven,
and I reckon I always will. I'm like the kid sister he never
had. He'd do anything for me, but . . ."

"But?" Sam prompted.

"Anything but want me again," Rae answered, the words soft and low and swift as a gust of wind. In the space of an instant the shadow was gone from her face, the devil-may-care expression back in place.

"Don't let it bother you none," she added. "I haven't let it hamper my social life any. From the time Matt walked down the aisle with Miss Priss, I've known it wasn't in the cards for him and me."

"Walked down the aisle?" Sam repeated in surprise. "He's married?"

"Oh yes, he's definitely married. Though you'd never know it by his lifestyle. He and Lucy haven't lived together in years, and he's got a long-standing reputation as one of the biggest heartbreakers in three states."

"You mean he's a philanderer," Sam observed in a hard tone.

"I don't know about that," Rae returned with a chuckle. "But it's for damn sure he's got a way with the ladies. And it's for damn sure he's got a thing for the new doc, too."

Sam looked sharply across the table. "I don't know about that. A new single woman on the scene always gets a flurry of attention. If Matt Tyler has a *thing*, I'm sure it's a passing one."

"You sound like you don't welcome his attentions."

"I don't," Sam replied, emphasizing the final word. "Does that surprise you?"

"Damn right. I don't think I've ever heard of anybody turning him down. Women have always liked Matt, and he's always been happy to oblige."

"I'm interested in a cordial, respectful acquaintance-ship with Matt Tyler. That's the only thing I'd like him to oblige me with."

Rae gave her a long, searching look. "Summertime down South," she murmured. "Passions run hot. People find themselves feeling and doing things they wouldn't expect."

"No offense, Rae. I know he's an old friend of yours, but Matt Tyler holds absolutely no interest for me."

"Is that right," Rae commented on a lingering note of doubt.

"That's right. For one thing he's married."

"Separated."

"Whatever. For another thing we have nothing in common. In fact, I can't think of two people who are more opposite."

"There's an old saying about opposites attracting."

"It doesn't apply in this case," Sam insisted.

Yet after Rae left, and Sam climbed into bed and turned out the light, nagging thoughts of Matt taunted her for a liar. Regardless of how she shifted and turned, images of him followed, foiling every attempt at sleep. On several occasions she'd crushed the impulse to relive the kiss in the street; now, against her wishes, her mind played it out in detail, and she faced the fact that she'd never felt quite like that in her life.

Matt Tyler's overpowering masculinity was unique, as was the impact he wielded on some female part of her so integral she hadn't known it existed until he kissed her and something seemed to explode.

"This is ridiculous," Sam muttered finally, and leaving the bedroom, went down to the kitchen for another magical glass of Rae's iced tea. Even that didn't chase away the heat that seemed to radiate as much from inside her body as without.

She wandered into the parlor. Moonlight gilded the spot where the man had stood mere hours before. At the time, she'd been so outraged by his brazen approach, she wouldn't have given him the satisfaction of even *considering* his invitation. Now, Sam imagined where a different course would have taken her.

What if she'd accepted? What if she'd put herself in the position of being alone with Matt Tyler? There was no doubt of where it would have led. The confrontation of man and woman. Straightforward. Bottom line. No glaze of getting to know one another, just raw confrontation. That was the word for Matt Tyler—raw.

Sam hastily swallowed a gulp of tea. Of course, there

was no question of how she would have handled the situation. After all, she was a creature of cerebral tastes, and he a rutting beast with a reputation for philandering that spanned the Southeast.

Still . . . she could see why he was so successful at it. With a look he made a woman feel as though she wore no clothes. With a smile he provoked the intimacy of bed. Everything about him screamed of sex until the word filled a woman's head and raced in her veins.

Summertime down South, Rae's words whispered. *Passions run hot . . .*

Of *course,* there was no question of how she'd have handled the situation! Reason and generations of New England moral fiber would certainly have taken charge. Just as they would anytime in the future that Matt Tyler sought to ply her with his renowned charms. Besides, he was married, and she had far more worthy ways to spend her energy than to waste it thinking about a married man.

Thus shoring herself up, Sam returned to bed—though she failed to find sleep before a distant rooster announced the approaching dawn.

Chapter Six

Labor Day, September 6

Patting her neck with a damp cloth, Sam followed Celie onto the porch. It was nearly seven, the sun disappearing behind distant treetops while the street continued to shimmer. Sam had never known heat like this. It filled the air, crept down her throat, settled in her lungs. They sat down on the steps, leaving plenty of room between them for any breeze that might stir.

In three days, the difference they'd wreaked in the old Daly house was laudable. Furniture and linens had been aired, hardwood floors polished, washrooms sterilized. All that remained downstairs was to organize the storage room adjoining the examining room—once the supplies were ordered and delivered. All that remained upstairs was the monumental task of sorting through the stacks of patients' files and papers and boxes that composed Dr. Daly's office.

Sam had paid Celie twice the rate she hesitantly quoted, and insisted on packing her a light supper to take home. As for herself, she was too hot and tired to eat. Shifting to lean against one of the porch's massive columns, Sam gazed across Main Street. As usual, the thoroughfare was quiet but for the voices drifting through the screened doors of Rae's Place.

"Sounds like a fair-sized supper crowd across the way," Celie said. Sam listlessly nodded.

"You should try it out," Celie went on. "Miz Washburn has got the two best cooks in the county. Fried chicken, black-eyed peas, turnip greens, and when the peaches are in—mmm, mmm!—you ain't ever had cobbler till you've had Georgia peach cobbler."

Draping the cloth around her neck, Sam smiled. "I'll try it out. It just won't be tonight. Tonight, all I want to do is soak in a nice, clean tub. Thanks for all your help, Celie. I'm awfully glad Rae brought us together."

"Me, too," the girl replied, her typical smile flashing, but swiftly dying. "I don't want it to end," she added quietly.

"It doesn't have to end, Celie. In fact, I was telling Rae just last night that I'd like to offer you an after-school job."

The girl's face lit up like a lantern. "I'd still work hard and clean for you, Dr. Sam. But I'd like to learn, too. You see, one day I'd like to be . . . well, I want to be a nurse."

"Do you really?" Sam asked happily.

"I get good grades in school. You don't think it's—you know—*above* me, do you?"

Reaching out, Sam covered the girl's hand with her own. "I think you'll make a fine nurse, Celie. And you know something? It won't look half bad on your résumé that you've had training with the local doctor."

"Training? Just like you had at Saint Elizabeth's?"

"Yes," Sam affirmed with a light laugh. "Just like that."

She accompanied Celie to the sagging front gate, and it was then that a drumroll sounded out, drawing their attention to the square down the street. There, Sam beheld the eeriest sight she'd ever seen—a small circle of people dressed in white hoods and robes, each of them holding a torch, each of them coming forward to touch a personal flame to the wooden structure already ablaze. As the flames licked against the dusk in the shape of a cross, she realized what she was looking at—the Ku Klux Klan.

"Oh, no," she mumbled, unaware that she'd voiced the words aloud until Celie spoke up.

"It's the heat," Celie said, drawing Sam's shocked gaze. Gone was the girl's typically bright expression; in its place, a blank look that didn't quite hide the sadness of her young face.

"Folks get rowdy in the summertime," she added quietly. "Like a bunch of firecrackers ready to pop. Reckon we're lucky they don't do no more than burn up a few sticks of wood."

Celie squared her shoulders as she started quickly down the street, staying carefully in the shadows. The sight of her against the backdrop of such a shameful display filled Sam with anger—the feeling escalating as the group at the square broke into song.

> *Well, I wish I was in the land of cotton,*
> *Old times there are not forgotten,*
> *Look away,*
> *Look away,*
> *Look away, Dixieland.*

As they continued to sing, people began emerging from buildings along Main Street. Some joined the hooded demonstrators and began to sing along. Most watched from their porches. When Sam noticed the constable, Larry Edison, among the onlookers outside Rae's Place, she stood and briskly crossed the street.

> *I wish I was in Dixie!*
> *Hooray! Hooray!*

Rae was there, too, along with six or seven men who were strangers to Sam. She paid them scant attention as she marched up to the constable.

"How dare you stand by and let this go on," she said.

Larry Edison straightened away from the porch rail. "What?" he asked, genuinely taken aback.

"That," she replied with a curt nod toward the square. "I'd call that a disturbance of the peace."

The constable shrugged. "Sorry, ma'am. There's nothing I can do about it. They filed for a permit weeks ago."

"But isn't there some kind of ordinance that prohibits their demonstrating here in town?"

"Nope," the man replied. "Just the opposite. Something to do with the Constitution, I believe."

"Why should people who are offended by them have to witness their actions?"

"Nobody forces anybody to watch."

In Dixieland, I'll take my stand,
To live and die in Dixie.

"You can't help but watch!" Sam answered in an exasperated tone. "That's the point."

As the constable looked uncomfortably aside, she became aware of the buzzing attention of the other onlookers. The men were scowling, and although Rae produced a smile, her expression suggested perplexity more than anything else.

"Isn't there a more discreet place they could meet?" Sam asked. "Do they have to do it at the square?"

"The square's been the place for meetin' ever since there's been a town," Larry said.

"But what if the townspeople objected?"

"They've had over a hundred years to object. Nobody has."

"Till now, you mean," Sam firmly replied. "How about a petition? If enough people signed, couldn't a petition legitimize some kind of action? A restraining order, perhaps?"

Pushing his hat to the back of his head, Larry Edison surrendered a friendly look. "It's an idea," he said. "Of course, it would take a lot of time and energy to gather signatures."

"Once the clinic is set up, I could find the time."

"And I'm not optimistic about the kind of response you'd get."

"Surely there are people just as outraged by this kind of thing as I am," Sam said.

Larry Edison's friendly expression gradually dissolved. "I don't know how much outrage you'll find," he said. "But if you're serious, I suggest you talk to Matt."

"Tyler?" Sam questioned.

"Why?" Rae demanded.

"Use your head, Rae," he replied. "I'm just the law in these parts. Matt's the power. Who do you think half the people around here work for?" Larry turned to look at Sam. "The Tylers have always held a special place in this town. I'd say if you can bring Matt around to your way of thinking, you've got a chance. If not, forget it."

"All right, then," Sam said with determined spirit. "I'll speak to him tomorrow. I'm going over there, anyway."

"To Matt's?" Rae interjected.

"Yes. He asked me, so I'm going."

"Slow down, Sam," Rae advised. "Don't you think you might be going overboard a little bit? This klan thing is just part of something you're not used to—coming from Boston and all."

"Boston is no haven, Rae. During the early days of the civil rights movement, my home city was the site of one of integration's bloodiest battles. Maybe that's why no one from around Boston takes the subject lightly."

"No one from around Riverbend takes it light, either," Rae said, and with the arch of a brow, cocked her head toward the other onlookers. Glancing aside, Sam had just enough time to note the number of narrowed eyes turned her way before the commotion down the street swelled to an uproar.

The marchers ended their song with a chorus of whoops, their white robes flapping as they jabbed torches at the sky. There was a sense of unreality about the scene, and yet Sam knew the ugliness it represented was real. It had existed throughout time—among the

Romans, the Nazis, the South Africans—it was one of the most abominable traits of the human species, and seeing it celebrated made her sick to her stomach.

"They're disgusting," Sam pronounced and started to turn.

"Best watch your tongue," came a male voice. Sam looked around as a brawny stranger in overalls shouldered forward.

"The name's Hal Carter," he added. "And I got kinfolk down the street."

"I'm sorry."

"That's better."

"I mean about your kinfolk," Sam clarified, and tried to ignore the angry exchange that erupted as the constable took hold of the man—apparently to prevent him from jumping her as she crossed the street. *God!* Sam thought as she stomped along. How in the world could she last a year in this racist, chauvanistic, culturally deprived hellhole of a place? *How?!*

Slamming her own door behind her, she was greeted by the scent of pine cleanser, and almost could have laughed—so paradoxical were her thoughts. Little by little, the house was coming together. Piece by piece, her life was falling apart. The conditions in which she was expected to work were deplorable, the people she was expected to treat were like foreigners who could no more speak her language than she could fathom theirs.

She couldn't believe it—the KKK, alive and kicking in Riverbend, Georgia. And the locals didn't even seem to mind.

Brushing the bangs from her forehead with a short stroke, Sam bolted the door, latched the downstairs windows, and climbed the stairs thinking she'd never been so thoroughly weary in either body or spirit. An hour later, after a cool bath, she lay down on clean sheets and soaked up every bit of breeze the meager fan could produce. Life's simple pleasures had never meant so much; still, they couldn't stave off the dark emotions that dwelled beneath the surface.

As Sam rested an arm across closed eyes, her mind recreated the image of hooded figures with torches, and she felt once more the horror she'd experienced on the street. It was hard to say which wrenched her more deeply—her anger on behalf of people like Celie Johnson, or her own misery at having been abandoned to such a place as Riverbend . . . condemned to a crude existence of which she had no understanding, and wanted no part.

Tuesday, September 7

As soon as the phone was hooked up by a grinning nineteen-year-old who moonlighted at the Shell station off Main, Sam spent the morning talking long distance to Savannah. The list of equipment and supplies was extensive; nonetheless, the supplier guaranteed shipment of on-hand inventory within twenty-four hours, and the full list by the weekend.

As Celie lingered downstairs, applying finishing touches to the storage room that would receive stock the next day, Sam walked into the second-floor room that once must have been Dr. Daly's sanctum. The walls were covered with photographs dating back to the forties, the desk with file folders that appeared to originate from the same era. Sam put on her glasses and sat down in the late doctor's swivel chair.

What started as a passing look at a few charts swiftly turned into voracious investigation. Daly's files were not simply medical charts, but mini-journals filled with rambling observation, speculation, and philosophy. Cases from the fifties chronicled a number of young soldiers who'd been killed abroad, and included the doctor's notes on the horrors of the Korean conflict. Files from the sixties provided a treatise on the "peace and love" generation. At the bottom of a stack, Sam came across a coffee-stained folder dating back to 1947. She scanned the handwriting.

I am not a religious man, but the suicide of Cora Swantee has made me think in terms of good and evil, God and Satan. Juda's curse on the Tylers is a well-known legend in Riverbend. Less known is what actually became of the voodoo priestess. The fact is, she was fruitful and multiplied, producing three daughters who inherited her dark beauty as well as her penchant for mysterious ways.

One of those daughters, Sybil, began working as a nanny for the Swantees two years back. Some months later, Cora began exhibiting symptoms of depression and paranoia. I referred her to a psychiatrist in Savannah, but her occasional checkups with me showed little progress. And now, she has hanged herself, and her widowed husband has been seen with Sybil on his arm.

Even a nonreligious man can't help but draw a connection between Juda and her daughter, and the violent ends met by the wives of the men they coveted.

"Ready for some lunch, Dr. Sam?"

Sam jumped as she looked up to see Celie's cheery face in the doorway. "You go ahead. I'll be down in a minute, okay?"

As it turned out, she grabbed a piece of Grace Whitehead's fried chicken from the fridge and returned to the upstairs office.

Ida was always such a meek little thing. Red, on the other hand, has always been volatile. He came into the world screaming, and most likely will leave it that way. I had my doubts when the two of them married, and now the worst of my fears has proven out.

At first it was just the occasional bruise I noticed when we happened to cross paths. Then came the burn on her hand, for which Ida slipped secretly into my office; then the violent miscarriage that left her unable to bear children. Red himself brought her in for that one, and explained she'd fallen down the stairs. Tonight, his story was that she fell off a loft at the mill.

I fail to see how a simple fall could have mangled an ankle so badly. It appeared to have been twisted to the point of breakage, and then allowed to become infected. If she'd been brought to me within a reasonable amount of time, I could have prevented the limp I fear she'll carry forever. As it is, I was challenged merely to save her leg. On the occasions when I say a prayer, I pray for the safety of Ida Carter.

Sitting back in the chair, Sam removed her glasses and pictured Red Carter. The despicable bully. Bigotry ... wife-beating ... What else had he been getting away with all these years? And why hadn't Dr. Daly intervened?

Even as the question formed, Sam sensed the answer. It had to do with an outlook that put men in some kind of sacred camaraderie with one another, and wives in subservience to husbands—as though females were owned property to be dealt with as their masters saw fit. Despite his knowledge and compassion and sense of morality, a male doctor apparently wouldn't expose another man.

She'd have liked to despise Dr. Daly at that moment, but she couldn't. The man had been a servant to his community, and a product of his times. The many ways he'd helped the people of Riverbend obviously outweighed the ways he'd slighted them ... she supposed.

It was late afternoon when Sam tore herself away from his records. Having worked most of the day in the examining and storage rooms, Celie had the place looking as though it really might become a clinic after all.

"You've done an amazing job," Sam complimented, and sending Celie off with a bonus in her pocket, dashed back upstairs where she swiftly changed out of shorts and T-shirt, and put on a medically correct ensemble of white blouse and slacks.

Pulling her hair back in a clasp, Sam gave herself a fleeting smile in the mirror. She looked merely the way she'd looked most days of her adult life. But it was the first day she'd looked like a doctor in Riverbend. Picking up her black bag, she trotted down to the van and departed for the vineyards.

After passing the square, she followed the road away from town in a northwesterly direction. To the left, cypress was a tall gray wall presiding over swampland that stretched out of sight toward the river. To the right, a series of farmhouses dotted brown and dusty fields. When the swamp ended, brown acres swelled across the road to present a barren landscape ... until she saw the sign, made the turn, and was confronted by a white fence bordering a sea of green.

Sam stomped on the brakes, her gaze sweeping the panorama, straining toward the horizon where seemingly endless emerald fields met the sapphire blue of the sky. It was beautiful. No, more than that. After the blandness of the countryside, it was like something unreal ... a Garden of Eden. Breathtaking.

Across the road a wrought-iron arch supported a sign announcing: RIVERBEND VINEYARDS. Sam drove slowly beneath it, and fancied she was entering another world where color became suddenly vivid, as did the invigorating smell of growing things. Still lush with the green of spring in the ebb of summer, the grapevines were trained along posted lengths of screen ... bank after bank, row after row, acre after acre. And far ahead, a white, castlelike house on a hill overlooked it all.

Keeping the van at a crawl, Sam peered along the columns of vines, occasionally spotting workers with their heads covered with straw hats or bandanas, occasionally hearing a cheery exchange of their voices. She was barely moving at all when she noticed the pickup parked by the road mere yards ahead. Standing beside it was a black man and ... Matt. Though his back was to her, there was no mistaking his powerful form—cowboy hat, jeans, boots, no shirt ... his massive shoulders browned to the hue of Georgia earth.

The sound of the van reached his ears, and he turned. With an uncharacteristic lack of interest, he gave a tug to the brim of his hat, turned back to the black man, and didn't so much as glance her way as she passed. Looking ahead toward the drive to the house, Sam increased her speed and tried to ignore an irritating sensation not unlike the sting of a bee.

The drive forked at the crest of the hill, one branch leading to a sprawling side building where a number of vehicles were parked. The winery, she imagined. Taking the fork to the house, she parked in a newly paved courtyard bordered by green lawn that rolled down the hill to the vineyards.

Sam paused and treated herself to a long look. Departing from the antebellum flavor that was standard in town, the Riverbend house had the fanciful appeal of a French chateau. Its roofline was steep and peaked and the color of slate; its walls, whitewashed; its windows trimmed in black wrought-iron, which was repeated in columns at an entrance cupola banked with flowers. Though grand in size—with two sweeping stories, a turret at one end, and a screened verandah at the other—it didn't suggest the impression of a mansion, but more of a country estate.

She was shocked by the idea of Matt Tyler in such a setting. If ever she might have pictured where he lived, it would have been in a rough-hewn cabin . . . or maybe a teepee.

Pushing aside the thought of him, Sam walked to the door and was met by a black woman with a face-splitting smile and snow white hair. She had cheeks as plump as a cherub's, and a girth that filled her tentlike dress.

"Do come in, honey," she said. "I'm Nadine, and I'm happy as can be to see you, though only the Lord knows why Matt insisted on calling you all the way out here."

The chateau was even more charming inside than out—tiled foyer, arched doorways, graceful rooms with antique furnishings, as well as a magnificent staircase and chandelier. Sam gazed around appreciatively as she followed Nadine to her quarters at the rear of the house. She also noted the woman's potential health problems.

For starters Nadine was not a young woman—well past seventy, Sam would guess. And overweight nearly to the point of obesity, her swollen legs carrying her at a slow, waddling pace.

As Sam performed a basic preliminary exam, Nadine talked of her daughter, Justine, who was married to George Waters, one of the "Riverbend bosses" . . . and their four children, the oldest of which, "little Crystal," was a real beauty . . . and her deceased husband, "God bless his soul," who had passed away some years ago.

"There never was a finer man," she concluded with a sigh.

Replacing the last of her instruments, Sam picked up her bag and strolled over to the bed. "Your blood pressure is high, Nadine."

She grimaced as she began buttoning up the top of her dress. "Always is in the summertime. Dr. Daly said it was my nature."

"Yes, well, I'm still going to prescribe a medication. Are your records among those I saw at the Daly house?"

"Reckon so. He's the only doctor I ever been to."

"Have you noticed any shortness of breath?"

"Honey, I don't get around fast enough to lose my breath."

In spite of herself, Sam couldn't prevent the flicker of a smile. "Do you have trouble getting around?"

"Only when my feet swell so bad," she replied and cast a look at the offending ankles.

"Elevate them," Sam advised. "Whenever you can, take a break, lie down, and prop them higher than your hips. And you shouldn't be going up and down that staircase all the time. I hope you don't take care of this big place all by yourself."

"Good gracious, no. We got us an upstairs maid, and a downstairs maid, and a yard man, and a cook I'd sorely like to chase out of my kitchen. All I do is piddle."

"There's something else," Sam said as Nadine fastened her collar beneath the folds of her throat. "You really need to lose some weight."

She looked up, her dark eyes flashing with indignation. "Now, I'd call *that* a matter of opinion. My man always appreciated a full figure."

"I don't mean for aesthetics," Sam replied, helplessly smiling. "I mean for your health. Cut out sweets, soft drinks, fat as much as possible. How about salt? Do you use a lot of it?"

"A pinch here and there."

"Try to do without the pinches."

"You sure do talk big for such a little thing," Nadine muttered, but as she pushed to her feet, she offered Sam a pearly smile, along with an assessing look that swept her from head to toe and back again.

"So, you're the one who slapped that big stud silly."

The comment took Sam by complete surprise. "What?" she managed.

"Saturday night, in front of Rae's. I hear you hauled off and knocked Matt winding."

"Is that what he told you?"

"Lord, no! He never tells me anything. I have to get all my gossip from Drew."

The name rang a bell. Drew ... the one with the picture-book smile. She'd met him at Rae's, then seen him again at the charade in the street.

"Drew Pierce, right?" she questioned.

"Uh-huh. Matt brought him along when he moved out here. I got me two big boys to look after, honey, and things have never been dull. But I got a feeling they're gonna get downright rowdy. Drew says you got hair like the blaze of fire, and a temper to match."

"Be that as it may ..." Sam began uncomfortably, letting the phrase hang as Nadine emitted a deep, rumbling laugh.

"I can see it," she said. "I can see it plain as day."

"See what?"

Her smile broadened to astonishing limits. "Matt Tyler's done met his match. *That's* what."

Sam shook her head. "My coming to Riverbend has

nothing to do with being anyone's match, Nadine. I'm a doctor."

Nadine's brows lifted as she showered Sam with another head-to-toe survey. "That ain't *all* you are, honey. Come on out to the kitchen, now. I got some fresh-baked cookies to send along."

"Cookies? What kind?"

"Georgia pecan. Homemade, and chock full of butter and sugar." She seemed to relish saying the forbidden ingredients, and the mere sound of the confections made Sam's mouth water. "No more of those for you, now," she cautioned Nadine, who responded with a scowl.

"Well, then," she said, her frown melting in a sunny smile. "You might as well take the whole batch."

Sam left the house with a tin of the most delicious-smelling cookies she'd ever imagined. She could hardly wait to reach the end of the drive before prying off the lid and pulling back the waxed paper. Driving along between the green walls of the vineyards, she heartily bit into the first warm taste of heaven and had just finished consuming it when she came upon the pickup blocking the road.

Slowing to a stop, she scanned the area and spotted the black man she'd seen earlier. She followed his gaze to a shirtless man who was crouched, working at the base of a nearby vine. An instant later, as sunshine flashed across his back, she recognized Matt. He was like part of the earth . . . a dark, moving mountain.

Suddenly, a cloud of smoke burst above his head as a deafening boom split the air. Instinctively clapping her hands over her ears, Sam stared as a huge flock of birds rose through the smoke and flapped swiftly into the distance. They must have been cawing to beat the band, but she didn't hear a thing as the sound of a thunderclap rang in her head.

She sat there a few more stunned seconds—feet planted on brake and clutch, palms planted on her ears. A trickle of perspiration slipped between her breasts. Irritably yanking her hands from her head, Sam grasped steering wheel and gear shift, and inched the van forward. A look of impatience that had been aimed at the impeding truck, now rested squarely on Matt. When she tapped a short honk on the horn, he rose to his feet and strode her way, dusting work-gloved hands against his pants legs as he came.

"What in the world was that earsplitting noise?" she demanded as he stopped beside her window.

"Propane cannon. I usually try to warn first-timers. Didn't realize you were here."

"Propane cannon?" Sam repeated.

"Um-hmmm. Look in the bed of the truck up ahead. See those blue cylinders? They look kind of like bazookas, don't they? And each one is a weapon in the grape-grower's battle against birds. Every year when the grapes get ripe, they come and stay for harvest. They'd steal you blind if you let them. Most growers space cannons throughout their vineyards. All they do is make a loud noise and a little smoke. But they scare the birds away . . . normally."

"Normally?"

Matt looked toward the western horizon. "Well, this damn bunch just doesn't seem to stay scared. Besides that, most birds feed in the morning. Look what time it is, and these are still at it. I've never seen the like."

Sam peered off into the distance, wondering about the peculiar behavior of the birds until the insufferable heat brought her around. Wiping swift fingers across her beaded lip, she looked to the left, her eyes lighting on the incredibly developed chest no more than an arm's length away.

"That's very interesting," she said. "But it's been a long day."

Matt's head snapped around. "Sorry. I'll move the truck. Just didn't want you getting away without me asking after Nadine."

Dark and sweaty, his skin shining as though it had been oiled, he swept the familiar cowboy hat from his head, and wiped a forearm across his brow. The simple gesture was accomplished with the most amazing play of muscle swelling to muscle . . .

"Well? How is she?"

Sam looked up with a start. "Fair, I would say. I'm glad you asked me to see her, though. Her blood pressure is pretty high."

"Can you do anything about it?"

She searched the glowing eyes, and saw more than a teasing look of challenge.

"Medication if necessary," Sam answered. "But I'd like to see what can be accomplished with diet first, and I want to review Dr. Daly's records."

Replacing the hat, Matt pulled the brim low on his brow. "Much obliged to you for coming out."

"Not at all. It was a pleasure meeting Nadine, and seeing the vineyards. You have quite a place here."

Propping a hand on the van roof, he leaned close to the window. In spite of herself, Sam caught her breath as he lifted a gloved finger to her face.

"How ya been sleeping?" he asked, his gaze meeting her eyes as his fingertip traced a light line across her cheek.

"None of your business," she returned.

"I only ask because you've got circles under your eyes," he said with a look of pure innocence.

Sinking back against the seat, Sam removed herself from his light touch. "It's the heat," she explained. "Even at night it doesn't go away; it just lies there and waits to get worse when the sun comes up."

"Now that you mention it, I noticed it was damn hot in the house the other day. Air conditioner on the blink?"

"Extinct is more like it," Sam answered on a weary note. "Just like every piece of machinery in that house."

"Sorry you came?"

She looked up. "To Riverbend?" When Matt nodded, she said, "It's a far cry from Boston."

"Maybe we'll grow on you," he said with the beginning of the sexy smile she'd come to associate with Matt Tyler.

It was interrupted as the black man stepped up, and Matt turned.

"Sam, I'd like you to meet one of my partners, George Waters."

"How do you do?" she said as he removed his straw hat to reveal curly black hair frosted with gray.

"My pleasure, ma'am. Sorry to interrupt." Replacing his hat, he looked up at Matt. "They ain't gone, brother. I just saw 'em set down at the west end."

"Dammit to hell," Matt muttered.

"We'd best be gettin' over there with some cannons." The two of them started to walk away.

"Matt, wait!" When he looked questioningly over his shoulder, she added, "Can you spare a minute?"

"About a minute, yeah," he answered, moseying her way once more as George Waters walked off toward the truck.

"I'll try to be brief," Sam said. "I'm thinking of organizing a petition. And Larry Edison suggested you're the place to start."

"Petition about what?"

"The KKK."

"What about them?"

"Well, they're disgraceful."

"I don't agree with their views either, but what do you want me to do about them?"

"Larry said that many of the people around here work for you. Maybe some of the klan members do."

"So?"

Losing patience with his disinterest, she sputtered, "So, maybe you could put your very important support behind a petition banning them from demonstrating in town."

Matt gave her a wry look. "Ban them," he repeated.

"That's right."

"If you want to stir up a hornets' nest, that's the way to do it. The klan has been holding their little get-togethers in these parts for a hundred years. Nobody pays them any attention."

"That's not true. You should have seen Celie Johnson's face."

"A few hurt feelings are nothing compared to what might happen if somebody tried to interfere. All that would do is get their backs up, and then you might really have a problem."

"I can think of less worthy risks than striking a blow against the Ku Klux Klan."

"Can you?" he returned with a lift of his dark brows. "Then, best of luck." Once again he stepped back.

"I can't believe you're so blasé about this," Sam cried.

He spread gloved palms to the sky. "And I can't believe you'd walk in here after four days and think you know how things stand."

"You sound like Red Carter," she accused and was awarded a swift scowl, as well as a warning index finger.

"Look, lady. I've got some very real birds here who are doing some very real harm to my land. Do me a favor, will ya? Leave well enough alone."

He moved away at a no-nonsense pace toward the pickup.

"One might wish you took human beings half as seriously as your damn birds!" Sam called to his back. There was the briefest hitch in his long stride, but other than that he surrendered no reaction as he climbed into the truck and pulled out of her way.

"Savage," Sam muttered under her breath as she sped toward the arch marking the boundary of Riverbend Vineyards.

*C*hapter Seven

Andrew Dunaway leaned back in his leather chair, his reflective gaze taking in the lavish appointments of his office. Against the backdrop of priceless *objets d'art* and antiques, the refined blonde in the tailored navy dress looked right at home. Strolling casually about as she spoke, she moved with the grace of one who had been trained at the finest of finishing schools. She might well have been discussing the plans for a garden party rather than a corporate coup.

Long considered one of the first ladies of Savannah, and one of its most beautiful, Lucy Beauregard Tyler led a public life of hostessing charity benefits, sponsoring historic society events, and patronizing the arts. Her picture was always showing up in the social pages for one reason or another, and she was always wearing just the right smile, along with just the right gown or dress or suit. Andrew should know. His own wife had spent thousands following the fashion trends set by Lucy Tyler.

Andrew saw through the veneer of impeccable grace. Beneath it Lucy was hard as nails, and well accustomed to wielding the power of both her beauty and her money to get what she wanted.

"Riverbend Vineyards has emerged as one of the top wine producers in the Southeast," she said. "And the

Riverbend property has been in the Tyler family for more than a century. It seems perfectly clear to me that I'm entitled to half the profits."

"Half," Andrew repeated on a doubtful note.

"That's the percentage I receive from other revenue-producing assets."

"Those that existed when the separation agreement was drawn up a dozen years ago."

"Things have changed," she replied with a light shrug.

Yes, they had. The word was that Matt Tyler had exiled himself to the countryside and worked like a madman to build Riverbend Vineyards into what it had become. Leaning forward, Andrew propped his elbows on his desk.

"Lucy, I was delighted when you made the appointment to see me, but I have to ask why you're not talking to Robert Larkin."

Her chin lifted a notch. "Robert is retired."

"I saw him just yesterday at the courthouse. It's my understanding that he continues to represent selected clients. I'd have thought you'd be one of them."

Her blue eyes seemed to narrow as they leveled on his. "I'll be frank, Andrew. I've already spoken with Robert."

"And?" he prodded.

"And he's lost the taste for blood. How about you?"

Making a temple of his hands, Andrew rested his chin on his fingertips. "I like lawsuits I think I can win. I'm not at all sure about this one."

"Would the idea of being retained to manage the sum of my legal affairs assuage your fear of risk?"

Andrew raised a brow. "You mean you're splitting entirely with Robert Larkin?"

"He and I simply don't see eye-to-eye any longer."

"So, you're willing to turn over the sum total of your business to me *if* I take on this suit."

"That's right."

"What if the hearing doesn't turn out the way you want it to?"

She paused in the midst of pulling on kid gloves. "I'm accustomed to things turning out the way I want them to, Andrew. If you plan on working for me, that's something you'd do well to remember. Do we have an agreement?"

Andrew's brows knitted together as he considered the proposition. On the one hand, he didn't like the feel of this lawsuit; on the other hand, if he turned down Lucy Beauregard Tyler, he'd be turning down one of the most enviable clients in Savannah. At forty-five he was a full partner in one of the city's leading firms, a success by anyone's measure. Lucy could make him a megasuccess.

"I'll have the contract drawn up," he said at last.

"Good. Now . . . how do you intend to proceed with the suit?"

"I'll have to subpoena the company records in order to formulate your complaint. There's only one logical strategy in a matter such as this . . ."

"Which is?" Lucy prompted impatiently.

"To go after Riverbend Vineyards, we're going to have to prove that Matt Tyler is hiding assets behind a facade of incorporation. It's called piercing the corporate veil."

"I like that," Lucy declared.

"A lot will depend on how the judge sees things, Lucy. After all, you've already amassed quite a fortune through Matt Tyler."

"Never mind about that. When can we take him to court?"

Andrew glanced at his calendar. "With some luck we might get a court date before Christmas."

"Christmas?" Lucy repeated with an airy laugh. "Oh, no. That's far too long. It will have to be much sooner—within the next few weeks."

"I can't possibly pull this together in a matter of—"

"Then perhaps I'm talking to the wrong man," she interrupted.

"Lucy," he said firmly, "even if I stay up nights to get the paperwork in order, the dockets are full. Hearings scheduled for the next few weeks were slated months ago."

She gave him a cool smile. "Use my name," she suggested. "You might be surprised at the weight it swings."

"I might be at that," Andrew murmured.

When she stepped over to his desk, he rose to his feet.

"You'll let me know as soon as an acceptable date is set," she said—not a request, but a command.

"Of course."

Offering a gloved hand, she joined him in a brief shake. "Also, I'd like to be contacted when the summons is prepared."

"We use a private investigator, Joe Riggs, to deliver most of our summons. You'll get a copy the same day Matt is served."

"Actually, I intend to be there."

"At Riverbend?"

"Yes. Inform Mr. Riggs that we'll be taking my car. I wouldn't miss the look on Matt's face for all the world."

Smiling prettily, Lucy turned toward the door. Hard as nails, Andrew thought as she glided gracefully out of the room.

Sam's temper continued to smolder as she drove from the vineyards to town. Matt Tyler could get a rise out of her faster than any man she'd ever known. Braking to a short halt in front of the Daly house, she leaped down from the van, and was halfway up the walk when she caught the first whiff of the stench.

Freezing in midstride, she sniffed the air—her nostrils withering as they registered the odor of animal dung. Sam made herself move closer. The brown pile on the porch was a foot high, and twice as wide; plus, the shape of a cross had been smeared on the door with the stuff. Whirling away, Sam stomped over to Rae's Place, and demanded the loan of a shovel.

"What for?" Rae questioned.

"Don't even ask," Sam returned.

Scarcely ten minutes had passed before Rae blustered across Main Street. By that time, Sam had filled a bucket with soapy cleanser, and set up her trenches on the porch.

"For God's sake, what *is* that?" Rae demanded, quickly applying her fingers to her nose.

"The feces of an animal," Sam answered. Scraping up a shovelful of the stuff, she carefully dumped it at the base of a bush by the porch. "I have no idea from what kind of animal, but it ought to make pretty good fertilizer."

"Smells like mule droppin's," Rae commented, her pinched nose giving her words a comical twang.

"Whatever," Sam muttered. Shoveling the rest of the stuff into the bushes, she reached for the bucket and poured a healthy amount of soap on the floor's reeking stain.

"Have you ever seen anything like that before?" Sam asked with a nod to the door.

"A cross," Rae observed.

"I know it's a cross, Rae. I *am* Catholic, after all. But who would have done such a thing?"

"I don't know. When did it happen?"

"While I was at the vineyards."

"What did you go out there for, anyway?"

Sam dragged the bucket to the desecrated door. "Matt wanted me to take a look at Nadine."

"Oh . . . well, you made an announcement yesterday you were going out there. Anybody could have slipped in here behind these weeds."

"But who is the most likely candidate?" Sam demanded with a glance over her shoulder. "Somebody whose toes I stepped on last night? Somebody involved with the KKK?"

Rae shrugged. "Maybe. I don't know. It *is* a cross. . . . Whatever the case, it looks like somebody's trying to scare you off."

"Well, somebody failed."

"You sound real brave, Sam. But sometimes the line between bravery and foolishness wears thin. You're alone here. And I don't agree with the others that the klan is

just a bunch of harmless old boys. Red Carter's their
leader, and I know for a fact that he's mean as a snake.
He'd just as soon take somebody's head off if he thought
he could get away with it. And he don't like you. He's
made that plain enough."

"That's the point, Rae. If I let him scare me with
something like this, Red Carter will have scored a victory. I'm not about to give him one. Go on back to your
place."

"But don't you want some help?"

"You can't get your hands in this mess. Within the hour
you'll have a supper crowd to serve."

As Rae reluctantly withdrew down the steps and out of
the yard, Sam soaked her cloth in the bucket, and pictured Red Carter's face as she slapped the door with a
ragful of suds.

The sun was low when Matt picked up Drew at the winery and drove the short distance to the house.

"We're going to have to start the cannons before day-
break and keep them going," Matt said as they stepped
inside. "I've never seen a flock like this, and it's getting
bigger by the day. They just damn well don't go away."

"I'll take the west acres," Drew replied as they removed their hats and hung them by the door.

"Okay, I'll go east. Then maybe George can spell us."
Matt looked around as he picked up a delicious aroma
drifting from the kitchen. "Something smells good. Let's
go see what it is."

They walked in to find Nadine seated at the table, her
feet pillowed on a neighboring chair as she busily diced
bell pepper into a mixing bowl.

"What's for supper?" Matt greeted.

"Pork chops, fried squash and okra, stewed tomatoes
and corn bread, and this here potato salad as soon as I
finish. It'll be ready by the time you two wash up."

"You look downright leisurely, Nadine," Drew observed with a smile.

"Doctor's orders. She says I'm supposed to *elevate* my feet."

Matt propped a shoulder against the doorjamb. "What do you think of her?"

"The lady doctor?" With a roll of her eyes, Nadine broke into one of her brilliant smiles. "Lord have mercy, honey. You done picked yourself a handful!"

When she chuckled, Drew joined in.

"Matt may have picked *her*," he said. "But it doesn't look like she's doing much in the way of picking him back."

Again, Drew and Nadine shared a laugh. Matt produced a small smile. "She'll come around," he announced and started to turn.

"Care to place a wager on that?" Drew taunted.

Facing him, Matt arched a brow.

"I'm serious," Drew went on enthusiastically. "You won twenty off me with that kiss in the street. Let me have a chance to get even. I'll give you ten-to-one you never get to first base with her. Come on. Let's shake on it."

"No."

"Why not? Do you admit you finally met a woman you can't charm the pants off of?"

"Nope. She's just not something I want to gamble over anymore."

"Aha-a-a-a!" Drew exclaimed, his voice rising and falling as though he'd uncovered a great secret.

"Shut up, Pierce," Matt muttered, and as he headed for the stairs, outdistanced the sound of a new duet of laughter.

The thought of Sam Kelly remained as he stripped and showered and dressed for supper. She was a handful, all right. It had been a long time since he got an erection in the middle of a cold shower—particularly over a woman who made no bones of telling him off every time they crossed paths. As he rolled up his shirtsleeves, Matt's gaze slid to the phone on the bedside table. On impulse, he crossed the room and dialed the operator.

"Clemmie? It's Matt. Is the new doctor's phone hooked up yet?"

Making a note of the number, he tucked it in his shirt pocket and went downstairs. After supper, he and Drew drove to Rae's Place and sat down at the front card table with Edwin and Larry. It was just after ten when Matt folded another uninteresting hand, his attention promptly departing the poker table and returning to the lighted windows across the street.

"Whatcha looking at, big brother?"

Turning with a start, Matt found that Drew was drilling him with a teasing look. So were the other two.

"Nothing," Matt replied with a grim grin. "I'm just ready to call it a night. You coming, Pierce?"

"No, I think I'll stay here awhile longer and see if I can catch a glimpse of her at the window."

As Edwin, Larry, and Drew erupted in laughter, Matt rose from the table.

"Thanks for the game, boys," he said with forced cheeriness. "But if you'll excuse me, I have prettier fish to fry."

It was nearly half-past ten when Matt retired to the privacy of his room, sat down on the bed, and dialed her number. He was beginning to think she wasn't going to answer when she picked up after the fourth ring.

"Hello, Sam."

"Hello, Matt," she readily replied.

"You recognize my voice. How flattering."

"Don't let it go to your head," she said. "To someone from Boston your voice sounds very distinctive."

"Am I disturbing you?" he asked.

"Not yet."

He laughed. "Now, that's positive thinking if ever I heard it."

"Cautious thinking," she replied. "I've quickly learned that caution should be one's guide when confronted with Matt Tyler. What's on your mind?"

Swiveling around, Matt stretched out on the bed. "You," he replied simply.

There was a brief pause before she said, "Excuse me, but is this the point at which the lady generally swoons?"

Matt laughed again. "It would be nice."

"Sorry to disappoint you."

He tried to imagine how she looked. Her voice sounded as though she were smiling. More than likely she was trying *not* to, but couldn't quite hide the beginnings of dimples.

"I called to say—about the klan and all—well, I'm sorry we ended up on a bad note today."

"You mean you've changed your mind?"

Matt arched a brow. "I didn't say that. I still believe that what you're suggesting would only open up a can of worms."

"I'd say the worms are already out of the can," she replied.

"You shouldn't let it bother you so much. These guys aren't part of the active klan. They don't go to national rallies. A few times a year they dress up and march around town. So what?" The heavy breath she expelled came clearly across the line.

"It doesn't matter if they keep a national profile. It's what they stand for that counts. Last night those people celebrated a tradition of bigotry, a history of cruelty, a vision of white supremacy. And everyone just stood by and watched."

Folding his arm behind his head, Matt leaned back against the pillow. "I'm beginning to see you're a woman of principle."

"That doesn't seem to matter much. Larry says I've no chance of restricting them from town without your support."

Grasping the phone cord, Matt threaded it through his fingers. "I might be willing to discuss the idea further."

There was a pregnant moment of silence. He could sense the suspicion building on the other end of the line even before she said, "Why do I get the feeling that the true reason for your call is about to surface?"

"I don't know," he lightly replied. "Are you psychic?"

"You tell me. Are you about to suggest some sort of rendezvous?"

"Well, if you insist, I'll see what I can do."

"What?" she said so shrilly that he laughed once more.

"Actually, I was going to say that I won't have time to discuss this klan thing until after harvest. But then there's a perfect opportunity."

"And what might that be?"

"The street dance. We always throw one when harvest is in. The whole town turns out. I was thinking you and I could go together."

A moment of quiet passed. "I'm thinking we'll just see each other there," she then said.

"Sounds like you don't trust me," he observed.

"Whatever could have given you that idea?"

Matt closed his eyes and pictured her—hair the color of the sky just after sunset, eyes the hue of spring leaves. Her looks were what first caught his eye, of course; but the attraction had gone swiftly deeper. Now it was hard to say what drew him most—her beauty, intelligence, wit, or the fiery spirit that made his blood come alive every time he was around her. He didn't know. It was all of it—it was just . . . her.

"Go with me, Sam," he urged. "You won't be sorry."

"You're wrong," she returned. "Sorry is exactly what I would be. I told you before, Matt. I'm not looking for entanglements here in Riverbend. I have no interest in any relationship with you that goes beyond friendship."

Opening his eyes, Matt directed a sly grin into the receiver. "The way you kiss says different."

"So, now you're back to that!"

His grin flashed wide.

"Honestly!" she railed on. "You are the most exasperating man! First, you force yourself on me—"

"Only at the beginning."

"Then you insist on manufacturing something out of nothing!"

"If that's nothing, I'd like to see what you call something."

"I'm not going to stand here any longer while you blithely drive me crazy. I have enough trouble as it is trying to sleep in this damn hothouse—"

"All right, all right," Matt interrupted on a chuckling note. "Relax. I'll let up."

"Thank you very much."

"For now. Maybe in a few weeks, after you've settled in, you'll be more receptive."

"I wouldn't bet on it."

"Okay. I'll just bank on it."

"Good night, Matt!"

"See you at the street dance," he said. There was a click, and then a dial tone. Replacing the receiver, Matt lay back on the bed, and released a rolling laugh. She was a handful, all right.

Wednesday morning the first wave of medical supplies arrived from Savannah. Continuing to demonstrate an interest in all things medical, Celie took great care in helping to unpack the crates, and then fervently undertaking the task of organizing the supply room. In the afternoon Sam was shocked when a truck from Pettigrew's Mercantile pulled up in front of the house to deliver three brand new air-conditioning units.

"For Riverbend Medical Clinic," Edwin Pettigrew announced somewhat grumpily. "From an anonymous donor."

After overseeing the delivery of the merchandise, he made a fast exit. But once inside the house, his workmen went beyond the duty of installing the units.

"How about some music?" one of them suggested, then toyed fruitlessly with the stereo of the old console TV.

"It's the antenna," another theorized. "It's been down since the storm of '89."

The next thing Sam heard was the trample of footsteps on the roof, and there was a decided difference in her sixth night in Georgia. The house was filled not only with the most delightfully cool air, but also with the rousing strains of a classical concert broadcast from Savannah. With these improvements, and scrubbed to the standards of a hawkeyed mother, the old Daly house was almost . . . livable.

What a difference a day could make. Last night at this hour, she'd been washing her hands for the umpteenth time—trying diligently to purge an imaginary stench from her fingers as well as a haunting fear from her mind. Tonight, the violation of her door front seemed less a threat than a tasteless prank. Tonight, she felt the closest thing to peace that she'd experienced in a long time.

Making her nightly round of checking doors and windows, Sam climbed the stairs with a faint smile on her face. She had no physical evidence that Matt Tyler was the anonymous donor behind her sudden good fortune. She just *knew* that he was.

Turning out the lights, she slipped beneath the covers and thought of Riverbend. At times it was like a Norman Rockwell scene come to life—woodsmoke on the air, cobblestones on the streets, front-porch visits, and homemade pie. At other times it was like a horror story from the past, complete with all the fearsomeness of masked marauders in white hoods and robes.

Then there were those few undeniable occasions when the magnificence of the place struck her with awe . . . like Saturday, when she looked across the glassy expanse of Ezra's Swamp . . . or yesterday, when she gazed on the green acres of Matt's vineyards against the sapphire Georgia sky. As she drifted, she decided there simply was no way to pinpoint how she felt about Riverbend. Like Matt Tyler, it repelled and drew her at the same time.

Falling abruptly asleep to the purr of air-conditioning, Sam found the rest that had eluded her since she first heard mention of Riverbend, Georgia.

A week passed, and then another. Summer was officially over, but the low-country heat remained stifling . . . and Sam's renovated clinic as empty as the town streets, now that Riverbend Vineyards harvest was in full swing.

At the end of the first week, Sam had opened the door one morning to discover Hannah Mathers and little Jason waiting on her front porch. When Hannah timidly offered to cook and clean in exchange for meals, Sam tried to insist on paying her.

"I got me a truck patch and a few chickens. And I take in the mendin' for Nadine. I get by. You been real good to us, Dr. Sam," she said. "And I don't mean to bring you no trouble, but home just ain't no place for us to be. Sometimes the kids going back from church school yell ugly words at Jason."

Looking at the adorable boy with the big brown eyes, Sam had been filled with sadness—not just for him, but for all the children of Riverbend.

Though the days of settling in had been preoccupied, Sam nonetheless had managed to gain a grasp of the stratified society in which she found herself. There were two distinct classes—those who were part of a self-proclaimed elite, and those who were not. Led by Eloise Pettigrew, the genteel ladies were the wives of the most successful men in town, lived in its grandest houses, and were the dignified caretakers of the exclusive Ladies Garden Club. The lower class encompassed everyone else.

However, since the medical insignia had been posted on the resurrected gate and Sam officially opened the clinic, neither the cream of society nor its dregs had darkened her doorway.

Of course, Hannah and Jason came on a daily basis, and Celie arrived each afternoon after school, still hoping for her first chance to assist a "real doctor." In a way, Sam supposed, she'd developed a sort of household, complete with a maid, a nurse in training, and a neighborly across-the-street friend in Rae. But both the clinic and Sam's purpose in coming to Riverbend had gone ignored.

"Bunch of stiff-necked old biddies," Rae pronounced.

Sam smiled and, taking a slow turn, trailed her fingers across the mirrorlike surface of water. They were shoulder-deep in the "swimmin' hole" Rae had bragged about for days. Finally, on this hot afternoon, Sam had taken her up on one of her lively spur-of-the-moment invites.

A cool clear pool, the pond was fed by a branch of the river, shaded by live oak and Spanish moss, and presided over by a family of beavers who'd built a glorious dam at the southernmost end. A rope hung from one of the massive oak limbs, dangling images of young boys swinging out in flight and splashing wildly into the water—although Rae had warned the rope was "old as Methusalah" and would come down with a good tug.

"Can you imagine anything more boring?" Rae continued. "Who the hell would want to spend every Wednesday scratching around the dirt with the Ladies Garden Club?"

"I might," Sam responded. "Maybe it would open a door. I've got to do something. These people are acting like I don't exist."

"Well, I'm sorry to tell you, honey, but you can be damn sure Eloise Pettigrew and them ain't gonna be coming to see no young, single, uppity-talkin', Yankee, Catholic, doctor woman."

Sam laughed. "You have a colorful way of putting things, Rae. I shouldn't be laughing, though, because I'm sure you're right. And it isn't just Eloise Pettigrew; it's everyone. Celie and I worked extremely hard to put the clinic in first-class shape. And now it doesn't seem to matter."

"All dressed up and no place to go, huh?"

"I guess so," Sam agreed.

"They just have to get to know you," Rae suggested. "There'll be a street dance when harvest is over. Matt always throws one. That's just a few weeks off."

"I don't want to wait a few weeks. If they won't come to me, I'll just have to go to them."

"What do you mean?"

"Pack my black bag and start making house calls. There are reportedly several hundred people living around here. I've never seen half of them."

"You don't *want* to see half of them," Rae said in a wry tone.

Again Sam laughed, her gaze settling on the buxom brunette in the black swimsuit. Propped against the bank, Rae had picked a number of yellow wildflowers and appeared to be weaving them together.

"I can't contain my curiosity, Rae. What on earth are you doing?"

"Dandelion chain. It's just something I do to pass the time." She looked up from her task. "Didn't you ever make a crown like this when you were a little girl?"

"There's not exactly a profusion of dandelions in Boston."

"Well then," Rae replied with a chuckle, "I'll just have to give you this one. Watch. It's easy. All you do is put a slit in the stem with your nail, then slip another stem through and pull . . ."

A short while later they climbed out of the sequestered pool, and Sam left the glade, crowned with wildflowers and feeling rather like a wood nymph. The path from the swimming hole led through a thicket of pine that backed up to the Daly property. Plowing through the tall weeds of the side yard, she and Rae broached Main Street just as a long, silver Mercedes purred by, its tinted windows hiding the occupants of the luxurious car.

"Oh, shit," Rae muttered.

"What's the matter?" Sam asked, her eyes following the sedan's progress toward the square.

"Lucy Beauregard Tyler's the matter," Rae answered on a note of doom. "That's her car, and she's on her way out to Matt's. Mark my words, fur is gonna fly."

In other parts of the fields, the water trucks were making their rounds, carefully sprinkling the grapes that would continue to ripen for the next two to three weeks. In the farthest acres to the south, harvest was underway.

Row by row, the pickers were slowly but steadily clearing the fields. As they filled their buckets they journeyed to the end of the row, where they dumped their yield in giant crates six feet across and five feet deep. Once those were full, they were transported by forklift to the winery, where the grapes were emptied into the crusher that culled skin and stems.

Matt was running one forklift, Drew another, and George a third. With two hundred pickers in the fields, the three of them had been kept busy most of the day.

But things were going well. Matt was humming under his breath as he returned from the winery—until he spotted the Mercedes moving smoothly between the columns of vines, oblivious to the pickers who had to move swiftly out of its way.

"Dammit," Matt muttered, and shifting into third gear, speeded up the thundering forklift so he could cut off the silver car at the end of the row. There, he shifted irritably into neutral, jumped down, and stalked to the center of the path.

A stranger got out of the Mercedes, followed quickly by Lucy, who remained by the car door, watching as the man in the brown suit walked toward Matt. Her hair was pinned up under a sun hat with a trailing ribbon the color of her pale blue dress. As usual, she looked like a picture in a magazine, not a flesh-and-blood woman.

"Matt Tyler?" the stranger questioned.

"I'm sure the lady told you I'm Matt Tyler."

"I'm private investigator Joe Riggs, sir," he said, and handed over a document. "Consider yourself served."

Quickly unfolding the summons and glancing over the front page, Matt stuffed the paper in his back pocket as he bypassed Joe Riggs on his way to Lucy. He was shirtless, dirty, sweaty. He hoped he offended every sensibility she had as he walked up to her and peered down on her perfection. Planting painted fingertips on the crown of her hat, she looked up to meet his eyes.

"Hello, Matt. It's nice to see you looking so . . . productive."

"Four weeks, huh?" he returned gruffly. "That's just fine. I'll have all the time in the world in four weeks.

Harvest will be in. I'd have thought you could manage to interrupt that."

"Believe me," she replied with an empty smile. "I did try."

"I'm sure you did."

"You know, Matt, sometimes I think we understand each other more than we admit."

"We understand each other, all right. We just don't like each other worth a damn. Now, why don't you get your car out of the way of my pickers? I may have to deal with you in four weeks, but I don't have to do it now."

"Certainly," she responded. "I wouldn't dream of interrupting such lucrative enterprise."

Stepping back, Matt flexed his fists as Joe Riggs offered her a hand and she prepared to climb into the back of the car.

"You know, Lucy," Matt called at the last instant. He waited for her to straighten and look his way before adding, "When I look at you, I sometimes think old Juda's curse actually lives."

"Of course it does, darling. In every heart that hates a Tyler." She offered another icy smile. "And that brings it down to you and me, doesn't it?"

Like so many times before, her open hatred struck him speechless, and Matt found himself helplessly staring as her car rolled out of view.

Chapter Eight

As Indian summer lingered, Sam spent her nights going through Dr. Daly's files, and her days knocking on doors. She made a point of calling at the Pettigrew house first, and succeeded in flustering Eloise to a degree that gave her mild satisfaction. She received similar responses from Lettie Campbell, Grace Whitehead, Sarah Bishop, and Clara Simon.

At Celie's rundown rowhouse on Oak Street, Sam left an analgesic for her grandfather, whose joints were so swollen with rheumatoid arthritis that she knew he must be in constant pain. Although he treated her with the utmost respect, the aging man was obviously embarrassed the entire time she was in the house.

At the Ingram place, where Celie worked on Saturdays, Sam met Patty Ingram who was well into pregnancy with her sixth child.

"Would you like me to assist you when the time comes?" Sam asked, and the woman blushed.

"Thank you, ma'am. But by now, birthing a baby is like rolling off a log. I'll do fine with my oldest girl to help."

Sam tried a few calls at rural houses in the surrounding area, but quickly discovered it was a futile idea. All those of an age to work were picking grapes at Matt Tyler's. Those left at home were small children and the elderly, who seemed to tolerate Sam's presence with the same embarrassment as Celie's grandfather.

Over the course of three weeks, the reception Sam received at thirty doors proved disturbingly uniform. Black, white, young, old. They were all friendly enough when she showed up on their doorsteps, but drew back in mortification when she tried to take on the role of doctor. The one exception was the home of George Waters, where she met Nadine's daughter and four grandchildren, and was gratified by their promise to come by for a checkup when harvest was through. But when fourteen-year-old Crystal—a beauty, as Nadine had said—started crying and ran out of the house, the visit came to a swift, distressing end.

The only time Sam really felt like a physician was when she stopped by to check on Nadine, whose blood pressure was definitely improving, but whose weight remained at the colossal level. On each of two visits Sam had seen Matt from a distance—both times amid the bustle of some harvesting business. The stirrings that had so bothered her upon her arrival seemed faded now and trivial.

On Thursday, the fourteenth of October, the news spread to town that the grape harvest was in, and Riverbend Vineyards was throwing a street dance on Saturday night.

"Are you going, Dr. Sam?" Celie asked eagerly. "There'll be music and dancing and good stuff to eat and drink."

"It sounds like fun," Sam replied noncommittally.

"*And,* Mr. Matt will be there," the girl added in a lilting voice.

"Celie!" she reprimanded, but couldn't deny a quick flutter in the vicinity of her abdomen.

"What's this about Mr. Matt?" Hannah asked with a timid smile.

"Absolutely nothing," Sam answered.

"He brought her flowers," Celie chimed in. "*And* asked her out to supper."

"Oh-h-h," Hannah responded with wide eyes.

"That's enough, you two," Sam chided, but her scolding failed to dispel the knowing smiles that circulated through the house for the rest of the day.

On Friday, Sam gathered her resolve and drove south toward the destination she'd been putting off for weeks, the sawmill and home place of the Carters. A month-and-a-half had passed since she arrived in Riverbend, first locking horns with Red Carter, and then scarce days later, with his brother Hal. Still, she clearly remembered their slovenly appearance and crude ways ... and the stench of animal dung on her porch. She had a bad taste in her mouth, and a bad feeling in the pit of her stomach, as she drove onto the property with the sprawling house and mill.

Parking in the dirt drive, Sam glanced to the left where stacks of lumber billowed across the landscape like myriad hills, and were overlooked by the two-story sawmill. Smoke rose from a series of metal chimneys on its roof, and the noise of machinery drifted from its open, barnlike doors. Praying that the Carter men were at work within, Sam climbed down from the van and turned in the opposite direction toward the house. She wanted to meet Ida, but—cowardly, though it may be—she hoped to get through this encounter without crossing paths with Red or his brother.

Like the Daly house, the Carters' was a white-frame two-story; unlike the Daly house, it had never been grand, but was more like a huge nesting place that had been added onto generation after generation to accommodate a burgeoning brood. Paradoxically, there was no brood in sight. As Sam walked across the sagging porch, she was struck with a feeling of isolation that was even worse than upon first sighting Riverbend.

She rang the bell twice before the door was finally opened—and then only an inch or two, just wide enough to allow a pair of tired-looking eyes to peer out.

"Can I help you?" the woman asked.

"I'm Dr. Kelly," Sam said. "You must be Ida."

Swinging the door wide, Ida wiped her palms down the front of her apron as Sam stepped inside. The interior of the Carter house was clean, sparsely furnished, and noticeably quiet—which made it noticeably different from most of the houses she'd visited. No children, Sam thought, and remembered Daly's notes about a violent miscarriage that left Ida barren. Sam turned with a smile.

"I apologize for showing up without notice," she said. "I'm trying to get to know the people around here. You haven't been to town, so I thought I'd drive out and introduce myself."

Once again, the poor woman's response was a sidelong glance and an absent palming of her apron. She was pale as though she never saw the sun, stooped as though constant cringing had taken inches from her height.

"Thanks for inviting me in," Sam added.

Finally, Ida Carter looked up long enough for a swift meeting of eyes. "I just made a pitcher of lemonade. Would you like some?"

"That would be nice," Sam replied, and received a fleeting smile before the woman turned and shuffled across the room, waving an inviting hand as she went. Sam followed into the kitchen and took a seat at the chair Ida indicated, her gaze turning out the side window toward the sawmill. She hoped not to see either Red or Hal, and wondered how many times Ida Carter had done the same thing.

As Ida poured glasses of lemonade, and delivered them to the table in bobbing fashion, Sam tried to keep her eyes off the damaged leg, but failed. According to Daly's notes, it had been broken more than ten years ago, and allowed to become horribly infected. Now, Ida Carter favored it to a great degree as she walked—and covered it with skirts that brushed the tops of lace-up work boots. As Ida sat down across the table, Sam lifted her glass with another smile.

"Cheers," she said. Again, there was no audible reply. Sam took a sip of the cool drink. "That's delicious," she pronounced.

"The secret is in the sweetenin'," Ida said. "I use a bit of sugarcane."

"How interesting," Sam returned, her gaze drifting over the woman across the table. Her dishwater-blond hair was streaked with gray and pulled behind her shoulders in a ponytail reaching halfway down her back. She might be forty-five or so. It was hard to tell when she so rarely looked up to meet one's eyes.

"Ida," Sam said. As she paused, searching for the right way to continue, the empty eyes lifted. "You know I'm a doctor, right?"

"Yes," she quietly affirmed.

"Are you doing well?"

"Well enough."

"How about your leg?" Sam asked.

"How about it?" Ida replied, a hint of sharpness in her low-pitched voice.

"I read Dr. Daly's notes. It seems you've had several serious accidents since you got married." Sam's gaze darted toward the window. "I know he hurts you, Ida. If you press charges . . ." Ida looked swiftly away. "Okay," Sam nodded. "That's your business. But could I at least look at your ankle?"

"What for?" the woman demanded.

"To see if something can be done," Sam replied.

"Like what?"

"Like corrective surgery." Slowly, Ida Carter extended her leg and lifted her skirts. Leaning around the table, Sam bent over the twisted limb.

"It could be done," she said after a moment. "It would take a specialist, but at a glance I'd say a great deal of your limp could be reduced, as well as the discomfort—" She broke off as the sound of baying dogs erupted from out back. Ida snatched her skirt down and rose from the chair a mere instant before the kitchen door flew open and her husband walked in.

"What's this?" he boomed. "You carryin' on behind my back?"

"No, Red. The doctor just—"

"I told you I didn't want you talkin' to no upstart woman!"

"But Red—" Ida's desperate attempt to respond was snuffed as the man backhanded her across the cheek. Her palm clamped to the side of her face, she limped swiftly past the table as Sam sprang to her feet.

"Ida!" she exclaimed, but the woman paid her no heed as she disappeared around the corner. Her eyes flashing, Sam directed an accusing glare at Red Carter. His belly hung over the waist of his work pants; his upper arms bulged at the sleeves of his T-shirt. Clearly, Ida was no match for him. As Sam regarded him, she thought she'd never come across such a loathsome creature. It seemed an insult to humanity to call him a man.

"There are laws against that kind of thing," Sam announced.

"Against what? Slapping the old gal around a little? You really *are* one of them damn Yankee liberals, ain't you, girl?" He chuckled around the butt of his cigar, and Sam's stomach lurched.

"I'm not a girl," she replied coldly. "I'm a doctor. And I came here to offer my services to your family. Now that I've done so, I'd like to be on my way." Walking swiftly to the back door, she pushed the screen open, started down the cement-block steps, and glanced across the way to a massive dog pen as a dozen or so hounds started yapping once more.

"Hear tell you got that Mathers trash over at your place."

Sam turned at the base of the steps, the disgust she felt showing clearly on her face as she looked up to find Red Carter grinning down on her from the open doorway.

"The only people at my place are friends of mine, Mr. Carter. I'll thank you to curb your tongue when you speak of them in my presence."

"Hear tell you been talkin' down the klan, too," he added obliviously. "I'd watch out if I was you. Little girls who play with fire are liable to get burnt."

Removing the cigar butt, he punctuated his threat with a perverse licking of his lips, as though he could barely wait for the chance to gobble her up. Spinning on her heel, Sam made quick progress around the side of the house to the van, and told herself it was only the intense revulsion she felt that had her insides shaking.

Saturday, October 16

As dusk settled over the town, Sam stood before the dresser mirror, gave herself a critical look, and stripped off the paisley skirt and teal blouse. What did one wear to a street dance in rural Georgia?

Night was falling, the string rhythms of a bluegrass band wafting down the street. She lost patience with herself, put on her best dress jeans and white cotton shirt, and set off for the square.

A bandstand had been erected near the gazebo, which was strung with Chinese lanterns, but what first drew Sam's eye were the torches lining the makeshift dance floor at the end of the street. The sight of flames flickering at the square took her back to Labor Day evening, when the KKK had been on center stage instead of a bluegrass band.

As she walked along, Sam did her best to push away the image. If ever she'd entertained delusions of changing the ways of Riverbend, she had none now. She couldn't even persuade these people to accept her as a doctor, much less a social influence. All she could do was maintain her own values, and perhaps manage to rub off on a few people along the way.

Bypassing the dozen or so dancers at the end of the street, Sam moved onto the grass of the square where most of the crowd was gathered—some before the bandstand, some on benches under the trees, and a fair number lined up at the gazebo, where Rae was presiding over a table of refreshments.

Sam headed in that direction, and as she threaded her way through the crowd, was heartened to receive a

number of friendly greetings. At least her efforts the past
few weeks had yielded something. Taking her place in
line behind Patty Ingram and two of her children, Sam
scaled the steps to the gazebo and watched as Rae—who
was wearing a white apron over a bright floral dress—
served with a practiced hand from a variety of steamers
and platters. When Patty and the children moved on,
Sam stepped into the light of the Chinese lanterns.

"This is quite a spread you've got here," she greeted.

"It's an annual event," Rae cheerily replied. "I've ca-
tered this thing for Matt ever since he started having it.
Each year it gets a little bigger. You've got to try my barbecue. Minced or sliced, I guarantee it'll be the best you
ever put in your mouth. Then there's country fries and
baked beans, cole slaw, watermelon, peach fritters. Beer
and tea are in the urns over there."

"I think I'll just settle for a cup of your legendary iced
tea at the moment," Sam said with a smile. "Could you
use some help serving?"

"Shucks, no, honey. This is what I do every day of my
life. And if I want a break, I'll get those lazy cooks of
mine up here. You go on over to the bandstand and enjoy
yourself."

Drawing a cup of tea from one of the giant urns flanking the table, Sam left the lantern light of the gazebo and
moseyed to the edge of the crowd clapping in time with
the fiddles of the band. She'd been there scarcely a minute when Drew Pierce approached.

"Hi ya, Sam," he said. Along with jeans and a white
shirt much like her own, he was wearing the perfect
smile she remembered.

"Hello, Drew."

"Long time, no see. What with harvest and all, I
haven't laid eyes on you since that—uh—night in the
street."

She would have known immediately the night to
which he was referring, even without the sheepish look.
The memory of Matt's earthshaking kiss flashed through
her mind.

"I owe you an apology for my part in that," Drew added.

"I don't remember your taking much part in it," Sam replied.

"Well, to be honest, it was Matt's idea, all right. But I bet him he couldn't do it."

Sam's eyes snapped to Drew's. "It was a *bet*?"

"Uh-oh. I haven't made things worse, have I?"

Sam gave him a sweet smile. "There's nothing to be made worse," she said. "I haven't given the incident a second thought. Tell me, how did harvest go?"

"Very well," he replied enthusiastically. "This is the best year we've ever had."

"What exactly is considered a good grape harvest?"

"Last year we produced thirty-two thousand cases of wine. This year we might make forty. *That's* a good harvest."

Finishing the lively tune to a round of applause, the band started up another.

"A two-step," Drew observed. "I was brought up on this kind of music, but I must confess I've acquired a new love—classical."

"You're kidding," Sam replied. "Classical is what *I* was brought up on. My mother was a piano teacher. The music around our house was always Tchaikovsky, Mozart, Chopin—"

"That's a coincidence. I've got tickets to the Savannah symphony tomorrow night. There's a featured pianist from Austria. They're doing selections from Chopin."

"One of my favorite composers."

"Would you like to come with me? I can never get anybody from around here to use my extra ticket."

"You mean, it will go unused?"

Drew tendered a broad smile. "Unless you save it from sure-and-certain waste."

"Then I'll certainly go," Sam replied with a laugh. "I couldn't bear the thought of wasting something as beautiful as Chopin."

"I'll pick you up about six-thirty, all right?"

"You're on," Sam agreed, and as they turned to watch the band, gave Drew a sidelong look. He was a tall man, though not nearly as tall as Matt. He was handsome, too; though once again Matt was in another league with his dark good looks. And although Drew was a charmer, he inspired none of the breathlessness she remembered experiencing when Matt was smiling down on her.

"Evenin', ma'm."

Sam jumped as she looked around. It was as though he'd materialized out of the night. He was dressed all in black—hat, jeans, open-throated shirt with sleeves rolled to the elbow. The first thing she noticed was that she'd forgotten how truly spectacular he was. The second thing, as he stepped close, was how wonderful he smelled. Whatever the after-shave was, he was wearing just enough to send her senses reeling.

"Good evening," she said at last.

He looked past her to Drew. "What's the matter with you, Pierce?" he asked. "Haven't you asked the lady to dance?"

"I was just about to."

"If you snooze, you lose," Matt returned, and taking hold of her hand, he looked down at Sam. "Will you do me the honor?" he asked gallantly.

With a swift glance at the massive hand engulfing hers, Sam cast a doubtful look at the couples moving in a smooth, flowing circle within the boundary of torches.

"I can't do that," she protested.

"It's easy. Come on, I'll show you." Leading her off the grass and into the street, Matt opened his arms for her to take her place within them.

"I'm sure you know this part," he prodded as she stood hesitatingly before him.

Moving forward, Sam placed one hand on his tall shoulder, the other in his waiting palm. His hand closed on her waist, his fingers curling halfway around her back. She looked up to meet his smiling eyes, and her cheeks turned hot despite her best intentions to remain infinitely cool. She'd also forgotten how being close to Matt

Tyler made her feel slight and fragile and unnervingly female.

"Just feel the music," he said. "One . . . two . . . one-two . . . One . . . two . . . one-two . . ."

As he crooned, he moved forward to the beat of his voice. It was the most natural thing in the world to follow along, stepping back as he advanced, falling in with his rhythm. In the space of a few musical bars Sam was moving smoothly to the steady pressure of his lead. She looked up with a bright smile, he smiled back, and a quivering flutter took hold of her stomach.

"See?" he said. "I told you it was easy."

"I have a feeling the ease depends on who's leading," Sam commented. "You seem to have an affinity for this kind of music."

"Affinity, huh?" His smile widened. "You have the damnedest way of talking."

"What's wrong with it?"

"Nothing's really *wrong* with it. But it's like you've got a dictionary tucked up there in your head somewhere. If you want folks around here to understand what you're talking about, you might tone it down a little. Nadine happened to mention you haven't been too pleased with the turnout over at your clinic. I reckon folks would come around a lot quicker if you'd just . . . relax."

"I *am* relaxed," Sam insisted and received a squeeze about her waist. Looking up with a start, she found Matt shaking his head.

"Nope," he pronounced. "Stiff as a board. Relax . . . enjoy yourself. There's a new moon tonight. Take a look at the sky. The stars always seem brighter on the night of a new moon."

Glancing up, she saw that he was right. The night sky was a canopy of twinkling stars.

"You look mighty pretty," he said. "No more circles under your eyes. What did you do—get used to the Georgia heat?"

Sam surrendered a smile. "You were the one who sent me those air conditioners, weren't you?"

"What if I was?"

"Then I'd have to say thank you very much."

"You're very welcome," he replied, his voice low and intimate and sending a shiver along her spine.

Swiftly changing the subject, Sam said, "I understand congratulations are in order. Drew says you've just concluded your most successful harvest."

"That's right. Everybody who had a hand in it deserves to celebrate."

"I imagine harvesting acres of grapes isn't the easiest job."

"No," Matt replied, his smile mesmerizing, his charisma captivating. "But there's something satisfying about it, too. There are times when I think it goes by too fast."

"I'm sorry."

"About what? Harvest being over?"

Sam brought herself into focus with a start. Damn! Where had she been the past few seconds? "I'm sorry," she said again, this time with a light laugh. "I don't know what's the matter with me."

"Maybe you're finally starting to relax."

"Maybe so," she admitted.

"I damn well hope so," he returned, his voice stirring the shivers once again. "It would be a shame for you to be tight as a hatband on a night like this."

Sam looked up and . . . what he'd said flew from her mind. All she could see was his face. All she could feel was his hands upon her. The air was filled with his scent.

"Sam?"

His voice was the only thing about him that was far away, as was the Georgia sky—dark and beautiful and spangled with stars . . . and the music, rhythmic and throbbing and guiding her feet when no conscious thought had moved them. One . . . two . . . one-two . . .

"Hello?"

She snapped back once again, was once again nonplussed, and had to laugh at herself.

"I like that," he said.

"What?"

"The sound of your laugh."

Sam looked into his eyes, steeled herself against being drawn to them, and was smitten anyway. Her laughter settling, she sighed.

"Boy," she murmured. "You sure are something."

"You think so?"

"I'm sure you *know* so."

"No. I don't think—"

"Matt," she said in a scolding tone. "Don't spoil the compliment with false modesty, hmmm?"

Beneath the black brim of his hat, his brows drew together in a puzzled frown. "Have you been sampling somebody's corn liquor?" he asked. Once more Sam dissolved into laughter. This time he joined in. And still they moved in the musical circle.

"Let's go somewhere," he suggested after a moment.

"Like where?"

"Anywhere you say, darlin'."

The music continued to play. The stars continued to sparkle. But suddenly the dreamlike moment began to unravel.

"I'm not sure what you mean," Sam said.

He gave her a knowing look, and in the seconds that passed, she had the chance to be summarily shocked at herself. For a spellbinding moment, she'd actually drifted right along with him, just as she was following his lead about the dance floor, just as she'd followed along the night he kissed her.

"I mean let's go someplace private," he answered. "My house, for instance."

"Your house."

"Yeah. We could put on some music, open a bottle of wine, share a little—" He paused as his gaze swept suggestively down the front of her. "Stimulating conversation," he supplied finally.

Sam could actually feel her vertebrae locking up—like a series of hands locking fingers and drawing tight. "Why must you insist on behaving like a wolf on the prowl?" she demanded.

" 'Cause that's what you bring out in me, I guess," Matt replied, still smiling.

"Me and a trail of women across Dixie, from what I hear."

Finally, his flirting smile disappeared. "I've been around, and that's a fact," he said. "But I never met anybody like you, and that's a fact, too."

Naive or not, at that moment Sam found his expression to be one of the purest, most sincere she'd ever seen.

"So, what do you say?" he added. "My Jeep's just down the street. Shall we go?"

"We've been over this before," Sam replied firmly. "The answer is still no."

He gazed down at her with solemn eyes. "Then I'm still trying to figure out why. Is there a boyfriend at home or something?"

"No, Matt," she returned on a note of impatience.

"Then what's the problem?"

"The problem, if you must put it that way, is *me*. I've come to Riverbend for one purpose, to be a doctor. And what I've found is a townful of people who'll have nothing to do with me. Things are hard enough for me as they are. I don't need the complications of an entanglement, particularly with a married man."

"Married," Matt said. "Who told you that?"

"This is a small town. The only thing people have to talk about is each other. It's true, isn't it? You *are* married."

"Barely."

"That's like claiming to be barely dead," she replied. "Either you are, or you're not."

His dark brows knitted in a foreboding line. "We've been legally separated for a dozen years, and I'd divorce her if I could."

"Why can't you?"

"Because I'd lose virtually everything I own."

The thought of Chad barreled into Sam's mind—*What did you expect me to do? Give up my inheritance?* North, South . . . city, country . . . Beacon Hill, Riverbend. Neither geography nor circumstance seemed to make a difference when it came to some things about men.

"I have the right to see any woman I choose," Matt went on. "I choose you, and the chemistry between us says you're not indifferent to me, either. If you don't want to leave the street dance, okay. Then let me take you to supper tomorrow night."

Sam looked up, a hard expression having formed on her face. "I can't tomorrow night. I'm going to Savannah with Drew."

For a few punishing instants, Matt merely stared.

"I don't get it," he then said, his deep voice rumbling like thunder.

"There's nothing to get," Sam returned obliquely. "He invited me to the symphony, and I accepted."

"But you won't go out with me?"

"No," she answered slowly.

"Why, Sam?"

Daring to search his amber eyes, she was captured once more. No one had a right to eyes that beautiful, like candles burning in the shadowed place, beckoning with the promise of a warming touch.

"Why Drew and not me?" he pressed.

The steady look she summoned belied her raucous pulse. "Maybe because he doesn't treat me like a notch about to be added to his bedpost."

"He's worse than I am!"

"It doesn't seem so to me."

Matt's eyes bored into hers. "I think you just put your finger on it, Doc. The difference is in you."

The music came to an end, and the dancers applauded. Taking a backward step, Matt dropped her hand and scrutinized her from head to toe. "The difference is that you're afraid," he said.

"I can't think of a single thing I'm afraid of," Sam returned.

"Really?" He startled her by stepping forward and lifting a hand toward her face. Acting on instinct, she moved quickly back.

"See what I mean?" he taunted.

"Of course I react every time you come near me," she snapped. "I never have any idea what you might do next—what outrageous proposition might roll out of your mouth."

"It's not outrageous for me to ask you to share a glass of wine, or go out to dinner."

"But everything else you imply *is*."

"Everything else . . . you mean, that I find you desirable? That I'd like to hold you and kiss you and make love to you?"

"You see? There you go again!"

"Do you have a hangup about sex, Sam?"

"No! I do *not* have a hangup about sex!" she exploded . . . and then became instantly aware of the staring eyes of the between-dance crowd. Her face flooded with heat. She was sure it must be the color of a ripe tomato to elicit the grin that broke across Matt's face.

"Glad to hear it," he drawled.

And once again she was the center of the locals' amused chuckles. Once again she found it necessary to dredge up a lighthearted smile when her insides felt like an erupting volcano.

"Thanks for the two-step," Sam said, her voice quietly directed to Matt's ears alone. "I'll try to be a little quicker on my feet next time."

Producing a friendly glance for the onlookers, she turned her back on him and merged with the crowd on the grassy commons of the square. She made herself stay another hour—refusing dance invitations from Larry Edison and Drew and a few others . . . chatting with Rae at the gazebo . . . and watching from the corner of her eye as Matt made a show of twirling one woman after another about the torchlit dance floor of the street.

It was well after midnight when Matt tapped on Drew's door and came in without waiting for an invitation. Sitting in the chair near the door to the bath, Drew was unlacing his shoes. As Matt walked in, he glanced up, smiled, and looked back to his laces.

"Hey, buddy," he said. "What's going on?"

"You knew I had the lady doctor staked out, Pierce."

Drew looked up once again. Matt was wearing a small smile that didn't reach his eyes.

"Now I find out you're taking her to Savannah tomorrow night," he added.

"Matt, if I steered clear of every lady you staked out, I'd hardly have anybody left to call on in three states."

"Sam's different."

"Oh?" Drew questioned with the arch of a brow.

"You don't come across somebody like her every day."

"I see," Drew commented and received a grimace, which he answered with a grin. "Relax, big brother. If I read the cards right, she's more interested in the dead man who wrote the music than the live one who's taking her to the concert." Discarding his shoes, Drew rose from the chair.

"How about you?" Matt questioned. When Drew looked his way, he added, "Does your interest lie in the music or the lady?"

Drew turned his back—his pleasant, after-party expression slipping. Only one lady held his interest—the same one who had grabbed it with slim, unrelenting fingers when he was all of twenty-two. He'd been the first one to take out Lucy Beauregard. Later he'd discovered she dated him only because he was Matt Tyler's college buddy. There had been only one date. Lucy didn't make a habit of mixing with those who were below her, and as the son of a struggling peach farmer, Drew Pierce didn't come close.

God, how he hated her. But even more than that he hated the gnawing hope that he might at least catch a glimpse of her at the upcoming concert. That stupid hope was the only reason he'd bought season tickets to the symphony in the first place.

"Relax," Drew said again. Pulling his shirt over his

head, he tossed it at the chair. "I won't be hitting on Sam. Like you said, she's different."

Nonetheless, Matt found a reason to be in town the next evening. Lolling about Rae's boardwalk with a copy of a newspaper he'd read twice, he kept an eye on the house across the street. Drew arrived at half-past six— spit-and-polished in a dark suit and tie, and looking every inch the lady killer he'd been at the University of Georgia.

Matt's eyes were trained over the top of the newspaper as Sam came out. Her hair was up, and she was wearing a simple black dress that hugged her slim body. The legs he'd admired on every occasion he'd had the chance to see them, were shown off by sheer stockings and black heels. In short, she was a damn knockout.

As Drew opened the car door for her, she cast a look across the street and waved. With a short tug on the brim of his hat, Matt turned and pushed through the saloon doors. The cafe was buzzing with a suppertime crowd. There was no one at the bar. He yanked out a stool and plopped down.

"Bourbon," he said when Rae approached with a smile.

"I know," she replied and poured him a shot. "What's the matter with you?" she added as he did away with it in a single gulp.

"Women," Matt muttered. "For a man who likes them so much, I sure have plenty of reason not to. Lucy's taking me to court in a week, and now—"

"And now, what?" Rae prodded when he broke off.

"Nothing," Matt responded, though he fired a telltale glance out the window just as Drew's car pulled away from the Daly house.

"I see," Rae commented knowingly.

Matt grimaced. "Pour me another one, will you?"

She released an audible sigh. "Happy to. But it ain't gonna do you no good."

"It'll take the edge off."

"For a while, maybe. But facts are facts. After the bourbon wears off, they'll still have the same old edge."

"You going philosophical on me, Rae?"

"Maybe," she admitted with a quick laugh that died as Matt tossed down the second drink. "But I can't help noticing," she went on with a solemn look, "that people are the damnedest critters. They go looking all over for some dream or other, and the whole time what's really good for them is right in front of their faces."

Setting down the shot glass, Matt lifted a brow as he studied the woman on the other side of the bar. Dark-haired, dark-eyed, voluptuous as the Georgia earth. Rae . . . he'd known her as long as he could remember knowing himself, and he knew exactly what she was saying. Rising to his feet, Matt shelled out a twenty, grabbed her behind the neck and planted a kiss on her cheek.

"Keep the change," he said and walked out into the fading sunshine of the October eve. As usual, Main Street was deserted—seeming even more intensely so since he knew the house across the way was empty. Climbing into his Jeep, Matt drove back to the vineyards, pulled over in the south acres, and killed the engine.

A breeze off the river rustled through the vines. Other than that, everything was quiet—the pickers departed for another year, the bosses free to do whatever they pleased for the night. One was home with his family, another was sitting alone in the fields that no longer required his hand. The third was escorting Sam to a night of music in Savannah. Starting up the Jeep with a rough hand, Matt scratched off the side of the road and drove up to the house.

"What are you doing here?" Nadine greeted as he walked inside.

"What do you mean?" he barked. "It's my house, isn't it?"

"Uh-huh," she responded, and with an arch look waddled off in the direction of her room.

Stalking into the dining room, Matt sprawled on the settee by the window and propped his boots on the footstool. As he gazed across the familiar landscape sweeping toward the river, a twilight from some weeks ago came to

mind. Ellen, her name had been . . . No, Eileen . . .
Whatever the case, he'd met her at the polo match in
Charleston, and had sobered up shortly after they blew
each other's minds.

The next week Sam Kelly had shown up in Riverbend,
and from the first time he set eyes on her, Matt had felt
something. Somehow, he'd known, things were going to
change. And they had. There had been no more Ellens
or Eileens since Sam came to town, and although Matt
knew he could clean up, take off, and find that kind of
action within a few hours, he just plain didn't want to.

The longings that had been creeping up on him for
years had finally taken a physical form . . . and that form
was on its way to Savannah with his best friend. "Dammit," Matt uttered and, pushing off the couch, proceeded
to the liquor cabinet where he poured himself another
drink.

Chapter Nine

The concert was being held in the performing arts theater of the Savannah Civic Center, which sprawled for a block between West Oglethorpe and West Liberty streets. Located "smack in the middle of the district"—as Drew said—the destination gave Sam a chance to view historic Savannah for the first time.

Laid out in a series of squares with names like Lafayette and Madison, the district was lined with old-fashioned street lamps and studded with historic site markers. They passed Colonial Park Cemetery, 1750–1853, second burial ground for colonists, including a signer of the Declaration of Independence; Chippewa Square, featuring the Savannah Theatre, the longest continuously operated theater in North America; and a variety of fine houses and magnificent churches dating back to both antebellum and Revolutionary times. The flavor of a heritage well-preserved permeated the air.

In sharp contrast, the Civic Center theater was equipped with modern seating and state-of-the-art acoustics. When the lights went down, Sam could almost pretend she was back in Boston. The Chopin was wonderful, as was the feeling of having returned to her element, however briefly.

Drew was the perfect escort. Attentive with a leading

hand as they entered, he seemed to become intensely absorbed in the music once the performance began. It wasn't until the concert ended and they crossed paths with Lucy Tyler that Sam began to think his absorption might have been with something else.

They'd exited the theater and were traversing the foyer of the Civic Center when the light hand Drew had placed at her back suddenly clenched about her waist. When Sam glanced up, she saw that he was staring toward the door.

"There she is," he announced.

"There *who* is?"

"Lucy," came the quiet reply. "Matt's wife."

Sam looked swiftly ahead. Although a number of people were chatting by the doorway, her gaze narrowed instinctively on the woman who was the unquestioned center of the group. She was blond and slender, her hair pinned up in a formal twist, her slimness shown off by a tailored black dress with white satin trim around its dropped shoulders. Lovely.

As she noted their approach, she excused herself from her entourage and moved into their path. It was then that Sam noticed there was a hardness about her lovely face. Flawless though her features may have been, they somehow evoked the impression of being as cold and unforgiving as granite.

"Good evening, Drew." Her gaze slid to Sam. "And Miss . . . ?"

"Samantha Kelly," Drew supplied. "Sam, I'd like you to meet Lucy Beauregard."

"Lucy Beauregard *Tyler,*" the woman corrected, and with a regal nod, looked once more at Drew. "Another barmaid?" she inquired with a smile as benign as it was maddening.

"*Doctor* Kelly, I should have said," Drew announced.

Lucy turned to Sam with an expression of surprise. "Doctor?" she repeated. "Of what field?"

"The medical field," Sam replied in short order.

"From Boston," Drew added with apparent satisfaction. "She's been sent to run a clinic in Riverbend."

The fine brows lifted. "How in the world, may I ask, did you end up in Riverbend?"

"Ever heard of the National Health Service Corps?" Sam asked.

"Don't they go about placing doctors here and there and everywhere?"

"I suppose that's one way of putting it," Sam replied.

She laughed—the sound as empty as the look in her blue eyes. "It appears my sources have fallen down on the job," she said. "I've heard nothing of a new doctor in Riverbend."

"I've been there only a matter of weeks," Sam pointed out.

"More than enough for Riverbend, wouldn't you say?"

"In some ways, perhaps. In others I feel I've barely scratched the surface."

"But you must have met my husband, Matt. He's always one of the first to want to scratch a new surface."

Sam's nostrils flared. "I've met him, yes. But he and Drew have been immersed in harvesting nearly the entire time I've been in Riverbend. From what I hear, they're to be congratulated for a bonanza crop."

"You have no idea how happy I am to hear that. You see, I intend to take Matt and Drew, and whomever else they bring along, to court within the week. Half of Riverbend Vineyards will belong to me after that."

"I wouldn't count on it, Lucy," Drew bristled.

"Why, Drew," she returned with a flutter of lashes. "Surely you don't mean to imply that you doubt my rights, *or* my influence."

"I have no doubts about your influence, Lucy. But unless you've managed to bribe the judge, I *do* have doubts that you'll walk out of court with anything other than attorneys' fees ... and maybe the satisfaction of putting Matt through one more mile of hell."

"Well, then," she returned. "I really can't lose, can I? *Au revoir,* you two."

"Charming," Sam murmured as the woman glided away.

"Isn't she, though?" Drew snapped. When Sam turned to look at him, he produced one of his engaging smiles. "Sorry. She always puts me in a bad mood. Would you like to stop off for a nightcap on the Riverfront?"

Declining the invitation, Sam found herself dwelling on the image of Lucy Tyler as they drove back toward Riverbend. And judging from Drew's atypical quietness, she sensed his thoughts were similarly preoccupied. When they were halfway home, he flipped down the visor, produced a pack of cigarettes, and lit up a smoke.

"I didn't realize you smoke," Sam observed.

"Only on occasion," he said. "Does it bother you?"

Sam glanced his way and smiled through the darkness of the car. "I don't suppose you'd like to hear my lecture for smokers."

"I don't suppose I would," he returned with an answering smile, and promptly flicked the cigarette out the window.

It was after eleven when they pulled up in front of the Daly house. Coming around in gentlemanly fashion, Drew opened her door, helped her out of the car, and guided her up to the darkness of the porch. Once there, he propped a forearm on the door sill while she fished in her purse for the key.

"Thanks for going with me," he said.

"Thanks for asking me," Sam replied. The October night closed about them with a cool breeze that whispered the end of Indian summer. As she withdrew her key, Sam looked up with the beginnings of a smile, only to find that Drew was leaning toward her—with the unmistakable intent of kissing her. Planting a swift hand against his silk tie, she looked up to meet his eyes.

"Do you think we could leave this on a basis of friendship, Drew? You and I both know I'm not the woman you want to be kissing right now." He backed away to arm's length.

"It is so obvious?" he asked after a moment.

Sam's brows lifted. "I'm afraid so. I guess I can't blame you. She's a beautiful woman."

"On the outside, yes."

"How long have you been in love with her?"

Once again looking down with open surprise, Drew threw back his head and laughed. But it was a quick laugh, swiftly begun and swiftly over. Silence ensued, and the katydids sang from the surrounding weeds as his smile died away.

"Am I this transparent to everyone?" he asked eventually. "Or is it just because you're a doctor?"

"Maybe I just happened to be at the right place at the right time. As they say, a picture is worth a thousand words. The picture of the two of you together seemed pretty clear."

"There *is* no two of us," he replied. "There never has been."

"There must have been something . . . sometime," Sam objected.

"One date a lifetime ago."

"That's it?"

Drew nodded. Even through the shroud of darkness, Sam detected the haunted look that covered his face.

"Have you ever seen such an utter fool, Sam? My best friend's wife. Matt hates Lucy, and so do I, but I can't seem to get around something else. Something over which I have no control. It's like a sickness. The more I can't stand her, the more I'm drawn to her. Do you know what I mean?"

The image of Matt leaped to her mind. "Yes," Sam murmured. "I guess I do." Her thoughts taking off on a journey all their own, she fitted the key in the lock and opened the door.

"Yeah," Drew said. "Maybe you do."

Lamplight streamed from the open doorway as Sam looked over her shoulder. "What's *that* supposed to mean?"

"Maybe you're not the only one who can read pictures," Drew responded with a smile.

"I have no idea what you're talking about."

"Then why are you on the defensive?" he countered, his fragile smile disappearing as he stepped up and rested light hands on her shoulders. "He's a good man, Sam."

She looked up, her eyes tracing the attractive lines of Drew's illumined face. "I won't pretend I don't know who you're talking about, Drew. But if you're thinking of drawing some connection between me and Matt, well . . ."

"Well, what?" he prompted.

"I'm not about to join the countless ladies who have become his paramours."

"He doesn't see you as one of them," Drew replied, and in spite of herself, Sam experienced a swift-running thrill along her spine.

"I'm sure he's felt that way about every one of them," she said. "In the beginning."

"No, he hasn't. And I should know. I've been his best buddy since college days. Last night he came to my room and confronted me about this little outing."

"Confronted you?"

"Frankly speaking, he was ticked off because I asked you to the concert. In fact, he backed me into a corner about my intentions."

Along with the feelings of defiance that erupted within Sam, there was also a hint of forbidden pleasure.

"Of all the arrogant things," she said. "As if Matt Tyler has a say over anything I should do, or anyone I want to see."

"Right," Drew agreed with the knowing arch of a brow.

"Honestly. A man sends you a few air conditioners, and what does he expect?"

"Air conditioners?" Drew questioned with a light laugh. "What do you mean?"

"You don't know about that?"

"About what?"

"The air conditioners."

"No. What about the air conditioners?"

"It doesn't *matter* about the air conditioners! I've told Matt, and I'll tell you, I'm not in the market for performing as anything but a doctor in Riverbend. After all, he *is* married!"

As soon as the words were out of her mouth, Sam longed to take them back. The mention of Matt's marriage summoned the image of his wife, and once again the haunted look dropped over Drew's face like a mask.

"Drew, I'm sorry—" she began, but he cut her off as he pressed a quick kiss to her forehead and backed into the darkness.

"The bottom line is you're right," he said. "They *are* married, even though in name only, even though Matt wishes it otherwise with all his heart. At least after meeting Lucy, you should have an idea of what he's up against. 'Night, Sam."

It wasn't until Drew pulled a screeching U-turn in the middle of Main Street that he realized what he was doing. A deadly look settling on his face, he pushed the car well above the speed limit as he drove back to Savannah . . . back to his favorite club on the Riverfront. . . . back to his favorite seat at the bar.

"Give me a double, will you, Ted?" he said as he arrived.

"Sure thing, Mr. Pierce."

As he downed drink after drink, Drew peered out the window at the lights of the river. Beautiful as the scene was, he found himself thinking of it as a prison. God, would he ever get out of here? Would he ever have the chance to move beyond the intangible, unyielding velvet of Lucy's clutches?

The later the hour waxed, the more he thought he heard his own voice—speaking to Ted . . . speaking to anyone within earshot. And then suddenly he was being borne along silent roads, dark but for the occasional lights of street lamps at intersections. When they stopped, he was aware of being carried.

"Tobias?" he asked at one point. For some reason the

aging face of Matt's black butler came to mind. For some reason, it seemed his voice answered: "Yessir."

"What the hell are you doing?" Drew's voice seemed to say.

"Taking you inside, Mr. Drew. You'll rest up just fine in your old room."

"Are you part of my dream?" Drew asked after a minute, and could have sworn he heard the black man laugh.

"Could be, Mr. Drew. Could be."

A short time later—Drew couldn't be sure how long—he was certain he was in the midst of a dream when he heard the unmistakable voice call his name.

"Drew, are you all right?"

He let the magical words sink in before replying: "Is that you, Lucy?"

"Of course it's me."

Time passed—a second or two . . . an hour or two . . .

"I can't see you," he pointed out.

"Maybe it would help if you opened your eyes."

Drew tried to laugh, but it seemed his lips wouldn't move.

"He really is the most disgusting thing," Drew then heard, but the insult barely penetrated his groggy mind. "Undress him, Tobias, and let him sleep it off."

After a few merciless minutes of yanking and pulling, the room, chamber, cave—whatever it was—was filled with the most wonderfully peaceful quiet.

As the sun climbed high with bright morning light, Matt paced the foyer like a surly lion.

"What's wrong with you?" Nadine asked as she came down the hall and spotted him.

"Nothing," he responded.

"You look like you ain't been to bed at all," she observed.

"No different from others around here," came the short reply.

"Where's Drew?" she asked.

"Good question," Matt responded. "Where *should* he be after a night celebrating a good harvest?"

Her eyes going wide, Nadine shrugged her shoulders. "Don't ask me," she replied.

"Exactly," Matt responded as though he'd uncovered a great truth. Bounding up the stairs, he splashed his face, brushed his teeth, and stripped off his shirt in favor of a new one.

"Uh-huh," Nadine mumbled when he came barreling down the staircase at half-past ten.

"Shut up, Nadine," he tossed back on his way to the door.

Speeding into town, Matt expected to see Drew's car parked in front of Sam's. It wasn't there. Hell, maybe they never even came back. Maybe they spent the night in Savannah.

Stalking up to the porch, Matt angrily rang the bell, and was surprised when Hannah Mathers opened the door.

"Mornin', Hannah. What are you doing here?"

"Me and Jason come most every day," she replied, and seemed to shrink back in the doorway.

Suddenly realizing he was scowling down on the poor woman, Matt brought a friendly look to his face. "Is Sam here?" he asked.

"No, sir."

The friendly expression dissolved. "Where is she, then?"

"Swimmin'."

"Swimming?" Matt hooted.

"Down at the old swimmin' hole—you know, through the pines."

"Yeah, I know." Matt arched a brow. "Is she alone?"

"I reckon so."

"Drew isn't with her?"

"Mr. Pierce? No, sir. At least I don't think so."

Matt gazed at her thoughtfully. "How long have you been here?"

"Most of an hour."

"Did you see Drew when you arrived?"

She shook her head emphatically, her eyes wide with what appeared to be fright. Matt smiled reassuringly as he backed away.

"Thank you, Hannah. You take care now, ya hear?"

"Yes, sir," she replied, and quickly closed the door.

Circling to the side of the house, Matt came upon a trail through the weeds. *Swimming,* he repeated to himself as he made quick progress to the familiar path through the pines. After all his wondering about where she might be and what she might be doing, it turned out she was taking a dip in the old swimming hole of his youth. Matt almost could have laughed, except that the night with Drew remained unexplained.

As he neared the end of the path he caught sounds of splashing, and when he arrived at the clearing, he saw that Hannah was right. Sam was alone. Moving quietly up to the giant oak by the edge of the water, he watched for a moment as she swam.

Sunlight sifted through the leaves to dapple the pool. It glistened on her hair and limbs, as well as the yellow swimsuit she was wearing. As she pushed off in a smooth stroke, she was like a sunbeam moving through the water. When she reached the other side, she dove and came up facing away, her hair shedding a cascade down her bare back and into the depths rippling about her waist.

In an impatient gesture Matt scooped up a pebble and sent it sailing to splash a few feet away from her. She spun around.

"It might be a good idea not to go swimming alone," he said.

She waded a step or two in his direction, into deeper water that concealed most of her body. "Why? More gators?"

"No, but there are some two-legged beasts who visit this watering hole from time to time."

"You're the first of those I've encountered," she announced with a slight smile.

Her skin was the color of honey; her eyes green as the

lush grass tufting the banks of the pool. Stepping over the gnarled roots of the oak, Matt came to stand at the water's edge, idly catching the old, swinging rope and toying with it as his gaze remained locked on the woman.

"Where's Drew?" he demanded abruptly.

"I don't know."

"I'll bet you can hazard a pretty good guess."

"Well, I'd *guess* he's at work in your vineyards."

Matt shook his head. "Nobody's working today. Nobody's working all week now that the harvest is in."

"Then, like I said—I don't know."

"Did he stay at your place last night?"

Her brows flew up. "What?"

"Drew hasn't been home since he picked you up. Did you two spend the night together? Just tell me the truth. I want to know."

"I'll be happy to tell you the truth," she replied indignantly. "No, we did *not* spend the night together. He dropped me off, and I assumed he went home. You don't suppose something's happened to him, do you?" Her face clouded with worry.

Matt shrugged, suddenly realizing the obvious. "He probably went back to Savannah. He overnights it there every now and then."

"He does?"

"Yeah. Especially when there's no work the next day."

"Then, why were you so concerned about his neglecting to come home?" she asked, her puzzled look swiftly changing to one of understanding. "I see."

"Do you?"

"You thought ... You actually believed ... You were jealous," she concluded.

Matt's penetrating gaze bored into her eyes. "Would it further my position in any way if I admitted it?"

"Matt ..." she began in a gentle tone.

Preparing himself for another of her lectures, Matt sighed, grabbed the rope with both hands, and leaned toward her across the water. A look of horror rose to her face.

"I don't think—"

That was all she had time to get out of her mouth before the old rope snapped. His balance centered beyond the shoreline, there was nothing Matt could do but fall face-first in the water. He came up sputtering, and the first thing to register on his surprised senses was the sound of Sam's bubbling laughter. Surrendering a grin, Matt gained his footing in thigh-high water and looked down at the useless trail of rope in his hands.

"Damn," he said. "It didn't do that the last time I put weight on it."

"When was that?" she asked, still shaking with laughter.

"Reckon I was a mite lighter," he returned. Tossing the rope to the bank, he unbuttoned his shirt and peeled off the soaked garment. Wringing the shirt into a coil as he went, he walked toward her into the deeper water. With a smile lighting up her face the way it was, she was the loveliest thing he'd ever seen.

"I hadn't planned on taking a swim," he said as he came to stand before her. "But the water feels pretty good . . . except for inside my boots."

Sam's expression of merriment dissipated as her gaze swept over him, and her thoughts began to drift in the strange fashion that this man, alone, provoked. Swirling about her shoulders, the water reached only to his rib cage, which swelled into the most remarkable chest, topped with the most remarkable set of bronze shoulders. Wet and shining, his black hair clung in tendrils to his neck, and even curled in a few places against his unshaven jaw. The fact that he needed a shave only enhanced the spectacle of manliness. He was like a dark god.

"How did you find out about the swimming hole?" he asked.

Snapping out of her reverie, Sam managed a light smile. "Rae brought me a few weeks ago. I've been out here nearly every day since then. But now . . . well, the heat I thought would last forever seems finally to be dying away. Look around. The leaves are beginning to turn. Each day I wake up and wonder if it will be the last day at the swimming hole. Each day I find myself out here a little earlier."

Matt shook his head. "I never would have pictured you here."

"Why not?"

"I don't know. A little too rugged, maybe."

Sam lifted a brow. "Since I arrived in Riverbend, I've been pitted against a broken-down house, a townful of skeptics, and an angry mother alligator. The swimming hole seems peaceful next to those."

"I see what you mean," he acceded with a chuckle.

Their eyes met. His smile faded. And Sam found herself breaking the look. It was just too strong—the sight of him standing there in the shifting sunlight, unencumbered by clothing from the waist up. In an effort to hide her discomfiture, she sank beneath the surface of water and when she resurfaced, had succeeded in putting an additional two feet of distance between them. He, on the other hand, seemed hell-bent on establishing the sense of intimacy he wielded like a weapon. Moving forward, he blithely annihilated the distance she'd achieved, and also managed to recapture her gaze.

"So, you and Drew didn't . . . ." When he trailed off on a questioning note, Sam gave him an arch look.

"No," she affirmed. "We didn't."

"Did he at least give it a shot?"

"Drew was a charming escort, but we're friends. That's all."

Matt raked her with a long, considering look. "I've thought about what you said the other night," he then said. "That bit about notches in bedposts."

"And?" Sam prodded.

"Maybe I *have* come on a little strong."

"Maybe?" she questioned. Twisting his shirt in powerful hands, he fixed her with glowing eyes. "I don't know how to be bashful, Sam. I feel what I feel, want what I want, and make no apologies for going after it. The

women I've known have never objected ... till now. It
kind of puts you in a class by yourself. I'm not sure how
to handle you."

"That's the point, Matt. I'm not something to be *handled*. I'm me, Sam Kelly—a member of the female sex,
yes, but that's not where it ends. I'm other things, too."

"I know. I'm aware of those other things."

"You don't act as though you are. Every time we cross
paths you behave as if the only thing on your mind is
how fast you can get me into bed."

"It is," he confirmed with a small smile.

Sam started to turn away. In an instant he'd flipped the
coil of his shirt over her head and lodged it around her
back, effectively imprisoning her within arm's length.
Grabbing the makeshift rope just below his dark fingers,
she looked up with flashing eyes.

"I'm not used to curbing my impulses," he said.

"So I see."

"But I'll try."

"Really," she returned with a sarcastic lilt.

"Yes, really. I know what you think," he went on, his
voice low and stirring. "You think we have nothing in
common, that nothing of importance can pass between
two people with such different backgrounds, such different views."

"Are you saying I'm wrong?"

"I'm saying you're ignoring the most basic link in the
world—the one between man and woman."

"And I'm saying that's quite a line," Sam replied and
tugged at the lassoing shirt.

"Don't."

Something about the timbre of his voice stopped her.
Looking slowly up, Sam met the challenge of his eyes
once more.

"I might not be saying or doing the right things," he
added. "But don't leave. Please."

Was it the final, supplicating word that did her in?
Sam didn't know, but the change that occurred then was
swift as the smash of glass, as though a solid barrier had

been obliterated. Perceptions flooded her senses—the sound of a breeze rustling through the trees, the smell of late-blooming honeysuckle, the warmth of sunshine mixing with the chill of the pool ... and surpassing all those, the hypnotic sensation of being lifted ever closer to the man before her.

"You're beautiful." She must have said the words aloud, because he smiled. Otherwise, he hadn't moved. Neither had she, although suddenly she found her fingers itching to slip along the muscles of his arms, to lock behind his neck ... As the image dawned, Sam looked sharply aside.

"Hey," he said. When she glanced up, he pulled the coiled shirt from around her back and threw it to the bank. "I'm not pushing anything," he added, his eyes settling on hers.

"You're not?"

"No. I've decided not to push anymore. Not with you."

The irony sliced like a blade—now that Matt was backing off, all she could think of was taking the lead herself.

"That's very interesting," Sam murmured.

"Is it?"

She gave him a thoughtful look. "From the first time I saw you, I thought: *savage*. And now, here you are, behaving with the most civilized restraint."

"I have my good days," he pointed out in a wry tone.

In spite of herself, Sam smiled.

Reaching out, he captured her chin and leaned down, so close that she felt his breath on her face.

Pulled by an irresistible force, Sam's gaze dropped to his mouth. Outlined by the dark shadow of beard, his lips appeared smooth and firm, and though she'd told herself to forget, she well remembered the magic of their touch. She realized now that she'd been wrong. Reason and moral fiber couldn't stand up to a secluded glade and Matt Tyler. Her eyelids drifted.

"But I'm not going to kiss you," he added. Her eyes springing open, Sam stared into the glowing orbs above hers. "If that's what you want, you're going to have to show me."

She twisted out of his grasp; Matt caught her by the arm and pulled her back. Swiftly cradling her face in giant hands, he sought her eyes.

"Show me, Sam," he commanded, his voice deep and resonant.

Her gaze dipped from his amber eyes to his mouth and returned to his eyes. "Damn," Sam muttered and, grasping his neck, lifted her mouth to his.

In the instant their lips met, Matt's arm was around her, claiming her hips and pulling her through the water between them. As he embraced her, he hoisted her up, securing her with iron grips about her back and bottom. His tongue searched her mouth, and Sam found herself opening to him as before—admitting in some dim corner of her mind that there were drives over which the reasoning mind simply held no rein.

Her legs were wrapped around his waist, her arms around his neck, and she was kissing him for all she was worth when a sharp noise rang out. Matt drew back just as the sound repeated itself.

"What's that?" Sam cried.

"Gunfire."

"Gunfire?" she echoed, alarm sweeping over her.

"About the caliber of Rae's Colt, I'd say. She keeps a forty-five under the bar. Come on. Let's go."

Having washed the stale tastes of tobacco and liquor out of his mouth, Drew slung his jacket over his shoulder and went downstairs. What he was doing in the Savannah Tyler house, he couldn't fathom. He found Lucy seated at the tea table in the Florida room where— dressed in bright green, and with sunlight in her hair— she was color-coordinated with the pots of yellow chrysanthemums lining the chamber.

"Good morning, Drew. Would you care for some brunch?"

"How did I end up here?" he demanded.

"You don't remember?"

"I was on the Riverfront. I'm sure I didn't drive here."

"The barkeep called you a cab, and the driver said you gave him this address. He and Tobias carried you in."

"Sorry for the intrusion," Drew replied curtly. "You could have sent the cabbie to a hotel."

She offered a light shrug of her shoulders. "It's a big house. There was no need to turn away a friend in need."

Arching a suspicious brow, Drew leaned against the doorjamb. "Friend?" he repeated. "We've known each other a lot of years. But we've never been friends."

For a passing instant, her face took on an uncharacteristic bloom of color. "I'm sorry to hear you say that. Particularly when I was thinking of making you a friendly proposition."

"Now we're getting to it."

"Getting to what?"

"The reason you didn't turn me away last night."

"You needn't make a simple act of hospitality sound as though it's steeped in intrigue."

"Stop dancing around, Lucy. What the hell do you want?"

With upturned palm she gestured to the adjacent chair at the tea table. "Why don't you have a seat?"

"I'll stand."

She gazed for a moment with her cold, pretty eyes. "All right then," she said, and rising to her feet, moved toward him. "I could make you a rich man, Drew."

"I'm doing all right as it is."

"You could do better than all right. You could do so well that you could live any kind of life you wanted, any-*where* you wanted."

"And what would I have to do in exchange for such luxury?"

"Nothing really. Just stay in touch with me. Let me know what goes on at the vineyards. Be my ally."

"Be your spy, you mean."

"Really, Drew! Do you have to twist everything I do or say into something tawdry?"

"It doesn't take any twisting," he answered bluntly.

Again, a lovely shade of pink invaded her cheeks. "Contrary to your prediction of last night, I fully intend to win the upcoming lawsuit," she said. "There is, however, no guarantee. If, by some chance, the judge doesn't see things my way . . ."

"Well?" Drew barked.

"Well, I certainly don't intend to let the matter drop."

"And it would be my job to feed you ammunition for a new lawsuit, is that it?"

"I'm entitled to half of whatever Matt has," she fired.

"I'd say you've taken a lot more than half."

"I'd hoped you'd see things reasonably, Drew. I'd hoped you'd grown up enough to see the opportunity I'm offering."

His gaze moved slowly over her body before returning to her eyes. "So far, you haven't offered anything that interests me."

"Oh?" she replied, the high-pitched tone of her voice betraying a nervousness he never would have imagined in Lucy Beauregard. "What *would* interest you, then?"

With a fleeting smile Drew tossed his jacket to the floor and stepped close. Although her eyes flared unusually wide, she tipped her head to look him in the face, and held her ground.

"Stocks? Bonds?" she questioned, still in that falsely bright tone. "A major interest in one of my holdings, perhaps?"

"Not even close," Drew replied, his eyes drilling into hers. Looking swiftly aside, she broke the intense look and started to turn. Almost as swiftly, Drew reached out, captured her by the shoulders, and turned her to face him once more.

"I'm trying to talk business," Lucy snapped. "I don't intend to continue playing these guessing games with you."

His hand rose to the back of her head, his fingers closing cruelly in her hair. "I'm not playing games," he muttered, so close that his breath stirred a blond curl at her cheek.

"Stop it, Drew," she commanded, her palms rising to his chest.

"No," he whispered, and buried his parting lips on hers.

She gasped as his tongue moved into her mouth, but she didn't push him away. Surprisingly, but also disappointingly, she remained still as stone and allowed his mouth to have its way. *Like some damn stoic enduring punishment,* Drew thought and abruptly released her.

"And you talk about growing up," he accused, swiftly scooping up his jacket. "You still kiss like a teenaged virgin."

"And you still want me anyway," she retaliated.

There was no doubt of the fiery color in her face now. She was off balance—Lucy Beauregard, the one who never lost a step, never missed a beat, was actually flustered. And she was right. He'd never wanted her more.

"To my everlasting shame," Drew admitted with burning eyes. When her chin went up, he couldn't resist grabbing it and wrenching her face close to his. "I don't want your damn money, Lucy. I tell you what—*when* you lose in court, and *if* you decide you're ready to give up more than a debutante's kiss, you let me know, all right?"

With that, Drew pushed her away and turned on his heel. Though he didn't look back, he sensed that Lucy stumbled, and clearly felt the steel of her deadly look spearing its way between his shoulder blades as he walked out of the house.

*C*hapter Ten

Grabbing up her terry cloth robe as she scrambled out of the swimming hole, Sam shrugged into it and followed Matt's loping lead through the pines. Though Riverbend was the kind of town where most folks stayed behind doors, by the time they reached Main Street, a sizable crowd had gathered in front of Rae's Place, where Rae was standing—like Annie Oakley—with a pistol in her hand. Near her feet lay the mad dog she'd brought down with two shots.

"Last week Ira killed a rabid coon trying to get in his chicken coop," Edwin Pettigrew was saying. "Now it's a dog coming down the middle of Main Street. I don't like the looks of this."

Following Matt's course, Sam skirted the crowd and found a place near Rae. "You always *were* hell with that Colt," Sam heard him murmur.

"You oughtta know," Rae replied. "You taught me to shoot."

"That's right, I did," he confirmed with a teasing look. "So, how come it took you two shots?"

"He moved," Rae answered, her sharp gaze turning to encompass Sam along with Matt. "Hot day, ain't it?" she added, squarely reminding Sam of her and Matt's equally dripping appearance. She felt the blood rush to her cheeks. When Matt looped an unexpected arm about her shoulders, she jumped away as though he'd struck her. Looking up, she watched his dark brows draw together as he lowered his arm to his side.

"Hey! This is one of Red Carter's bitches!" a man in the surrounding crowd announced.

"He's right," Matt said, his frown deepening as Sam sidled another step away from him. "This is one of Carter's pack."

"Then all his dogs should be examined," Sam suggested, and was gratified that a sensible idea had rolled from her mouth beneath Matt's smoldering scrutiny. Everyone's eyes turned her way.

"It takes approximately thirty days for rabies to incubate," she added. "Who knows when this dog was infected, or how many others have been infected since then?"

"She's right," Larry Edison spoke up. "If this dog got to the others, there's no telling how many could be rabid."

"We don't know what we're dealing with until we look," Matt said with a cautioning hand. "Anybody seen the Carters around town today?" A ripple of negative answers made its way through the crowd. "Then I reckon we ought to drive out there and let them know what's happened," he suggested.

"Want to ride with me, Matt?" the constable invited.

"No, I'll go with the Doc," he answered with a pointed look at Sam. "It might be a good idea to have a medic on hand."

The crowd split up at that point—some staying behind to help Rae dispose of the dog, others heading home or in the directions of various cars and trucks. Sam wished she had the time and opportunity to change into something more presentable than a damp, knee-length robe, but Matt fell in beside her and walked straight for the van. He didn't say a word until she pulled her keys from her pocket and started around to the driver's side.

"I'll drive," he announced then, and stepping into her

path, extended an open palm. His wet shirt hung draped about his neck, his bare shoulders gleamed in the sun, and the memory of their passion barreled to the surface.

"What on earth for?" Sam asked, a fresh wave of heat pricking at her cheeks.

"I'd just be more comfortable driving, that's all."

"Why? Because you happen to be a man?"

There was no doubt of the anger in the look he flashed down on her. "Must you make an issue of everything?"

"Must you?" she countered.

"Forget it," he muttered and, stalking around to the passenger's side, didn't speak again until she'd made the turn in the middle of Main Street and started the van toward the south end of town.

"What the hell's happening?" he then demanded. "Twenty minutes ago we were all over each other at the swimming hole. Now? I have the distinct feeling that if I reached for your hand right now, you'd jump out the window."

Sam expelled a shaky breath. "Matt, please. I realize you have a right to be puzzled."

"I'm glad you realize that."

"But you can't go around holding my hand or putting your arm around me as if we were . . . you know."

"No. I don't know."

"As if we were *involved*," Sam returned on a note of impatience.

"I'd say we were pretty involved a short while ago, and you didn't seem to mind a bit. *You* kissed *me*, remember?"

"Look, Matt. I'm sorry I got a little carried away—"

"*A little carried away*? If we're going to talk about this, let's talk straight. If not for those gunshots, we'd be making love right now. I know it, and so do you."

"I do not!" Sam cried. "One little slip, and you—"

"*One little slip!*" Matt barked with a short laugh. "Forgive me for repeating everything you say, but I can't seem to help it. Is that what you call what happened at the pond? A *little slip*?!"

"Yes! I do!"

Seconds of electrified quiet crackled by. When Sam chanced a look in his direction, she found Matt gazing at her with an expression suggesting utter bewilderment. With another snort of a laugh he shook his head and turned to look out the window.

"A little slip," she heard him mumble a moment later.

"All right then, dammit," Sam said softly. "I'll do as you say. I'll talk straight. I lost my senses out at the swimming hole, I admit, but I'm thinking clearly now and the fact is I'm not the type to have casual sex. I never have been, and I don't want to be."

From the corner of her eye, she watched Matt's head slowly turn in her direction. "Who said anything about casual sex?"

"What else could it have been?"

"The start of something nice," came his deep reply.

"Nice in what way? I met your wife last night at the symphony, Matt."

He held up a quick palm. "Don't say anything else, okay?" He paused for a moment as if curbing some powerful feelings, then said, "My marriage was a disaster from the beginning. I've paid the price for that mistake a hundred times over. Don't make me pay it again."

"I'm not trying to make you do anything."

"Like hell. I told you at the street dance how things stand. My marriage means nothing. The affairs mean nothing. The way things are between you and me—the way they've been since the beginning, *and* out at the pond. Now, *that* means something."

"What, Matt?" she demanded. "What could it possibly mean that's any different—"

"It could mean we belong together, dammit!" he thundered.

Sam cast another glance in his direction. His face was flushed with anger, his eyes flashing beneath furrowed brows. Looking back to the road, she tightened her grip on the wheel.

"I've been looking for something for a long time,

Sam," he added. "Something real. When I met you, I thought I might've found it."

The emotions thrashing through Sam included longing and regret, and a dose of self-recrimination for feeling either. In ten months she'd be dusting the dirt of Riverbend from her feet. An affair with a Georgia grapegrower simply wasn't part of the plan.

"I'm not looking for the same thing you are, Matt," she said finally. "So, please . . . either be my friend, or leave me alone."

"You got it, lady," he said tightly.

Sam didn't look his way again, and when they reached the Carter place, he slammed the van door and strode off to meet the others without a backward glance.

She watched from the drive as a flock of men gathered at the porch, called out Red and his brother, Hal, and then proceeded around the corner of the house. Allowing them a fair lead, Sam slowly followed. By the time she arrived at the dog pen in the back lot, Larry Edison was taking aim with a rifle. There was a shot, and then an uproar of baying and howling.

Edging around the men, Sam drew near the pen. A black-and-white dog lay near the fence as a half dozen or more others continued to bark and jump about. Crouching down, she took a closer look. There was foam on the dead dog's jowls.

"Sorry, Red," she heard Larry say. "It was obvious the bitch was as mad as the one in town."

Rising to her feet, Sam surveyed the milling hounds. There appeared to be no signs of rabies in the others, but then the blatant symptoms of the salivary disease didn't manifest until the final phases. Any number of the dogs could be in the early stages of infection, and could, in turn, infect the others. She turned and looked at the men, who continued to discuss the two shootings. No one was paying attention to the pack in the pen. Drawing a deep breath, Sam stepped forward.

"You've got to separate those dogs if you want to save any of them," she announced. The men turned to look at her—Matt among them—and she felt suddenly as David must have felt when faced with Goliath.

"What do you know about it, Miss Hot Shot?" Red challenged.

"Yeah, what do you know about it?" Hal chimed in.

"Quiet, you two," Matt said.

"What I know," Sam added with a flash of her eyes, "is that rabies is generally undetectable but highly contagious in the incubation stage. Any number of these dogs could already have it."

"We might have a serious problem here," Larry Edison said.

"What are you saying, Constable?" Red demanded. "That on the word of a little Yankee girl, I should shoot my dogs?"

What followed was an explosion of voices—all male, all uniform in accusing that a lone, upstart female was suggesting the annihilation of Red Carter's hounds.

"I said, *separate them,*" Sam objected, trying to raise her voice above the clamor. "Not shoot them."

"The hell you say, girl!" Red Carter thundered. "You're the one who brought it up! If you're suggesting I should shoot my dogs, you can go straight to hell!"

"She's suggesting just the opposite," Matt tried to intervene.

"It don't sound like the opposite to me!" Hal joined in.

"God," Sam muttered, and brushing away her bangs with a frustrated hand, happened to look in the direction of the house ... and caught sight of the pale, hopeless face of Ida Carter at the window. That was it.

"All of you, shut up!" she shouted. "Right now!" Suddenly she had every male eye upon her, and she glared back at them fearlessly until they were as silent as they were still.

"It's like this," she said briskly. "You can take my advice, separate these dogs, and get a vet out here to test every one of them, or you know what? You can ignore me, and go right on being the most backward bunch of redneck chauvinists ever to turn up in the twentieth century! Within a week, you might have a full-scale rabies epidemic on your hands, but then, hey! That's okay! You *men* know best, right?"

With that, Sam turned and made swift progress around the side of the house. In unison, the men gravitated along her path, curiously watching as she started up the van and roared out of the Carter property in a southerly direction.

"Where the hell is she going?" Edwin questioned.

"Who the hell gives a damn?" Red replied.

Letting the wind rip through her hair, Sam drove aimlessly along the highway for a half hour or so, until the gas gauge registered only a quarter full, and the desolate emptiness of the countryside began to take its toll. She had mixed feelings about turning around and heading back to Riverbend. True, it was better than the nothingness surrounding her; but it also meant Matt Tyler and a plethora of other challenges she felt both unwilling and unable to address.

Returning home to the cheery sounds of Hannah and Celie playing ball on the porch with Jason, she felt a little better. But as daylight faded and her friends departed, the house closed about her with loneliness and Sam escaped to the outdoors.

Pausing in the front yard, she gazed for a moment across the empty street. The supper hour was past, and even Rae's Place seemed tranquil in the deepening dusk. Meandering about the side of the house, Sam ended up taking the familiar path to the swimming hole. Once there, she sat down by the presiding oak and gazed across the mirrorlike water.

Now, at twilight, the pool had a different character—a soft, dreamy air very different from the sun-dappled brightness of midday. The image of Matt's glistening body materialized in the pool, and she remembered the passionate way she'd clung to him. There was no denying the unprecedented effect he had on her. When she was alone with him, she found herself floating along . . . finding reasons not to object, thinking that the way she was feeling couldn't be wrong, and even if it was, she didn't care.

He was right. If not for the interruption, they probably would have made love right there in that pool—with her exhibiting no more self-control than the rest of Matt Tyler's legendary bevy of conquests. She simply didn't think straight when he touched her. Maybe no woman did.

Putting a hand to her forehead, Sam massaged an ache between her brows. Now that she was entirely herself, she could see quite clearly the total wrongness—on every plane—of becoming involved with Matt. But when he held her in spellbinding closeness, it was a different story.

Pushing to her feet, Sam stared into the gathering darkness. Anyway, it was over. He'd taken her blunt rejection to heart, and he wouldn't be back. She couldn't blame him for being enraged. After today's hot-and-cold performance, she was just as angry with herself as he was.

As she turned away from the pool, Sam noticed a patch of late dandelions blooming at the water's edge. Stooping to pick two of the wildflowers, she slowly straightened, made a slit in the stem of one and pulled the other one through. She smiled as she recalled a hot afternoon when Rae had demonstrated the technique.

It's easy. I'll show you, her voice seemed to echo—but only for a moment before the October night began to descend, its crisp edge erasing the image of soft summer days. Dropping the dandelions onto the shining surface of water, Sam started back through the pines. The encroaching darkness gave the path the same new spirit as that of the pool—cool, dark, serene.

As she entered the house, she was thinking she might even turn off the air conditioners, might even open the upstairs windows and air the house overnight. She made the usual check of windows and doors, and climbed the stairs with a long, hot bath in mind.

Flipping on the light as she walked into the bedroom, Sam stepped in front of the dresser mirror and started to pin up her hair. When she reached for the brush, her gaze trailed across the reflection in the mirror, halted, and went hurtling back. A scream escaped her as she whirled and stared in horror at the bed.

Someone had pulled back the covers, and there on her pillow lay the carcass of a chicken—its slashed throat having spilled a river of blood that ran along the pillow and pooled on the sheet. Sam stood there, frozen, until it dawned that whoever had done this could still be in the house.

The broom was propped in the corner. She grabbed it, and pointing it ahead of her like a bayonet, made a thorough search of every hiding place on both levels. As soon as she was sure the perpetrator had gone, Sam dropped the broom and hurried across the street to Rae's.

"Sam, honey," Rae greeted from behind the bar. "I been wondering when you were gonna pay me a visit."

"Good evening, Rae." Casting a swift look about the place, Sam saw that it was empty but for a couple of barflies perched a few stools away. "I was hoping I could borrow you for a minute."

"Borrow me?" Rae returned with a questioning look.

Catching her lip between her teeth, Sam nodded. In a heartbeat, Rae was whipping the apron from her hips and rounding the bar.

"Your face is white as a sheet," she said as they crossed the street. "What the hell's going on?"

"Just wait and see," Sam replied. Latching onto Rae's arm, she drew her up the stairs.

"For God's sake!" Rae exclaimed as they walked into the bedroom.

"Gruesome, isn't it?"

"I'll say. When did it happen?"

"Pretty recently. The blood hasn't had time to dry. Maybe when I took a walk a while ago."

"Any signs of breaking and entering?"

Sam glanced to her toes. "No. Whoever did it came through the front door."

"It wasn't locked?"

Sam looked up. "I didn't think of it. I was outside and decided on the spur of the moment to take a quick walk. I couldn't have been gone more than a half hour."

Planting her hands on her hips, Rae shook her head as she surveyed the bloody mess. "Damn," she muttered. "It looks like they killed the damn chicken right on your bed."

Sam shivered and fixed Rae with a searching look. "Does this look like more klan stuff? I made a bit of a scene today out at the Carter place. Do you think Red and his bunch have been at work again?"

"I don't know," Rae replied. "Maybe. It doesn't matter."

"It doesn't *matter*?"

Rae regarded her with dark, solemn eyes. "It seems to me that what's important here is the message, not the messenger. Somebody wants you gone, Sam. After something like this, nobody would blame you if you lit out."

"You mean leave Riverbend?"

"First your door. Now your bed. Whoever's doing this seems to be getting closer. Who knows what could happen next?"

"Is that what you think I should do, Rae? Leave?"

Rae thought a minute, her gaze sweeping Sam from head to toe and back again. "I think you're smart and young and have everything ahead of you," she said ultimately. "You don't belong here, Sam. The world is your oyster, and Riverbend ain't no pearl. Have you thought about calling Larry Edison?"

"To report what? A dead chicken in my bed? Whoever did it is long gone, Rae."

"They could still be watching." As Sam glanced up with a look of alarm, Rae added, "It might not hurt for the constable to pay you a visit."

Within mere minutes of Rae's call, Larry's official car screeched to a halt in front of the house, its blue light flashing. Shaking his head as Sam admitted to having left the house unlocked, the constable made a thorough check of the path from the door to the bedroom, with Rae and Sam trailing his every step.

"Wish I had more to go on," he said. Tipping his hat back on his head, he gazed down at the bloody bed. "Looks like whoever did this slipped in and out without leaving a trace."

"You know I've criticized the KKK," Sam spoke up. "Does this look like something they might do?"

Larry turned her way with a look of surprise. "The klan? Nah!"

"How can you be sure?"

"It's not their style. If they wanted to single somebody out—and I emphasize *if*—they might burn a cross in front of his house or something. And maybe years ago they might have done worse. But not these days. No, this looks like a malicious prank. Hey! You know what this *does* remind me of, Rae? All that voodoo devil-worship stuff. Remember Juda's curse?"

"Really, Larry," Rae muttered.

"What's Juda's curse?" Sam demanded, swiftly recalling the phrase she'd read in Dr. Daly's records.

"It happened back in the twenties," Larry began. "Juda came from Haiti and took a job as nanny out at the Tyler place. Little did anyone know she was a voodoo witch, and worse yet, she decided she wanted Mary Tyler's husband, Jonathan. The story goes that she cast a spell on Mary, and drove her to hang herself by killing a chicken in her—"

"Larry," Rae broke in on a scolding note. "I don't think anyone is trying to drive Sam to suicide. And she's got plenty to think about without tossing Juda's curse into the pot."

"Sorry," Larry responded with a light blush. "The least I can do is get rid of this thing for you, Sam. Do you have an old towel or something I could use?"

Wrapped in the blood-soaked pillow and taped securely in a trash bag, the dead chicken left the house under the arm of the constable. "It's just a kid's prank," Larry said on his way out. "I'm sure of it. Even so, don't forget to lock your door."

Having stripped the bed, Rae carried the bundle of soiled linen and followed Larry to the door. "I'll either get these clean or burn them," she said. "Wish I could stay longer, but I gotta get back to my place before it falls apart."

"Thanks for coming over, Rae."

"You sure you'll be all right?"

"I'm sure," Sam replied, and mustered a smile from somewhere as she was left alone in the creeping shadows of the house.

Klansmen? Curses? Dead chickens? *Damn!*

Securely locking the door, Sam coursed through the downstairs and turned on every lamp. With mounting dread she gathered bucket and scrub brush and returned to the bedroom, where the bloodstain on the mattress gaped with the morbidity of a crime scene. *Damn,* she thought over and over again as she scrubbed at the awful stain. When the entire right side of the mattress was sodden, she turned on the fan and took her remaining pillow down to the parlor, where she determined to sleep on the couch.

Lights blared from every corner. Still, the house seemed spooky. Sam turned on the old TV stereo, and music wafted through the rooms. But nothing really helped. As fear and anger began to subside, depression set in, dragging her spirits deeper and deeper. She was accomplishing nothing in Riverbend. No one came to the clinic. No one regarded her as a physician. And someone hated her enough to leave a pile of crap on her porch, and a mutilated bird in her bed.

It had to be Red Carter. The two of them had been clashing since the day she arrived. And judging from the condition of poor Ida, Sam knew the man was capable of a kind of cruelty that went beyond her powers of imagination. Rae's words came back: *Who knows what could happen next?*

A chill spread over her, and Sam went into the kitchen to put on the tea kettle. As the water warmed she propped herself against the counter and allowed a tantalizing thought to take root. Why should she go on beating her head against a wall—fighting to win acceptance from people who didn't want to give it? There were other places out there, other people who would welcome her services. Strings could be pulled. Chad had said so.

How much time had he given her? A month? Not much more than that had passed, and here she was— ready to run. All it would take was a phone call to Chad, and he'd have her out of here and back home in Boston.

Home . . . God, it seemed so far away. On impulse Sam set the kettle off the stove, went into the parlor, and called her parents. Her father answered.

"Sam! How's my Southern belle?"

She smiled into the phone. "It's good to hear your voice, Father. I've missed you."

"Just a minute . . . For heaven's sake, your mother's grabbing the phone. Are you okay?"

"I'm fine," Sam barely had time to say before her mother's voice came on the line.

"Darling! I must say your letters have all of us positively enthralled with the idea of Georgia!"

"Do they?"

"All this talk of swamps and cypress and Spanish moss—very intriguing, though it sounds decidedly uncivilized."

"No doubt of that," Sam responded. "Although, funnily enough, I attended the symphony in Savannah last night."

"The symphony?" her mother repeated in surprise.

"They did your favorite—Chopin's Fantasia for piano and orchestra. And they performed quite admirably."

"How amazing!"

Indeed, Sam thought. What was amazing was that a mere twenty-four hours had passed since she sat comfortably in the Savannah concert hall. It seemed a lifetime's worth of events had taken place since then.

"Sam?"

"Yes?"

"Somehow I sense there's something wrong."

"No. Nothing," Sam lied. "I just wanted to touch base with the outside world."

"Then I know you'll be happy to hear that poor Ellen's daughter, Inez, finally has a boyfriend . . ."

With that, her mother began filling her in on all the neighborhood news. Tears sprang to Sam's eyes as she remembered the impatient way she used to pat her foot when Mother launched into one of her "chatty news" monologues. She'd taken the good things so terribly for granted.

"And Mrs. Durante asked about you. You know, Sam . . . if you'd decided to be a ditch digger, I'd have been proud for you to be the best ditch digger ever born. As it is, you're a fine doctor, an answer to every parent's prayer. Your father and I are very proud, you know."

"I know," Sam responded, her eyes brimming.

"I hope those Georgians realize what a treasure has fallen into their laps."

"They're a little . . . hesitant about me, Mother."

"Hesitant? In what way?"

"Most of the people in Riverbend have lived here all their lives. I'm sort of a foreigner."

"Well," her mother crooned. "You've never been one to let something like that stand in your way, have you?"

"No," Sam replied, swiping at her eye as a tear spilled over. "I never have."

"You'll bring them around."

"Sure."

"And there are barely two months left before you'll be home for Christmas."

Two months? Sam thought, her eyes blurring all the more fiercely. At the moment two months seemed like two centuries.

"Sam, are you certain there's nothing the matter?"

She bit at her lip. It was now or never. Either spill the truth of how miserable she was, or forget the idea of engineering an early escape. As the question loomed, Sam saw that there never really had been any question at all. She'd stay because she couldn't bear the thought of crawling to Chad, or the notion of letting Riverbend beat her. She'd stay because she'd never be able to look herself in the eye again if she didn't.

"I just miss everyone, that's all," she ended up saying.

"And we miss you. See you at Christmas, darling."

"See you at Christmas," Sam replied, doing her best to keep the tears that were streaming down her face out of her voice. When she hung up the phone, she plopped down on the couch, grabbed her solitary pillow, and cried until no more tears would come.

Chapter Eleven

Matt had fallen asleep thinking of Sam—how hungry she could make him. How angry. And how damnably proud. No matter how he sought to dwell on the memory of her passion at the swimming hole, the picture he ended up returning to time and again was that of her out at the Carter place. Barefoot, and still damp, and clothed in nothing more than a swimsuit and robe, she'd stood up to a dozen hostile men—including himself—and faced them down. It took quite a woman to pull off something like that.

The next morning when he opened the newspaper, he thought of Sam again. The rabid animal population had reached epidemic proportions in the Georgia low country. She was right. Carter *should* separate his dogs, *and* get a vet. Anybody with any sense knew it, and if one of the men had suggested it, the rest undoubtedly would have agreed. But since it was Sam who brought it up, well . . . once again she was right. They'd acted like a bunch of rednecks. Continuing to scan the headlines, Matt was on his second cup of coffee when Drew strolled in.

"Mornin', big brother," he greeted.

"Mornin'," Matt replied, and watched from beneath hooded lids as Drew poured a cup of coffee and sat down across the table. Folding the newspaper, Matt set it by his plate. "Mind if I ask you where you've been since Sunday evening?"

Drew's brows lifted as he peered over the rim of his cup. "I got back yesterday. You weren't here."

"Where did you spend Sunday night?"

Drew replaced his cup in his saucer. "It wasn't with Sam," he answered with a thoughtful look. "Is that enough for you to know?"

"Yeah," Matt agreed, slipping into a grin. "That's enough."

The two of them were still at the dining table when the phone rang, and Nadine came in to announce that it was Matt's attorney. A scowl furrowing his brow, Matt rose from the table and picked up the extension in the hall. Minutes later he stalked back into the dining room; rather than sitting, he grabbed the back of his chair as though he might throttle it.

"What's new on the legal front?" Drew asked.

"Nothing, really. She subpoenaed our company records. We submitted the separation agreement. Nothing can be traded, sold, or bought until this matter is cleared up. In short, it's a mess for no reason that anyone but Lucy can understand."

"She can't win, Matt. I know it."

Once again Matt surrendered a grin, albeit a short one. "My attorney says it all depends on the judge, and that it's good of you and George to want to come along with me."

"*Good* of us?" Drew repeated with a comical lilt.

"Don't forget, now," Matt chided. "Friday afternoon. Two o'clock. Chatham County Courthouse."

Rising to his feet, Drew rounded the table and placed a hand on Matt's shoulder. "Don't worry. Both George and I will be ready. It's high time Lucy learned that if she tangles with Riverbend Vineyards, she's tangling with all of us."

On the appointed day, Drew—who wanted the freedom of his own car—led the way to Savannah. Matt and

George followed in Matt's Jeep, equally uncomfortable in suits and ties. The three of them walked into the court-room together. Lucy and her attorney were seated at the plaintiff's table. She was wearing a black suit and hat, both of which were trimmed in red.

"The colors of a black widow suit you, Lucy," Matt said as he passed.

"How kind of you to notice," she coolly replied.

It was at that exact moment that the fear set in. God, what if she won? What if she managed to poison the only good thing he'd done with his life? Forcing a smile, Matt joined his attorney at the opposing table, and tried to draw strength from the moral support Drew and George offered as they took seats behind him in the front row.

"Case of Tyler versus Tyler," the bailiff announced. "The honorable Judge Henrietta Brown presiding. All stand."

Along with everyone else, Matt rose to his feet as a black female judge with silvering hair walked into the courtroom. He didn't know her. Whether Lucy did remained to be seen.

Each attorney had his turn. Andrew Dunaway made things sound infuriatingly as though Matt had tried to hide Lucy's rightful assets behind a corporate mask. Matt's own attorney countered with a truthful statement of how things were—Riverbend Vineyards had been nothing before being incorporated a dozen years ago . . . at which time, any deficits or profits had become expressly the responsibility of the corporation.

After less than a half-hour's deliberation, Judge Brown was back from her chambers with a judgment. "I must say that, being new to Savannah, I hope this caliber of case is not the norm."

Unable to help himself, Matt tipped a sidelong glance toward Lucy. She was smirking, as though she could already taste the flavor of victory in her mouth.

"In the case of Tyler versus Tyler," the judge went on, "I find in favor of the defendant."

Defendant, Matt thought. *That's me!* Spinning in his

seat, he clapped his attorney on the back as Drew and
George leaned over the banister to add their congratulations. A moment later their spontaneous celebration
ended as Lucy sprang to her feet.

"Judge Brown!" she exclaimed, swiftly quelling every
voice in the courtroom. "I wonder if you've had time to
review—"

"Mrs. Tyler, I've *made time* to review every record
submitted to this court," the judge broke in. "Including
your very interesting separation agreement. I must say
I've never seen a man fleeced to quite such a degree. If
I were to speak frankly, I'd have to say that I find your
suit for further reimbursement not just unfounded, but
bordering on the laughable."

As Lucy clenched her fists, Judge Brown banged her
gavel. "This court is adjourned," she pronounced, and
with a frowning look for the plaintiff, exited the courtroom.

Snatching up her purse, Lucy turned to her attorney.
"You're fired," she announced.

"I expected that," Dunaway returned. "And I can honestly say I've never been happier to lose a client." With
that, he picked up his briefcase and strode up the aisle.

Taking a few brisk steps in his wake, Lucy halted before Matt. "This isn't over, darling," she said.

"Do your damnedest," Matt jubilantly replied, and as
he turned to shake hands with George, was unaware of
the long look that passed between Lucy and Drew before
she marched out of the courtroom.

The victors shared a toast at Drew's favorite Riverfront
bar, where Drew decided to remain and begin a celebratory weekend. After dropping George off at home, Matt
changed out of his suit and into comfortable jeans, and
drove to Rae's Place. He pushed through the saloon
doors in high spirits. It was nearly six, and the beginnings of a Friday night crowd was gathered at the bar—
Edwin, Larry, a few others ... including Red and Hal
Carter. What the hell.

"I'd like to buy the house a drink," Matt announced, smiling at Rae as he strode forward.

"Oh, Matt!" she exclaimed. "You won?" Hurrying around the bar, she threw her arms about his neck. "Serves the bitch right," she whispered in his ear.

After serving up the other drinks, Rae poured herself a beer and joined Matt at the front table. He had just finished recounting the story of Lucy's angry exit from the courtroom when Sam came out of her house and turned the old van around to head south.

"Where do you reckon she's going?" Matt said.

"Probably more house calls, not that they're doing her much good. Folks around here don't take her for a doctor."

"So she's said," he commented distractedly, his gaze following the van out of sight.

"You look like a mooning schoolboy," Rae observed.

Meeting her eyes, Matt produced a small smile. "Feel like one, too," he replied. "The last time Sam and I parted, it wasn't on the best of terms."

"I wish you wouldn't pull one of your love-'em-and-leave-'em routines on her, Matt."

His feeble smile disappeared. "I wasn't planning to."

Rae arched a brow. "You mean, you haven't been trying to sweep her off her feet ever since she got here?"

"I didn't say that. But I'm not planning some kind of short-term affair."

"What else could it be . . . You don't mean you've gotten *serious* over her!"

Matt's eyes narrowed as they steadfastly returned Rae's searching gaze. "Maybe," he admitted. "But like I said, we parted on bad terms."

"Just as well. She's not for you, Matt."

Leaning back, he slung an arm over the back of the chair. "What makes you say that?"

Rae spread her palms. "She doesn't belong here. Anybody can see that. She'll go back to Boston, and then what?"

"I don't know. I just know how I feel, and this is different."

Rae shook her head. "She'll break your heart," she warned.

"Reckon I'm due, don't you?" Matt replied. "And now if you've finished grilling me about my love life, how about another drink?"

With a parting look of disapproval, Rae went to do his bidding. Awaiting her return, Matt was gazing absently out the window when Sam's van sped into view and came to a screeching halt across the way. Getting to his feet, Matt moved to the saloon doors. Sam's urgency was apparent as she ran around the van to the passenger's side.

"Looks like somebody's hurt," Matt called over his shoulder. Pushing through the swinging doors, he strode off the boardwalk, and was quickly followed by the rest of the crowd in Rae's Place. By the time they crossed the street, Sam was helping Ida Carter down from the van. The woman's leg was bleeding. So was her arm.

A noisy chorus of questions arose. Planting a supportive arm about Ida, Sam raised her free hand. "Quiet," she said. "If you'll please be quiet, I'll try and tell you what happened. Ida was taking the wash to the clothesline when one of the dogs got out of the pen. I arrived just as he attacked, and I managed to scare him off by charging at him with the van and blowing the horn. Even so, she's been bitten several times. And the dog was rabid."

"I'll be all right," Ida mumbled.

"Yes, you will," Sam confirmed. "As soon as you're treated."

"Guess I need to drive out there and take care of that dog," Larry commented.

"I'll shoot my own damn dog!" Red bellowed. Shouldering through the crowd, he stomped up to Sam. "I separated the dogs like you said, Miss Fancy Pants. And look how much good it did."

"I'm tired of how you address me," Sam replied with

a curt look. "Either call me Doctor Kelly, or don't call me at all."

"She also told you to get a vet over there," Matt pointed out. "Did you have the dogs tested, Red?"

"No, I didn't! I didn't see the need!"

"Damn," Larry muttered. "I'll have to go out to your place with you, Red. Could be the whole pack has to be taken down."

"The hell you say!" Red thundered, his angry gaze sweeping back to Sam. "What were you doing out at my place, anyway?"

"Just passing by," Sam returned vaguely. She'd never admit in a hundred years that she'd seen Red and his brother go into Rae's, and had driven out to the Carter place expressly to check on Ida.

"Anyway, what does it matter?" she went on. "The point is that Ida has been infected, and the rest of you—particularly those of you who hunt, or have animals about the home—are in legitimate danger. Rabies has reached epidemic levels all around us. I have a certain amount of vaccine on hand, but not enough to inoculate everyone who qualifies as high-risk. If I order a supply now, it can be here in a few days."

"You mean all of us take a shot?" Red questioned with a sneer.

"A series of shots, actually," Sam answered forthrightly.

"Ain't no woman doctor sticking no needle in me!" he bellowed, and there were a few rumbling affirmations.

"Order the vaccine," Matt spoke up. "I, for one, will be happy not to have to worry about foaming at the mouth."

There were a few supportive comments. Still, the general consensus remained unclear. As Ida suddenly slumped, Sam grabbed for her, and was swiftly assisted by Matt, who scooped the woman up in his arms.

"We can talk about this later," Sam said, turning away. "Come with me, Matt."

"Where you going with my wife?"

"This woman needs treatment," Sam tossed back as

she started toward the gate. "I'd like to keep her a few days."

"You can forget it!" Red boomed. "I know my rights! You can't keep her without my say-so!"

Pausing as she passed through the gate, Sam fired a blazing look at the man. "One would hope your concern is with your wife's welfare, Mr. Carter. I need at least one night."

"You can have a coupla hours," he conceded as she walked away.

"Don't show up before morning!" she hurled over her shoulder.

"Do as she says," Matt commanded. "This probably wouldn't have happened if you'd listened to her in the first place."

"Shut up, Tyler," Red snarled. "You don't give the orders around here."

Matt glanced around as he followed Sam up the walk. "Then maybe Larry, here, could give you one. I reckon the idea of endangering your wife's life might call for a night in jail."

Sam paid little attention to the ensuing uproar as she stalked into the house and sent Celie scurrying to turn the sheet on one of the examining tables.

"Put her right there, Matt," Sam instructed, and pulled on a pair of surgical gloves while he carefully unloaded Ida onto the padded table. "Celie? In the cabinet where the vaccines are stored, there's a box labeled *immunoglobulin*."

"Immuno-what?" the girl questioned with round eyes.

"Never mind. I'll get it in a minute," Sam replied. "I want to take a look at these wounds first. Thanks for your help, Matt, but we need privacy now. Celie, could you get the door?"

As Celie escorted Matt out of the room, Sam's attention was riveted on her patient, who had clamped her lip between her teeth in an effort to confine the occasional, pitiful moan that escaped anyway. It occurred to Sam that Ida Carter was well accustomed to hiding agony;

otherwise, she probably would have been screaming at the top of her lungs. She'd sustained three bites—one on her calf, the other two on the forearm she'd used to try and defend herself. The gashing wound on her calf was the worst, and to add insult to injury, it was on the weak leg.

"Celie," Sam said without looking up. "I'll need a bowl of water, cotton swabs, and betadine." As the girl dashed away, Sam moved along the side of the table and gazed down at Ida, whose eyes were glinting with the pain she otherwise managed to conceal. Sam put a hand on her shoulder.

"You'll be just fine, Ida," she said. "First, I'm going to clean the wounds. Then I'll administer the injections you need to fight the rabies. Okay?"

"Will it be . . . bad?"

Sam smiled down on her. "The worst part was being bitten. The rest is a piece of cake."

The reassuring statement wasn't entirely accurate, although the treatment Ida was about to undergo was certainly more tolerable than victims of years past had faced. It used to be true that the cure for rabies was as horrible as the disease itself. For many years treatment had depended on a number of injections made directly into the abdomen. Thankfully, that painful procedure was outmoded, but the current method still involved a series of vaccinations, as well as an immediate dose of immunoglobulin, or deactivated rabies.

After a thorough cleansing and debridement of the wounds, Sam went to the cabinet for the serum, measured out the appropriate units, and returned to the table with the hypodermic. Carefully slipping the needle beneath the skin surrounding the bites, she divided half the dosage among the three sites.

"You'll have to turn on your side now, Ida. The rest goes in the traditional spot." When she gingerly shifted, Sam lifted the heavy fabric of Ida's skirt, and injected the remaining immunoglobulin into glutial muscle.

"There now," she said as she helped Ida turn once more onto her back. "That wasn't too bad, was it?"

"Are you finished?" Ida mumbled.

"Not quite," Sam replied with an encouraging smile. "But that's the worst of it. Celie? Can you bring me some gauze and tape?"

As Sam bandaged the wounds, Celie made up one of the cots from the supply room with crisp white linens; then assisted with such items as cotton and alcohol as Sam administered a tetanus shot, and then the first of the vaccine injections that would also be required on days three, seven, fourteen, and twenty-eight. It was dark, and well past a suppertime neither had noticed, when they settled Ida on the cot, and Sam walked Celie to the door.

"Will she be okay?" Celie asked as she stepped onto the porch.

"Spoken like a true nurse," Sam returned with a smile. "Yes. She'll be fine."

Celie's eyes searched through the darkness. "Did I—you know—did I do all right for you, Dr. Sam?"

"You were great, Celie. I couldn't have managed without you," she truthfully replied, and sent the girl into the night with a smile on her face. Locking the door behind Celie, Sam strolled back to the examining room to find Ida peering at the doorway.

"Are you comfortable, Ida?" she asked. "If not, I can try to arrange something other than the cot."

"It's fine. Did I hear you say I'm staying here overnight?" she asked in a shaky voice.

"That's right. I just want to keep an eye on you. There's nothing to worry about."

"But what if Red comes?"

"I'm sure he won't," Sam replied in a tone of conviction. "But if he does, I'll insist that he leave." With the flicker of a smile, Ida closed her pain-glazed eyes.

As the night wore on, she drifted in and out of sleep, her only signs of discomfort occurring when she slept and could not control her groans. From her station in the worn easy chair in the corner, Sam kept watch, and figured that Dr. Daly had probably spent many a vigil in the enveloping chair. At two in the morning, she approached the cot to find Ida looking up at her.

"How are you feeling?" Sam asked.

"Well enough. You're a good doctor." When Sam smiled, she added, "Did you mean what you said before? About my leg?"

Sam rested a hip against the cot. "You mean about corrective surgery?" When Ida nodded, she said, "I know someone in Savannah, an orthopedic specialist. His name is Dr. Brooks, and he's got a reputation as one of the best in the business. If I talked to him, I'm sure he'd agree to see you."

"And if I got an operation, I could walk normal again?"

"I don't know that the limp would completely disappear, but I believe it could be greatly reduced. I won't lie to you, Ida—there would be extensive testing and X-rays before surgery, and recovery would be long and painful."

"I can handle pain."

"So I've noticed," Sam returned with a slight smile.

"But I couldn't tell Red."

Sam's smile faded. "He'd have to be told. It's not the kind of thing you could keep a secret." Turning her head on the pillow, Ida stared at the wall.

"Ida," Sam said in the gentlest of tones. "Have you ever thought of leaving him?" She slowly turned her head and looked up.

"Red took a likin' to me when I was a girl. Believe it or not, I used to be right pretty."

"I can believe it," Sam replied.

"Mama was dead, and it was just me and my pa. I was sixteen when he gave me over to Red to get married. He wanted one of Red's hound dogs, you see." Sam bit her lip to hold back a shriek of outrage. "Pa left town after that," Ida went on. "I ain't got nothing of my own, Dr. Sam. No family. No place to go. Better the devil you know than the one you don't, my daddy always said."

"Judging from what you just told me about your daddy, I wouldn't put much stock in his advice."

Ida turned her head and closed her eyes. "I'm right tired now."

Reaching out, Sam pushed a tendril of hair from the side of her face. As her fingertips made contact with Ida's skin, the poor woman flinched as though she expected the touch to turn into a blow. Other than that she didn't make a move. Releasing a heavy breath, Sam tucked her hand in her pocket.

"Rest now, Ida," she said quietly. "Just rest."

Red appeared to collect his wife before the sun was fully up. Nonetheless, Sam felt a sense of victory the next couple of days as he adhered to the schedule of bringing her each afternoon for the checking and redressing of her wounds. Sam sensed it wasn't concern for Ida that made Red comply, but rather the peer pressure of the townfolk, who had taken great interest in her condition—and the proof of how real a threat rabies had become.

Two days after the attack, a vet brought in from Savannah ordered the destruction of all but four of Red's dogs. Three-quarters of the pack had fallen victim, and Sam couldn't help but think that some of them could have been saved if only their despicable owner had acted sooner.

When the supply of vaccine arrived, Sam posted a notice on the gate offering free inoculations. Matt was the first to show up, followed by Drew and the entire Waters family. Behind them, some of the locals began to form a line. Celie, who looked very official in the white medical coat Sam had given her, showed Matt into the examining room and bade him take a seat on the table.

Except for the preoccupied day when he'd carried Ida into the clinic, it was the first time in two weeks that Sam had been in close proximity with the man. He was wearing boots, jeans, and a long-sleeved white shirt; the cowboy hat he'd removed dangled from his fingers. As usual, his presence seemed to dominate the room. When she approached the examining table, Sam sought his eyes. But if he noticed, he didn't show it.

"Should I roll up my sleeve?" he asked.

"I need to inject you in the shoulder," she replied. "Perhaps you could remove your shirt for a minute."

He did, and she was confronted once more with the muscular perfection of his physical form. For a fleeting instant, Sam was standing once again in the swimming hole, and he was smiling down on her, his shoulders gleaming like bronze in the sunlight. Shrugging off the image, she reached for the vaccine.

"I'd like to thank you for leading the way today," she said.

"My pleasure, Dr. Kelly."

Sam paused as she lifted the hypodermic. "That's the first time you've addressed me as doctor."

"This is the first time you've been getting ready to stick me with a big needle," he replied with a hint of the old Matt Tyler humor. But he still didn't look up, only sat there still as stone while she performed the injection.

"That's it," she murmured, smoothly withdrawing the needle, then walking across the room to dispose of it. When she looked around once more, Matt had risen from the table and was shrugging into his shirt.

"This was just the first of five necessary injections," she said. "You'll need to come back in three days for the second."

"I'll be back," he replied. Leaving his shirtfronts gaping, he seated the cowboy hat low over his brow, and took a step toward the door.

"Matt," she called. When he turned, Sam clasped her gloved hands and shrugged. "Thanks again."

"Sure," he returned. "What are friends for?"

The poignancy of his remark struck home, and for a heart-stopping moment his eyes searched hers with familiar, burning intensity. Sam almost expected him to lunge forward and take her in his arms, but then just as her breath caught in her throat . . . he tipped the brim of his hat and strode from the room.

In retrospect, Sam would see that it was in the space of that day that everything turned around. With Matt's acceptance of her as a doctor, it seemed she gained the town's acceptance as well. One after another the high-risk candidates filed through to be inoculated, with Red Carter the notable exception.

A week passed, and Tully Simon was bitten by a rabid bat that had gotten into his storeroom. But Tully had already received three injections, and the bite quickly healed.

October bowed to November, Ida Carter recovered, and the rabies scare ended. But even when the cycle of vaccinations was complete, Sam found herself kept busy by her newfound flock. November's crisp days turned increasingly cold; December dawned with a freezing rain that coated trees with a sparkling glaze; and with the chilling winds of winter came the expected eruption of colds and viruses and, in a few cases, the threat of pneumonia.

All who could, made their way to the clinic. Those who couldn't were paid a personal visit, and the weathered van zooming about town became a familiar and welcome sight. When Eloise Pettigrew slipped on a patch of ice, hurt her ankle, and instructed the mayor to call Sam to their house, Rae announced that Dr. Sam had truly arrived in Riverbend.

Hannah, Jason, and Celie became more deeply entrenched as Sam's Riverbend family, Rae as the kind of friend she hadn't had since college days. Nadine, too, became a sort of grandmotherly chum. Since the vineyards were between seasons, Matt and Drew were usually about when Sam called in on her. Drew was his typical charming self; Matt, a gracious stranger. Since their quarrel after the swimming hole, he'd treated her with nothing short of the greatest respect. She tried not to notice that she wasn't thrilled with his respectful distance.

The lives of Riverbend were in her hands now, and if Sam sometimes felt a pang of longing in the woman's spirit Matt had awakened, at least she had the fulfillment of living as a doctor. She told herself that was all she'd wanted all along. She convinced herself it was enough.

Chapter Twelve

Friday, December 17

Only five days remained before Sam returned to Boston for the long-awaited holiday. The thought of home had been a mirage for so long, it was hard to believe she was actually going.

But the plane tickets that arrived a few days ago were real enough—as was the phone number she'd posted in the examining room. Dr. Brooks had located a Candler Memorial resident who was spending the holidays at his parents' farm across the Savannah River. In the case of a medical emergency he could be in Riverbend in twenty minutes.

Celie had the spare key to the clinic and had promised to check in every day. Rae, too, had offered to keep an eye on the place. Even Sam's patients were cooperating toward her exit; there were a few colds, one ear infection, and Eloise's slow-healing sprained ankle, but nothing to make Sam hesitant about leaving. Her bases were covered. Still, there was a sense of unreality about the idea of her departure, as well as an aura of excitement.

After a week of cloud-banked skies and icy rain, the day was clear, although piercingly cold, the high temperature at noon failing to crest thirty-five degrees. While

Sam spent the morning on paperwork, Celie and Hannah had decorated the perfectly shaped green fir Tully Simon brought by the previous day. Now, the old parlor was filled with the cheery spirit of Christmas lights and Jason's bubbling chatter about Santa Claus.

Shortly after lunch Sam bundled up in a heavy jacket, and decided to drive out to the chateau and check on Nadine, who was doing quite well—blood pressure stable, the swelling of her legs admirably reduced thanks to a diuretic Sam had prescribed. The truth was, she didn't need to be quite so solicitous of Nadine. The truth was there was an additional lure at the chateau that Sam could deny to everyone but herself. And on this bright afternoon when the outdoors called, she couldn't get Riverbend Vineyards out of her mind.

Turning off the highway, she drove beneath the white arch. Even garbed in the drabness of winter, the vineyards were impressive, though she couldn't help recalling how spectacular they were when lush with the green of summer. Up ahead, the house and winery seemed to loom larger than when framed with the leafy fields.

As Sam took the fork toward the house, her gaze wandered toward the winery. The sprawling structure looked deserted, though Sam knew that inside the business of winemaking was underway. Through Nadine, she'd learned that some of the wine was now aging in great oak barrels, other vintages being bottled, and the entire process overseen by a trusted crew, which—she complained, left Matt, Drew, and George with time to be continually underfoot.

Sam parked the van in the familiar courtyard, and as she walked toward the house, looked once more in the direction of the winery. She'd like to take a tour of that place some day. Maybe even today. Who knew? The day was sunny, the cold air stinging her cheeks and whipping her spirits toward lightheartedness. There was a smile on her face as she rang the bell.

"Is this a good time?" she asked when Nadine opened the door.

"It's always a good time for you to come by, honey," Nadine said with one of her beaming smiles. "Come on in out of the cold."

"Actually, it's kind of nice out today," Sam replied. "At least it's not raining." As Nadine swiftly closed the door, Sam walked into the foyer and became aware of the men gathered in the neighboring room. Matt, Drew, and George were seated about the dining table, which was littered with files and papers. They rose to their feet as she looked their way.

"Hello, everyone," she said, and received a chorus of greetings.

"How ya doing?" Matt added in friendly fashion. Sam's gaze raced over him. Handsome as ever, he looked particularly striking in the black flannel shirt he was wearing.

"Fine," she answered. "I'm doing fine, thanks." The men continued to smile in her direction. "Well," Sam added. "I just came by to check on Nadine. I'll let you get back to your work."

"See ya around, Sam," Matt offered with the utmost pleasantness.

"Sure," she replied, and as she turned to follow Nadine, watched from the corner of her eye as Matt and the others resumed their seats and returned to business.

There was absolutely nothing wrong in the pleasant way he'd treated her. Nowadays, he was *always* pleasant. Sometimes, she found it hard to believe the old, brazen Matt Tyler had ever existed . . . or that anything more intimate than a friendly smile had ever passed between them.

She thought of the old adage: *Be careful what you wish for—you just might get it.* She'd told Matt to be her friend, or leave her alone. He'd done both. And she had no right to complain. Still, as Sam walked with Nadine to the rear of the house, she couldn't deny the way her buoyant spirits had fallen.

Having performed the perfunctory examination, Sam was closing up her medical bag when a sharp crack sounded from outdoors. She looked up with a start, the memory of gunfire on an October afternoon barreling to mind.

"Was that a gun?" she asked.

"Rifle," Nadine acknowledged. "Deer season's open, and one of the best hunting grounds in Georgia is those woods out back."

But as the shots continued, Nadine's round face settled in frowning lines. "How many is that in a row?" she asked finally. "Five or six shots?"

"About that, yes," Sam affirmed.

"Something's wrong. Let's tell the boys." By the time they reached the foyer, the "boys" were already heading for the door.

"That shootin' don't sound right," Nadine announced.

"We're on our way," Matt replied, his gaze sweeping to Sam as she pulled on her jacket and prepared to follow them out. "Where do you think you're going?"

Sam looked up. Having donned a sheepskin jacket and the familiar hat, Matt looked like an advertisement out of some macho magazine.

"With you," she replied. When he arched a doubtful brow, she added, "If someone's in trouble, maybe I can help."

"All right, then," he conceded. "Come on."

They took the Jeep to the edge of the woods, then trotted through the trees in the direction of the continuing gunshots.

"It's coming from over by the creek," Matt called, and launched into a loping lead. Drew was right behind him, George and Sam bringing up the rear. They reached the bank of the creek to discover an ancient-looking black man in the midst of frenziedly reloading his rifle.

"It's Paw Greenfield," George said.

Just then the old man noticed their presence and threw down his weapon. "Thank the Lord y'all are here!" he cried. "I can't git to her! She's stuck out there, holding onto a tree root, and about to git swept on down to the river!"

Matt moved swiftly to the edge of the bank as George stepped over to the man. "Who, Paw?" he asked. "Who's stuck?"

"George!" the old man exclaimed, his voice breaking. "Why, it's your girl! Little Crystal!"

"Crystal!" George boomed and vaulted toward the bank.

Sam hurried over as well, arriving just as Matt started wading into the rushing waters. Sam's gaze flew cross the rain-swollen creek. The girl was desperately trying to maintain her hold, the bright shape of her red jacket bobbing with the current. And then everything happened at once. Matt lost his footing and stumbled, the swirling water closing about his waist. Drew caught him by the arm and yanked him back to the bank as Crystal's grip gave way.

"Daddy!" she shrieked as—like a macabre water slide—the creek took her barreling past.

"Crystal!" George thundered once more, and would have gone thrashing into the water after her. Sam grabbed his shoulder and pulled with all her might to stop him.

"That's not the way! Follow me!" she cried, and started running downstream along the bank, trying her best to keep Crystal in sight as the water seemed to carry her ever more swiftly.

It seemed like an age, but it must have been scarcely more than a minute when Drew and Matt galloped past, bypassing Sam and George, equaling and then outdistancing the red splash of color marking Crystal's position. Occasionally the girl managed to grab a handhold, slow her wild flight, and release a terrified scream. But before anyone could even think of trying to get to her, she'd be swept on once more.

The farther they dashed downstream toward the river, the wilder the floodwater became. Brimming with horror, minutes seemed to stretch into hours as Sam sought to keep track of the girl's flailing arms. She and George were about even with Crystal; up ahead, Matt and Drew established a human dam as they locked arms and took position in the frothing water.

George stumbled in front of her. Lunging around, Sam stopped, helped him regain his footing, and they carried on. By the time they arrived at the point where Matt and Drew had ventured into the creek, Matt had plucked Crystal from the water by the neck of her jacket, and he and Drew were hauling her onto the bank. And suddenly, Sam realized, she hadn't heard a scream for far too long.

"Crystal," George moaned, and fell to his knees.

Dropping down beside the girl, Sam grasped her face and noted the blue cast beneath her skin, as well as the stillness of her chest. When George started to gather his daughter in his arms, Sam pushed his hands away. "Wait!" she commanded.

Straddling the girl's body and planting her palms on Crystal's chest, Sam pushed once ... twice ... a third time. There was a faint gurgle as a trickle of water slipped from the girl's mouth. Moving swiftly, Sam cradled her head, closed her nostrils and administered mouth-to-mouth—one ... two ... three breaths against cold lips. She moved back to the chest and pumped ... returned to the mouth and breathed ... rhythmically performing the duty of lungs that were no longer working.

She worked on and on, until she realized it was no use. There was no bringing her back. Crystal Waters was dead. Slowly lifting her head, Sam turned sad eyes to George.

"I ... I'm so sorry."

"Oh, God, no!" George wailed. As he reached for the girl and clasped her close, Sam shifted to her feet and turned away from the sight of the dangling arms in the red jacket sleeves.

Sinking to a crouch, Matt put an arm around George's shaking shoulders. "Let's take her home, George," he suggested quietly. "Come on. I'll help you."

"No!" the grieving man cried, clutching his daughter closer still. "I can do it!"

Shifting back on his haunches, Matt kept his supporting arm where it was. "I know you can, George. Whenever you're ready, we'll go, okay?"

Despite his claims, George's knees buckled as he sought to rise to his feet. Matt and Drew hurried to lend helping hands, and as they backtracked along the creekbank, the dead girl was carried primarily by her father, but supported by all three men.

When they reached the Jeep, they found the old man who had summoned them standing nearby. As the solemn group approached, he swept a worn cap from his head. "Lord have mercy," Sam heard him say before she and Drew climbed into the back of the Jeep. After Matt settled George and his daughter in the passenger's seat, Paw Greenfield stepped hesitantly forward.

"I couldn't git to her, George," he said with tears spilling down his cheeks.

From her seat behind the grief-stricken father, Sam watched with a lump in her throat as George produced a smile for the old man.

"I know you couldn't, Paw," he said. "Thanks for your help."

It was an admirable gesture, and apparently all George could manage before hugging Crystal close, and burying his face in her wet hair. He was quiet until Matt stopped in front of his house. Though it was not yet dark, the cheery flicker of Christmas lights shone through the windows.

"Oh, God," George groaned in a voice as lifeless as Crystal's body. "Justine's gonna lose her mind. She's just gonna lose it. You go and tell her, Sam. You're a woman. Maybe it'll go down easier, coming from you."

And so Sam inherited the task of telling a mother her child was dead. At least when Justine went into hysterics, she had the means to administer a sedative. At least by the time the men came into the house with Crystal, she'd made the girl's mother sit down on the couch, along with her tearful children. Even so, Justine leaped to her feet and began to shriek as Matt carried her daughter through the den and into an adjoining bedroom.

George gathered her in his arms. Still, Justine continued to wail, lamenting bitterly that her baby was cold and wet. Sam stepped forward.

"I know you'll want to pick out something special for her to wear, Justine," she said gently. "But for now, why don't I get Crystal out of those wet things and into a nice dry nightgown?"

The woman peeped over her husband's shoulder, and for a moment, a look of lucidity returned to her tearing eyes.

"The white one with lace, Dr. Sam. It's in the top left drawer." With that, she hid her face in her husband's shoulder once more.

A half hour passed. Just as Sam emerged from the bedroom, respectfully closing the door on Crystal's resting place, Larry Edison arrived with Nadine in tow. The old woman's typically beaming face was twisted in sorrow as she tried to fight back the tears, ultimately losing the battle when she sank to the couch and enfolded her daughter.

Feeling as though her heavy heart had dropped to her feet, Sam remained woodenly at the bedroom door. The scene before her took on a sense of distance. She was aware of the weeping women on the couch, the children gathered at their feet, the group of men who had gravitated to the hearth where Matt was building a fire. But there was a dimness about it all as her mind's eye dwelled on the fixed image of Crystal's face. Sam had no concept of the time that passed before she looked up to see Matt walking her way.

"You need to put on some dry clothes," she said as he joined her. He glanced absently down the front of himself before searching out her eyes.

"I'll be all right. Will you?"

"Sure," Sam bleakly replied. Matt studied her for a moment.

"I'm going to hang around here awhile," he then said. "Why don't I get Drew to drive you back to your van?"

With that same sense of foggy distance surrounding her, Sam shrugged into her jacket, and made the rounds of saying goodbye to the bereaved family—concluding with a long hug for Nadine.

"Call me if you need me," Sam murmured against the silver hair, and walked swiftly out of the house.

The sun was going down as Drew pulled up beside the van in the chateau courtyard. The drive had been accomplished in silence. Now, as Sam climbed out of the Jeep and circled around, she looked Drew's way.

"This day started so differently," she said. "Clear. Bright. The first sunny day we've had in a week. Who would have dreamed it could turn into such a nightmare?"

"Nobody," Drew replied. "You hear about things like this, but when it happens up close, well ... it's damn hard to take."

"It's damn hard, all right."

Drew gave her a thoughtful look. "I reckon the thing to remember is that we all tried our best. You included."

"My best," Sam repeated in a brittle tone. "It doesn't seem to have been enough, does it?"

"It was all you could do, Sam. It was all anybody could have done, and a lot more than most." A cold wind whipped about the two of them. Sam started to turn, and ended up spinning around and gaining Drew's consoling embrace.

"It'll pass," he whispered.

With a quick, silent nod against his neck, she backed out of his arms, slung her medical bag into the van, and drove slowly away from the vineyards.

As the frigid December evening waxed on, Nadine retired to the guest room with her three remaining grandchildren. After settling Justine in bed, George eventually returned to the den where Matt and Larry were sitting before the hearth.

"I'll have to get Sam to issue a certificate of death," Larry was saying.

"Let it wait till tomorrow, huh?" Matt replied, looking up as George came to stand by the fireplace. "You okay, George?"

"Yeah," George said, his gaze turning across the room to the closed door marking the room where his daughter lay. "I think so," he added.

"Do you feel up to answering a question?" Larry asked.

George looked around. "What question?"

"What was Crystal doing out by the creek?"

Lifting a hand, George rubbed at his brow. "I don't know," he muttered finally. "None of the kids are supposed to go in the woods. Especially during hunting season."

The three men talked another half hour or so, with George growing increasingly quiet. Finally Matt suggested that he and Larry be on their way, and George didn't object.

It was too late for a social call when he left the Waters house, but Matt drove to Sam's anyway. She'd acted strangely when she came out of Crystal's room—as if the lack of life in the girl had somehow drained her of her own.

Pulling off Main Street, he peered up at the old house. The downstairs lamps were still on, as well as the colored lights of a Christmas tree at the window. Killing the engine, Matt trotted through the freezing night and rang her bell. A moment later he heard fumbling at the lock, and then the door was swept wide.

"Matt!" she greeted in a cheery tone. "Come in! Come in!"

Sweeping off his hat, he walked inside, his curious gaze traveling over her. Sam's hair was loose about the shoulders of a fuzzy, pink robe—its sash cinched her waist; its hem disclosed bare feet. She was holding an empty shot glass, and as she closed the door and moved toward him, it was with a swaying gait.

"Are you all right?" he asked.

"Me?" she replied with a theatrical hand to her breast. "Of course! Mind you, there's a dead girl at the Waters house, but I'm just fine."

Her words were thick, her expression lazy. It was obvious she was well on her way to being raging drunk.

"I just came from the Waters place," Matt said. "When I told George I was coming to see you, he told me to thank you for all your help."

She sighed and shook her head. "First patient I ever lost."

"You didn't lose a patient, Sam. You did everything you could to save a dying girl."

Her drifting eyes met his. "I discovered something when I examined her, Matt. Something I decided not to share with her parents. Crystal was pregnant. Close to three months, I'd say."

"Pregnant?" Matt repeated quietly. "She was only fourteen."

"Yes. I know." Abruptly turning her back, Sam moved to the table and picked up a bottle. "Can I offer you a drink?" she asked over her shoulder and proceeded to refill her glass. "My brother, Harry, gave me this as a going-away present when I left Boston."

She turned and leaned back, resting her hips against the table. "Did you know I have seven brothers and sisters?"

"No."

"I'm the oldest," she went on. "Then Harry and James, Maureen, Bobby, the twins Jerry and Erin, and finally Frances. She just turned nineteen. And of course, there's Mother and Father. One big, happy, Catholic family."

"Sounds nice. I'd like to meet them some time."

She laughed lightly. "Now, there's a picture—you in Boston. Kind of like Paul Bunyan coming to the big city."

Still smiling, Sam downed a respectable gulp of whiskey. Shrugging out of his jacket with a frown, Matt tossed it with his hat to the sofa and moved in her direction.

"I'm not sure I like that comparison," he said.

"Oh, now, don't be offended," she replied in a chiding tone. "For heaven's sake, Matt. You must know you're magnificent."

"Magnificent," he repeated with a wry look.

"That's right. But picturing you in Boston—in my family's parlor, for instance? No. It just doesn't work."

"Why not?"

Flinging her arms wide, she sent the remaining whiskey in her glass flying to splash someplace near the hearth. "It just doesn't!" she insisted, her voice slurring over the words. "You don't fit that picture any more than I fit Riverbend."

"I don't know," Matt slowly responded. "You seem to have carved yourself a nice little niche here. I could see you settling in."

"Me? Here? My life is in Boston. This," Sam added with the sweep of a hand, "is but a dream."

"So, you plan to leave when your year is up?"

"Of course."

"I'm sorry to hear that. I've grown to like you, Sam. A lot."

She gave him a slow smile. "I like you, too, Matt." Looking suddenly into her glass, she saw that it was empty. "Uh-oh," she murmured and turned to reach for the bottle.

"Don't you think you've had enough?" Matt asked.

"Not quite," came the mumbled reply, but at least when she turned to face him, he saw there was hardly a finger's width of liquor in the glass.

"Have you ever thought how completely opposite we are?" she asked, her green eyes undeniably sleepy. "We're opposites in every way. I'm Boston, you're Riverbend. I'm classical music, you're country western. I'm pro-gun control, you drive a Jeep with an NRA sticker on the back. Can you get any more opposite than that?"

His reply was a scowl.

"Come on. Lighten up," she urged, her gaze boldly

roaming the length of him before returning to his eyes.
"Rae says opposites attract."

Matt must have looked as surprised as he felt. With
another of those light, lilting laughs of hers, Sam raised
her glass in a silent toast, eyed him over its rim as she
did away with the whiskey, and set the glass down with
a smack.

"Do you have a prophylactic with you?"

His eyes flew wide. "What?"

"Wait right here," she commanded. Weaving her way
from chair to doorway, she disappeared into the examining room. She returned in the same weaving fashion,
swaying against him as she tucked a condom in his shirt
pocket. Matt put steadying hands at her waist.

"There you go," she said, one hand planted on his
chest, the other patting his pocket. "A man with your reputation should never leave home without one. Now,
you're ready for anything. And so am I," she concluded,
lifting her mouth toward his.

Grabbing her by the shoulders, Matt put a backward
step between them. "What the hell are you trying to do?"

"Well, I'm trying to seduce you. But it doesn't look like
I'm getting very far at the moment."

"You're drunk," Matt accused.

"Inebriated," she corrected. "I'm Irish, you know. Fine
whiskey is mother's milk to me."

"You're drunk, Sam."

"Maybe a little," she admitted. "But not blind drunk. I
can still see how big and beautiful you are." Stepping forward, she reached to loop her wrists about his neck. Matt
caught them and gathered them against his ribs.

"I think it's time for me to put you to bed," he said.

"Now, you're talking."

"Stop it, Sam," he said firmly. "I know it wouldn't be
right, but I'm not made of stone either." Stretching beyond his grip, she spread her fingers against his chest.

"No," she replied. "Although you do feel rather like a
mountain. Anyway, why wouldn't it be right? Don't you
find me attractive? At least a little?"

"I think you know the answer to that."

"Well then," she pronounced with a lazy smile. "You want me, and I want you. *Now*." Shifting forward once more, she rested her body full-length against his.

"You wouldn't be doing this if you weren't drunk," Matt insisted, feeling his valiance slip with every second that passed. "If I make love to you now, I'll be taking advantage."

"But I want you to take advantage."

"Yeah, and then you'll hate me in the morning. That's not what I want, Sam. I won't have you thinking I used you."

She looked up, the bleary smile gone from her face. "I won't think that. Not when it's the other way around. Please, Matt. Can you block it out? Can you make me stop seeing Crystal's face? I don't think I can bear it much longer."

Her heavy-lidded eyes filled with tears. Staring into them, Matt felt her pain and was lost. Releasing her wrists, he smoothed the hair from her brow, threaded his fingers into the auburn mass, and tipped her face to his. He kissed her forehead, her eyelids, and traced the path of a tear along her cheek. When he claimed her mouth, it was open and seeking.

Matt kissed her with the fierceness of long pent-up desire set free. He'd have had it otherwise—he'd have had her stone-cold sober and wanting him this way. But whatever his preferences might have been, it was too late to think about them. He could no more stop himself now than he could stem a flood after a summer storm.

Tearing his mouth from hers, Matt swept her up in his arms and took the stairs two at a time to her bedroom. Once there he deposited her on the bed, pulled his shirt over his head, and dropped it to the floor. Moonlight spilled through the windows, silvering her face and sparkling in her half-open eyes. He sat down on the bed beside her, propping a forearm on the far side of her waist as he peered heatedly down at her.

"Are you sure you want this?" he asked. She lifted a

hand to run it caressingly over his chest. His flesh trembled with chills.

"Are you?" she replied.

"Oh, yeah," he murmured. Stretching her arms about his neck, she pulled herself up until they were nose-to-nose.

"Then let's stop talking," she whispered, and slipped her tongue across his lips.

Grabbing a fistful of bedspread with one hand, his knee with the other, Matt willed himself not to rip off her robe. He remained stock-still, except for opening his mouth to her kiss. He wanted to taste every inch of her, possess every part of her, be inside of her, and he wanted it all *now*. He also wanted this to go on for as long as he could make himself last.

Pulling him with her, Sam fell back to the pillow and went on kissing him, her hands caressing his neck, moving into his hair. Matt reached for his belt buckle.

A moment later her fingers pushed his aside. Unsnapping his jeans, she pulled down the zipper, her hand pressing along his hardness. Her fingers returned to graze his stomach, roaming lower ... lower.... Matt held his breath. And then finally her fingertips wandered onto the hot flesh that had strained above the waistband of his underwear.

He couldn't help but end the kiss then. Breaking free of her embrace with a ragged breath, Matt rose to his feet, pulled off his boots, peeled off his fettering clothes, and snatched up his shirt to pull the condom out of the pocket. Tearing open the package with his teeth, he turned to find her perusing him. Though her lids were nearly closed, her eyes glittered between them.

"I haven't been able to keep myself from wondering what you were like in your entirety," she said, her voice as lazy as her eyes.

Matt stood before her in unashamed arousal. "So, what do you think?" he asked.

"Like I said before ... magnificent."

Catching his lip between his teeth, he positioned the

protective sheath on the tip of his erection and swiftly unrolled it as far as it would go.

"So are you," he then replied.

"No," Sam murmured. "I'm ordinary."

Matt's gaze swept over her. The lapels of the pink robe had fallen open to disclose the curving line of a breast, the skirt to reveal a shapely leg. Moonlight shimmered on her hair and glistened on her skin. He released a low laugh.

"You're anything but ordinary, Sam."

Sitting down beside her, he placed a palm between the lapels of the robe, and moved it steadily downward to the barrier of the sash. His free hand loosened the tie, and joined the other on the warm velvet of her skin—his fingers fanning across her ribs, curling around her sides. As he caressed his way up her body, the robe was brushed aside. When he reached the swells of her breasts, he cupped them in his hands, and bent to taste the valley in between. She smelled of scented soap and powder, and his racing blood began to thunder through his veins.

Running his thumb across one tautening nipple, Matt left a wet, kissing trail to the other and took it in his mouth. As Sam cradled his head to her bosom, he gradually stretched out on the bed, pressed his hardness into the bedspread, and willed himself to stay under control.

His hand moved from her breast along the hollow of her waist, on to the curve of her hip, where it met the line of lacy panties. Hooking an arm beneath her knees, Matt lifted until her feet rested on the bed, then caught the back of the underwear and spirited it down her bent legs. Tossing the panties in the air behind him, he gazed on her nakedness. Her body was beautiful—slim, perfect, glistening as though it had materialized out of the moonlight. And it was his to claim. God, he was going to be hard-pressed to move slowly. But he was going to, dammit. He was going to.

Leaning down once more, he pressed his mouth to her stomach and kissed a path around her navel. She shivered, and Matt continued in earnest, his tongue stroking

her flesh as he proceeded to explore her the way he'd
been longing to for months. Much later, after he'd put
her in a state of moaning delirium, he shifted up the bed,
turned on his back, and pulled her on top of him. Her
legs straddled his rib cage. Her robe hung at her elbows.

"You wanna get rid of that?" he asked as he reached up
to run his fingers through her hair. With a slight smile
she withdrew her arms from the encumbering sleeves,
and returned his gesture—her fingers shifting into his
hair as she bent to kiss him. Matt's arms encircled her,
urging her to lie full-length atop him. When she did, his
hands roamed her back, eventually clasping her buttocks
to pull her seductively along his body until she was
poised against his manhood. The first touch was mind-
blowing.

Instinct took over. As they kissed, Matt directed her
hips like a conductor—crescendo . . . pianissimo . . . Little by little he entered her body. Little by little the
breaths she gasped against his mouth became more fevered; and his own powerful drive, harder to contain.

She was tight, and Matt was only halfway inside when
he sat up, supporting himself with one trembling arm
while he folded her legs about his torso. Pushing all the
way up, he gained a cross-legged Indian seat, and planted her hands on his shoulders.

"Hang on," he mumbled, and delivered the first, slow
lunge.

Her head fell back, her arms locking about his neck as
he caught her around the waist. He began to move—his
hips thrusting and falling with the rhythm of a mustang
on the run . . . and Sam its impassioned rider. She was
grace and sensuality incarnate—her hands and mouth caressing him, her body enveloping him like a sleek glove.
Matt had known it would be good between them. He
hadn't expected anything quite like this. On and on they
went, driving each other higher and higher.

And then her slick heat closed convulsively around
him. Going abruptly still, Matt crushed her to his chest,
holding her tightly as the spasms shook her, and him as

well. Sweat broke out on his lip as he fought to maintain his self-control and nearly lost it. A well of fortitude he didn't know he had carried him through.

When Sam relaxed in his arms, he rolled her to her back. Propping on his forearms above her, he looked down, quiet and still but for the throbbing deep inside her he could do nothing about. For a second she opened her eyes a fraction of an inch, but then as though the effort were too much, her eyelids closed.

"Can you handle one more round?" Matt murmured.

A faint smile appeared on her lips. "Don't worry about me," she whispered. "Just take care of yourself."

"I want you to be there with me."

"But I can't—"

"I'll bet you can."

He blew hot kisses in her ear, trailed them across her throat, and then covered her mouth. When she put her arms around his neck and started kissing him back, Matt began to move once more—slowly, seductively . . . filling, and pulling away . . . again and again. Her legs climbed around his back, and he moved an arm to cradle her hips, his thrusts taking on an ungovernable urgency.

Minutes later Sam wrenched her mouth from his, and panted for breath as her head twisted on the pillow. She grabbed his shoulders, her nails digging into his flesh. Matt could feel her building tremors as well as his own. Plunging deep, he held fast. Once again she climaxed, this time crying out in ecstasy.

"Sam," he mumbled before his mouth closed fiercely on the side of her neck. His eyes slammed shut as the hot waves burst over him, crashing up and down his body, racking him with their intensity. Time and space ceased to exist as Matt was suspended in pure sensation. Gradually the tempest began to calm, the raucous waves smoothing out one into the other, engulfing him in a warm, undulating tide.

"Damn." The word came out in a rasping voice. When Matt recognized it as his own, he snapped back to reality.

Swiftly lifting his head, he peered down at Sam. Her

face was turned away, her eyes closed, her lips slightly agape. Reaching up, he brushed a curl from her cheek.

"Sam?" he said. She didn't budge. Nor did she stir when he carefully withdrew, settled her on her side, and shimmied the covers from underneath her. Crawling up beside her, he pulled the sheet and blanket over them. Only then did she move as, inching up against him, she curled at his side.

Prying an arm beneath her shoulders, Matt drew her close and nestled his chin in her hair. *Damn,* he thought once more, and closing his eyes, surrendered to sleep with a satisfied smile on his lips.

Sam woke with a start, her mind blasting into consciousness with the knowledge of what she would see when her eyes sprang open. And there it was—Matt Tyler's muscular arm stretched across her rib cage, lodged familiarly against her bare breasts.

Oh, my God! Sam only mouthed the words; even so, they thundered in her head, and triggered a crashing throb in her temples. Everything came flooding back from a misty distance—the whiskey, Matt's arrival, his shoulders above her, his powerful body moving on hers, filling her over and over again until she cried out—

Oh, my God, she thought once more, her gaze flying to the neighboring pillow. He was lying on his stomach, his face turned in her direction, peacefully sleeping.

Carefully lifting the massive forearm with both hands, she slipped off the bed. As she stood, the throb in her head escalated to a sharp banging. As she took a step, the ache between her thighs testified with a vengeance to the way she'd passed the night. Sam hobbled to the bathroom, swallowed two aspirin, and took a long hot shower.

She had nothing to wear but a towel when she left the steam-filled bath and crept back to the slightly open bedroom door. Matt had turned on his back, but continued to sleep. Tiptoeing inside, Sam quietly opened and closed drawers, pulling out the most available pairs of jeans, underwear, and socks. Slipping across the room to the closet, she retrieved the handiest sweater and shoes, and made a swift, silent exit.

An hour passed, and she downed a pot of coffee while he continued to slumber in her bed. It was after eight when she heard his footsteps on the floor above her.

Sam cast an anxious look at the ceiling—her ears following his movements as he crossed the bedroom, opened the door, proceeded to the bath, closed the door. . . . Moments later came the flush of the toilet, and then the drum of the shower. Minutes stretched out—five . . . ten. The shower stopped. His barefoot steps returned to the bedroom. By the time she heard the tap of his booted feet coming down the stairs, she was a nervous wreck.

He strolled into the kitchen—black hair wet and shining, a smile on his unshaven face. Though he was fully clothed, as Sam looked at him the barriers of shirt and jeans seemed to dissolve, leaving him standing before her in the naked splendor of the night before.

"Mornin'," he greeted in that deep, rolling voice of his.

"Good morning, Matt. Would you like some coffee? I've made a fresh pot." Even to her own ears, her voice sounded high-pitched and unnatural.

"Sure," he replied, his smile spreading.

Shifting his weight to one leg, he ran a palm over his gleaming hair. The gesture struck Sam as scaldingly sexy, as did the look in his eyes. Turning her back, she reached for the coffeepot, her pulse racing like a thing gone mad. She told herself it was just nerves. She squashed the whispering truth that the sheer animal magnetism of the man made her giddy.

She'd nearly finished filling his coffee mug when he came up behind her. And then his bearlike arms were reaching around her waist. She jumped, and a spew of coffee splashed across the counter.

"Sorry," he murmured with a soft chuckle. "Didn't mean to startle you." The last words stirred the hair at her ear as he moved closer to enfold her, his body settling familiarly against her back, his arms closing familiarly across her stomach.

Setting down the coffeepot, Sam stepped swiftly away before he could complete the embrace, and didn't turn to face him until she'd put half the room between them. By then he was eyeing her with a knowing look.

"Uh-huh," he muttered. "I figured this was going to happen. I told you last night you were going to hate me in the morning."

"I don't hate you, Matt, for heaven's sake. And I don't blame you in any way. I'm aware of what happened. I know I was the one who asked you to . . ." She trailed off, unable to make herself recount the shameless way she'd thrown herself at him.

"I was happy to oblige," he said, the remark—as well as his expression—pricking her temper.

"So I noticed," Sam returned.

"But . . . ?" Matt said after a brief silence. "I'm sure I feel a 'but' coming on here."

"But last night was last night," she supplied briskly. "And today is a new day."

"And today I'm not supposed to touch you, is that it?" Sam turned away from his searing gaze. "You're angry."

"You could say that."

"Look," she began, staring blindly at the floor. "I realize my behavior last night was questionable, but—"

"I didn't find anything questionable in your behavior last night," Matt broke in, drawing her eyes back to his. "Although I'm beginning to have my doubts about this morning."

Sam's cheeks began to burn. "This morning I'm cold sober and fully cognizant of the difference between appropriate and inappropriate behavior—a condition which, you may remember, did not apply to me last night."

"Uh-huh," he responded, the innocuous utterance seeming to discredit everything she'd said with infuriating ease.

"We're *friends*, Matt," she announced, pointedly emphasizing the word. "It took a long time for us to forge a friendship. I'd like to preserve it." Shifting his weight, he gained a new, sexy stance that whipped her sparking nerves to flame.

"We're not just friends anymore, Sam," he said.

"If we want to be, we can be."

"You know," he replied after a moment, "for somebody who doesn't have casual sex, you're sure trying to make this whole thing pretty damn casual."

Her chin went up. "I don't mean to be callous in any way, or to imply that what happened was unimportant . . ."

"But," he prodded once more.

"But we're friends, Matt. Not lovers."

"No?" he questioned with a deepening frown. "Then I'd like to know what you call what we did most of the night."

"Something that happened one night."

Cocking his jaw, Matt gave her a scathing once-over. "You know, I think I'll skip the coffee. I usually don't hang around for it with one-nighters." With that, he stalked out of the kitchen. Sam followed, glaring at his back with every step.

"That's not a very nice way of putting it," she snapped.

Arriving at the sofa, he reached for his jacket and hat. "It's no different from the way you're putting it."

"Yes, it is. The way you say it makes what happened sound cheap and tawdry."

He straightened, his gaze raking over her as he shrugged into his jacket and crammed the hat low on his head.

"And the way you say it doesn't?"

"No. Sometimes people need people. I'm not ashamed to admit that I'm human, that last night I needed someone."

"Someone," he repeated. "It didn't have to be me, right? Any man could have filled the bill."

"You're being deliberately spiteful, Matt."

"You're right," he agreed quietly. "You know, Sam,

you're the first woman I've liked—I mean, *really liked*—in a long time. You're like a thoroughbred filly— fiery, spirited, full of life ... bursting on the scene from out of the blue, busting into my thoughts until it's all I can do to put my mind to anything else."

Sam peered up at him, mesmerized by his words, consumed by a feeling of rising warmth.

"But I've finally realized something," Matt went on. "As thoroughbreds can sometimes prove, you're a damn snob."

"What?" Sam hooted, her dreamy state shattering.

"You had me cast a certain way from the minute you laid eyes on me," Matt replied, his tone quiet despite the angry color in his cheeks. "And Paul Bunyan doesn't fit into your Boston-china-shop of a life, does he? And so you'll turn me away and pretend you were too drunk to remember last night. Well, let me tell you, Sam. *I* won't forget. I'll remember that you might have been drunk when we started, but you were far from it when we finished. I'll remember the way you threw back your head and screamed because it was so damn good between us you couldn't stand it."

"Stop it, Matt!"

"But I can see that you purposely won't recall any of that," he accused with a wry look. "You'll bury the whole thing with that clinical mind of yours, and pretend it never happened. And all because you can't see me sitting in your family's parlor, all because Matt Tyler just doesn't fit into the refined picture you've got all planned out for yourself."

Sam's head ached, her throat ached. Beneath his damning gaze, she felt as though her very soul ached.

"You make me sound like the lowest creature on earth," she managed to say.

"On the contrary," Matt returned. "That's why I don't like this a damn bit. I think you're one hell of a woman. But I've never had anybody look down on me before, and I'm not sure I can get past it. In fact, I don't even want to try. So, if you'll excuse me, ma'am, I'd like to say thanks for a most unforgettable time, and be on my way."

With a curt tug at the brim of his hat, he turned and strode out of the house.

The days passed and Sam didn't see Matt after that, except from a distance at Crystal's funeral. But the memory of his burning eyes stayed with her, haunting her morning and night, and stealing the joy from the moment she boarded the plane to Boston.

Chapter Thirteen

Friday, December 24

At five o'clock Robert Larkin bundled up against the clear December cold and walked the short distance to the Tyler home place. Lucy's annual Christmas Eve open house was one of the society events of the season, and the town house was dressed for the part—garland draped along the wrought-iron fence, a candle in every window, a wreath with a huge red ribbon on the door.

He hadn't missed one of these affairs since Lucy started throwing them a dozen years ago. This year, however, was different. He and Lucy hadn't spoken since that evening months ago on the Riverfront, although he'd learned of course that Judge Brown had thrown her case out of court. Knowing Lucy, he imagined she was still furious. But it was Christmas, his own children were miles away, and Robert wanted to make peace.

As he climbed the front steps, he picked up the sound of violins accented by the deep notes of cello and bass. Glancing into the adjacent window, he spotted the chamber musicians. Dressed all in black and ensconced in the traditional performing spot by the fireplace in the parlor, they were performing a string rendition of a popular Christmas carol. Robert fleetingly smiled. Lucy was a staunch patron of the symphony who didn't hesitate to call in her markers when it came to both procuring and scheduling music for her social fetes. She could have made them play "Jimmy Crack Corn, And I Don't Care," if she'd wanted to.

When he rang the bell, Tobias opened the door and greeted him with a beaming smile.

"Evening, Mr. Larkin."

"Good evening, Tobias. Merry Christmas."

"Same to you, sir. Come in and let me take your hat and coat."

As usual during one of Lucy's soirees, the stately home was filled with light, music, and a chattering crowd of Savannah's most prominent citizens.

"There's music in the parlor," Tobias offered. "Hors d'oeuvres in the dining room, and Miss Lucy is overseeing the bar at the back of the house."

"Thank you, Tobias. I suppose I'd better see Lucy before I assume I'm welcome to partake of the music and refreshments."

"Lord have mercy, Mr. Larkin," Tobias replied with a laugh. "How you go on!"

With a parting smile for Tobias, Robert made his way to the Florida room, which was decked with poinsettias, their dark green leaves the shade of the velvet gown Lucy was wearing. Her fair hair was swept up in curls at the crown of her head, baring her graceful neck and shoulders, where the neckline of the long-sleeved gown was frothed with ecru lace. Perfectly lovely as always, she was chatting with several board members of the Historic Society. When she spotted him, she excused herself from the group and came to meet him.

"Hello, Robert," she said crisply. "It's been a long time."

"Yes. It has."

"Have you come to gloat?"

Robert gave her a look that was both tolerant and admonishing. "Actually, I came to wish you a merry Christmas, Lucy. I haven't missed doing that since you were knee-high."

"You mean there isn't even a little bit of an *I-told-you-so* itching to burst from your lips?"

He chuckled. "Maybe a little. Can you forgive an old man such an indulgence?"

"*Any* old man? No. But since it's you . . ." Leaning forward, she brushed a kiss past his cheek. "Merry Christmas, Uncle Bob."

"And a happy new year," he replied with a smile. "Now that you've dropped this Riverbend business, perhaps you can—"

"I haven't dropped anything," she cut in. "Quite the opposite. I've come up with a new strategy."

"A new strategy for what?" Robert questioned with a frown. "Torturing Matt Tyler?"

Lucy arched a brow. "For gaining what's rightfully mine," she replied. "Now, before we get into another quarrel, why don't you let me get you a drink?"

With a resigned sigh, Robert followed her to the other side of the room where a waiter in formal livery was tending bar. While Lucy ordered him a Scotch and water, Robert scanned the crowd, lifting his hand in greeting as he caught the eyes of a few people he knew. Then, across the way by the window overlooking the garden, he spotted Drew Pierce in smiling conversation with socialite Elizabeth Childers.

Robert's gaze hovered on them. Though older than Drew by several years, the raven-haired widow had retained her sinewy figure through constant hours on the tennis court, and was considered one of Savannah's most attractive women. Tonight, she was wearing a clinging black gown that meshed with the formal black of Drew's tuxedo. The two of them made a striking couple.

"Here you go," Lucy said, handing Robert a cocktail glass.

"I've been coming to your parties for years, and I've never seen Drew Pierce among your guests," he commented, and watched her gaze fly directly to the couple.

Obviously it had traveled that way before. "What are you doing with poor Drew?" Robert added on a suspicious note. "Or did he come with Elizabeth?"

"No, he did *not* come with Elizabeth," Lucy answered testily. "She descended on him like a bird of prey the moment he walked in. And he's certainly not 'poor Drew.' He's crafty and obstinate and unconscionably brash."

Robert's brows lifted as he traced Lucy's tense profile. If he didn't know better, he'd think . . . "Drew always was a handsome lad," he said. "As I recall, you went out with him once or twice years ago."

"Once," she returned tersely. "And he was as nervous as a schoolboy who'd never seen a girl before."

"He doesn't look nervous now," Robert pointed out.

Her gaze lingering on the man in question, Lucy pursed her lips as Elizabeth leaned to whisper something in his ear, and Drew responded with a flashing smile.

"Honestly," Lucy pronounced huffily. "If Elizabeth continues to drool over him that way, she's going to leave a puddle on the floor."

As if on cue, Drew put a hand to Elizabeth's elbow and they departed the sunroom, apparently on their way to the front door.

"For heaven's sake, they're leaving?" Lucy exclaimed with a quick glance at the jeweled watch on her wrist. "It's five-thirty. He's only been here twenty minutes."

"Why, Lucy," Robert remarked with a light laugh. "Maybe there's hope for you after all. You're actually jealous."

She looked up with a start. "Uncle Bob," she replied. "I do believe you've grown senile. Excuse me, won't you?"

Drew was helping Elizabeth Childers into her coat when Lucy walked into the foyer. As always, his blood ran a little faster at the sight of her. And tonight she was quite a sight, all decked out in velvet and lace, glistening pearls at her ears and throat.

"Leaving so soon?" she asked.

"It's a lovely party," Elizabeth responded before he could answer. "But Drew and I have decided our appetites call for more than hors d'oeuvres."

Lucy shocked Drew by slipping her hand in the crook of his arm.

"There's a business matter I must discuss with Drew before he goes," she said to Elizabeth. "I hope you don't mind."

"How long will it take?"

"Not long, dear," Lucy replied as she pulled Drew into the privacy of the study. "If rumor is to be believed, I'm certain your appetite will only have grown more keen."

"On that you can depend," Elizabeth returned with a flash of her eyes before Lucy closed the study door in her face.

"What was that about?" Drew asked with a look of surprise. "I thought Elizabeth was a friend of yours."

Releasing his arm, Lucy strolled a few paces away and turned. "She comes to my parties, that's all. And she's the most notorious jezebel in Savannah."

"Jezebel, huh? Maybe I'm in for a better time than I thought."

"If you can tear your attention away from Elizabeth, I'd like you to give it to me for a moment," she snapped.

Drew's eyes traveled the length of her. "You've got it."

"Good," she said. Clasping her hands before her, she gave him a long, assessing look. "I've been doing some thinking, Drew . . . about you."

"You mean you've been fantasizing about me? How flattering."

"I'd appreciate it if you could be serious for a minute," she returned briskly.

Drew expelled a heavy breath. "So, once again we get down to the nitty-gritty of why you invited me here. Okay, Lucy. What's on your mind?"

"As I said, I've been thinking. And I've decided you don't belong in Riverbend."

"No?"

"No. You're not a country bumpkin, Drew. You enjoy the city—the symphony, the galleries, the clubs. I understand you spend quite a bit of time on the Riverfront, and I know you've got a talent for dealing with the public."

"So?"

"So, there's a sweet little club that just went up for sale. Decent price. Perfect location. With some refurbishing, it could be a showplace."

"Cut to the chase, Lucy."

"All right," she said, folding her arms beneath her breasts as she steadily gazed at him. "I can easily picture you as the owner of the hottest new nightclub on the river."

"You can, huh?"

"Yes. Have I struck a nerve?"

"The picture isn't altogether unappealing," he admitted.

"I could buy it, Drew. And finance the renovations. And give you starting capital."

"And all I have to do in return is be your *ally* against Matt. Is that it?"

"I have an idea. It won't work unless you help me."

"What's the idea?"

"Nothing so terrible. Just a little something to let Matt know he's vulnerable."

"What's your idea, Lucy?" Drew repeated sternly.

"What's your decision, Drew?" she countered, equally stern. "Are you going to live forever in Matt's shadow, or forge a life of your own?"

Flicking the fronts of his jacket behind his hips, Drew crammed his hands in his trouser pockets. "Why me? Knowing how close Matt and I are, why do you keep coming to me with these propositions of yours?"

"There are several reasons why you're the logical choice."

"Name one."

"Frankly, the very closeness you just mentioned. No

one would suspect you if something happened to go wrong at the vineyards."

Drew just stared at her a moment, appalled. "You are such a bitch," he said at last. He started walking toward her, and fancied Lucy's cheeks turned pink. As he drew near, she unfolded her arms and began backing away.

"Name another reason," he challenged. Stalwartly looking him in the eye, she continued to retreat as he advanced.

"As I said, I can see you living a different sort of life. I could give you that life."

"What else?" Drew demanded. Running out of space, Lucy backed into the massive oak desk that had been handed down through generations of Tylers. There was no doubt about it now. Her cheeks were bright red. Taking his hands from his pockets, Drew planted them on the desk at each side of her.

"Well?" he prodded.

"You've led me to believe I hold a certain influence with you," she said in a rush, her eyes sparkling like blue diamonds.

Closing the distance between them, Drew leaned down and rested the front of his body brazenly against hers. "Then why don't you just offer me what you know I want?" he murmured.

Shrinking away, Lucy achieved a near backbend across the desk. Nonetheless, she glared up at him with rebellion in her eyes. "And what—specifically—is it that you want, Drew? A roll in the hay with your best friend's wife?"

Drew frowned down at her. "Your marriage has been nothing but a sham from the beginning. Everyone knows it, especially Matt. So don't try to play the role of loyal wife, Lucy. It doesn't fit. And besides, what you're asking me to do is a far worse betrayal. Matt loves Riverbend Vineyards; he couldn't care less about you."

"Get off me," she whispered on a note of fury.

"With pleasure," Drew returned. Backing swiftly away,

he straightened his cuffs with a few curt jerks. "If you'll excuse me, I have a date," he added and started to turn.

"It would have been easiest with you," Lucy said, her shrill tone drawing his eyes back to hers. "But I wager there are plenty of vineyard hands who'll be interested in making a fortune."

"You can try, Lucy. But I doubt you'll have any success. The people at Riverbend owe Matt. I can't think of one who would turn on him. *Some* people have a thing called scruples."

"The way you say it suggests you include yourself in the group," she retorted. "Tell me, Drew, what's so scrupulous about the way you're trying to turn me into a whore?"

"Not a whore," he replied with a burning look. "A woman. It's a shame you don't know the difference."

Turning on his heel, Drew strode out of the room and left the door gaping. Elizabeth was waiting just outside. With a smile, Drew offered her an arm.

"Sorry for the delay," he said.

"What's going on between you and Lucy?" she asked with a pointed look into the study.

Drew glanced over his shoulder. Lucy was gliding in their direction, looking her normally cool, collected, ice-maiden self. He turned back to meet Elizabeth's dark eyes.

"Not a thing," he answered. "Let's get the hell out of here."

"I'm with you," she replied, and clung with provocative closeness to his side as Drew ushered her out of the house.

Evening was closing in, and the Boston streets twinkled with lights, rang with the sounds of music and bells, and bustled with last-minute Christmas shoppers. The four women—Sam, Maureen, and their sisters-in-law, Kate and Helen—were laughing as they weaved their way through the package-laden horde. It wasn't until they boarded the rail for Dorcester, and snow flurries began to fall, that Sam retreated into the pensive mood that was prone to overtake her these days.

As Maureen, Helen, and Kate gabbed away, Sam gazed out the window of the train—studying the way the snowflakes flew past. Farther away, the veil of white fluttered over the skyline, obscuring familiar buildings, enhancing the city with wintry beauty. Boston . . . She'd longed for it for months. And there was no doubt it was wonderful being with the family again. But somehow the homecoming seemed a letdown, perhaps because at every unguarded moment her mind turned to Riverbend.

She thought of Celie, Hannah, and Jason (Santa Claus was coming!) and wondered what busy preparations Rae was in the midst of for the party she was throwing at her place tonight. Sam thought of George and Justine, and how sad a Christmas was in store for the Waters family. She wondered how Nadine was faring, and Ida Carter, and a host of others.

But of all the faces Sam imagined, the one that loomed before her most often was Matt's—smiling as he slipped her a flirting wink . . . smiling in a different way as he shifted off her naked body and drew her to his own. The final image in her repertoire was the angry look on his face when he turned and walked out the next morning.

She told herself it was for the best. Matt Tyler simply was not part of her real life, just as she was not part of his. Still, she couldn't stop thinking about him—despite Boston, despite family, despite everything.

"You're daydreaming again," came Maureen's lilting voice. Sam looked around to meet the green eyes so like her own.

"You can deny it again if you want to," her sister added. "But I *know* something's going on."

"For the hundredth time, there is absolutely nothing going on," Sam insisted.

"Yes, there is."

"No, there isn't."

"I'll find out."

Sam surrendered a smile. "No, you won't."

"Ten-to-one it's a man," Maureen returned insistently.

"Whenever there's a problem, you *always* say it's a man."

"Aha! So, there *is* a problem!"

Sam broke into laughter. "Maureen?"

"Yes?" she eagerly replied.

"Shut up," Sam concluded, and laughed once more at the exaggerated look of hurt her sister turned her way.

Her good spirits restored, Sam joined in the ebullient chatter as they walked from Dorcester station toward the Kelly house. When they drew near, they stared curiously at the long, silver, Lincoln limousine parked out front. A driver in chauffeur's livery stood beside it smoking a cigarette.

"Do we know anybody with a fancy limo?" Kate asked.

"And a fancy driver?" Helen added.

The four of them looked at one another. "No," they agreed in unison, and bustled up to the stoop.

As they stepped inside they were greeted by the familiar noise of a houseful of people. Kate and Helen hurried up the stairs to hide Christmas surprises. As Sam and Maureen hung their coats and mufflers on the long row of pegs by the door, Frances was the first of a stream of family members to emerge from the adjacent, crowded parlor.

"Your friend from Georgia is here," Frances announced. Tucking her gloves in the pocket of her coat, Sam turned with a puzzled look. "Boy, is he ever dreamy!" Frances added as Erin came up behind her.

"Spectacular is more like it," Erin corrected, and with a roll of her eyes for Sam, pushed Frances along toward the kitchen. Glancing back, the two of them burst into giggles when they saw Sam looking after them with an expression of bewilderment.

"What *I* appreciate is his manners."

Head swiveling, Sam watched with surprise as her mother passed by with a tea tray. "Now I know where the phrase *Southern gentleman* comes from," she called as she proceeded along the hall after the girls.

"He's got a good head on his shoulders."

Pivoting once more, Sam stared into her father's face.

"His political views might be conservative, but he's got solid reasons to back them up. I like a man who makes up his own mind."

"Wait a minute, Father!" Sam exclaimed as he started to turn. "Will you please tell me who you're talking about?"

"Matt Tyler, of course."

"Matt?" she repeated in a stunned tone. "Here?"

"Sitting right there in my chair. He's been here the better part of an hour ... waiting for you." With a twinkling smile suggesting mischief was afoot, her father moseyed off in the direction her mother had taken.

Sam moved to the parlor doorway, scarcely aware Maureen walked along beside her. Harry, James, and Jerry were gathered around the facing leather chair where Matt was ensconced. Though Sam could pick up the stream of his deep voice, she couldn't decipher what he was saying. It must have been a funny story, for the boys suddenly burst into laughter.

Glancing up with a smile, Matt spotted her in the doorway and rose to his feet. Sam's breath caught in her throat. He was wearing a white turtleneck, gray slacks, and navy blazer, his raven hair sleekly brushed back and confined at the nape of his neck. The man she'd once labeled a savage looked as though he could walk into any boardroom in the city ... and take charge.

The boys turned to follow his line of vision. Matt towered over them, his presence filling the room.

"So, *that's* how they grow them in Georgia," Maureen whispered. "And *you* said there was nothing going on."

The teasing remark jarred Sam out of her trancelike state. With a quick scolding look for her sister, she summoned a smile, and did her best to ignore her thundering heartbeat as she walked into the room and offered a hand.

"This is quite a surprise," she greeted.

"Hello, Sam," he replied, his massive hand grasping

hers. "I hope you don't mind me dropping in like this. When I happened to be in the neighborhood, I decided to take a chance on inviting myself over."

Giving her hand a parting squeeze, Matt stuffed his own in his trouser pocket. His stance, his expression, everything about him said he was greeting a casual acquaintance. But there was an intensity in his eyes, a kind of knowing glow that brought the intimacy of a week ago spinning into the present.

"When you happened to be in the neighborhood?" Sam questioned. "In Boston?"

"Didn't I ever mention I have interest in a little shipping firm up here?"

"No. You never did. What little shipping firm might that be?"

"You may have heard of it. Simpson and Tyler."

"Of course I've heard of it. Simpson and Tyler has been around for a hundred years, and it's no little—" Sam broke off, her face turning warm. "Tyler . . . as in Matt Tyler?"

He grinned like the Cheshire cat. "Actually, it was my great-great-grandfather. The Tyler half ended up coming down to me."

"Matt was just telling us the story of the alligator that nearly took you for a swim," Harry interjected, ending in a laugh that Jerry and James echoed.

The temperature of Sam's face climbed a notch. "It didn't seem so funny at the time," she answered stiffly.

"Well, it is now," Harry returned with unabashed glee. "You know, I can't wait to see this Riverbend. Matt has been kind enough to invite us down to go hunting."

"*Hunting!*" Sam cried. "You boys have never hunted anything in your lives!"

"That's because we've never lived anywhere but Boston in our lives," James returned.

"That's right," Jerry chimed in. "I can't wait to go, too."

Sam's horrified gaze moved from brother to brother to

brother, ending up on Harry, who continued to beam at her.

"I never would have guessed the kind of adventure you were going to find in Georgia," he said, his gaze darting meaningfully to Matt. "Come on," he added, planting his hands on James and Jerry's shoulders. "Let's give Sis some privacy with her guest."

With a parting wink, Harry hustled his brothers out of the parlor. The room was suddenly still and cloistered, its silence enhancing the overwhelming impact of the man before her.

"Well," Sam offered quietly.

"Well," he repeated.

"You look very different from what I would have expected, standing here in my family's parlor."

He lifted a brow. "You mean, Paul Bunyan doesn't come to mind?"

"Not in the least."

His gaze swept over her. "You look different today, too."

"Do I?" she said with a quick glance down the front of herself. She was wearing a cream turtleneck sweater dress that reached to midcalf, and fawn suede boots.

"It occurs to me that I've rarely seen you in anything but jeans and sneakers and a white coat," Matt added. "You're mighty pretty, Sam. I guess the difference between us is that, to me, you look just as good in jeans."

Expelling a heavy breath, Sam lifted her gaze. "All right. You've made your point in spades, Matt. I'm a snob, and my brothers a bunch of repressed animal killers."

He tipped his head and laughed.

"Why didn't you tell me you have business connections in Boston?" she demanded.

"You never asked."

"Are there others? Business interests, I mean?"

He shrugged. "The Tylers have been in this country since before the Revolution, and they've done all right over the years. There are real estate holdings in Florida and the Carolinas, a lumber company in the Appalachians, a paper mill in the low country. Assorted other things."

"And you run it all?"

"I run Riverbend Vineyards. The rest runs itself."

"I wish I weren't so damn impressed," Sam muttered. He laughed once more. "No, I mean it," she countered. "You were right about me. The first time I saw you, I made up my mind about who you were and struck it in stone. I didn't think I was the kind to prejudge people that way. You've shown me a side of myself I never knew was there, Matt. I don't like it much."

"I wouldn't worry," he responded, his smile disappearing. "Your other sides almost make up for it. Anyway, I don't believe you have a judgmental bone in your body, not as far as people in general are concerned."

"What *do* you believe, then? That I saved my judgmental bones just for you?"

"Me and any other man who looks at you as a woman instead of a doctor."

Sam searched his eyes and found herself swiftly captured once more, held by the glimmering depths as they showered her with memories of a night of unbridled passion. He was thinking of that night, too; she could feel it.

"It's a shock to see you here, Matt. You seemed so furious the last time we met."

"There wasn't any 'seeming' about it. I *was* furious. But I couldn't get around thinking you were worth one more shot." He glanced at his watch, which was gold . . . which was something else Sam had never seen before.

"I've got only two more hours, Sam," he went on. "Jack Simpson was gracious enough to grant me the use of the company jet. But I've got to be back at the airstrip at eight. I knew I was taking a chance showing up like this, especially on Christmas Eve. You may already have plans you don't want to change . . . Do you?"

"Well, Christmas Eve supper *is* kind of a family tradition—"

"Would you consider spending the next couple of hours with me instead?" Matt abruptly asked.

It would lead to things, she knew. The man was just as irresistible here in Boston as he was in Riverbend. To go with him would be to open the door on their drawing close once more. But after his grand gesture of showing up the way he had, she couldn't imagine refusing him. Nor did she want to, regardless of how unwise it might be.

"What do you want to do?" she asked, and offered a smile.

"I was hoping for dinner. But it looks like we'll barely have time for a drink."

"There's a pub across the street from Saint Elizabeth's. It's sort of a medical community hangout. The owner is a friend of mine. I'm sure he'd manage a table for us."

"Let's go," Matt said, and retrieved a handsome overcoat from the back of her father's chair.

They paused in the threshold as everyone poured out of adjoining rooms to converge on Matt, who smilingly issued handshake after handshake, delivering the *coup de grâce* when he bowed over Mother's hand to bestow a kiss. It was then that Frances piped up.

"Mistletoe! Mistletoe!" she chanted, pointing to the greenery nailed above the door.

Sam glanced up with a start. The sprig of Christmas greenery cleared Matt's head by a mere inch. When her gaze lowered to his face, she found his eyes leveled on her, and as he stepped forward and grasped her by the shoulders, there was a heart-stopping moment when Sam expected his mouth to come crashing down on hers.

But when he bent to her, it was only to brush his lips across her cheek so lightly that she couldn't be sure they actually touched. Descending the front steps into the twilight, they were peppered with snow flurries, and trailed by a chorus of her entire family's best wishes. On this evening of surprises, Sam was hardly fazed when Matt directed her toward the sleek limousine.

"That's yours, of course," she observed in a wry tone.

"It sort of came with the jet," he replied.

As they rode in sinful luxury toward the city, Sam began pointing out landmarks. Matt let her go on for a while before stretching an arm across the back of the seat and tapping her on the shoulder. She turned from the window with a questioning look.

"You can put a hold on the tour guide routine," he said gently. "It's been a number of years, but I used to come up here fairly often. I know my way around Boston."

"Oh," Sam murmured.

"But I don't know anything about Saint Elizabeth's. It's a hospital, I presume."

Sam smiled as she nodded. "I did my training at Saint Elizabeth's—five years' worth. It may not be the newest or fanciest facility in Boston, but to my way of thinking, it's the best. I have a lot of friends there. It's my professional home."

"The one you'll return to when you leave Riverbend?"

Her smile faded as she met his searching eyes. "That's right," she admitted.

"I'm glad I'll have the chance to take a look at it," Matt commented with an enigmatic smile.

When the limo pulled up in front of The Jolly Roger, it drew interested looks from passersby, as well as from patrons seated by the pub's expansive, street-facing window. The place was jammed. Sam was heartened when they went inside and the owner, Dave O'Leary, hurried to meet her.

"Sam!" he exclaimed, and enfolded her in a bear hug.

"Hello, Dave," she said with a laugh. "It's good to see you."

"It's good to see my favorite customer. I thought you'd forgotten me. Who's this?" he concluded with a look at Matt.

"A friend from out-of-town. Unfortunately, we don't have much time before he has to catch a plane. What do you think, Dave? The place is pretty crowded. Can you squeeze us in somewhere?"

"How about your old table up front?" he replied.

Her "old table" had been *their* table—hers and Chad's.
It was impossible to guess how many times they'd sat at
the third booth by the window, holding hands across the
tabletop, gazing into each other's eyes. As Dave settled
her and Matt in the familiar spot, Sam expected to have
to force down a wave of stubborn sadness. But it didn't
come. Matt's presence seemed to exorcise Chad's spirit.
In fact, she couldn't even picture his face.

Declaring that he'd put a rush on two of the best burgers in the city, Dave hurried away toward the kitchen.

"You're a sweetheart!" Sam called, and turned to find
Matt peering across the street at the hospital. A mix of
old and modern architecture, the massive complex suggested both the solidity of having stood the test of time,
and the progressiveness of an institution moving
surefootedly toward the future.

"So, that's Saint Elizabeth's," Matt said. "Very impressive."

"I think so," Sam replied. "A lot of good work goes on
there."

A waiter arrived with a round of beer on the house.
Taking a drink, Matt gazed at her over the rim of the
mug.

"You were sent to Riverbend by the National Health
Service Corps, right?"

"That's right," Sam answered with another flash of surprise. "Most civilians don't know anything about the
corps, much less its formal name."

"I made it a point to inquire," he replied with a considering look. "From what I understand, the goal of the
corps is to transplant doctors in areas that really need
them."

"That's the theory, yes."

Glancing out the window toward St. Elizabeth's, Matt
seemed to study the busy, floodlit entrance before again
meeting her eyes. "How many doctors do you figure
they've got over there?" he asked, and the simple question drove his point squarely home. There were hundreds of physicians and specialists and surgeons, and

medical personnel of every variety at St. Elizabeth's. In Riverbend, she was the only doctor for miles. Sam cocked her head to one side.

"My father thinks you've got a good head on your shoulders," she said. "I'm beginning to see that he's right."

"Nice of you to say so," Matt replied with a grin.

"Contrary to what you might assume, I've thought a great deal about Riverbend the past couple of days. How is everyone?"

"Fine as far as I know."

"Are you going to Rae's party tonight?"

"If I didn't, she'd shoot me with her Colt."

Sam smiled. "Tell her I wish her a happy Christmas."

When they were halfway through their burgers, Will Bennett burst through the door, brandishing a fistful of cigars.

"It's a boy!" he announced, and was greeted with a round of cheers and applause. Handing out cigars as he went, Will swiftly made his way to their table.

"Yo, Sam!" he greeted. "I heard you were back for Christmas."

"Congratulations, Will," she returned, and chuckled as he shoved cigars at both her and Matt. "Tell me about this son of yours."

"He's going to be a basketball player. Weighing in at nine pounds, he's almost twenty-four inches long."

"That's one big boy you've got there," Sam responded.

"I'll say. Gotta get moving. I want to get back to the hospital. Yo, Dave!" Will boomed as he moved away. "It's a boy!"

With another light chuckle, Sam looked across the table to find Matt gazing pensively at the cigar lying by his plate.

"Is something wrong?" she asked.

He looked up with a small smile. "No. Nothing."

"Yes, there is. Even though you're smiling, you somehow look extremely sad."

He shrugged, his eyes turning once more to the cigar. "I almost had a son once," he said.

"You did?"

"I married Lucy because she was pregnant. But she miscarried in the seventh month. I was told it was a boy."

Reaching across the table, Sam placed her hand on his. "I'm sorry, Matt."

"Me, too. Lately, I've been thinking about him quite a bit, and about the fact that I'm the last of the Tylers." Gazing down at her hand, he turned his own beneath it. As their palms met, he folded warm fingers around hers and began stroking the back of her hand with his thumb. He had such a wonderful touch. Sam realized she should pull away, but couldn't make herself do it. Looking up, he met her eyes.

"The family is cursed, you see."

"Don't tell me you give any credence to the legend of Juda's curse."

"How do you know about Juda's curse?"

"I have my ways," Sam said with a slight smile. "And I don't imagine for one second that you believe in voodoo magic."

"All I can say is that everything Juda predicted has come about, starting with Mary Tyler's suicide."

"I'm certain there's a logical explanation for everything that's occurred."

Matt finally flashed an open smile. "The scientist speaks," he said. "But you must agree there are still mysteries in the world that science can't explain, Sam—like how the first spark of life came into existence, or where we all go when we leave this lifetime. And what about miracles? As a doctor, you probably know of patients whose recoveries have been nothing short of miraculous."

"Yes," Sam responded. "I guess I do."

"If you concede the possibility of miracles, can you refute the idea of magic?"

Propping her elbow on the table, Sam rested her chin in her free hand. "My, my," she said with a thoughtful

look. "I certainly am learning a great deal about you tonight."

"Anything you like?"

"What do you think?"

He slipped her one of his sexy winks before taking a
look at his watch. "Oh, man. It's a quarter of eight, and
the airstrip is thirty minutes away. The pilot's got a hot
date lined up; he's gonna be mad as hell. You're riding
with me, by the way."

"Oh, am I?" Sam queried.

"I hope so," Matt returned, and planting a swift kiss on
her hand, signaled the waiter for the check. He'd just finished settling the tab when the pub door swung open,
and a noisy bunch of men came in—loud and rowdy and
obviously drunk. Sam looked up, and her heart fell. It
was a group from the Etheridge Center, and Chad was
among them.

"Oh, no," she murmured.

"What is it?" Matt asked.

"Someone I used to know."

"Someone you don't want to see?"

"Exactly."

"Then let's get going."

"It's too late," Sam said. "Here he comes."

"Well, well," Chad muttered, swaying on his feet as he
came to an abrupt halt by the booth. His coat was hanging halfway off his shoulder, his tie askew and his cheeks
red from the cold. "I knew you'd be back."

"Just for the holidays," Sam replied in a brittle tone.

"Ah, yes. The holidays. My buddies and I have been
making the rounds and celebrating the holidays ever
since we left the center."

"So, I see," Sam returned dryly. "You'll have to excuse
us, Chad. We were just leaving."

"We?" he repeated, and feigned a look of surprise as
his gaze slid to Matt. "My goodness, what have we here?
A new stud at the old trough?"

Sam rolled her eyes at the ceiling. "This is a friend of
mine from Georgia. Matt Tyler, meet Chad Etheridge."

"Matt Tyler, huh?"

"That's right," Matt replied with a stony look.

Chad's sloppy smile disappeared. "Tell me, Tyler. Is she still as good in the sack as she used to be?"

"Chad!" Sam exclaimed. "You have no right—"

"Where I come from," Matt curtly broke in, "folks would say you just insulted a lady."

"Uh-oh," Chad muttered with a mock look of alarm. "I'm in trouble now."

Matt rose from his seat and glared down at the shorter man. "You sure as hell could be."

Swiftly gaining her feet, Sam stepped between the two men as they squared off.

"You should learn to hold your liquor, boy," Matt added.

Chad glared through bloodshot eyes. "I'm still sober enough to take a dim-witted redneck."

"The fact that you're *not* is the only reason I'm not decking you right now."

"Don't do me any favors, cowboy."

"Don't press your luck, Yankee."

"Stop it, you two," Sam commanded quietly. "Everyone's looking at us. Thank you for coming to my defense, Matt, but I can fight my own battles."

She pivoted to meet the familiar eyes. "He's right, Chad. You're drunk, and you insulted me. In fact, it occurs to me that every minute I've known you has been an insult." Sam looked pointedly from him to Matt and back again. "I didn't realize till now how very small you are."

Chad grinned with infuriating arrogance. "All it would take is one minute alone with you for me to change your tune."

At that remark, Matt shouldered forward, a menacing look on his face. Sam planted a palm on his chest as she looked over her shoulder.

"Get someone to drive you home, Chad," she snapped, and taking Matt firmly by the arm, pulled him out the door. When they climbed into the back of the limo, Sam slid to the far door and peered miserably out the window.

"To the airstrip," Matt instructed the driver. "And step on it."

The privacy glass rose, and the passengers' compartment was plunged into quiet. Matt said nothing until they pulled away from The Jolly Roger and merged with the traffic of the Boston street.

"Old flame, huh?" he then questioned. "Was it serious?" he added as Sam looked around.

"At the time, yes."

"How about now? Is the flame completely out?"

Sam regarded him through the shifting shadows. "If I ever had doubts, they're gone."

"Good," Matt responded in a satisfied tone. "Then let's forget him." Sliding to the middle of the seat, he stretched an arm around her shoulders and began drawing her to his side. Sam stiffened.

"Come on," he urged. "It's not going to hurt you to ride like this, is it?"

Like before, his magnetism made any reasons to resist seem vague and irrelevant. A valiant moment of indecision died swiftly away, and Sam surrendered. Relaxing against his massive chest, she tucked her head on his shoulder. Matt rested a cheek against her hair, his hand traveling her arm in a slow caress. The lights of the street flashed by, along with the snowy wind—sweeping away thoughts of Chad and Boston and everything but the man who held her.

"Did you really have business at Simpson and Tyler?" Sam asked eventually.

"Nothing I couldn't have handled by fax or phone."

"So, you came all this way just to see me?"

"Are you flattered?" he returned.

"Yes," she answered, and smiled into the darkness. "My family will never let me hear the end of it. You made quite an impression on them."

Taking her chin in his fingers, Matt tipped her head against his shoulder until they were face-to-face. "How about you?" he murmured, trailing his fingertips along her cheek. "Have I finally managed to make an impression?"

"For heaven's sake, Matt," she responded with a sigh. "I doubt there's a woman on earth who could *help* being impressed by you. It's just that—"

"Shhh." Placing a single finger against her lips, he bent close and set her heart pounding. "Let's not spar tonight, okay?" he said, his whispered words fanning her face. "I've come a long way, and I have very little time. Kiss me, Sam."

His fingertip pressed between her lips, opening them to meet his own as he claimed her in the remembered, thrilling way. While his tongue roamed her mouth, his arms engulfed her body, lifting and guiding until she lay across his lap. And then she was lying on the plush limousine seat, her head cushioned in one of Matt's palms as he settled atop her.

Sam melted beneath him—it was as though she became part of him—and once again all sense of time and place vanished as she was swept away in the man's magic. Hours could have transpired when Matt lifted his head, and she opened heavy lids to gaze into his glowing eyes.

"We're here," he announced quietly, and Sam suddenly noticed that the car was no longer moving.

"Where is 'here'?" she murmured dreamily.

"The airstrip. I'm late, but there's something I want to say before I go."

Lifting a hand, Sam ran her palm over his shining hair. "What is it that you want to say?"

"That this is my last card. My final play. Now, it's up to you."

"What's up to me?"

"Us," he replied, and sent a shiver scurrying down her spine.

"Maybe I should sit up for this," Sam suggested. Helping her shift to a seat, Matt maintained a firm arm around her shoulders.

"I'm not going to beat around the bush, Sam."

"I don't recall that you ever have."

"A week ago we were as close as a man and woman can be. That's how I want it to be again. And the way you just kissed me says you want it, too."

"It's not as simple as that," Sam replied quietly.

"It can be," Matt returned, his eyes boring into hers. "Like I said, this is my last play. I won't be showing up on your doorstep again; so if you want me, you're going to have to come and get me. And I don't mean for one night. There's a fair number of ladies who would faint dead away if they heard me say this, but I'm not playing around anymore. I happen to love you, Sam."

While she stared in speechless silence, he glanced at his watch. "That pilot is going to have my head. I gotta go."

Grasping her by the nape of the neck, Matt held her steady and planted a final, searing kiss on her mouth. When he pulled away, Sam's dazed eyes followed his movements as he tapped at the driver's window.

"The lady goes back to Dorcester," Matt announced and got out of the limo, only to lean back into the open doorway. Snowflakes swirled around him, catching on his hair and shoulders.

"I want to hear from you when you get back," he said. "Will you call me?" Studying her face as she gave a nod of assent, he broke into a smile. "You look a little shocked."

"Only a little?" Sam managed.

His smile flashed wide before he closed the car door and turned to stride through the softly falling snow.

The drive back to Dorcester passed with a sense of unreality. Sam sat in the back alone, but continued to feel Matt's arms about her. The limousine was silent, but she still heard his voice—*I happen to love you, Sam.* She turned with a start when the chauffeur opened the door, and she looked up to see she was home.

Sometime along the way the snow had stopped. Sam climbed the front steps beneath a clearing sky to find a note from her mother on the door. The family had gone to candlelight mass. There was also a poinsettia on the stoop, with a small white card propped at its base. *Sorry. I still love you,* it said. Though clumsily executed, the handwriting was unmistakably Chad's.

Letting herself into the uncharacteristically quiet house, Sam placed the poinsettia by the hearth, and dropped the card in the trash on her way upstairs.

It was nearly midnight when Matt arrived at Rae's. Drink was flowing, music blaring. The gentle folk had retired, leaving a couple of dozen die-hard partiers who had the place in full swing—half of them carousing about the bar, the other half dancing to the jukebox.

Rae marched up to him with a frown on her face. She was wearing a red dress that showed off her curves, and was very pretty despite her glowering look. Tossing his overcoat at a nearby chair, Matt gave her a whistle.

"Lord, Rae. You're enough to make a man's knees go weak."

"That almost makes up for how late you are," she returned.

With a light laugh, he leaned down and pressed a kiss to her cheek. "Merry Christmas."

"Well," she said grudgingly, "at least you're here. Better late than never, I guess."

"Sam said to wish you a merry Christmas, too."

"You spoke to her?"

"I just got back from Boston," he announced, his face beaming as Rae's insides seemed to turn to stone.

"What were you doing up there?"

"I went to see Sam."

"How?"

"I hitchhiked," he answered with another laugh. "Come on. Let's dance."

"You certainly seem in high spirits," she commented as he twirled her in a series of turns.

"I've got a good feeling, Rae. Tonight, I'm thinking maybe things just might work out."

"Things? What things?"

He met her eyes. "Between Sam and me. I told you a long time ago how I wanted things to be."

"And I told you it was impossible."

For the first time since he arrived, his cheery smile faded. "Where there's a will, there's a way," he replied.

The tune on the jukebox changed to a slow number, and Matt gathered her close. Rae hid her stinging eyes against his shoulder. She might be holding him in her arms, but his heart and mind were in Boston. She was wondering if she was going to be able to hold back the tears when Ida Carter walked in sporting a bruise on her cheek and a busted lip. With a discreet swipe at her eyes, Rae hurried over to her, closely followed by Matt.

"For God's sake," Rae said, lifting hesitant fingers to the purpling bruise. "What happened to you?"

"The same as always. I was hoping for a big favor, Rae. If I worked for lodging, could you put me up for a while?"

" 'Course I can!"

"Thank you." Expelling an audible breath of relief, Ida glanced toward the bar. "Is Dr. Sam here?"

"She won't be back till New Year's," Matt answered. "You sure you're all right, Ida?"

"Oh, yes," she replied, smiling despite her swollen lip. "Dr. Sam can fix my leg, now. I've just left Red."

Chapter Fourteen

Friday, December 31

Sam spent the morning at St. Elizabeth's, saying hello to friends, and having lunch in the cafeteria with John Thomason, who assured her the worst of her ordeal in Georgia was over, and she'd soon be back home where she belonged. They were halfway through the meal when he was paged. She watched with longing as the Chief of Surgery bade her farewell and hurried to respond.

Storing up as much of the familiar, bustling atmosphere as she could, Sam left the hospital and headed back to Dorcester. The winter day was sunny, but it wasn't long before cloudy thoughts closed in, muffling the buoyant effects of St. Elizabeth's, and dimming the brightness of her last day in Boston.

When she reached the Kelly house, she found it unusually peaceful. The only person in sight was her mother, who was arranging a centerpiece on the dining table.

"Hello, dear," she called.

Lifting a hand in greeting, Sam turned the opposite way, strolled into the parlor, and plopped down on the couch. A few minutes later her mother walked in with a cheery expression.

"Did it feel good to be back at Saint Elizabeth's?" she asked.

"Wonderful," Sam replied.

"You don't look like you feel wonderful."

Sam mustered a smile. "I guess the blues are setting in. I have to leave tomorrow, you know."

Tipping her head to one side, her mother considered her thoughtfully. "Forgive me for saying so, Sam, but this mood didn't pop up just today."

"What do you mean?"

Her mother smiled. "My dear Samantha, you're a Kelly through and through," she said. "You have the auburn hair, and you have the Irish temperament, which gives you strength and passion and a tendency to wear your feelings like a neon sign. You've been preoccupied ever since you came back from Riverbend. Could it be that you miss it?"

"*Me* miss *Riverbend*? I wouldn't say that."

"What would you say?"

Sam's gaze drifted to her clasped hands. "I'd say it's like summer camp. You meet new people, see new things, have new experiences. But you wouldn't want to spend your life there."

"And Matt is asking you to?"

Sam looked up. "Not exactly."

"He didn't fly up here on Christmas Eve to discuss the weather," her mother commented with the arch of a brow.

"No," Sam admitted.

"It occurred to me that he wanted to meet the family, and give us a chance to meet him. When a man does something like that, it usually suggests a certain amount of seriousness."

Sam mutely returned her searching gaze.

"Well?" her mother prodded. "Did he propose to you, Sam? If my daughter is contemplating a move to Georgia, I'd like to know about it."

"He did *not* propose, and I certainly am not contemplating a move to Georgia. My life and future are here. You know that."

"But Matt Tyler *is* serious about you, isn't he?"

"He sounds like it . . . I think so . . . I don't know." Releasing a sigh, Sam slumped back against the couch. "I don't know anything."

"Do you know how you feel about him?"

Sam's eyes lifted. "Wild," she replied in a whispering tone. "When I'm with him, my common sense goes out the window. He's all I can see, or hear, or feel. He . . . takes my breath away."

"That sounds like the kind of man every woman dreams of."

"He's married, Mother."

"Married?" Her mother sank to the couch with a look of dismay.

"They've been separated for years, but apparently, if Matt divorced her, she'd take virtually everything he owns."

"Oh," her mother uttered in the same dismal tone.

"You see? It's hopeless. I don't know what I was thinking on Christmas Eve. How could I have been swept away all over again?"

"You told me *how* just a moment ago, Sam."

"Just like Chad," Sam muttered. "Both of them say they love me. Both of them belong to someone else."

"I don't think Matt is the least bit like Chad," her mother replied. "I don't believe you do, either."

"No," Sam answered slowly. "The situations are ironically similar, the men entirely different. Matt is fine and strong and . . ." She rubbed a hand across her eyes. "And I don't belong with him any more than I do in Riverbend. I promised to call him when I get back. What am I supposed to say?"

Reaching over, her mother took her hand and patted it reassuringly. "Matt isn't the only one who's fine and strong. Whatever you say, I'm sure it will be the right thing."

"Are you?" Sam returned with a solemn look, and fervently hoped her mother was right.

Saturday, January 1, 1994

After seeing in the new year at Rae's Place—and sticking around with a few regulars until two—Matt was awakened first by a pounding downpour of rain at five in the morning, then by the persistent ring of the doorbell a scant two hours later. On and on it went; each time he managed to slip back toward slumber, it came again. Finally, he climbed out of bed and walked grumpily to the head of the stairs. By that time Nadine had opened the door, and Larry Edison was standing below in the foyer.

"What's the matter?" Matt called with a yawn.

"I think you oughtta get dressed and come take a look for yourself," Larry replied.

"A look at what?"

"There's been an incident at the cemetery."

"What kind of incident?"

"I don't know whether to call it vandalism or theft."

"Stop talking in riddles, Larry. What the hell happened, and what does it have to do with me?" Larry twisted his hat in his hands as he gazed up the stairs.

"It's about Mary Tyler, Matt. Last night somebody opened her grave and made off with her skull."

After dumping torrents in the black hour before dawn, the rain clouds had scattered. Though cold and damp, the morning was clear, the sky a brilliant blue. When Larry's official car pulled up by the cemetery, Reverend Bishop came running from the neighboring parsonage to meet them—his black coat flapping in the wind, his white hair shining in the sun.

"As soon as I got up this morning, I had a feeling something was wrong," he announced as he arrived. "And then to discover this! It's horrible, just horrible!"

"The reverend called me at six-thirty," Larry said with a hooded look for Matt.

"I'd gone out to walk the dog," Reverend Bishop chattered. "And I saw the disturbed monument, and went closer, and—well—it's a sacrilege. That's what it is. What do you propose doing about it?"

"For the moment I've covered the memorial and taped off that section of the graveyard," Larry said. "As for Mary Tyler's remains, Matt's here to decide how to proceed."

Turning to Matt, the reverend looked up with flashing eyes. "No offense, but maybe you could consider moving your ancestor's remains to the chateau. This is holy ground, and the woman was a mortal sinner who never should have been buried here. Now, look what's happened."

Matt peered down on the much smaller man. "Preacher," he began slowly. "I haven't had much sleep, and I'm in a rotten mood. So, I hope you'll forgive me when I ask you to shut up and go home."

"Well!" the man returned in a huff, and swiftly departed.

Turning through the iron gate, Larry and Matt proceeded to the desecrated gravesite.

"Prepare yourself," Larry said as he bent to remove a plastic tarp. "It's not a cheery sight."

Matt stepped up to the uncovered sepulcher and looked down. Four or five inches of water had collected in the open tomb. The remnants of a white nightgown floated on the surface, along with the occasionally surfacing bone of an index finger. The eerie impression was that the headless skeleton was trying to point to some conclusion—perhaps the identity of its violator.

"Pretty grisly prank," Matt muttered as he glanced around the site. "Any signs of who did it?"

"Not that I could find," Larry replied. "It's my guess this was done before the storm hit. Whatever tracks there might have been were washed away by the rain."

"And there's no sign of the skull."

"Nope. What do you want to do with her, Matt?"

"Seal her up again, I guess."

"Without a head?"

"I doubt she misses it much at this point, Larry. Besides, what else can I do? It'll take a few days to make the arrangements. Maybe by then the skull will have turned up somewhere."

They anchored the tarp in place, and drove back to the chateau. "By the way," Larry said. "Happy New Year."

"Seems more like Halloween, doesn't it?" Matt replied.

The plane touched down in Savannah at a quarter-past three. It was nearly five when Sam cleared the Riverbend town limits, proceeded along Main Street, and deliberately bypassed her house. There was a sense of homecoming as she drove the familiar street, but like most recent sensations, it flitted by in a subliminal sort of way. Throughout her journey—in fact, ever since Christmas Eve—Matt Tyler had filled her mind so intensely that there hardly seemed room for anything else.

For days, muddled thoughts had circled her brain like debris in a roiling whirlpool. It wasn't until last night that the scientist in her had risen in frustration to take control. A process of elimination had proved the key, along with employing the principle of cause and effect. By tracking each potential course of action to its logical end, she'd been able to discard the many possible scenarios one by one until only a single choice remained.

There was a kind of peace in having reached a conclusion. There was also an undeniable dread in the idea of approaching Matt. But approach him, she must. The situation called for more than a conversation over the phone. Circling around the square, Sam continued determinedly to the chateau.

Nadine met her at the door with a hug and hearty wishes for a happy new year. "Lord, honey, don't you look pretty!" she added as she pulled Sam into the foyer and swiftly closed the door against the cold.

"Thanks," Sam replied with a smile. She was wearing a cashmere turtleneck of hunter's green, matching skirt, camel-hair duster, and Italian leather boots. It was a sophisticated, businesslike ensemble, selected with deliberate care. She felt entirely like Sam Kelly of Boston, which was precisely who she needed to be at this moment.

"How are you feeling?" Sam added.

Nadine took on a scolding look. "Don't tell me you came out here on New Year's Day to take my blood pressure."

"No," Sam replied with a light laugh. "Although I can if you like. My bag is outside in the van."

"And that's just where it can stay. Did you have a nice Christmas?"

"Yes, but I thought about you, Nadine. And George and Justine. I hoped you would have happy times, but I knew there would be terrible sadness as well."

"It was hard, and that's a fact," Nadine replied. "We'll never stop missing Crystal, but we gotta carry on." With an undeniable sheen in her eyes, she produced one of her broadest smiles. "Enough about that. Did you hear the latest news in town?"

"No. I drove directly here from the airport. What happened?"

"Lord, honey, Ida Carter up and left Red. She's staying over at Rae's, and telling everybody you're gonna get that crippled leg of hers fixed. Red's fit to be tied."

"I'll bet he is," Sam replied with a flare of anxiety that was quickly doused by a wave of happiness for poor Ida Carter. "Good for Ida," she added. "I'm sure it took great courage—"

Sam halted as the sound of a closing door came from upstairs, followed by masculine footsteps. Her gaze flew up the staircase, her heart began to pound, and then Drew came into view and she breathed a secret sigh of relief.

"Hey, Sam, how ya doin'?" he greeted with a friendly hug.

"I'm fine," she smilingly replied. "Happy New Year."

"Same to you. Did you just get back?" When she nodded, he said: "Matt's been chomping at the bit waiting for a phone call."

"Is he around?" Sam asked.

"I chased him out of the house about an hour ago. He was beginning to wear a path in the rug." Sam returned Drew's teasing grin with a wry look. "He's tinkering around in the wine cellars," Drew said with a laugh. "Give me a minute to get my jacket, and I'll take you over."

The sun was low and golden in the clear sky, casting long shadows across the side yard as the two of them hurried through a biting wind to the winery. When Drew pulled open the door, Sam stepped quickly inside, her cheeks stinging with cold.

"It's not much warmer in here than outside," Sam commented as they entered the vast, shadow-filled structure.

"The winery's kept at forty-five degrees," Drew explained. When he switched on the lights, Sam's eyes turned across the rambling room appointed with elaborate machinery.

"I've been wanting to take a look in here for quite some time," she said.

"Yeah? Then allow me to give you a brief rundown."

As they walked through the cavernous building, Drew pointed out the crusher—which separated skin and stems from the grapes—and the giant press, from which juice was extracted and transported via motorized pump to a group of twenty huge, metal fermentation tanks. From there, he explained, the filtered wine was piped to the cellar below, where it was aged in oak barrels.

"Over there is the bottling room and warehouse," he said eventually. "But come this way if you want to see something interesting." Sam followed him behind one of the fermentation tanks to a concealed door, which he opened to reveal a pantry stocked with mops and brooms and cleaning supplies.

"You're right, Drew," she said with a lift of her brows. "It's the most interesting broom closet I've ever seen."

"Watch this," he advised and, reaching up to the top shelf, twisted what looked like one of the braces. To

Sam's surprise, the back wall of the pantry creaked open to disclose a hidden room. In its center was a ramshackle structure with a stove belly and tubes and pipes funneling in and out of it.

"What is it?" she asked.

"Lady, you're looking at a genuine moonshine still. Estimates are it was built around the turn of the century."

Stepping into the musty chamber, Sam took a scrutinizing look at the contraption. "You mean, people actually *drank* what came out of this thing?"

"Oh, yeah," Drew replied in a tone of great earnestness. "Especially during Prohibition. That's when Jonathan and Mary Tyler lived here. Word has it that great-aunt Mary was right fond of the white lightnin' that came from this still."

"Poor woman," Sam said. "As if she didn't have enough problems."

"You heard about Juda's curse, huh?"

"I imagine anyone who's been in Riverbend for more than a few hours has heard about it."

"Yeah," Drew agreed. "I reckon it's the biggest local legend we've got around here."

When they exited the secret room, Drew replaced the lever, and the back wall of the pantry creaked shut with an echoing bang.

"Who's up there?"

As Matt's voice ran from the invisible bowels of the place, Sam jumped as though someone had fired a shot.

"Shhh," Drew whispered with a finger to his lips and a mischievous look on his face. "It's me, big brother!" he called, and began leading Sam on tiptoe toward the corner of the building.

"Who were you talking to?" Matt boomed.

"Just myself," Drew replied as they reached the recessed entrance to a set of steps leading down to the cellar. "Thought I'd stop by and see how you're doing," Drew added.

"I'm doing fine, but this damn line of pipe is gonna have to go," came the muttered response.

"Just tell him I'm here," Sam whispered, only to have Drew respond with an emphatic shake of his head.

"Did Sam call?" Matt's voice rose again.

Drew broke into a devilish grin. "Nope. The phone hasn't rung all afternoon. Reckon I'll head on back to the house now."

"Let me know if she calls!" Matt yelled.

"You've only told me ten times," Drew returned. Still grinning from ear to ear, he stomped noisily away, slammed the door, and left Sam alone in the winery with unsuspecting Matt.

The soles of her boots muffled her steps, and though she didn't intentionally sneak down the stairs, she could see that Matt hadn't heard her as she entered the softly lit cellar. Kneeling with his back to her near the base of a giant barrel, he appeared to be examining a length of pipe. Sam's gaze raced over him. He was wearing boots, jeans, cowboy hat, and a hefty leather jacket. The sight of him shook her resolve.

"Hi," she said.

Spinning around as he leaped to his feet, Matt bumped his head on one of the exposed beams of the low ceiling.

"Ow," he complained as Sam stifled the reflex to laugh.

"Matt, I'm sorry," she said, and moved quickly toward him as he swept off his hat and put a hand to the crown of his head. "Are you all right?" she added.

As he met her eyes, his wincing expression gradually settled into a smile. "I'll live," he said. "When did you get here?"

"Drew brought me over. I guess it was his idea of a joke to surprise you."

"Yeah. That sounds like Drew."

Having been momentarily sidetracked by her own silly entrance, Sam's nervousness suddenly returned. She crammed her hands in her coat pockets.

"So, this is your wine cellar," she said.

"This is it."

"Exactly what kinds of wine are you producing?"

Lifting an arm, Matt pointed across the room. "Over

there is the merlot. To the left, chardonnay. Right behind me is the cabernet, which happens to be my personal favorite . . . and who gives a damn, anyway?"

Stepping swiftly forward, he took her face in his long fingers, and before Sam could do so much as pull her hands from her pockets, his mouth came down on hers. The shock of the kiss was swiftly overtaken by its thrill. As Matt's arm stole around her, the sensation swelled like a building wave. All she need do was surrender a few more seconds to be completely carried away once more.

Turning abruptly away from his mouth, Sam planted her palms against his jacket and backed firmly out of reach. Matt's arms dropped to his sides.

"What's going on?" he asked, his voice deep and rumbling.

Once again Sam's nervous hands found their way into her pockets. "I've thought of a dozen ways to start this conversation," she said. "And now, none of them seems right."

"Why don't you just jump right in?" Matt suggested, his eyes warily searching her face.

"You must know that I regard you as a very special man," Sam began slowly. "You're one of a kind—like some . . ." She faltered under his grim scrutiny but forced herself to go on. "I've never met a man like you, and I don't expect to again."

"Sounds like a nice buildup to a kiss-off," he responded, his face hard as stone.

"That's a crude way of putting it," she returned. "I've given this situation a great deal of thought, and—"

"Shut up, Sam. The way we are together is plain as day. It doesn't need to be intellectualized to death. After that night in Boston I expected you to come back with a different answer."

"Answer to what, Matt? I have no idea what you expect from me."

"I expect you to act the way you feel. Is that so tough?"

"Yes," she answered with a flash of her eyes. "It is."

"Why?"

"Because it would go against the way I've always lived my life."

Matt peered at her, his eyes glittering like sunstruck gold in the gloomy cellar. "Maybe you should change the way you live your life," he said.

Her ragged nerves erupted in a flare of temper, and Sam plunged to the heart of the matter. "And do what?" she challenged. "Enter into a hot little love affair with you? A few months worth of clandestine rendezvous—is that what you want?"

"I told you in Boston I'm through playing around," he barked. "Unlike you, I know exactly how I feel, and exactly what I want. A little love affair, as you put it, is *not* it."

"Then what the hell *do* you want from me?" Sam shrilly demanded.

"I want everything I've been looking for, and I see it in you!" Matt yelled back. "I want what other men have—a lifetime of happiness with one woman!"

"You know I can't give you that!"

"Then I want nothing at all!" he thundered. Sam stared at him with burning eyes. "I mean it, Sam! It's all or nothing!"

"Then it'll have to be nothing."

"Shit!" Matt exploded, and with a quick sidestep, slammed his fist into the nearest oak barrel. As he bowed his head and cradled the violated hand, Sam hurried over and started to reach for him. He jerked away.

"Let me see—"

"No!" he boomed, and lifted eyes filled with such anger and pain that her own filled immediately with stinging tears. They peered at each other for a tense moment.

"Don't do that," he commanded when a tear spilled over. Sam wiped at her eyes. "I said, stop it!"

"I'm trying!" she cried, and spinning around, buried her face in her hands. A minute later something floated over her shoulder and brushed the backs of her fingers. Sam blindly swatted it away.

"It's a handkerchief," Matt said, his voice coming from just behind her. "Take it."

Snatching the thing out of the air, Sam mopped the tears from her cheeks and took a few deep, steadying breaths. When she turned, she found Matt standing a few feet away, his hands planted on his hips as he fixed her with a piercing look.

"In case you haven't noticed," she said, "I sometimes let my emotions get the better of me."

"Not often enough, if you ask me," Matt replied in a growling tone. When her eyes promptly filled once more, he glanced sharply aside before adding, "There's no call for that. And there's nothing more to say. Come on. I'll walk you out."

Putting an arm around her shoulders, he escorted her out of the dank recesses of the cellars and into the cold, cutting air of the first twilight of the new year. Neither said a word as he walked her to the van. Climbing into the driver's seat, Sam started up the engine and looked bleakly at him out the open door.

"Rae's a smart lady," Matt said. "She told me months ago you were gonna break my heart." With that, he closed the van door and stalked off toward the house.

Feeling as though she'd been drained of every emotion she would ever have, Sam carried her bags into the house and turned on the lights. The little Christmas tree was gone, the place in perfect order. Celie's efforts showed. At the thought of Celie, a flickering smile crossed her face, but was quickly chased away by the returning image of Matt. She unpacked in a sort of preoccupied daze, and it wasn't until she washed her face and went back downstairs that Sam noticed the house was uncomfortably chilly. In fact, there was a definite draft.

Following the air current to the rear of the house, she discovered a broken window, and was gripped by a sudden sense of danger. She scurried back to the parlor, armed herself with a heavy iron poker from the fireplace, and walked through the room. The house was secure. And as far as she could tell, nothing was missing.

Sam returned to the window. The jagged hole was about the size of a softball, the broken pieces of glass lying on the floor below. She told herself not to be paranoid. It could have happened any one of a hundred accidental ways—a child throwing a rock . . . a branch blown from a tree. . . . Birds were known to smash into windows, weren't they? She tried not to dwell on the niggling idea that Red Carter might have done it out of spite.

After taping a piece of cardboard over the vented pane, Sam went into the kitchen and put on the kettle. As the tea steeped, she leaned against the counter, her thoughts settling once again on Matt. She'd done the only possible thing. She knew she had. But the memory of his pain-filled eyes once again brought the threat of tears to her own.

Crossing to the refrigerator, Sam opened the door and reached absentmindedly within for the creamer. As her hand closed on something smooth and round, she bent to turn a puzzled look inside. Screaming and leaping back, she knocked the thing onto the floor where it rocked morbidly to and fro on the linoleum.

As her mind shrieked, *A skull!*, her eyes watched a scrap of paper flutter to the floor beside it. Even upside down and scrawled in what appeared to be blood, the two words were easy to read: *Go Home.*

Leaving the things where they lay, Sam hurried into the parlor and called Larry Edison. When he arrived, she showed him the fractured windowpane before leading him to the kitchen.

"Obviously, whoever did this broke the window to get in," Sam said. "But I don't know when it could have happened. Celie checked on the place every day I was gone."

"I know when it happened," Larry replied. "Sometime between eleven last night and five this morning."

"How do you know?"

"Because we had us a grave-robbing last night, Sam. That skull you're looking at belongs to Mary Tyler."

"Mary Tyler?" she repeated with surprise. "That's the second time I've heard that name today." Crouching beside the skull, Sam started to reach out and set it upright.

"Don't touch it," Larry cautioned. "I doubt I'll find anything, but I'd like to dust it for fingerprints."

"I'll put on gloves, then." Swiftly returning from the supply closet, Sam snapped on a pair of surgical gloves and lifted the skull to the kitchen table. "Very interesting," she murmured.

"Interesting?" Larry said with a short laugh. "I don't know another woman who would call finding a human skull in her refrigerator *interesting.*"

"Maybe you don't know another woman who's a doctor," Sam replied. "When did Mary Tyler die?"

"Sometime in the early twenties. I'm not sure of the year."

Taking a seat in one of the kitchen chairs, Sam turned the skull to face her. "A seventy-year-old mystery," she softly said.

"I wouldn't call it a mystery. Mary Tyler committed suicide."

"But why?"

"Because a voodoo witch who was after her husband used things like dead chickens and human bones to put a spell on her, that's why."

Sam looked up to meet the constable's eyes. "Surely, you don't believe in such nonsense, Larry."

"I believe somebody's threatening you," he replied in a no-nonsense tone. "And using Juda's methods to do it. Seventy years ago, those methods led to Mary Tyler hanging herself."

"I'm sure there's another explanation."

"If there is, I doubt it will ever be found."

"Maybe *I* can find it," Sam said. "If you allow me to hold onto this for a few days."

"Hold onto what?" Larry said with a shocked look. "Mary Tyler's skull?"

"I'd like the chance to examine it—maybe run a few tests."

Larry tipped his hat to the back of his head. "We might need Matt's permission for that. Technically speaking, I reckon the skull belongs to him."

"Technically speaking, I would think it's evidence in a case of breaking and entering," Sam returned. "That would put it under *your* jurisdiction, wouldn't it?"

Larry arched a brow as he studied her. "I'll have to let Matt know you've got it," he said eventually. "If he has any objections, I'll be back."

"Fair enough."

"And I want to come over tomorrow and try a quick dust for fingerprints. Don't be touching it without gloves."

"Yes, sir!" Sam said with a smile that lasted all the way to the door, where Larry turned to her with a look of concern.

"I'm a fair tracker, Sam," he said. "If the perpetrator had left any signs, I feel sure I'd have picked them up. But just like last time with the chicken, he seems to have gotten away without leaving a trace."

"At least I didn't make it easy for him by leaving the door unlocked this time," she said.

"I wish you wouldn't take this lightly," Larry replied. "I don't know who we're dealing with here, or what he's capable of."

"Apparently he's not capable of dealing with me face-to-face, or he would have done it already. Somehow, instead of frightening me, this latest incident makes me feel . . . safe."

Shaking his head, Larry left the house with a final warning: "Keep things locked up now, ya hear?"

"I will," Sam promised. When he was gone, she transported the skull from the kitchen to her makeshift lab. An hour later she looked up with a start when Rae bustled into the room, hugging an overcoat about her shoulders and sporting rosy spots of cold on her cheeks.

"Hi, Sam. Welcome back."

"Hi. You startled me."

"Sorry. I knocked, but I guess you didn't hear me. The door was unlocked, so I came on in."

The door unlocked? Sam thought with chagrin. Larry would have killed her.

"How was Boston?" Rae asked.

"Good. How was everything around here?"

"Good. What are you do—" Rae broke off as her gaze drifted to the table where Sam's hands were poised. "What the hell *is* that?"

"Mary Tyler's skull. Someone left it for me in the refrigerator."

"How awful! I heard about Mary getting dug up, of course. The story's all over town. So, the missing skull turns up in your *refrigerator?*"

"Uh-huh," Sam mumbled as she bent once more over the magnifying glass.

"What's this?" Rae asked, stepping closer. "*Go home?*"

"Oh. That's the note that came with it," Sam absently replied.

"Are you going to?"

"Going to what?"

"Go home."

"In August, yes."

"August may be too late."

Setting the glass aside, Sam looked up to meet Rae's dark eyes. "First of all, it's not that easy to manage a transfer. The corps placed me in Riverbend. I'm supposed to stay here for the duration of my contract."

"I'd imagine the fact that you're being terrorized might swing some weight with your contractors," Rae returned.

"It might," Sam replied with a casual lift of her brows.

"I must say you seem mighty cool and collected about the whole thing. Doesn't it matter that somebody's been stalking you ever since you got here?"

Sam leaned back in her chair. "Rae ... I can either buckle under to scare tactics and leave. Or I can stay. If I'm going to stay, it doesn't do me any good to be scared to death, does it?"

Rae gave her a long, considering look. "I said from the beginning you were tough," she murmured. "I only hope that whoever's doing this doesn't start thinking they've got to hurt you to get your attention."

"That's a horrid thing to say."

"I know. I wouldn't say it if I didn't like you so much. Come on. Walk me to the door, and lock it behind me."

As she stepped onto the porch, Rae turned and directed a searching look through the darkness. "Does Matt figure into your decision to stay in Riverbend?"

"No. He doesn't."

"It didn't sound that way to me on Christmas Eve. When he came back from Boston, he was very . . . optimistic."

Sam released a heavy breath. "I admit I've changed my mind about Matt over the past few months. I like and respect him tremendously. But I can't let things go beyond friendship."

"That's something else that could change by August," Rae commented. Turning away, she descended the steps and hurried through the freezing night toward the lights across the street.

Sunday, January 2

Nadine's cheery humming drifted through the open door to the kitchen. Finishing off the last of a plateful of eggs, country ham, and grits, Drew leaned back in his chair and gazed across the dining table.

"Nobody makes redeye gravy like Nadine," he pronounced with satisfaction. Matt's eyes remained on the newspaper by his plate as he responded with an absentminded grunt. Propping his elbows on the table, Drew rested his chin atop folded hands as he perused the scene. The hearty breakfast on Matt's plate was barely touched, and he'd been staring at the same page of the newspaper for ten minutes.

"What's in the news?" Drew asked.

"Not much."

"I gather it didn't go well."

"What?"

"Your meeting with Sam."

Matt swiftly looked up. "I don't want to talk about it, Pierce. Do you mind?"

"Hey, no problem," Drew said with a lift of his brows. A few seconds later Matt pushed away from the table and rose to his feet.

"I think I'll take a spin around the vineyards," he said.

"For what?"

"For the hell of it."

"Want some company?" Drew asked.

"What do you think?" Matt replied, his face looking like a thundercloud about to erupt. Gaining his feet, Drew cracked a smile.

"I think I'll walk you out, take a look at this beautiful winter morning, and come back here where it's safe."

"Funny, Pierce. Real funny."

"Thank you," Drew replied, undaunted.

As they stepped out on the porch, Larry's car pulled up in the courtyard. Zipping their jackets against the breathtaking cold, Matt and Drew descended the front steps.

"Guess what I just finished doing," Larry greeted as he got out of the car.

"Let's see," Drew replied. "You just finished winning the lottery, and you've come to say goodbye before you set off on a trip around the world."

"You're in high spirits this morning," Larry commented.

"That makes one of us," Drew returned with a sly look toward Matt, who ignored the jab as he hung an arm on the open car door and glared at Larry.

"This is the second morning in a row you've shown up out here," Matt stated. "What's happened now?"

"What's happened is that Mary Tyler's skull turned up, and I just finished dusting it for fingerprints."

"Did you find out who opened her grave?" Matt asked.

"Nope. But guess where he left the skull?"

"On a stake at the entrance to town?" Drew put in, and received a fleeting scowl from Matt. "It was just a thought," Drew added with a mock look of apology.

"Where the hell did you find the damn skull?" Matt demanded.

"I didn't find it," Larry answered. "Sam did."

"Sam?!"

"She wants to keep it for a few days to run some tests. I told her I'd have to ask your permission."

Matt's eyes shone like the morning sun. "You tell Sam I want that thing back by day after tomorrow. That's when they're sealing up Mary Tyler, and I'd prefer that it be with her head."

"I'll tell her," Larry replied agreeably.

"Where did Sam find it?" Drew asked.

"You'll never believe this—in her refrigerator."

"Her *refrigerator*?" Matt exclaimed. "How did it end up there?"

"Somebody broke into her house and put it there, along with a note warning her to go back to Boston."

Seemingly stunned, Matt stared at Larry in silence.

"This isn't the first time something like this has happened," Larry added. "A few months ago somebody walked into her house when she wasn't there, and slashed a chicken's throat on her bed."

"For God's sake, who?" Matt thundered.

"Don't know. There hasn't been any evidence either time."

"Why didn't you tell me before?!"

"You never asked," Larry replied with a look of innocence.

"I want you patrolling that house every night, Larry. Look at it as private duty. I'll make it worth your while."

"You could always stake it out yourself," Larry suggested with a grin.

"No. I couldn't," Matt replied sharply and stalked off toward the side yard where his Jeep was parked.

"What did I say?" Larry asked with a questioning look for Drew, who clapped a hand on his shoulder.

"Big brother's got it bad," Drew said, his quick smile disappearing as he watched Matt speed away in the Jeep.

Two mornings later Drew was gazing absently out the study window while Matt sat nearby, cleaning his rifle in preparation for the upcoming Friday-night hunt. Drew had been there a mere minute or two when he spotted the white van heading up the drive.

"Here comes Sam," he announced, and wasn't surprised when Matt set the rifle aside and swiftly joined him by the window.

"Oops," Drew murmured. "She just took the turn to the winery."

"What does she want at the winery?"

"I don't know."

"I'll go see," Matt stated. Crossing the room, he grabbed his jacket from the back of a chair, and glanced over his shoulder. "You stay here," he added.

"I figured that," Drew replied.

Clearing the side yard with long strides, Matt bypassed the van parked at the winery entrance and went swiftly inside. The winery crew was diligently at work, the building filled with the sounds of rumbling machinery. Matt walked swiftly up to the foreman.

"Did a woman just come through here, Jake?" he asked, lifting his voice above the noise.

"You mean Dr. Sam? Yeah. She headed back yonderway. Said there was something she wanted to check out. I figured it was okay!" Jake called to Matt's back, as he had already moved off in the direction Jake had indicated.

Matt found her—of all places—in the hidden room behind the supply closet, where she was crouched by the old moonshine still, apparently in the midst of examining it.

"If you're in the mood for a drink, we've got better stuff in the cellars," he said.

She slowly straightened. Bundled from head to toe, she was wearing jeans and boots and a gray, hooded sweatshirt emblazoned with the phrase: *Property of St. Elizabeth's.*

"Do you mind if I ask what you're doing here?" Matt added.

"I came to bring you that," she replied, pointing to the corner where—neatly wrapped in plastic—Mary Tyler's skull was sitting on a wooden stool.

With an indifferent glance in that direction, Matt looked back to Sam, met her eyes, and was struck anew by how green they were ... and how desperately he wanted her. His very heartbeat seemed to thunder her name.

"How did you find out about this room?" he asked.

"Drew showed me the other day. I didn't think you'd mind if I took a closer look at the still. I needed to examine it in order to verify a theory."

"Have you finished?"

"Yes."

"Good," Matt muttered. Walking over to the stool, he tucked the skull in the crook of his arm and returned to the doorway. "After you," he added.

"Don't you want to know what I found out?"

"About a seventy-year-old skull and a ninety-year-old still? Not particularly."

Her eyes flashed green fire. "Well, I'm going to tell you anyway," she stated curtly. "You said you wanted the skull back today, and I stayed up most of the night concluding my tests in order to accommodate you. I'd at least like the courtesy of relating my findings."

"Suit yourself."

"I've disproven the legend of Juda's curse," she announced.

"No way," he mildly replied. Sam folded her arms in a quick, exasperated gesture.

"There's a logical, medical explanation for the state of mind that led Mary Tyler to commit suicide, Matt. The woman wasn't cursed, she was mad."

"And you decided that after taking a look at a skull that's been buried for three-quarters of a century?"

"Buried *above ground*," she pointed out. "Elevated tombs have a distinct advantage in terms of protecting their contents from the elements. Even after seventy years, there are things about bone matter that don't change."

"Like what?"

"Like an unduly high quotient of lead."

Matt frowned. "Go on."

"The loss of mental stability is a common symptom of lead poisoning, and Mary Tyler was unquestionably a victim. Considering the levels of lead in her skull, I'd say she absorbed it over a period of years during which she grew increasingly delusional and paranoid, and finally incapable of holding onto any sense of reality whatsoever."

"Where did she contract lead poisoning?"

"Right here," Sam replied, flourishing a hand to the still. "The other day when Drew showed me this room, he mentioned that Mary regularly consumed the liquor produced in this deathtrap. Look at the pipes. They're lined with lead. Juda may have manipulated a woman in a highly suggestible state, but these pipes were the ultimate instrument of Mary Tyler's death, not a voodoo spell."

"Very impressive," Matt said with a dark look. "So, science wins in the end, and there's no magic after all."

Sam's arm dropped to her side. "Is that all you have to say?"

"No. I'd like to know if there have been any other incidents besides the dead chicken on your bed and the skull in your refrigerator."

"Not really," she replied after a moment.

"That doesn't sound very convincing."

"Well, one day somebody left a mess on my porch."

"What kind of mess?"

"Animal . . . droppings." Matt cocked a brow. "They left a pile of dung on my porch, and smeared it on the door," she added.

"Any idea who's doing these things?"

"I have my theories."

"Don't you always?" he shot back in a decidedly cutting tone. She gazed at him in silence, her eyes reaching . . .

"Just be careful," Matt gruffly added. "And now if you'll excuse me, I've got a funeral to attend to."

"Matt, wait." Releasing a heavy breath, he turned to face her. "Is this how it's going to be?" she added.

"What do you mean?"

"I mean you and me—hardly speaking, barely looking each other in the eye."

"I don't know, Sam. I've never been here before. You tell me. What's supposed to happen next?"

Once again she could only mutely stare.

"It seems that for once, the doctor is out of theories," Matt concluded, and leaving her behind in the old secret room, made a swift departure from the bustling winery.

Chapter Fifteen

Thursday, March 17

The St. Patrick's Day Parade was one of the biggest annual events in Savannah; the tradition dated back to the 1800s, and was the second largest in the nation. Every year, thousands turned out to celebrate, following the parade through downtown and ending up on the Riverfront, where there were food booths and live music and a party in every pub.

Each year Robert waited for the parade crowds to die down before making the walk to River Street and lifting a celebratory glass at Wet Willy's. Although the place was especially crowded this year, Willy had saved his usual barstool.

"Happy Saint Patrick's Day to you, Willy," he greeted.

"Here's wishing you the same," the barkeep replied in his best Irish accent. "And will you be having a glass of fine Irish whiskey to toast the day?"

"I wouldn't dare have anything else," Robert returned. As he waited for his drink, he cast a look along the crowded bar, his gaze halting as he spotted Drew Pierce a few stools over. When the whiskey arrived, Robert took a sip, and turned again to look in Drew's direction.

It didn't take long to realize the young man was covertly watching someone across the room. Robert wasn't surprised when he followed Drew's line of vision to discover Lucy and a group of comrades at a table across the way. What *was* surprising was that she was being no more successful at hiding surreptitious glances in Drew's direction than he was in hers.

Lifting a hand, Robert called Willy over. "Drew Pierce is seated a few stools over," he said. "Send him a shot of whiskey with my compliments, will you?"

When the drink was delivered, Drew looked around with surprise, then walked over to shake hands. "Thanks, Mr. Larkin," he said. "How have you been?"

"I can't complain for an old man," Robert replied with a smile. "Happy Saint Patrick's Day."

"Same to you." Clinking glasses, they took a drink, and as if magnetized, Drew's gaze flickered across the room once more.

"Why don't you go over to her?" Robert asked.

"Who?"

"The woman you can't take your eyes off of—Lucy." Though Drew's face turned rosy, he met Robert's eyes with a steady look.

"She's here with a private party, Mr. Larkin. But even if she were alone, I wouldn't make the effort."

"Why not?"

"Because it would be pointless. Every time we speak, we end up in a fight."

"Sometimes that can be a sign of love."

Drew laughed. "I never realized you're such a romantic."

"Maybe," Robert said. "But I'm also a lawyer with a good deal of experience at reading people. I've known Lucy all her life, and I've never seen her react the way she did on Christmas Eve when you walked out of her party with Elizabeth Childers."

Drew's smiled faded. "I'm not sure what you're suggesting."

"I'm suggesting that Lucy has feelings for you, Drew. Maybe they were there all along, and she never knew it.

Maybe she's finally outgrown the shell she's worn all these years. I don't know. But of one thing I'm certain—she didn't like it when you disappeared with another woman."

"She didn't like the fact that I turned down a business proposition. That's all."

"I don't know what business you're referring to," Robert said. "But I know what I saw, and for the first time in years I believe there's hope for Lucy, after all. Maybe she doesn't have to live the rest of her life as a cold, embittered woman. Maybe if you came to Savannah on a consistent basis, and made a concerted effort, you could bring her completely out of that shell."

Tossing down the remainder of his drink, Drew set the shot glass on the bar. "I learned my lesson long ago, Mr. Larkin. As far as Lucy and I are concerned, there wasn't any chance from the beginning, and there isn't any chance now."

"In 1975, they said that about the University of Georgia's hopes of beating Ohio State. But in the final seconds, the Georgia quarterback—a young star named Drew Pierce—pulled an unexpected play and ran for a touchdown. What was the final score again?"

"Georgia, 21–20."

"Exactly," Robert said. Taking the last gulp of his whiskey, he rose from the stool and clapped the boy on the shoulder. "You've got a good brain, Drew," he added. "Use it, and you might be able to win more than you think."

Exiting Wet Willy's, Robert paused by the front window and looked within. Drew was peering straight in Lucy's direction. Laughing and chatting with her friends, Lucy was making a great show of pretending not to notice. With a sly smile on his face, Robert dapperly tapped his walking cane along the cobblestones as he strolled down River Street.

Saturday, March 19

Eleven weeks had passed since Sam returned from Boston. At first, she'd looked for ways to stay busy, then soon found she didn't have to look anymore. Clara Tully gave herself a nasty cut on the hand with a butcher knife; Sarah Bishop suffered a gallstone attack; Edwin Pettigrew developed a blister on his heel, and didn't come to the clinic until it became dangerously infected. In addition to treating a host of other patients for typical winter ailments, Sam had spent every spare minute making arrangements for Ida Carter's surgery at Candler Memorial.

The two of them had made a half-dozen trips back and forth to Savannah for X-rays, examinations, and consultations with Dr. Gary Brooks, who reminded Sam of John Thomason not only in appearance, but also in the easygoing air of confidence with which he conducted himself. Ida loved him—which was a definite plus, considering the ordeal that lay ahead of her.

The severe ankle fracture she'd sustained so many years ago had resulted in traumatic arthritis in the joint space, which in turn had led to the angular deformity and painful limp. Though fairly complex, the corrective surgery would be accomplished in a single procedure during which the bone would be straightened, the joint fused, and a supporting plate and screws installed.

Ida would be in the initial cast for four weeks; a walking cast for an additional eight. After that, her program of physical therapy would begin. She was facing months of discomfort with wheelchairs and crutches, but as the date of surgery drew near, Ida only became more excited.

On the night before she was to be admitted, Red showed up at Rae's Place and created a brawl as he attempted to drag her out of the inn.

But even her husband's bellowing failed to dampen Ida's spirits. As Larry hauled Red away to let him cool his heels in jail overnight, Ida blithely commented that she'd expected more trouble out of Red than that. She and Sam left for Savannah the next day before he was released.

The surgery required most of the following afternoon. When it was over, Gary Brooks pronounced that everything had gone well. Nonetheless, Sam had camped out in the doctors' lounge, checking on Ida from time to time through the night. The sun had been up a scant hour when she walked into the hospital room to find Ida smiling up at her. Sam was amazed. Though she was still unquestionably frail, the downtrodden air that had always shadowed Ida's face was gone, in its place a shining aura of happiness.

"I don't have to ask how you feel," Sam said. "You look great."

"Take a gander at this," Ida replied and swept away the sheet to reveal the leg with the white cast from toe-to-knee. "Look how straight it is."

"Straight as an arrow," Sam smilingly agreed. "Dr. Brook says the procedure went extremely well."

"I know he did the surgery, and I'm real grateful. But I ain't forgettin' who got me here. It was you, Dr. Sam, and I thank God every day for sending you to my door."

Swallowing down the lump that rose to her throat, Sam perched on the side of the bed. "I'm very happy for you, Ida. I sense a whole new life opening up for you. In three days you'll be out of here, and when we get back to Riverbend—"

"Dr. Sam," she interrupted.

"Yes?"

"I've decided not to go back."

"You have?" Sam said, her brows lifting with surprise.

"There's nothing there for me but bad memories, and more on the way if Red has anything to do with it."

"I suppose you're right, but where do you intend going, if not back to Riverbend?"

"I'm staying here in Savannah," Ida stated. "The night nurse, Maria, is real good to me. She told me about a place, a shelter where women like me can go. She lived there herself for a while after she left her husband. Maria says she'll take me there, and bring me back and forth when I need to come to the hospital. Soon, when I'm all healed up, I'd like to get a job."

"I think that's wonderful," Sam said warmly. "I've got

to say it, Ida—you're like an entirely different person. When I first met you months ago, I never would have expected you to strike out on your own like this."

"Me neither. Used to be I was so down deep in a hole, I couldn't see anything but black. Now, everything seems so clear. As soon as I get settled in the shelter, I'm gonna write Red a letter and tell him I want a divorce."

Reaching out, Sam put a light hand atop hers. Ida caught and held it.

"And all this is happening because of you," she murmured.

"No, Ida," Sam returned solemnly. "It's happening because of you, because you have great courage and strength."

She shook her head on the pillow. "I might be doing the flying, but you're the one who opened the window. I'll never forget you, Dr. Sam. No matter how much time goes by, I'll never forget."

Despite her sleepless night, Sam drove back to Riverbend with a song in her heart. It was midday when she parked in front of the clinic, glanced aimlessly across the street, and froze. Sitting alone on Rae's boardwalk, Matt was propped back in a chair with a guitar lodged across his lap. Snapping around, Sam stared ahead.

Regardless of the way she'd worked herself to distraction the past weeks, the thought of him had stayed in the back of her mind day and night. One day at the end of January, she'd driven out to see Nadine, and spotted him in the fields alongside a line of workers busily cutting back the brown vines. Matt had been on the end of the line nearest the vineyard road, and she was sure he must have noticed the van. But he showed no sign of it. As she drove slowly past, preparing to wave when he looked in her direction, he kept his eyes on his work and delivered a murderous whack that sheared a vine to its main stalk in one swoop.

She'd also observed him from a distance a few times, coming and going at Rae's Place. But they hadn't spoken to each other since that day in the hidden room of the winery. On the few occasions they'd found themselves in the same vicinity, whether at the chateau or in town, Matt had executed a quick disappearance. It was painfully obvious he was avoiding her.

The sun was high, the day bright and blustery. Getting out of the van, Sam walked determinedly across the street, her coattails flapping. As she arrived, Matt looked up from the guitar—dark and beautiful as ever. A thrill jolted through her.

"Hello," he said.

"Hello, Matt. I didn't know you play the guitar."

"I fiddle with it from time to time," he replied. "How's Ida getting along?"

"You know her surgery was yesterday?"

"Everybody does."

"She came through it really well. She'll be recuperating for a number of months, but I've never known a patient with higher morale. It's as if she's been reborn."

"That's great. I can't think of anyone who deserves a new life more than Ida."

A gust of wind whistled by. Sam stuffed her hands in her pockets.

"How are things at the vineyards?"

"The vines have started budding. As long as we don't get a spring frost, we should be in good shape."

Sam gave him a smile, but he didn't return it—only searched her face in a way that went beneath the polite level of their conversation. She expelled a heavy breath as her smile died away.

"Thanks for not disappearing on me this time," she said. "I half expected you to run down the street when I headed your way." Making no reply, he looked back to the guitar.

"Dammit, Matt," she added. "Why do you have to make this so difficult?"

"I thought I was making it easy," he replied, accenting the statement with a strummed chord.

"I don't find this easy."

"Gee. I'm sorry, Sam."

"Would you look at me, please?" Resting his arm atop the guitar, he slowly lifted his gaze. "You know that I care for you, Matt," she added quietly. "Do you think I enjoy watching you avoid me every time we happen to cross paths?"

"I don't know what else to do."

"You could be my friend," Sam declared.

"Be serious," he returned with a snort of a laugh.

"I *am* being serious."

The halfhearted look of levity vanished from his face. "We're not friends, Sam. We're lovers."

"For one night we were lovers."

Matt arched a dark brow. "I'd say Boston qualifies as a second night. That was a pretty intense ride in the limo."

Sam could think of no reply to that. She peered at him, her cheeks flooding with heat.

"Look, Sam," he continued, "for whatever reasons, we agree on one thing—neither of us wants a casual affair. But that doesn't change the fact that every time I look at you, I go nearly crazy with wanting you. I thought that as the weeks went by, the feelings might die down, but they only get worse. It's best if I'm just not around."

"So, you want to cut me out of your life. Is that it?"

"What I want is to have you *in* my life from now on, every day in my house, every night in my bed."

"How can you say something like that?" Sam sputtered. "You know, whether or not you choose to regard yourself as such, you happen to be a married man."

"I don't have to be."

"You said you can't divorce her, that you'd lose everything if you tried."

"Lucy hasn't got her hooks in Riverbend, yet. If I could walk away with that and you, I'd figure I made out like a bandit."

Sam gazed at him with wide eyes. "Is that a proposal?"

"If I thought it would make any difference, I could make it one," Matt replied with a solemn look. "But the fact is I've got the picture down pretty well. You'll be gone in a few months, and I'll still be here."

"It doesn't have to be so cut and dried," Sam said after a moment. "People do visit other people, you know."

"I told you before, part-time isn't enough for me."

"I still say there's no need to be so fatalistic. You've got connections in Boston. Did you ever think you could—"

"What? Move up north and sit behind a desk somewhere? It took me a long time to find my purpose, Sam. The vineyards are my life, and have been for a dozen years. A man needs a life."

"So does a woman."

"You can be a doctor anywhere—even here, where you're needed a helluva lot more than you'll ever be in Boston."

His quiet words struck the blow of a club. Sam put a hand to her brow as her temples began to throb. Setting the guitar aside, Matt rose to his feet.

"I'm a number of years older than you," he added. "And it's for damn sure I've been around a lot more. Maybe our paths crossed at the wrong time. Maybe you haven't had time to realize just how special a thing it is you're throwing away."

Sam scrubbed at her aching forehead. Stepping down from the boardwalk, Matt reached out and lifted her chin until she looked into his amber eyes.

"I love you," he said in a rumbling tone. "And it follows that I want you to be happy. So if I have to let you go, then that's the way it'll be. But don't ask me to treat you like my best buddy in the meantime, okay?"

With that, Matt turned and ambled away. Sam remained in the street, watching with a thudding heart as his Jeep disappeared beyond the square.

Having witnessed the scene from the table by the front window, Drew looked up as Rae delivered his sandwich and fries.

"Thanks," he said, his eyes turning back out the win-

dow and lighting on Sam as she started across the street
with a heavy step. "Now, that's a sad sight," he added.

"What?" Rae questioned.

"Sam ... Matt ... the whole thing." Glancing up,
Drew met Rae's eyes and offered a small smile. "Star-
crossed lovers," he added.

"Is there any other kind?" she replied.

Drew propped his elbows on the table and perused
her. "That's a pretty cynical outlook, Rae."

"Just realistic," she returned as she placed a coaster on
the felt tabletop and put down a giant glass of iced tea.
Drew continued to study her as she straightened and
wiped her palms across her apron. Finally, her eyes
lifted.

"What are you looking at me like that for?" she asked.

"I don't know. I just didn't figure you for such a hard-
ened viewpoint."

Rae gave him a searching look. "You should know the
lesson as well as I do, Drew. Sometimes it doesn't matter
how much you love somebody. Sometimes it just isn't in
the cards."

The hooded reference to Lucy straightened his spine.
"Maybe," he said. "Or maybe sometimes all the player
needs is a new deal."

Rae arched a brow. "You've always had a gambler's
spirit, Drew. Careful you don't let it make off with your
good sense."

With that, she returned to the lunchtime diners across
the room. Drew looked at the plate of food, his appetite
waning as his thoughts lingered on Lucy. Since Robert
Larkin spoke to him night before last, he'd done quite a
bit of thinking. Until then, Drew hadn't allowed the puz-
zling reactions he'd noticed in Lucy to mean anything—
like the uncharacteristic blush when he came near, or the
flustered response when he kissed her months ago. But
since talking to Larkin, there was no doubt a locked door
in his mind had swung open. *Maybe*, he'd started thinking. *Just maybe the old man was right.*

Drew took a gulp of iced tea, his gaze straying to the pay phone in the back. The glass was halfway drained when he abruptly rose from his chair. As he reached the phone, he glanced at his watch. One o'clock. Unless she was at one of her charity luncheons, he ought to be able to catch her.

"Tyler residence," Tobias answered.

"Hello, Tobias. It's Drew."

"Well, hello, Mr. Drew. How y'all doing?"

"Fine, thanks. Is Lucy in?"

"Sure thing. Just hold on while I have her pick up." Seconds ticked by. Drew stared unseeingly at the wall above the phone. There was a click, and then . . .

"To what do I owe this honor?"

"I've been thinking about what you said," Drew answered straightforwardly. "Is that Riverfront club still for sale?"

"Well, well," she returned in a lilting tone. "Yes. I believe it is. Have you changed your mind?"

"If you want to talk, I'll talk," Drew gruffly announced. "But it'll be on my terms, and on my home turf."

"What home turf?"

"The chateau."

"Drew, it hardly makes sense to set up a meeting at a location where Matt could walk in at any minute."

Drew rubbed his fingers across his aching forehead. "He's going to Atlanta in a couple of weeks to meet with our advertising people. He'll be gone overnight. I'll agree to see you then at the chateau, or not at all."

There was a moment of silence. Beads of sweat broke out on his upper lip.

"All right," she finally agreed. "It'll be as you say, although I still think—"

"I'll talk to you then, Lucy. Goodbye."

God, Drew thought when he hung up the phone. *What the hell was he doing?* Leaving his lunch untouched, he dropped a ten by the table on his way out of Rea's.

Friday, March 25

It was suppertime when the last patient left the examining table. Sam stripped off her gloves as Celie hung her white coat in the supply room, and prepared to depart after yet another long afternoon. There had been an outbreak of chicken pox, and for the past two weeks, the clinic had been inundated with children between the ages of two and seven.

"How many does that make?" Celie asked as Sam walked with her onto the porch. The sun was newly set, the glow of twilight hanging over the town.

"Thirteen including Jason," Sam replied. "The Ingram girl has the worst case. I think I'll drive out there tomorrow and take another look at her."

With a thoughtful nod, Celie strolled to the head of the steps, took a deep breath, and looked over her shoulder with a smile.

"Isn't that nice?" she said.

Sam followed to the edge of the porch. "Isn't what nice?"

"Spring air," Celie replied. "The days are getting longer, the nights milder, and it won't be long before you've got flowers popping up in your front yard."

"Flowers?" Sam repeated with a smile. "What kind?"

"Buttercups and tulips, as I recall. It must have been twenty years ago when old Doc Daly's wife planted the bulbs. They still come up every year. I like that."

"Me, too," Sam agreed, her smile lingering as she glanced across the street to the lights of Rae's Place. Her passing gaze halted, then backtracked to the broad, street-facing window. Matt . . . She easily distinguished his cowboy-hatted silhouette at the front table. He was sitting with a few other men, apparently playing cards. Her attention thoroughly arrested, Sam failed to notice Red Carter's approach along Main Street until he blustered through the gate and up the walk.

"What you lookin' at, girl?!" he demanded of Celie.

"N-nothing," she stammered, shrinking back. Stepping

swiftly forward, Sam pushed Celie behind her as she glared down at Red.

"So," she said. "You finally have the nerve to confront me in the open."

"One thing I've never run short on is nerve, girlie. See this?"

Holding out a letter of some sort, he started up the steps. In spite of herself, Sam began backing away, and prodding Celie along with her. Clad in his typical T-shirt and overalls, Red Carter was big and slovenly, and as usual, had a cigar clamped in his mouth. The sight of him made Sam sick to her stomach.

"It's a letter from my wife saying she wants a divorce," he said when he reached the top. "*You* did this, and you know what I think of it?"

Taking a few brisk puffs on his cigar, he touched the smoldering tip to the corner of the letter. The paper began to black and curl as he brandished it in her face. Sam swatted the thing out of his hand.

"That doesn't matter, Red. You could burn up a hundred letters, and it wouldn't matter. Ida wants a divorce, and she's going to get one. The days of your taking satisfaction from abusing your wife are over."

"Then maybe I'll just take my satisfaction out of your hide instead," he growled, and advanced menacingly on Sam.

The street, the gate, the porch front . . . everything was veiled in a red haze as Matt stormed toward the clinic, his eyes fixed on the back of Red Carter and beginning to burn as the bastard raised a threatening fist toward Sam and Celie. A few last long strides, and Matt grabbed hold of the back of Carter's overalls and summarily tossed him off the porch. He landed in a roll, and was on his feet by the time Matt moved from the steps to face him.

"That redheaded bitch ain't done nothin' but stir up trouble since she got here, Tyler!" he thundered. "And now she's fixed it so my wife walked out on me!"

Grabbing him by the neck of his shirt with both fists, Matt snatched the man forward so they were nose-to-nose. "Ida should have walked out on you years ago," he said quietly. "And if you come around Sam's place again, I'll make you sorry you were ever born. You got that?"

Sam's hand was planted over her mouth, her eyes glued on the men. In a swift move Red fanned his forearms, broke Matt's hold, and punched him in the nose. Matt stumbled back a pace, his hat falling to the ground. Sam started forward, but Celie grabbed her shoulder and pulled her back as Matt flashed a dangerous smile.

"Thanks for the invitation, you son of a bitch," he said, then drew back and landed an upper cut to the jaw that knocked Red off his feet and squarely on his backside. Still, the man got quickly to his feet, balled up his fists, and started toward Matt with the unmistakable intention of continuing the fracas.

But then a number of men who had run out of Rae's Place poured into the yard. Larry Edison latched onto Red as Drew and Edwin Pettigrew each grabbed one of Matt's arms. But they were no match for the enraged giant, who shook them off like flies and took a threatening step toward Red Carter.

"Hold it right there, Matt," Larry cautioned as Drew and Edwin joined him between the two angry men. "This thing needs to end here and now."

"It wasn't none of his business, no how!" Red accused.

"And what *business* did you have here at the clinic?" Matt returned heatedly. "The business of beating up on another couple of females? You want a piece of something, Carter? Come on, and try to take it out of me."

Carter strained forward. So did Matt. The men in the yard jumped on both of them and dragged them apart.

"You want to spend another night in jail, Red?" Larry demanded.

"Me?! What about Tyler? He started it."

"You threw the first punch," Larry returned.

"He threw me off the damn porch!"

"What were you doing on the damn porch in the first place?"

At that, Red finally went still, his narrow eyes turning to the porch and finding Sam through the gathering darkness.

"Nothin'," he answered eventually. "Nothin' I plan to do anything about right now."

Twisting out of Larry's grasp, the man stomped out of the yard and proceeded out of view down Main Street. Only then did the half dozen men who'd piled on Matt move off of him.

"Thanks a lot, boys," he muttered. "You stepped on my hat." Straightening his shirt cuffs, he bent to the ground, picked up the violated hat, and dusted it against his pants leg.

"Lord, have mercy," Celie murmured. "I'd never want to be on the wrong side of either one of *those* men."

As though surfacing from a dream, Sam snapped to alertness and started down the steps. But by that time Matt had passed through the gate without a backward glance. Larry moved to meet her as she walked into the yard.

"Anything you want to press charges about, Sam?" he asked.

"No, nothing," she murmured absently as her eyes followed Matt's progress across the street, where he pushed through the saloon doors and disappeared inside Rae's Place.

Night closed in. As Sam put together a light supper, she considered the idea of going over to Rae's, thanking Matt for his gallant action, and inquiring after the condition of his affronted nose. With anyone else, that's what she would have done. But with Matt, she couldn't make the scenario work.

He didn't want her thanks. In fact, he didn't even want her presence. He'd made that abundantly clear on a number of occasions, including an hour ago when he stalked away without a word. If she walked into Rae's,

Matt would only glower at her with those beautiful eyes that were at once sad and angry. And once again she would be flooded with the same sense of helplessness and loss that came over her every time she looked at him.

Last week he'd stated that—albeit for different reasons—neither of them wanted an affair. What would he say if he knew the way the idea had started teasing her mind? The fact was that deep down where her true desires smoldered, it didn't matter anymore that he was married, or that what they could share could only be temporary, or that such a thing went against the code of morality that had always governed her life. Down deep, her craving throbbed so urgently, it was as though the need arose from within her very soul. Sam never would have imagined that the want of a man could ache so profoundly—so that every day without him became a day lived with the feeling that part of her was missing.

She'd suggested that he be her friend. The truth was she pined for Matt as a lover. What would he say to such a proposition? She didn't really have to wonder. *All or nothing*, his words echoed in her brain. And as much as she wanted him, she wasn't ready to give him all.

Halfheartedly consuming her meal, Sam washed up the dishes and started through the downstairs, turning off lamps as she went. As fate would have it, just as she plunged the parlor into darkness and glanced across the street, Matt came out of Rae's Place. Lingering by the window, she watched as he climbed into the Jeep and turned it north toward the vineyards. He'd be home in a matter of minutes.

Sam went upstairs, washed her face, brushed her teeth—the thought of him lingering all the while. By the time she finished dressing for bed, her mind was made up. Marching downstairs to the phone, she dialed the chateau. When his deep voice answered, her stomach did a flip.

"Hello, Matt. It's Sam."

There was a brief, stunned silence on the other end of the line.

"I know who it is," he then said. "Did you want to speak to me?"

"Yes, I did . . . I do."

"What about?"

"About this evening. Thank you for coming to my aid."

"No thanks are necessary."

Sam caught her lip before answering, "I disagree. After all, it wasn't the first time you've nearly come to blows on my behalf."

"What are you talking about?"

"Remember when Chad showed up at The Jolly Roger in Boston?"

"Boston was a long time ago," Matt replied after a moment. "I try *not* to remember it."

Putting a hand to her forehead, Sam paced back and forth in front of the phone. "That's ironic," she replied. "I find myself remembering it quite often."

"Stop it," Matt commanded.

"Stop what?"

"Stop trying to dredge up what's past. Things aren't like they were in Boston, Sam. Since then we reached a fork in the road, and we made a turn. There's no going back."

"I just . . ." Sam closed her eyes as she tried to force sense to her words. "I just wish there were a way around this impasse that seems to grow bigger by the day."

"Well, there isn't," he returned stiffly. "So, thanks for the call, but don't do it again. As a matter of fact, I'd appreciate it if you didn't come out to the chateau so often."

Her eyes springing open, Sam yanked her hand away from her brow. "I don't come out *so often*. I come *occasionally* to see Nadine. In fact, I was planning to stop by at the first of the week."

"Why don't you make it Thursday or Friday? I'll be in Atlanta on business."

"Fine," she snapped.

"Fine," Matt returned. There were a few tense seconds of silence. "I guess I'll be going now."

"Don't you think you're taking this whole thing to an extreme?" she demanded.

"I'm not taking it anywhere, Sam. Things have been *extreme* between you and me from the beginning. You know how I feel, I know how you feel, and the way things are, well . . . frankly speaking, I'd prefer not to see you at all. So, if you don't mind, I'd like to say goodbye."

"All right, then. Goodbye!"

The incensed feelings Sam experienced at that moment remained through the following days, swelling instead of ebbing while she waited—as instructed—for Thursday to arrive before driving out to see Nadine. It was midafternoon when she pulled up at the chateau, and was surprised by the sight of a silver Mercedes parked in the courtyard. Lucy Tyler? Sam thought as she walked to the door.

"Does that car belong to who I think it does?" she asked when Nadine welcomed her inside.

Nadine's round face took on a scowl. "She's here, all right. Showed up fifteen minutes ago, and she's been locked in the study with Drew ever since."

Sam cast an interested look at the study door as they started toward the hall to Nadine's room.

"I got a worrisome feelin' about this," Nadine added over her shoulder. "Lucy never comes here, and then soon as Matt leaves, she turns up like a bad penny and pounces on Drew." Nadine shook her silver head. "Worrisome," she repeated under her breath.

Sam found the premonition hanging in the back of her mind as she checked Nadine's vitals and found her continuing along a much-improved path.

"Your pressure has stabilized admirably," she said. Closing up her bag, she walked to the bedroom door as Nadine buttoned her dress. "Now," Sam added, "if only you'd agree to lose—shall we say—five pounds over the next two weeks. That's less than half a pound a day,

Nadine. I'm sure you could manage it if you put your mind to it."

"Hmph!" Nadine replied. "You ain't gonna be satisfied till I look like one of those half-starved girls in the magazines."

With a light chuckle, Sam started down the hall. "See you in a couple of weeks," she called, her smile dying away as she reached the foyer and once again noted the closed study door. Directing a swift glance over her shoulder, she confirmed that Nadine had not yet emerged. Unable to resist the impulse, Sam tiptoed across the foyer and pressed her ear to the door.

"I thought you wanted a part in Riverbend," Drew was saying. "That kind of thing only hurts everyone involved."

"In the short term perhaps," Lucy replied. "But look at the long term, Drew. You must see there's no other way—"

Nadine's humming floated down the hall. Leaping back from the door, Sam scurried across the foyer and out of the chateau. But as she drove away, the secretive exchange resounded in her ears. There was no doubt of the ominous portent of Lucy's words; nor of the questionable timing of her showing up when Matt left town; nor of her greedy hunger for Riverbend Vineyards.

Sam consoled herself with the reminder of Matt and Drew's closeness. Drew shared some of Matt's better qualities—he was strong, smart, dedicated. Lucy couldn't work her wiles on him any more successfully than on Matt . . . Could she?

"Worrisome," Sam murmured, as she turned off the vineyard road and took the highway toward town.

Atlanta

Springs, Howard, and Rush was one of the top advertising agencies in Atlanta, their client list including several Fortune 500 companies, their offices lodged in one of the most prestigious buildings of the city. But that wasn't why Matt hired them on. He simply liked Tim Springs—a self-made man like himself—and trusted his judgment. When Tim personally presented a multimedia campaign targeting an audience ten times the size Riverbend Vineyards heretofore had reached, Matt was all ears.

The meeting lasted beyond the usual business hours. It was well past six when Tim leaned back in his chair. He sat at one end of a massive table; Matt at the other; the creative team and account execs in between.

"That's it," Tim said, spreading his palms. "What do you think?"

"I think it's obvious you and your team are giving me my money's worth," Matt replied. "Let's go for it."

A round of applause erupted about the conference table. Rising from his chair, Tim crossed the room with a beaming smile, and clapped a hand on Matt's shoulder.

"Hope you haven't made plans for supper, buddy," he said. "I've got reservations for the whole team at 103 West."

"What's that?" Matt asked.

Tim shifted his brows in Groucho Marx fashion. "Where those in the know go," he answered. "You're riding with me from here; I'll drop you back at the hotel afterward."

Located in distinguished Buckhead, 103 West offered linen-covered tables, impeccable service, and excellent continental cuisine. Tim had reserved a table that accommodated ten. One of the group was a willowy redhead—a writer, Tim whispered when Matt discreetly inquired.

As the night wore on, and the wine flowed, Matt thought she began to look more and more like Sam. And the two of them began playing eye games across the table. When she went to the ladies room, Matt excused himself minutes later and waited for her in the hall.

"Well, hello, Mr. Tyler," she said, the unmistakable lilt of interest in her voice.

"Call me Matt." Propping an arm on the wall by her

head, he created a sense of intimacy as he bent closer. "What did you say your name is, darlin'?"

"Summer."

"Summer," he repeated. Reaching up to push an auburn curl behind her shoulder, he grazed his fingertips across her collar bone. "That's a hot name," he added.

"Some people I've known say it fits me to a tee."

"I'll bet they do," Matt replied, his eyes settling on hers. "I wonder if you're feeling at all *hot* tonight."

"Honey, if I got any hotter, I'd catch fire."

When the dinner broke up, he rode with her to her apartment in Dunwoody. Romantically lit and stylishly furnished, it was like one of any number of places he'd been welcomed into over the years.

"Can I offer you a drink?" Summer asked.

"I'm not thirsty," Matt replied, his gaze trailing suggestively down her body. "Sure am hungry, though."

With a seductive smile, she walked up to him and looped her arms around his neck. "I'll have to see what I can do about that," she murmured, and pulled him down to her seeking mouth.

It had been months. The first time was fast and furious; the second, she teased him to new life with her mouth, and when he returned the favor she was rewarded with a climax that apparently knocked her out. She slept while he dressed in the neighboring room. The feeling was as familiar as slipping into a well-worn overcoat. After all, this was the life he'd led for fifteen years.

Matt called a cab, and as he rode back to his hotel in the city, the old feeling of loneliness enshrouded him, but with a new edge. He thought of a saying: *Even bad sex is good.* And sex with Summer had been far from bad. In fact, on a purely physical plane, it had been pretty damn good. But that was all it was. Sex.

While he once had wondered what he might be missing, Matt now knew, and the craving cut like a blade. He loved Sam, and the one night they'd spent in each other's arms meant more than the past fifteen years put together.

In the hotel lobby he stopped by the night desk and made arrangements for flowers to be delivered to Summer the next morning. Wearily letting himself into his room, Matt flopped down on the bed and folded an arm beneath his head.

He'd done some good business, had some good sex, and he felt like he'd just lost his best friend. Sam's image materialized before him. Since he met her, there had been no one else until tonight. And regardless of the insurmountable distance between them, Matt felt as though he'd betrayed something precious.

Closing his eyes, he willed sleep to enfold him in a blanket of numbness.

Chapter Sixteen

April transformed Riverbend into a springtime fairyland. As lawns and live oak turned green, flowering pear and peach trees burst into snowy bloom, their frothy branches nodding over the bright yellows, reds, and purples of jonquils, tulips, and violets. The days were sunny and mild; the cool nighttime breezes laden with the scent of freshly mowed grass. Sam had never felt the season so keenly.

Although she'd never been particularly interested in yard work, she found herself consumed with a passion for it. What started with a meager trip to Simon's Produce for gardening gloves turned into a mission during which she ended up stocking the old shed out back with tools from Pettigrew's Mercantile. With Rae's help she cleared the lot of weeds, mended the front gate, and painted the fence a fresh white.

As early spring flowers faded and the flowering trees lost their blossoms—their petals fluttering through the air like snow flurries—Sam was delighted when the bushes in front of the house began to show tiny fuschia buds. By the end of the month they'd opened in the full flower of hot pink azaleas, and she had taken to spending every spare moment laboring about the yard—often into the elongating twilight hours.

On one such dusky evening, she was perched on a ladder by the giant magnolia out front—busily pruning away dead limbs as she estimated how many years the tree had presided in this spot. She was sure it was a century old, probably older.

"You've got the place looking mighty nice, Sam."

At the sound of Matt's voice, she spun around and nearly fell off the ladder.

"Whoa," he cautioned, and surrendered a smile as her startled gaze lit upon him. He was standing on the walk on the other side of her fence. Climbing nimbly down from the ladder, Sam discarded her pruning shears and started in his direction. The white of his shirt glowed in the twilight, along with the smile that faded as she drew near.

"Didn't mean to interrupt your work," he said. "Just wanted to compliment your efforts."

"Thank you, kind sir," she said with exaggerated politeness. "Of course, my little garden doesn't hold a candle to *yours,* but I do what I can."

Their eyes met, and Sam's pulse began its familiar race. She hadn't seen him up close since the day weeks ago when he threw Red Carter off her porch. As usual, Matt in the flesh was something spectacular.

"How have you been?" he asked.

"Good. How about you?"

"No more visits from Carter?" he asked, ignoring her question.

"No," Sam replied. He nodded, and took a backward step. "Are you leaving?" she added, a bit too shrilly.

Pulling the brim of his hat low on his brow, he tipped his head and looked at her. "I only stopped by to say hello, Sam. And I can already see it's a mistake. Take care of yourself, huh?"

As he walked away, Sam spun around, grabbed her shears, and scaled the ladder into the limbs of the magnolia. But the peaceful pleasure of her task had evaporated, along with the last of the fading light. Storing her equipment in the shed, Sam returned to the house still fuming with indignation.

Was there no sense to the world? Was there no divine purpose? No guiding hand of fate? No logical plan to anything? If things were going to be like this, why had she ever crossed paths with Matt Tyler, anyway? And how had the matter become so inextricably confused and mixed-up that the whole thing was enough to give her a damn headache? Slamming the door behind her, Sam went upstairs and took two aspirin—knowing it wouldn't help. Her enjoyment of spring was severely impaired, and would be over the next few days.

But then April turned into May, and the town began to buzz with excitement over the upcoming Grape Parade. The first time Rae mentioned it, Sam couldn't help but smile.

"*Grape* Parade?" she repeated, as visions of townfolk dressed as giant fruit danced through her head.

"Oh, it's probably the biggest annual event we have around here," Rae replied in all seriousness. "The tradition started a hundred years ago, supposedly to wish a healthy growing season to the Riverbend Vineyards crop. The last Saturday of May the parade starts south of town, with school bands, pretty girls on the backs of cars, and so on. They proceed up Main Street, and the whole town follows past the square and out to the vineyards, where a pig-pickin' and games and music generally go on till after dark."

"Grape Parade, huh?" Sam murmured, still unable to dispel a flash of amusement at the thought . . . until the sophomore class of the district school elected Celie to the Grape Princess Court.

Then the weeks flew as Sam juggled medical duties with the preparation of Celie's costume. Nimble-fingered Hannah was the seamstress; she, the designer and critic. All the princesses were supposed to wear full-length gowns in the style of Greecian tunics—in homage to the ancient god of wine, Bacchus, Sam presumed. Color and accessories were up to the individual princesses, of which there were six.

Clara Simon produced a bolt of lilac chiffon—which was beautiful against Celie's dark coloring—as well as a matching length of silk lining, and yards of elasticized gold lace. On the way out of the store, Sam spotted a decorative cluster of purple grapes attached to the crown of a sun hat.

"It'll be perfect," Clara said, and without hesitation, detached the ornament from the hat and pressed it in Sam's hand. "You take this to Celie with my compliments, ya hear?"

The afternoon before the event, Hannah and Sam stood back and surveyed the girl all dressed up in her finery. Gathered at one shoulder with the cluster of grapes, the flowing, lilac gown was crisscrossed over the bodice and cinched at Celie's waist with gold lace—which was repeated like a ribbon around her dark up-swept hair.

"You look every inch a princess," Sam commented, and received a glowing smile that completed the dazzling effect, and struck Sam with the bittersweet notion of how Celie was turning from a girl to a woman right before her eyes.

Later that day, Sam had promised to help Rae load the van with supplies for the next day's festivities, and haul them out to the vineyards. The "supplies" included checkered tablecloths; boxes of napkins, cups, and utensils; jugs of barbecue sauce; two giant urns of tea and lemonade; and several kegs of beer.

"Heavens!" Sam exclaimed as the two of them carted one of the urns to the van. "I hope you're being well-paid for this."

"Want me to get some of the men to help us load?" Rae asked with a quick look of concern.

"No, no," Sam said, dusting her hands against the seat of her jeans. "Two able-bodied women can handle the job, right?"

"Right," Rae agreed cheerfully. "You heave pretty good for such a skinny little thing."

"I have wiry strength," Sam replied with a sardonic grin.

"I have the feeling it has less to do with wiry strength than stubbornness," Rae returned.

It was nearly seven o'clock, but on this evening in late May the sun was only just starting to set as they turned off the highway and drove beneath the familiar archway of Riverbend Vineyards.

"Look how green they are," Rae said as they drove between the leafy banks of grapevines. "It's been a good spring."

Her arm propped in the open window, Sam surveyed the quiet fields—acre after acre, flooded with the fiery light of sunset. "What makes a good spring?" she asked.

"No late frost and plenty of rain. Hey," Rae added, her head swinging around. "Want to stop and take a closer look?"

Pulling over to the side of the road, Sam climbed down from the van and walked with Rae into one of the corridors between the vines. The smells of earth and growth went beyond the olfactory to surround all the senses. Rae reached out to gather the frond of a leaf in her hand.

"Next month the grapes will begin to show up," she said. "You should see them, Sam. All of a sudden they pop out in green bunches, some of them so tight you couldn't pry them apart with a butter knife. You know, the grapes don't turn purple until just before harvest at the end of summer."

"You seem to know a great deal about grape-growing, Rae."

She shrugged. "I've lived here all my life, and the vineyards have always been the backbone of this town, even through the many years when they weren't operating." She scanned the fields, a smile spreading across her face.

"As I look back, it's hard to believe what Matt has

done. When we were kids, these vines were nothing but a big, brown thicket twice as tall as we are. One summer we cut a tunnel all the way down to the riverfront. When we were halfway done, I thought we'd never make it, and was all for giving up. But even then Matt wasn't the type to let go of something he'd started."

Lifting an arm, Rae pointed toward the distant strip of river. "Right over there, the two of us drank our first beers," she said. "And that spot there beneath that big oak? Well . . . never mind, you don't want to know what happened over there. Come on. Let's get this stuff delivered."

When they reached the fork leading to the chateau, Rae instructed Sam to drive to the back of the house. Sam picked up a mouth-watering aroma long before they rounded the corner of the house and came upon a series of picnic tables set end to end beneath a green, tentlike awning. A column of smoke rose from the distant stone barbecue pit.

"What is that delicious smell?" she asked.

"Pig, o'course."

"Pig," Sam repeated with a sidelong glance.

"Whole pig. He'll roast all night long, and be prime by tomorrow afternoon. Haven't you ever been to a pig-pickin' before?"

"I can't say that I have." Parking the van near the picnic tables, Sam killed the engine and looked around to find Rae studying her.

"What *do* you all do up in Boston, anyway?" she said.

"Miss out on a lot, apparently," Sam returned with a smile.

Opening up the back of the van, Sam hoisted a box of paper supplies while Rae grabbed jugs of sauce. Depositing their burdens under the awning, they were returning for more when Matt's Jeep careened to a halt in the side yard. Looking over with obvious surprise, he got out and started their way—shirtless and sweaty, his skin gleaming in the light of the setting sun.

"Evenin', ladies," he said. "Need some help?"

With that, he began unloading the van, easily carting away the urns it had taken the two of them to lift. Propping against the side of the van, Rae regarded him with a bemused expression.

"Nice to know you're good for something," she said when he approached for another load. With a pang of envy, Sam caught the easy grin he turned Rae's way, and felt suddenly awkward, just standing back and observing the two of them. When Matt shouldered one of the beer kegs and walked away, she reached into the van, gathered up the armful of tablecloths, and followed his path toward the awning.

His careless stride made three of hers. She was merely halfway there when Matt set the keg on one of the tables, and started back in her direction.

"I could have gotten that," he tossed as he sauntered past.

"I don't mind," Sam returned in a matching, breezy manner.

When she walked back to the van, she was awarded a spectacular picture. Behind Matt the cloud-streaked sky was on fire in the wake of the sun's descent—limning his silhouette as he stood leisurely cradling a beer keg in each massive arm.

"That's it, ladies," he said as she arrived. "I'll be heading on into the house now. As you can tell, I could use some cleaning up."

"Are you going to the parade tomorrow?" Rae asked.

"I doubt it. There are some things I need to do around here."

"Well then, I'll probably see you in the morning," Rae said. "I plan to be out here around ten to help Nadine set up."

"Okay. See ya," Matt replied, and ambled off. "Night, Sam," he added as an afterthought.

"Good night," she responded, but by that time he was yards away, and more than likely out of earshot.

Climbing swiftly into the van, Sam started up the engine—an increasingly familiar sense of frustration vi-

brating within her like the plucked string of a guitar. As
soon as Rae closed the passenger's door, she executed a
sharp turn and made rapid progress down the chateau
drive.

"Clouds are rolling in," Rae commented as they turned
onto the vineyard road.

"Yes. It looks that way," Sam replied.

"Hope the parade doesn't get rained out."

"Me, too."

They drove the rest of the way to town in silence, but
Sam had the distinct impression both their minds were
lingering on the provocative image of Matt's incredible
body—bare to the waist, and astounding in both form
and power.

Parade day dawned beneath cloudy skies, and although
the morning turned typically warm, there were occasional gusty breezes that hinted of approaching rain. As
Sam dressed in a light khaki outfit of walking shorts and
matching shirt, she cast an anxious look out the window
at the sky. But although the clouds seemed to grow increasingly heavy, they held their own. At noon she joined
an impressive crowd turned out along both sides of Main
Street.

Stepping outside the front gate, she moved to the edge
of the walk and peered south. Just then a drum roll
sounded out, and was followed with a marching cadence.
The parade started forward, led by the two Pettigrew
boys supporting a banner announcing: GRAPE PARADE, and
accompanied by their friend, Philip Whitehead, who was
beating his drum with notable precision.

As they passed, the crowd clapped and cheered. Sam
joined in, her gaze turning to the first vehicle of the
cavalcade—a flatbed truck draped with garlands of flowers. Seated in the back were the members of the Ladies
Garden Club. Sam stifled a grin at the sight of Eloise,
Sarah, Grace, and the others gaily smiling and tossing
flower petals into the street like a bunch of young maid-
ens. Following them was a Boy Scout troop decked out in

uniform, and led by the Reverend Bishop ... and then the district school's marching band, who launched into a rousing rendition of "The Girl From Ipanema."

Sam had attended gigantic parades in Boston, New York, and even one in California. But despite the sour notes of the band, and the relatively modest floats of trucks and convertibles decorated with streamers, Riverbend's Grape Parade was the most entertaining she'd ever witnessed. As Celie's car drew near, Sam strained toward the street, waving furiously.

"Celie!" she yelled, and when the girl turned and smiled, Sam plugged two fingers in her mouth, and released a ringing whistle. Celie laughed and waved, and Sam madly applauded as the convertible continued past.

"Juicy-lookin' little gal, ain't she?"

Spinning around, Sam confronted the smirking face of Red Carter. He was standing mere feet behind her, and there was no telling how long he'd been there ... watching. The fleeting thought made her skin crawl.

"Mr. Carter," she began in a cutting tone, "there are hundreds of other spots from which to view the parade. I'd be grateful if you'd choose one."

He propped a hip against her gate. "I like it fine right here."

"Then, I'll go," Sam snapped. Turning on her heel, she proceeded up Main Street and joined Clara and Tully in front of Simon's Produce. She watched the rest of the parade from there, and consciously restrained herself from looking over her shoulder to see if, perchance, Red Carter had followed.

The finale of the parade was Larry Edison's official car—headlights shining, blue lights flashing. Accompanying him and dashing from one side of the street to the other, a clown gave out balloons to onlooking children. As they passed, the crowd broke up and began moving toward various vehicles to follow the parade out to the vineyards.

"Want to ride out with us, Dr. Sam?" Tully asked. "You're more than welcome."

"Thanks, Tully," she said with a smile. "But that's okay. I'll take the van."

"We'll see you there, then," Clara put in. "And by the way, Celie sure did look pretty in the parade."

"Yes, she did, didn't she?" Sam replied.

Her beaming smile faded as she turned and started down the street, instinctively scanning the crowd for the hulking figure of Red Carter as she went. When she reached the van, she even peered cautiously inside, gripped with a childlike fear of his jumping out at her like the boogeyman.

But he was nowhere to be seen. Taking a steadying breath, Sam circled around to the driver's side, and was preparing to climb in when Patty Ingram rushed over, her three-year-old son, Randy, in her arms.

"Help me, Dr. Sam!" she cried. "He swallowed some candy and it stuck! He can't breathe! Oh, Lord! He can't breathe!"

"All right, Patty," she said, and hurriedly stepped forward. "Give him to me." The anxious mother shifted the boy to Sam's arms. He stared up at her with terror-stricken eyes, his mouth hanging open, lips turning blue.

"It's okay, Randy," she murmured as she strode to the back of the van. "We'll have you fixed up in no time."

Flinging open the back doors, Sam sat down on the floor of the van with the boy in her lap, reached around to his diaphragm, and applied the sharp thrust of the Heimlich maneuver. A green ball of candy shot out of his mouth and rolled along the pavement behind the van. Randy burst into tears. Sam hugged him close.

"It's over, Randy," she murmured. "You're fine." Twisting in her grasp, the boy threw his arms about her neck and continued to wail. Hoisting him up as she got out of the van, Sam cradled him comfortingly as she smiled at Patty.

"He's all right now. Why don't we go inside and sit down for a few minutes?"

Randy had a glass of milk; Patty, a cup of tea. When both had calmed down sufficiently, Sam drove them out to the vineyards. The courtyard was packed with cars and trucks. Parking behind the last vehicle in a line formed on the shoulder of the drive, Sam was met by a swell of music, voices, and laughter issuing from the crowd that spilled across the lawns of the chateau. After profuse expressions of gratitude, Patty bustled off with Randy to find the rest of her family.

As she meandered up the driveway, Sam surveyed the festive scene, which struck her as a page of Americana come to life. To the left, a congregation of silver-haired seniors were tossing horseshoes; to the right, a throng of children played football. A sizable group of mixed ages were gathered before a country-western band in the side yard; still others picknicked on blankets spread beneath the trees. Stopping and chatting along the way, Sam took a leisurely path to the backyard, where she discovered Rae and Nadine on a bench beneath the awning— apparently taking a break from their labors at the serving tables.

"Hey, Sam," Rae said and rose to her feet. "It's about time you showed up. Most everybody's already been through the line at least once. Still got plenty o' pig left, though. Would you like mild sauce? Or do you want to live dangerously and go for the hot?"

Following Nadine's suggestion to try the mild before venturing any further, Sam took her first bite of Georgia pig. The meat was, in fact, one of the most succulent morsels she'd ever tasted; the sauce brought tears to her eyes.

Over the course of the next couple of hours, Sam made slow-moving progress through the majority of the crowd—stopping to visit with Celie, Hannah, the Ingrams, and others. Of one thing she was certain—Matt wasn't in attendance. She crossed paths with Drew on the side yard near the band. He looped a friendly arm about her shoulders, and they listened to the remainder of a lively number together. When the musicians took a break, they chatted about the parade, and the way the rain had held off, although it looked like a storm was closing in.

Finally, Sam decided to broach the question she'd been burning to ask since she first walked up to him. "So," she said in as nonchalant a fashion as she could manage. "Where's Matt today?"

Drew didn't quite conceal the flicker of a smile. "We've got a bunch of clients coming to call on Monday. He's in the winery, picking out vintages for the tasting."

"I see," Sam returned, once again in that light, casual tone.

"Frankly, he's not in much of a party mood these days, anyway," Drew commented with the arch of a brow. "*If* you catch my drift."

Before Sam could respond, a peal of thunder rumbled from the west. She looked swiftly up at the sky. The clouds were low and rolling, and turning darker by the second.

"It won't be long now," Drew said. "I think I'll go help the ladies pack up."

"I'll go with you," Sam replied.

As they proceeded to the rear of the chateau, the wind picked up, and people started folding blankets and gathering belongings. By the time they finished packing the last of Rae's supplies in the back of one of the Pettigrew's Mercantile trucks, the crowd was breaking up in the directions of their cars. Rae climbed into the driver's seat of the truck, started the engine, and looked out the window as Sam and Drew backed away.

"Thanks for the help, you two," she said. "Looks like the clouds are about ready to bust open. Don't get caught in it."

With a quick look at the sky, Drew turned abruptly to Sam. "It's gonna be a bad one," he observed. "While I finish helping Nadine, why don't you go warn Matt the storm's about to break?"

"I don't know—"

"Where is he?" Rae broke in.

"At the winery," Drew answered.

"Why don't I help Nadine," Sam suggested, "and you warn Matt?"

Drew shook his head and grinned. "Nope. All that's left out back is the heavy stuff. Go on, now. Git!" he concluded, and punctuated the command with a playful swat to her bottom.

"Honestly, Drew," Sam complained as she walked around the truck, and was unaware of the way Rae's eyes followed her every move as she launched into a trot toward the winery.

At the far corner of the building, light beckoned from the recessed entrance to the cellar. Moving quietly down the steps, Sam entered the cryptlike room, looked beyond the giant barrels, and saw Matt across the way, where wine racks monopolized the wall from floor to ceiling. Standing before a table set with an assortment of bottles, he was in the process of lifting a wine glass to his mouth, purportedly to sample the vintage. She took a hesitant step forward.

"Matt?" she said quietly, but he reacted as though someone had yelled in his ear. With a choking noise, he spewed forth the wine and spun around.

"That's twice you've done that to me," he sputtered, and wiped the back of a hand across his mouth. Like before, Sam couldn't entirely squash the impulse to laugh. Like before, the urge died as Matt walked up to her—a frown furrowing his dark brows.

"What are you doing here, Sam?"

She pushed a swallow down her dry throat. "Drew told me to come and find you."

"I recall another occasion when he sent you down here to scare the life out of me. What is it this time?"

"The storm."

"What storm?"

"The one that's probably breaking as we speak. Haven't you heard the thunder?"

Slouching to one leg, he attained that inimitable, sexy stance. "As you can probably tell, it's fairly soundproof

down here. Let's go upstairs and take a look. After you,"
he suggested, and Sam had the sensation his gaze was
planted firmly on her backside while she led the way up
the stone steps.

When they reached the main floor of the winery, the
noise of the tempest became apparent. Wind whined
about the eaves; rain pounded on the roof. As Sam scurried along in his wake, Matt stalked to the door and
hauled it open. A wet wind swept inside. Sam stepped
back and peered around Matt's shoulders. Mere minutes
ago the parade crowd had been scattering across the
lawns. Now there was no one—no movement but the
thrashing of tree limbs as the wind whipped the rain in
stormy gusts.

"Everyone surely cleared out in a hurry," Sam commented.

Matt turned and gave her a wry look. "Everyone with
the sense God gave a mule."

"Thanks a lot, Matt. I thought I was doing you a favor."

"Uh-huh," he replied in the way that had always
pricked her ire. "Where's your van?" he added.

"Parked halfway down the drive."

"That's no help."

"Sorry," Sam returned with a flash of her eyes. "I suppose I should have hopped over the hundred other vehicles in the way, and parked it here."

One of his dark brows lifted. "Temper, temper," he
chided, only heightening her irritation.

"At least we've got shelter," she snapped. "Why don't
we just sit it out for a while?"

The place grew suddenly still and intimate as Matt's
gaze roamed down her body. By the time his eyes lifted
to hers once more, Sam's cheeks were prickling with
heat.

"I don't think that's a good idea," he said and—
latching onto her arm—gave no further warning before
yanking her out the door and into the driving rain.

"Matt!" she cried objectingly, but then turned her attention to shielding her face and scrambling to keep up with his long legs as he trotted toward the chateau. When they finally burst through the front doors, Sam was breathless and drenched from head to toe.

Nadine bustled into the foyer. "Lord, have mercy!" she exclaimed. "What in the world happened to you two?!"

Sam could only stare and heave for breath. Dropping her arm, Matt stepped forward.

"Obviously, we got caught in the rain. Why don't you show Sam to a room where she can clean up?" With the merest of parting glances, he started toward the staircase. "Give her something dry to put on," he added to Nadine, and vaulted swiftly out of sight.

"You come right along with me," Nadine said with a worried look. "You're sopping wet."

"I noticed," Sam managed to mutter. "Honestly, sometimes I could wring Matt Tyler's neck."

"Uh-huh," Nadine returned in doubting fashion. Pursing her lips, Sam followed the old woman upstairs to a guest room charmingly furnished in French Provincial, the adjoining bath continuing the theme with a gilded mirror and fixtures.

"Why don't you give me those wet things, honey?" Nadine suggested. "I'll get 'em dried up for you while you take a nice, hot shower."

"Great," Sam mumbled. Quickly stripping down, she handed her clothes out the door to Nadine and turned on the water.

"There's a bathrobe in the closet," Nadine called. "Put that on and come downstairs when you're done."

After luxuriating in a steaming shower, Sam towel-dried her hair and sought out the robe—which was a huge, white, terry cloth thing that must have been bought with Matt in mind. It swallowed her frame and reached to her ankles. But it was soft and warm, and the masculine size of it stirred a feminine thrill. Anchoring the sash around her waist with a trailing bow, Sam went downstairs and found Nadine in the kitchen. The room was filled with the cozy smell of fresh-brewed coffee.

"Feel better?" Nadine asked.

"Much," Sam answered with a smile.

"It'll take a while longer for your clothes to dry. I fixed a fresh pot of coffee. Thought you might like some."

"That would be perfect," Sam replied, and sat down at the kitchen table. Moving over to the counter, Nadine took down a mug . . . and then another.

"Thought Matt might like some, too," she added matter-of-factly. When she finished pouring the two cups, she brought them over and set them on the table in front of Sam.

"How do you like yours?" Nadine asked.

Sam reached for one of the mugs. "Black is fine."

"Matt likes a little sugar in his," the old woman replied, and reached for the sugar bowl. Sam lifted the cup toward her mouth.

"You don't mind taking this up to him, do you?" Nadine asked with a hooded look.

Sam gazed across the top of the steaming cup. "I don't think he'd like that, Nadine."

"Hmph! You know better than that."

"No, really," Sam insisted. "He doesn't want me around. He's told me so point-blank."

"What he says and what he wants are two different things, honey," Nadine said knowingly. "I'd like for you children to work things out. The way he feels about you has changed Matt. Some of it I like, some I don't."

Sam put down the cup and searched the old woman's eyes. "What do you mean, changed? Changed how?"

Nadine shrugged. "He's not wild and woolly and tomcatting around every weekend like he used to. But he ain't laughing much, either. Go on, Sam. Take the man a cup of coffee. What can it hurt?"

"I'm not sure—"

"It's the first door on the right at the top of the stairs," Nadine broke in, and turning her back, waddled across the room to the sink as though the matter were settled.

Sam climbed the stairs with mixed feelings. She knew she was right. Matt wouldn't like this, but that didn't change the fact that the idea of seeing him again had her blood singing through her veins. Balancing a full cup in each hand, she tapped clumsily at the portal with the back of her heel. A moment later the door swung open and he was standing there, wearing nothing but a towel around his hips. She tried not to stare, and failed.

"Come in, if you dare," he challenged.

Her eyes ungovernably fastened on the spectacle of his bare chest, Sam moved inside, only to have him send the door flying shut with a bang. She jumped, the coffee sloshing over the rims of both cups.

"I brought you this," she said and extended a hand, which to her dismay, began to tremble.

"Thanks." Taking the mug, he arched a suspicious brow at her.

"Nadine made it the way you like it."

"Thanks to Nadine, too, then."

She offered a small smile. He didn't return it. Turning her back to him, Sam secretly rolled her eyes at the ceiling and moved across the master suite with open doors disclosing both a spacious bath and an expansive dressing area. Contrasting with the light, French Provincial furnishings of the guest room, Matt's bedroom was decorated in deep colors of burgundy and forest green, and was equipped with an elaborate entertainment center, as well as a king-size bed. The stereo was on, the blues-y notes of a saxophone mixing with the drum of the rain.

"So, this is your room," Sam said, finally turning when she'd put the breadth of the chamber between them.

"This is it," he responded. "Like it?"

"Yes." Sam's gaze trailed about the room. "It suits you."

Watching her over the rim of his mug, he took a gulp of coffee. Sam nervously lifted her cup as well.

"I'd almost forgotten how beautiful you are," he said, making her look up with a start. "But then, you don't want to hear that your eyes are the color of spring leaves, and your hair like the fire of sunset. You wouldn't want

me to say that once a man has touched you, he can't stop
wanting more. Or *would* you?"

Every nerve ending in her body seemed to catch fire.
Sam did her best to return Matt's steady look. "Maybe I
would," she answered. "If you didn't seem so angry when
you said it."

Setting his coffee mug aside, Matt swaggered up to
her. Sam tipped her head to meet his eyes, her breathing
gone shallow, her heartbeat racing.

"But you want me, angry or not," his deep voice rumbled. "And that's why you're here . . . Isn't it?"

The trembling of Sam's hands turned into violent shaking as she stared up at him. "Yes," she finally whispered.

Taking the cup from her hands, Matt set it on a shelf
by the stereo, and peered down on her. Endless seconds
passed as Sam gazed into the amber lights of his eyes.
When he reached for her, it was fast and fierce—
gathering her up so that her feet left the floor as his
mouth swept down on hers.

Sam would have no recollection of how she came once
more to be standing on the floor . . . nor of the moment
his mouth moved along her throat, his hands pulling the
neck of the robe until it fell down her arms and loose to
the waist. Matt's palm cupped a breast. His mouth closed
on her nipple. She gasped, her fingers burying themselves in his raven hair.

"No, dammit!" Straightening sharply to his feet, Matt
yanked the robe up around her shoulders, and whirled
away.

A shard of pain sliced at Sam, digging deeper as he
turned back to her with a burning gaze.

"Is Boston still what you want?" he demanded.

"It's . . . what I feel I was born to do."

"That's not what I asked."

"I know," she murmured, her gaze dropping to her
toes.

"I thought you understood, Sam. Once more around
the park isn't enough for me. If it's not going to happen

between us from now on, I don't want it happening at all."

"I know," she said again.

"Then why the hell are you following me around? First, the winery. Now, this."

Her eyes lifted. "Maybe I couldn't help myself. I miss you, Matt."

"Don't you think I miss you?" he angrily returned. "But I'm through with stolen moments when your guard is down, lady. It's too damn hard coming back to reality when the ride is over."

Sam clutched the robe about her neck as her eyes began to sting. "I guess I should go."

"Yeah," Matt agreed after a tense moment. "I guess you should."

She dashed out, leaving the door gaping. Minutes later Matt was standing by the window, peering moodily across the courtyard when she ran through the rain to her van.

"Be careful, dammit," he muttered as she pulled a skidding turn in the drive, and sped away from the chateau. He was still there, peering into the rainy emptiness, when Drew walked in.

"I just saw Sam race out of here in one of your bathrobes."

"Yeah," Matt muttered, turning away from the window.

"So, what's up, big brother?"

"Nothing."

"Nadine said she came up here to bring you some coffee. What did you do? Chase her off?"

"Something like that."

Drew dropped to a seat on the foot of the bed. "You've been trying to corral that filly in your stall for months, and when she arrives—gift-wrapped in one of your robes I might add—you let her get away?"

"She's leaving, Drew!" Matt boomed. "This time next year she'll be nothing but a memory."

"Next *year*?" Drew questioned with surprise. "It used

to be that when it came to ladies, you didn't think beyond next *week*."

"Did it? I don't remember back that far."

"Oh, man," Drew murmured, shaking his head. "You're
worse off than I thought. When is Sam going?"

"August."

Drew's typical optimism reasserted itself. "That leaves
you three good months. Why don't you make the most of
them?"

"What do you mean?"

"I'm supposed to tell *you* how to make the most of
your time with a lady?" Drew asked with a chuckle that
quickly died in the face of Matt's scowl. "For one thing,
stop chasing her out of your bedroom," Drew continued
on a serious note. "She'll be here three more months.
Maybe you can bring her around."

Matt barked a short laugh. "The only person who can
bring Sam around is herself, and she's not giving up Boston."

"Then take what you can get," Drew suggested.

"No."

"Why not?"

"I might be new at this love stuff, but I figured out
one thing in a hurry. What I can get only makes me crazy
for what I can't have."

With a parting look that matched the fury of the outdoors, Matt walked into the adjoining bath and closed
the door.

Though it was barely six o'clock, the darkness of the
storm made the highway black as night. Wind howled
about the van as its headlights strained to probe through
the slanting rain, along with Sam's aching eyes—which
felt as though they burned to the back of her skull. Grip-
ping the steering wheel in viselike fingers, she blinked
furiously against a resurfacing veil of tears.

When she reached the clinic, she braked to an abrupt
halt, leaned forward, and rolled her forehead against the
backs of her hands. Matt was right. God, she wanted

him—angry or not, right or wrong. Gathering the long folds of his robe, Sam leaped out of the van and scurried to the house.

Her head was bowed, her gaze trained on the puddled path as her bare feet flew along the walk ... up the steps ... Reaching the shelter of the porch, Sam looked up just as something floated past her face. She leaped back with a gasp, nearly tumbled down the steps, and grabbed hold of a porch column.

Sam's heart pounded along with the storm as her startled gaze rose. The hanging effigy was simply crafted—a mere sheet with a noose cinched beneath a makeshift head ... the kind of thing people hung on their porches at Halloween. But this was no Halloween joke. This was a giant voodoo doll swinging in the wind.

The tears Sam had been holding back broke like floodwater through a dam. She whirled on the top step.

"I'm not leaving, do you hear me?" she shrieked at the pouring rain. But there was no reply but the whistle of the wind sweeping across the porch, setting the doll fluttering in a macabre dance.

"Why don't you show yourself, you disgusting coward?" Sam added, her voice breaking before she could finish the words. Tears streamed down her face as she fumbled with the lock and hurried into the house, returning to the porch with a kitchen chair and a butcher knife. Thunder rolled as she sawed away at the rope.

When the thing came free, she dragged it inside, slammed the door, and proceeded briskly into the parlor—where she swiftly if somewhat sloppily laid the makings of a fire. Striking a match with shaking fingers, Sam set it alight. As the flames crackled and climbed, she draped the sheet—along with its insidious trail of robe—on the spearlike tip of the fireside poker, and thrust them into the heart of the blaze.

Like everything else that had been exposed to the storm, the fabric was damp. For an infuriating measure of time, it merely sizzled. Finally it caught, and she replaced the poker with a feeling of dark satisfaction.

Minutes passed with Sam pacing back and forth before the fireplace, watching the ugly threat go up in smoke. Then, as she turned, the long robe wrapped about her ankles—drawing her eye to the hem, turning her mind abruptly back to Matt . . . his image, his kiss, his touch. And then, neither Red Carter's vicious gesture, nor her resulting rage, could stem the melancholia that returned to engulf her.

Abruptly losing her angry steam, Sam sank to a cross-legged seat before the hearth and ran a weary hand over her wet hair. How she longed for the peace of science—the sublime predictability of equations working out to an invariable sum . . . of results inevitably adhering to the principles that governed them.

When she returned from Boston, she'd tried applying those laws to her personal life, only to find that they shifted and twisted and writhed further out of her grasp with each passing day. There was no handhold in this mercurial world of emotion, no haven of sensibility or logic—just unchartable seas of confusion and desire, longing and remorse . . . churning and tossing until the brain was dizzied.

She wanted them both—the future in surgical medicine she'd dreamed of and worked toward for years . . . and the searing passion Matt had brought into her life. Whether or not he admitted it, he wanted it all, too—his beloved vineyards, as well as a family life he'd never had . . . a life in which he envisioned her a full-time partner.

Mentally forcing herself to a clinical distance, Sam gave the situation a pitiless look. Regardless of the way her heart bucked at the conclusion, the result came up the same as always.

"And never the twain shall meet," she murmured. Hugging Matt's damp bathrobe close, Sam stared into the flickering flames.

Chapter Seventeen

The thunderstorm that lasted through the night of the Grape Parade marked the end of the spring rains, and the advent of a period of arid heat. The first week of June passed in a series of uniform days with record-high temperatures and barometric pressure hanging far below average. The second week continued in the same blue-skied, desertlike fashion. Unlike the humid heat of late summer that Sam had known, this was the kind that parched the lips if a person stood too long in the dry wind that coursed gently, constantly, from the west.

Sam drove out to the chateau to see Nadine, whose blood pressure had climbed along with the daily temperatures. Determining to upgrade her medication for a week, Sam cautioned Nadine against exertion of any sort.

"Don't even go outdoors during this heat wave if you can help it," Sam concluded as Nadine walked her to the door.

"I sure hope it lets up soon," the elderly woman replied. "After the storm, Matt was worried about flooding. Now he's worried about a drought. He's got the water trucks going from sunup to sundown."

Sam couldn't resist a searching look toward the grape fields as she stepped outside.

"I thought you two were gonna patch things up a

coupla weeks back," Nadine said. Looking swiftly around, Sam met her steady look.

"Now things are worse than ever," Nadine added on a note of accusation. Sam released a heavy breath.

"That's not necessarily true," she said.

"Hmph! Looking at the way Matt's turned into a grizzly bear, I'd say it's true."

Sam's gaze leveled on the dark, indignant eyes. "It hasn't been easy for either of us, Nadine. But in a way, what happened two weeks ago was good. It opened my eyes to something I hadn't been able to see before."

"Ain't opened 'em enough if you ask me," she sniffed.

Sam backed away with a closed-off expression. "Goodbye, Nadine," she said firmly. "I'll be back to see you in a week."

Gazing across the fields as she drove along the vineyard road, Sam noted the three white tankers cutting slow, steady paths through the acres. She stopped the van and watched for a few minutes. Long, metallic arms extended from each side of the water tanks, spraying a shimmering mist that shone like a rainbow above the leafy vines. One of the trucks turned between the rows and started moving toward the vineyard road. When Sam recognized the broad-shouldered figure in the driver's seat, she shifted into gear and moved on.

Since that night two weeks ago she'd come to believe Matt was right in his avoiding her. The energy between them was a powerful force. But they would never be together. Rather than circling like attracting magnets, forever straining against the urge to fly into each other's arms, it was best simply to stay out of reach.

At times, a stubborn frustration rose to rebel against such thinking. Matt Tyler was unique—the most amazing man she'd ever known. When she was around him, she came alive to a degree she never would have dreamed possible. How could she deny herself that life? *Why* should she?

But then wiser thoughts would return. She'd learned something that stormy afternoon in Matt's room. Every time they were together it became more intense—in both the desire of the moment, and the forlornness that came afterward. If it was this hard *now* to deal with the idea of losing Matt when she left Riverbend, what would it be like if they drew close only to be ripped apart?

No. It was best for them to go their separate ways. But the certainty did nothing to prevent Matt's constant presence in Sam's mind, nor the radiant rush that showered her if she so much as chanced to spot him from a distance.

School was dismissed at noon on the third Wednesday of the month, heralding the beginning of summer vacation. Celie came to the clinic early that afternoon, and stayed through supper. Sam looked for her the next morning, but was called in on a boating accident downriver. She didn't realize until that night that she hadn't seen Celie all day.

Hannah and Jason arrived the following morning at nine-thirty. After lunch, when Celie still hadn't shown up, Sam planned to stop by her house. But then Reverend Bishop suffered heat prostration and collapsed in the middle of Main Street. The sun was low when Sam finally felt comfortable in turning him over to his hovering wife.

Leaving the parsonage, Sam proceeded along the hot pavement toward the clinic. An occasional vehicle passed. Three out of four drivers honked and waved. Not bad, she thought and almost smiled to herself when she looked up, realized she was bypassing Celie's street, and swiftly made the turn. Arriving at the old rowhouse at the end of the block, Sam gingerly climbed the broken brick of the front steps, and rang the bell. When Celie opened the door, it was only the few inches allowed by a chain lock.

"Are you all right, Celie?"

"Sure," she replied, although she didn't look all right. Her face was missing its usual cheery smile, and her eyes looked puffy, as though she might have been crying.

"May I come in?" Sam asked.

"Better not. Grandpa's asleep," she said, and Sam got the immediate impression it was a lie.

"Why haven't you been to the clinic the past two days?"

"I'm sorry. I should have told you. Now that school's out, Miz Ingram can use me full-time."

Sam stared through the crack in the doorjamb. "But we talked about your coming to the clinic on a full-time basis."

"I don't want to be a nurse anymore, Dr. Sam."

"What changed your mind?"

"Just getting waked up to the truth. I ain't ever gonna get outta here. And I ain't ever gonna be no nurse. I'm gonna clean houses just like my mama and her mama." Celie's brown eyes took on a sheen. "And Miz Ingram pays me a good wage."

"Something's wrong, Celie. I know it. Come on. Let me in."

"No, Dr. Sam," she said, her eyes swimming with tears. "I got supper to fix and laundry to do, and I gotta be over at the Ingrams' bright and early. Please, just go away."

With that, she closed the door, and Sam walked back to the clinic with a sharp sense of anxiety. Over the course of the next couple of weeks she stopped by the rowhouse several times, but Celie was never home. On one occasion Sam asked the girl's grandfather if something was wrong.

"No, ma'am," he replied with round eyes. "She's just working hard. That's all."

But Sam knew that wasn't all. As Nadine would say, she could feel it in her bones.

Saturday, July 2

With the Fourth-of-July weekend underway—and everyone's nerves ragged from the continuing heat wave—Saturday night in Riverbend turned rowdy when a water pipe burst in front of Rae's Place, and became a Mecca to a crowd of tipsy revelers.

Having grown tired of light suppers consumed alone, Sam had chosen this night to indulge herself with Rae's cuisine, soak up a little jukebox music, and visit with a best friend. It was after nine when she settled the tab and prepared to depart. By that time the group out front had narrowed to a half-dozen men dancing through the geyser in crazed abandon—their singing and laughter resounding along Main Street.

"Look at that," Sam said, as Rae paused with her just inside the saloon doors. "There's Drew, and Larry, and even the mayor, for heaven's sake . . . all acting like a bunch of barefoot boys."

"I've seen worse," Rae replied with a wry smile. "Even so, you be careful crossing the street. Barefoot boys have been known to act up on hot summer nights."

As Rae returned to finish up with the last of the supper crowd, Sam pushed through the saloon doors. True to Rae's prediction, as soon as she stepped down from the boardwalk, she was drawn into the melee. Drew grabbed her playfully and then she was passed from one man to the other through the spiraling water, becoming drenched in less than a minute.

"That's enough," she sputtered. "Let me go." But her objections went unheeded as the men's laughter roared around her.

"That's quite enough!" Sam added in a ringing tone.

Ignoring her shout, Edwin Pettigrew passed her laughingly back to Drew, who had the misfortune to grab her around the waist just as Sam's temper snapped. She drove a knee into his groin. When Drew doubled over, Sam draped his arm about her shoulders and helped him to a seat on the steps while the drunken men stared.

"There now," she murmured as she patted Drew on the back. "Just sit tight, and you'll be all right in a minute."

"Thanks, Sam," he replied in a rasping groan that started his comrades laughing once again. But not a single one came near her as, with a scolding look for the lot of them, Sam proceeded across the street.

Their howls went on into the night, the men cavorting through the flume of water like children. Peeking across the street through the curtains, Sam saw that Matt had joined them.

No sooner had she turned out her lights than a banging came on her door that would have roused the dead. Pulling on a light wrapper over her T-shirt, Sam went downstairs and opened the door, only to start immediately backtracking as Matt strode inside.

"I just heard the boys gave you a hard time," he announced in a slurring voice. "You all right?"

"Yes," she replied. "Thanks for your concern."

He kicked the door closed behind him, and an air of electricity jolted into the room. Big ... dark ... masculine beyond belief, Matt was soaked from head to toe—his white shirt like transparent gauze over his sun-browned shoulders ... his jeans clinging to the rest of him with X-rated clarity. When he stripped the cowboy hat from his head and threw it heedlessly over his shoulder, an alarm went off inside Sam.

"You can go, Matt," she said, unconsciously reaching up to close the neck of her wrapper about her throat. "Really ... I'm fine. They were just kicking up their heels a little."

"And you kicked back, from what I hear."

He took a few swaggering steps in her direction, leaving a trail of water across the hardwood floor. Sam backed away as he approached.

"I've got enough brothers to know boys will be boys," she said. "And the heat gets to everybody."

"How about you, Sam? Does the heat get to you?"

He reached out, cupped a cheek, and moved close. "Yep. You're damn warm," he said, his voice rumbling suggestively. When she started to turn away, he captured the other side of her face as well. For an instant his eyes burned down on her, and then he grabbed her up to him—his mouth seeking hers as she twisted aside.

"You know you want me," he mumbled against her cheek. "You told me so, yourself."

"Not like this."

Lifting his head, he bestowed a fleeting grin. "This is how I am, darlin'," he said just before his lips crashed bruisingly on hers. After a punishing few seconds Sam managed to wrench away.

"No, you're not," she protested breathlessly. "I don't believe that."

"Believe it," Matt replied, and swept her up in his arms. Before Sam knew what was happening, he'd dropped to his knees, she was on the floor, and he was stretching out on top of her.

"Stop it, Matt. You're behaving like a beast," she managed between panting breaths as she pushed with all her might against his chest.

"Not exactly," he mumbled. His bleary eyes rose lazily to hers as a hand imprisoned her wrists with contrasting speed and positioned them above her head. "You might be able to scare off a beast. That won't be happening with me."

His free hand ripped open the neck of her wrapper, and his mouth settled hungrily on her throat, its hot wetness sending shocks down her spine. Sam's eyelids slammed shut. She'd thought he was better than this. She'd thought she could trust him. . . . When his searing mouth moved below her collarbone, her eyes flew open and she stopped berating her poor judgment. Matt was sopping wet and stinking drunk, and if she didn't do something to stop him, he was going to tear her clothes off and take her here on the floor.

She tried to move her legs, but they were pinned beneath his far more muscular ones. She struggled to move her hands, but his grip was an iron band.

"You're frightening me, Matt," she gasped.

"Sometimes being scared can be a thrill," he replied huskily. "Just let it happen."

"I don't want it to happen," Sam returned, her voice shaking despite her best efforts. "Not this way."

"You say that now, but you won't be saying it in a few minutes. I'm fed up with wanting you and not having you."

"This isn't happening because you want me."

Matt uttered a short laugh, the gust of breath sending chills across her naked flesh. "The hell you say."

"This is happening because you're angry, and you want to hurt me," Sam went on pleadingly. "This is rape." Her eyes filled with tears as he obliviously ripped the T-shirt up her body and bent toward her bared breast.

"Matt!" she cried, her voice heavy with a sob. His breath fanned a rigid nipple as he hesitated.

"Please don't!" Sam added in the same desperate tone.

Matt slowly lifted his head. As his gaze settled on her tearful eyes, his grip on her clothing loosened, his fingers uncurling against her breast. A moment later he was climbing off her, reeling above her, impaling her with a look of fury.

"Damn you, woman," he muttered, and stumbled out of the house.

Early the next morning Matt appeared on her porch with a single gardenia. Though his eyes looked tired, they were clear.

"I'm sorry," he said and offered the flower through the doorway.

Taking the gardenia, Sam looked up with a small smile. "It's okay," she said.

"No, it isn't." Glancing aside, Matt tugged the brim of the familiar cowboy hat to his brow. "I don't know what got into me. I've never done anything like that before."

"It's okay," Sam repeated, drawing the door wide. "Come in."

He met her eyes once more. "No, thanks. I just came by to tell you nothing like that will happen again. Ever."

He started to turn.

"Matt, wait." When he looked around, she added, "Are you sure you won't come in for a minute?"

"Why?"

"To have a cup of coffee, maybe?"

"What would that accomplish?"

Sam lifted her palms, unable to explain her need to talk things out, not to leave this awful tension hanging between them.

"Thanks anyway," he added. When he started to turn once more, Sam stepped forward and put a quick hand on his arm. Looking first at her hand, he lifted his eyes to her face.

"I just . . ." Sam hesitated as she gazed up at him. "I just wish you wouldn't go."

"I have to."

"No, you don't."

"We're both better off dropping it."

"Why?" she demanded irritably. "Why can't you come in and have a simple cup of coffee? Or tea? Or—"

"Because it hurts, okay?" Matt broke in, his eyes flashing. "Being around you—knowing that with every day that passes, there's one less left before you're gone. And you expect me to sit down and have *tea*? I can't handle it! Don't you understand?"

Sam peered up at him for a tense moment, and then she was throwing her arms around his neck, burying her face against his chest. His arms slowly made their way around her back, and hovering on tiptoe, Sam clasped him closer still—flooded with emotion, filled with a dreadful sense of loss. For this desperate moment she held Matt, against all the forces of right and wrong and destiny that had stood between them from the start . . . all the forces that would rise anew as soon as the futile embrace came to an end.

Matt's hands traveled up her back and along her arms. When Sam resisted, he firmly disengaged her wrists from behind his neck. Grasping her balled-up fists in his palms, he brushed a kiss across the backs of her fingers.

He didn't meet her eyes again. Turning swiftly away, he leaped down from the porch, and took long, rapid strides to the Jeep parked out front. With his every step,

Sam felt the terrible distance swell until, once again, there seemed no way across it.

Sam remained in a despondent mood throughout the day. At sundown she hoped to roust her spirits by going outside and finding some yard work to do. She'd just started watering the parched lawn when she was rewarded with the unexpected sight of Celie a mere block or so up the street.

It had been weeks since Sam had caught so much as a glimpse of the girl. At the moment Celie was clutching a bundle and scurrying along the pavement. Her head was bowed, and everything about her demeanor said she didn't want to be seen, much less waylaid. Nonetheless, Sam dropped the watering hose, hurried out the gate, and caught up to her.

"Hi, Celie," she greeted, and kept walking as the girl failed to slow her pace. "What have you got there?"

"Some mendin' for Miz Simon," she mumbled without glancing up. Sam's cheery smile drained away.

"I want to talk to you, Celie."

"I can't stop—"

Reaching out, Sam took firm hold of the girl's arm. "Surely you can spare a minute," she said.

Finally, Celie looked up. Her eyes were full of tears. "Please let me go, Dr. Sam. If he sees me talking to you, he's gonna hurt me something fierce."

"Who?! I won't let anyone hurt you, Celie. I promise."

"Whatcha gonna do?" Celie returned as the tears spilled over. "By the end of next month you'll be in Boston, and I'll be here—right where he wants me. Whatcha gonna do, huh?"

"Something . . . anything," Sam replied urgently. "I'll help you *somehow*. Believe me."

Suddenly the girl broke down. Planting a supporting arm around her slight frame, Sam ushered her swiftly down the street, into the house, and back to the kitchen—where Celie collapsed at the table, buried her head in folded arms, and proceeded to cry her eyes out. Sam sat down beside her, extending as much comfort as she could through a light embrace about her heaving shoulders. When the sobs finally subsided, Sam dampened a cloth and gently mopped Celie's tear-streaked face.

"Now," she said after a moment. "Tell me what's going on."

The girl released a shuddering breath. "Only if you swear to keep it between you and me."

"If that's the way you want it."

"Give me your word," Celie insisted.

"All right," Sam supplied impatiently. "You have my word. Now, what's wrong?"

"He told me to stay away from you and the clinic, and he . . ." Celie hesitated as her eyes began to glitter once again. "He did things to me," she finished in a rush.

"You mean someone molested you?" The girl vigorously nodded. "Who?" Sam added in a deadly tone.

"He'll kill me if I tell! I know he will! He's already caught me twice, and he says he can get me anytime he wants!"

Sam shook her head. "Whoever *he* is, he's a despicable bully, and can't be believed. I wish you had come to me, Celie. I could have examined you for signs of forcible entry, analyzed the semen—"

"He used his *hands!*" she interrupted in a strangled tone. "He said he learned his lesson getting Crystal pregnant, and didn't want to have to throw me in the river, too!"

Sam straightened in the kitchen chair, her head buzzing so that she barely heard her own voice. "What did you say?"

"He raped Crystal, got her pregnant, and then got her drowned," Celie answered. "And he'll do the same thing to me if he finds out I told."

"Who?" Sam murmured from between stiff lips. "Who did this?" Celie's frightened gaze darted between her eyes. "Come on," Sam prodded. "Tell me."

"It was Red Carter!" the girl blurted. Sam's stomach lurched to her throat. With the severest of efforts, she held onto her self-control and swallowed hard against the taste of bile.

"That bastard," she hissed when she was able to speak. "We'll see what Larry Edison has to say about this." At that remark, Celie's dark eyes flew wide.

"No, Dr. Sam! You swore you wouldn't tell!"

Sam gazed at the girl in disbelief. "But I didn't realize what you were going to tell me. The man is a rapist and a murderer. He has to be locked up."

"You gave me your word!" Celie cried. "Doesn't it matter that you gave your word?"

After a moment of staring into the girl's horrified eyes, Sam buried her forehead in her hands. "Yes, it matters," she admitted. The two of them sat there in silence. Finally Sam got up, went into the parlor, and returned with the fireside poker in hand.

"Come on, Celie," she said. "I'll walk you home."

"Then who's gonna walk you back?" the girl said shrilly. "Red hates you more than anybody. What if he jumps on you just like he did to me?"

"I hope he tries," Sam responded. "I'd like to knock his brains out with this poker."

Through that night and the next day, Sam steeled herself against rivaling urges—one, to call Larry Edison; the other, to drive out to the Carter sawmill, plant some dynamite, and blow the place to smithereens. But she did neither as Celie's cry rang in her mind: *Doesn't it matter that you gave your word?*

Night fell, and the pops of firecrackers and Roman candles split the air as teenagers who'd crossed the state line into South Carolina to procure illegal fireworks set off their booty. Sam paced the parlor floor in frustration. If she didn't do something soon, she was going to *pop!* like one of those Fourth-of-July firecrackers. Still, she continued to bite her tongue. . . .

Until the KKK marched through town on their way to the square. As the dozen or so klansmen passed in single file, Sam stepped out on the porch, her ire burning hotter than the blaze of the torches they carried.

Red Carter was out there, probably at the head of the line. The nerve of that monster—marching self-righteously down the street while the innocent girl he was destroying cringed behind locked doors. The fury that exploded in Sam was blinding. All she could see was Red Carter's smirking face as she stormed down from the porch and headed for the square.

The procession of the klan had stirred barely a ripple in Rae's Place. The saloon was full of Fourth-of-July celebrators more interested in drinking than paying attention to a bunch of costumed bigots singing Confederate songs.

The typical foursome was playing cards at the front table, and Matt was losing. Rae stepped up behind his chair and put a hand on his shoulder. "Bring me some luck, darlin'," he said, and happened to glance out the window just as Sam burst through the gate and turned down Main Street, her arms swinging with her angry stride.

"Uh-oh," Matt muttered and rose to his feet. "Come on, boys. I have a feeling we're in for some trouble."

Pushing through the saloon doors, Matt dropped from the boardwalk and broke into a loping trot—followed moments later by a stream of people pouring out of Rae's Place. By the time he reached the square, where a few onlookers had gathered to watch, the klansmen had laid their torches to a bonfire, and Sam had begun to shout— her voice ringing above the melody of "Dixie" until gradually they stopped singing and looked in her direction.

Matt skirted around a few people until he stood at the edge of the gathering crowd. Yards away, Sam struck quite a heroic figure as she stood alone, shouting into the face of the formidable KKK.

"Show yourself, Red Carter!" she cried. "I know you're out here! You're the leader of this illustrious group, right?"

There was a moment of stillness—the only sound, the crackling of the bonfire. Rae appeared behind Matt's left shoulder; Larry and Drew at his right.

"What the hell's going on?" Larry asked.

"Something about Carter," Matt replied with a frown.

"Or are you too cowardly to show your face?" Sam challenged.

"Oh, man," Matt added, his frown deepening as one of the klansmen separated from the bunch and snatched off his white hood.

"What's your problem, girlie?" Red Carter growled.

"You're the one with the problem," Sam fired back. "You're a wife-beating, child-molesting bigot, and your sins have finally caught up with you."

A chorus of angry objections rose from the white-robed group.

"It's true!" Sam shouted. "And his latest victim is Celie Johnson. She told me last night what you've been doing to her, and that you terrified her into silence by threatening she'd end up like Crystal Waters."

"Shut up, you lying bitch!" Red bellowed above a swelling clamor. "You've had it in for me ever since you got here!"

"I'd say it's the other way around," Sam yelled in return. "Some day I'd like to talk to you about dead chickens and human skulls, but right now I don't care about that. Right now, all I care about is the fourteen-year-old girl you raped and murdered!"

The entire crowd gasped as Red shot back, "I ain't done no such thing!"

At that point Sam lifted her arms for quiet, the glare of the blaze painting her silhouette with fire. "Please, everyone!" she cried. "I have proof of what I'm saying. Please! Give me a moment of quiet!"

Like everyone else, Matt fell into a mesmerized silence.

"What do you think you've got proof of?" Red said with a sneer.

Sam folded her arms across her breasts. Once again, like every person there, Matt found himself holding his breath.

"If you didn't violate Crystal Waters," she stated in a ringing tone, "then how did you know she was pregnant?

Crystal kept the matter such a secret that she went into hysterics at the suggestion of a medical exam. I didn't discover it until I examined her after her death. And I told only one person."

Matt stepped forward. "And I told no one."

"So, how did you know, Mr. Carter?" Sam persisted. "How *could* you know to threaten Celie with the atrocity of what happened to Crystal unless you yourself committed it?"

The image of Red Carter forcing his bulk on little Crystal seared through Matt's brain. "God," he rasped. As similar mutterings flashed through the rest of the crowd, all eyes settled on Red.

"You truly are the foulest excuse for a man, Red Carter," Sam uttered, her bright eyes sweeping along the line of hooded klansmen. "I've never been able to understand why you people think the way you do. How far does your hatred go? Will you continue to follow a leader who rapes and kills defenseless young girls?"

Matt was astonished as, one by one, the klansmen began removing their hoods. Everyone knew their identities, of course, except for Sam—who stared as though she couldn't believe the revealed faces she was seeing. Finally, there was only one hooded man left.

"You can't pin nothin' on me about Crystal!" Red boomed.

"He's right," Larry said, leaning to Matt's ear. "The things he told Celie would be considered hearsay in a court of law."

"That won't matter much to George," Matt announced grimly. "In fact, it doesn't matter a lick to me, either."

When Matt started toward the firelit stage, Larry tried to pull him back. Yanking free, Matt kept going . . . and everything seemed to dissolve into slow, unfolding motion.

There was the background roar of the crowd, and Red's ugly smile . . . And then Matt saw him reach beneath the white robe. A moment later, a rifle appeared— the black holes of the barrel shocking Matt as they rose to point directly at him. His booted feet came to an abrupt halt, but it was too late. A sharp crack sounded out, and white-hot pain seared his right arm. Matt grabbed his bicep, felt the warm moisture of blood, and was catapulted back to real time. He looked up with a murderous expression.

"Come ahead, Tyler," Red snarled. "The next one'll be in the gut."

"Have you gone plumb crazy, Red?" Larry shouted. "Put the gun down!" The rifle swerved to fix Larry in its sites.

"Not tonight, Edison. I ain't about to git locked up on the say-so of this Yankee bitch, so don't think about trying nothin'. I can outshoot you any day, and you know it. You coming with me, Hal?"

The last of the klansmen removed his hood. "No, Red. I ain't," his brother said. "I went along with you sampling the black girls that took your fancy, but I never knew you killed any of 'em."

The onlookers broke into a new wave of shouts. Pointing the gun to the sky, Red fired three times, then swiftly leveled the barrel toward the crowd as he backed out of the light of the bonfire.

"The first one that follows me gets it point-blank," he warned, and proceeded to hold the gaping throng at gunpoint until he reached the edge of the street, turned, and fled into the pines. As soon as he disappeared, the crowd exploded in chaos.

"Hold on, everybody!" Larry shouted. "The thing to do is form a posse as quick as we can. Who's got the best dogs?"

Within minutes, a group of men had assembled with rifles, flashlights, and leashfuls of baying hounds. When Matt prepared to go with them, Rae stepped in his path.

"Where do you think you're going?" she asked.

"What do you mean?" Matt returned with a scowl.

"You've been shot, big brother," Drew put in. "You don't need to be traipsing through the woods spilling blood."

"Besides," Larry added. "Carter knows those woods better than anybody. Chances are we won't be finding him. Not with him having a headstart in the dark."

Drew turned with a frown. "Love that optimism, Larry," Matt heard him say as the two of them walked off to join the others.

And so he stayed reluctantly behind, watching with a sense of frustration as the bobbing beams of the flashlights melted into the trees. The voices of the hounds gradually dimmed into the distance, and the crowd on the street began to scatter, streaming off in various directions among flurries of shocked whispers.

"Would a drink help?" Rae asked.

Matt turned, his careless glance sweeping the street, and then backtracking as he saw Sam approaching them.

"I'm sorry," she said as she arrived.

"For what?" Matt questioned.

"For getting you shot. Why don't you let me take a look at that arm?"

He lifted his eyes, met hers, and felt the bolt of emotion strike him to his toes. God, how he loved her, and admired her, and was awed by her. The feelings pounded so fiercely inside him, he thought he might explode.

"It's just a graze," Matt replied. Stepping closer, she lifted a hand. He flinched away. "It's all right, Sam," he added in an irritated tone.

"It should be cleaned and bandaged," she returned firmly.

"I don't feel like it."

"It would only take a minute—"

"Dammit to hell! Would you drop it?" he thundered. Swinging around, Sam walked stiffly away.

"All I want to do is go home," Matt announced to her retreating back. "Rae . . . would you mind driving me out?"

The hot night flew by in silence as they drove to the chateau in the topless Jeep. Rae cast the occasional glance in

Matt's direction, but he only sat like a lump of stone in the passenger's seat, wordlessly staring ahead.

"How about me?" she asked as they walked into the chateau to find it quietly deserted. "Would you bite *my* head off if I suggested cleaning up that gunshot wound?"

They went into the kitchen. While Rae gathered iodine and a bandage, Matt took off his shirt and sat down at the table.

"There you go," she said when she finished. "I don't know if it's as good as Sam would have done, but I reckon it's good enough."

"Thanks," he replied, gazing off into the distance. Rae's eyes fastened on his bare shoulders. Stepping to the back of the chair, she succumbed to the overwhelming temptation and began massaging his neck.

"You're tight as a hatband," she murmured, her fingers kneading their way along the crest of his shoulders. His only reply was to turn his head from side to side, as though he sought to work some misery out of his neck.

"Be still, Matt," she chided. As he complied, Rae's hands roamed his back and his arms, returning along the crest of his shoulders, moving beneath the black veil of his long hair. As if hypnotized, she stared down at the gleaming expanse of his chest. Touch followed desire as, spreading her fingers wide, Rae ran her palms sensually down the front of his body.

"Stop it, Rae."

"It was always good between us, Matt," she replied in a breathless tone, her fingers continuing hungrily across his flesh.

"It's not gonna happen."

She bent to his ear as her hands grazed the waistband of his jeans. "It could be so nice," she whispered.

Abruptly grabbing her wrists, Matt threw her hands aside and sprang from the chair.

"Dammit, Rae! Don't you understand? I don't want anybody but Sam! I'll *never* want anybody but Sam!"

"She'll be gone in a few weeks!" Rae cried.

"Not from my heart!" Matt boomed in return. "Never from my heart! Now, leave me alone!"

He stalked out of the kitchen. Rae stood there stunned. It was as though the blow of his words had knocked her silly. Her life passed before her eyes, all in images of Matt, starting with the first time she'd laid eyes on him ... continuing with treasured memories of his smile, his touch ... concluding with the painful recollection of his glaring eyes.

She didn't remember driving home, although she must have, for her next lucid thought occurred as she was standing in the dark by her bedroom window, peering at the Jeep parked out front. Matt's Jeep. How many times had her heart leapt at the sight of it? Now, it felt as though she had no heart ... as though it had been crushed to dust, along with every naive hope that had lived within it for thirty years.

Walking slowly to the bed, Rae curled up in the fetal position and stared blindly into the darkness.

Two weeks passed, and Red Carter wasn't seen—although Simon's Produce was broken into, the night raider making off with a well-selected haul of provisions. Larry espoused the theory that Red was lying low in the woods somewhere, remaining close enough to slip into town when the need arose.

"Don't worry," Larry said to Sam. "It might take some time, but we'll get him."

But Sam had her doubts. Red Carter was a cunning animal—a predator with a savage sense of knowing when to strike. Until he was caught Celie would remain terrified, and Sam would continue to jump at every bump in the night. The situation was her doing, and regardless of Celie's heartfelt exclamations of forgiveness, Sam felt the weighty responsibility of having set up both the girl and herself as targets for Red Carter's vengeance.

"You stopped him, Dr. Sam," Celie insisted. "And you taught me something important. Giving in to somebody like that is worse than anything else that can happen. I'm still scared, all right. But I'm not letting Red Carter push me around anymore. I'll testify against him in court and I'm coming back to the clinic."

And so Sam got her nurse back, and the household became more closely knit than ever. Even Hannah seemed to exude a new air of determination.

The Simons installed a watchdog at their store; Patty Ingram took on the responsibility of chauffeuring Celie to and from her door; Reverend Bishop's Boy Scout troop toured the sidewalks during the day; and Larry Edison's car was on constant patrol through the night. There was a difference in the townfolk of Riverbend, as though they'd wakened from a long sleep.

The morning of Saturday, the twenty-third of July, was hot and dry like so many others in the long line preceding it. No one was hesitant in calling the heat wave a drought anymore. The entire Southeast was suffering—farmers of every sort in fear of losing their crops; and the news full of warnings against any type of burning as the danger of wildfire escalated.

Dressing in a cool pair of shorts and a light shirt, Sam went down to the kitchen, poured a glass of iced tea, and peered out across the sun-drenched side yard. This was the kind of day she'd have longed to go to the swimming hole—if not for the threat of Red Carter running loose in the woods. Still, she might consider going if Rae would agree to accompany her. But even as the idea dawned, Sam knew she wouldn't.

Just as there was a difference in the town, there was a change in Rae. Oh, she bustled about the inn as usual, but the old lively spirit was missing. Ever since that night at the square . . . The image of Matt's furious eyes flashed through her mind. Shaking off the memory, Sam walked into the parlor, looked aimlessly out the window, and was surprised to see a silver Mercedes parked at the inn.

Lucy Tyler's Mercedes? Sam wondered. Slipping into a pair of sandals, she donned her sun hat and crossed the blazing street. The place was empty but for Rae, who was polishing the bar.

"Is that Lucy Tyler's car out front?" Sam asked as she perched on a barstool.

"It's hers, all right."

"What's she doing in town?"

Rae shrugged as she continued with her polishing. "Who knows? She arrives about fifteen minutes ago, hoity-toity as usual, makes a phone call out to the vine-yards, and then rents a room. Whatever she's doing, you can bet she's up to no good."

Just as Rae finished, the saloon doors swung open, and Drew walked in.

"Mornin', ladies," he greeted, and proceeded directly to the staircase—presumably on his way to Lucy Tyler's room.

Sam and Rae exchanged an arch look as the sound of his footsteps receded up the stairs.

"Well, what do you know about *that*?" Rae murmured.

"I've got a bad feeling about this," Sam replied. "This isn't their first private meeting. Lucy was out at Riverbend one day a few months ago when Matt was out of town. You don't think they could be—you know—*conspiring* against him, do you?"

"Drew conspiring against Matt?" Rae said, her voice heavy with doubt. "Not in a million years. They're like brothers."

"I know," Sam admitted. "But Lucy seems to have some sort of hold over Drew."

"Everybody including Matt knows that Drew's always had a thing for Lucy. Maybe the guy's finally getting lucky." Stashing her cloth behind the bar, Rae started to move away. "And now if you'll excuse me, Sam I've gotta get busy in the back."

"Wait a minute, Rae . . . I've been meaning to talk to you," Sam added when she turned and lifted her gaze. The dark eyes had never looked so dark—as though a light that had burned within them had gone completely out.

"The past few days you haven't seemed at all like yourself," Sam went on. "Are you all right?"

"As all right as I'll ever be," Rae returned with a hint of the old smile, and walked off in the direction of the kitchen.

Drew paused in the open doorway and surveyed the cozy chamber. The fact that Lucy had left the door open didn't surprise him; the fact that she'd drawn the blinds did. She was standing on the far side of the bed, wearing a crisp white dress with black buttons down the front, her hair confined on top of her head with a black ribbon. Picture-perfect as always, she looked as though she were on her way to a fashionable tea.

But she wasn't. She was alone in a motel room . . . waiting for him. Stepping inside, Drew closed the door and tossed his hat to the seat of a nearby chair.

"Nice choice of meeting places," he commented.

"Actually, I had no choice whatsoever," she snapped. "I've tried calling you a dozen times."

"I've been busy."

"It's been nearly three months, Drew. It occurred to me you might have had an attack of cold feet."

His brows furrowed. "I've just been waiting for the right time."

"I want you to do what's necessary, and do it now."

Shifting his weight to one leg, Drew planted his hands on his hips. "Are you absolutely sure you want to continue this, Lucy? After all, sabotage is no light-weight crime."

"I know what I'm doing. And if I weren't sure, I wouldn't be here, would I?"

"So, you have no misgivings about this plan of yours, even though you know full well that it could land us both behind bars."

She released an exasperated breath. "I tried the *lawful* way, and it got me nowhere. The time for this discussion is past, Drew. I've already made a bid on that Riverfront club you like in Savannah. There's nothing more for us to talk about, except the question of when you're finally going to take action."

"I'd say there's one more thing for us to talk about."

"What would that be?"

"My incentive bonus."

"What incentive bonus?" she said, her stance suddenly wary.

Drew's gaze traveled over her, the desire he felt showing clearly in his eyes. A look of shock rose to her face as he started unbuttoning his shirt.

"You can't be serious," she said.

Shrugging out of the shirt, Drew lay it across the arm of the chair. "It's the perfect place, the perfect opportunity. Are you sure you didn't have this in mind when you came out here?"

"Oh!" she exclaimed and turned her back in a huff. "You are detestable!"

Drew walked up behind her. "Used to be I would have taken those words to heart. Now, I don't know. The past few times we've met, I've noticed a difference in you, Lucy."

"I can't imagine what you mean," she muttered to the wall.

"I mean I'm not so sure you really want to say no anymore. Are you?"

"Oh course, I want to say——"

She broke off as Drew reached up to pull the ribbon from her hair. The tresses spilled over his fingers in a golden cloud.

"What are you doing?" she demanded. As her hands rose to the back of her head, Drew dropped the ribbon to the floor and reached around her, his arms closing beneath her breasts. Her palms flew to the backs of his hands.

"Let me go, Drew," she said shrilly.

In reply, he began nuzzling the side of her neck. She smelled like flowers on a summer day. His pulse began to race, and he could feel her pounding heartbeat beneath his fingers.

"Let me go," she said again, this time her voice soft and unmistakably breathless.

God, Drew thought. *She does feel something. She does!* One of his hands traveled to her hip, pulling her close as he pressed the front of his body intimately against her back. He moved to her ear, slipping his tongue in and around as he sent hot breath coursing down the shaft. Anchoring her across the hip, he ran a familiar palm over her breast on his way to the top button of her dress. He moved on to the second . . . the third . . . his fingertips grazing her skin. Lucy's head fell back on his shoulder as he slipped a hand inside the open front of her dress.

"I can't do this," she mumbled.

"I think you already are," he whispered back. She was wearing something silky underneath. Reluctantly leaving the touch of it, Drew returned to the buttons and swiftly unfastened them down to the barrier of his own arm. He released her then, but only to reach up and shift the dress off her shoulders so that it fell with a rustle to the floor.

Still, she continued to face away from him. Drew stepped unabashedly around, swallowing hard as he took in the sight of her from the front. Golden hair waving about her shoulders, she was wearing black heels, shimmering stockings, a lacy white bra and a matching thing so short it could hardly be called a slip. He mutely extended a palm. After a hesitant moment, Lucy placed her hand in his and stepped out of the discarded dress. Inch by inch, Drew's heated gaze moved along her legs, over the curves of hips and breasts, and finally lifted to her face—which, once again, had turned the color of a blushing rose.

"Well?" she said, her blue eyes bright and shining. "Do you intend to make love to me or not?"

"What do you think?" Drew returned in a husky voice.

"Then stop staring, and kiss me."

Stepping forward, he swept her up in his arms. "Yes,

ma'am," he murmured as his seeking mouth closed on hers.

How he managed to hold back as long as he did, Drew would never know. Lucy felt like silk, her body meshing with his as though made purely for that purpose.

Over the years, he'd wondered—if he ever *did* have a chance like this, would it be a letdown? It wasn't. The sharp-tongued bitch was gone, and in her place a soft, tremulous girl wrapped up in the seductive body of a beautiful woman. Her hands played hesitantly over him, igniting a fire he suspected she didn't really fathom, and it occurred to Drew that this could very well be her first lovemaking experience since the tempestuous years of her marriage. The thought only enhanced his drive to make it so damn good she'd never want to do without it.

Extending the foreplay far beyond what he thought he could endure, Drew kissed her from head to toe, his tongue trailing across her skin as he led her hand to explore his body. When he finally entered, he had to go still for a moment, so intense was the sensation.

"Is something wrong?" Lucy gasped.

Drew gazed down at her. "No, baby," he managed with a slight smile. "It's just hard to hold back."

She shocked him by looping her arms about his neck and pulling him down until their lips touched. "Then don't," she murmured.

But he did anyway, and was repaid in full for the effort when he managed to bring Lucy to resounding climax. As soon as hers began, his own burst upon him. They held each other as the intensity raged, and then gradually ebbed into serenity.

Drew's eyes drifted shut, only to spring open as Lucy sat up—swiftly gathering the sheet about her in the process—swung her legs over the side of the bed, and presented her back.

"Are you okay?" he asked.

"I suppose so."

"You don't sound too convincing."

Her shoulders lifted and fell. "Was I . . . ? Was it . . . ?"

"Was it good for me?" Drew supplied teasingly. She shot to her feet at that, dragging the bedclothes with her, and whirled to glare down at him. Lucy Beauregard Tyler—dressed in a sheet, hair tangled with passion, and the light of afterglow shining in her eyes. He never thought he'd see the day.

"Well?" she snapped. "Was it?"

Drew's grin broadened. "You're not bad for a beginner," he said. "But I'd recommend consistent practice. In fact, I'm thinking of making it part of our bargain."

"You'll do nothing of the sort," Lucy returned and glided off in sheet-clad glory toward the bathroom.

"Why not?" Drew called after her. "I couldn't help but notice you kind of enjoyed it, particularly at the end."

Pausing in the doorway to the bath, she swept the skirt of the sheet around like the long train of a gown.

"You truly are detestable!" she then announced.

Drew laughed as she closed the door in his face. But his merry expression soon evaporated as he remembered the momentous reckoning that lay ahead.

Chapter Eighteen

Sam woke with a start and bolted up in the bed. Something was wrong—some noise ... something ... Her gaze flew to the clock on the bedside table. One-thirty in the morning. The image of Red Carter dawned, and she was crawling with chills. She strained to see through the dark bedroom. Just as she noted the blue light flashing beyond the window, she heard the sound that had roused her—Larry Edison's voice, blaring over a bullhorn. Despite closed windows and the purr of air-conditioning, Sam clearly heard his words as she came fully awake: *"Fire! Fire at the vineyards!"*

Hurriedly getting into jeans, shirt, and sneakers, Sam checked off a mental list of things she should take—oxygen, bandages, salve, blankets ... By the time she ran outside, Larry's car was gone, and Main Street was alive with vehicles rushing in the direction of the square. Swiftly loading her supplies in the back of the van, Sam darted around to the driver's side ... halting when she noticed Rae standing idly on her boardwalk.

"Rae!" she called. "Do you want to ride with me?"

"No thanks," she called back.

Waiting for a truck to pass, Sam trotted to the middle of the street. "But aren't you going out there?"

"No," Rae replied, her voice brittle. "I'm never going

to the vineyards again." With that, she turned and
headed for the saloon doors.

"Rae!" Sam called once more. But if she heard, she
didn't show it as she disappeared inside the inn. With a
last mystified look, Sam ran back to the van and joined
the line of cars and trucks streaming toward the highway.
As soon as she cleared the outskirts of town, she spotted
the orange glow in the distance.

"Oh, no," she muttered, mindlessly repeating the
phrase over and over as she turned onto the vineyard
road and gained her first clear view of the blaze. Like an
orange-red sea, it roiled against the night, licking its way
across the southernmost fields.

Up ahead, illuminated by the flashing lights of his car,
Larry was yelling through the bullhorn, directing everyone to park there on the road, well outside the area of
danger. As people spilled out of vehicles, and started running toward the fire, Sam pulled the van around and
screeched to a stop by Larry.

"I've got medical supplies in here," she announced. "I
need to take the van closer."

"Not too close," Larry cautioned. "The wind is from
the west. See to it that you stay well behind the eastern
line."

When he briskly waved her on, Sam turned between
columns of vines and sped toward the site. The vineyard
water trucks flanked the wall of flame, their long arms
replaced with hoses spraying arcs of water. Beneath the
area, firelit silhouettes milled—some hauling buckets of
water, others flailing at the edge of the blaze with wet
blankets, still others busily shoveling a trench.

Swiftly parking by one of the water trucks, Sam leaped
to the ground and snatched a blanket from the rear of the
van. The air was filled with heat and smoke, the bellowing of voices, and the roar of the fire. Running to the side
of the tanker, Sam found George Waters manning the
hose.

"How did this happen?" Sam asked as she quickly
soaked the blanket.

"The Lord only knows," George returned, his eyes trained on the gushing stream of water he aimed at the flames.

Spinning around, Sam started toward the inferno. Just then a gust of wind sent the fire leaping, and there was a scream. The men at the trenchline fell back—all but one, who dashed along the edge of the blaze. Following his movement, Sam recognized Matt just as he grabbed someone, whirled away from the flames, and fell to the ground. Dropping the blanket, Sam ran toward them, realizing as she ran that the victim's shirtsleeve was on fire, and Matt was smothering it with his hands. She arrived just as he climbed to his feet with Clara Simon in his arms.

"We've got to move!" he yelled above the howl of the fire, and stalked to the safety of the line of water trucks before depositing Clara and swiftly looking around. "Sam!" he barked.

"I've got her," she replied, and looped an arm around Clara's waist as Matt trotted toward the firefighting crowd.

"Fall back and start a new trench!" Sam heard him yell as she started toward the van. Throwing open the rear doors, she helped Clara to a seat and reached for her bag.

"Let's see that arm," she said. Lucky for Clara, Matt's action had been so quick that the flames had barely had time to burn through the fabric of her blouse. The hair on her forearm was singed, the flesh having sustained a third-degree burn. Sam was applying salve when George Waters appeared at the back of the van.

"We're pulling out, Sam. You gotta come with us."

"Okay," she answered. "I'm right behind you."

But for the threat of shock, Clara would be fine. Wrapping a blanket around her, Sam climbed through the cab of the van to the driver's seat. A moment later the water truck engines revved, and the forces mobilized—some of the firefighters jumping onto the sides of the trucks, others following on foot. Sam was dismayed as they passed

column after column of leafy vines, the sacrifices that
would fall in order that others might be saved. Finally,
when the lights of the chateau were visible in the distance, the lead truck turned, and they set up new
battlelines against the glowing foe on the western horizon.

Women took stations at the water trucks, soaking the
vines beyond the line where a force of men cleared a
frenzied path ten feet wide. Axes whirled, and posts were
leveled; shovels flew, and clumps of earth and vine
sailed. And all the while, the west wind blew—sending
smoke billowing in their direction as surely as it carried
the flames. Edwin Pettigrew was the first to stumble
away from the ditch, violently coughing. He was followed
by several others. By the time Sam attended to them in
the van and emerged, the fire had marched frighteningly
close—its breadth outstripping the length of the trench
by half. Still, the diggers continued at a furious pace.

Time became distorted as Sam darted back and forth
between the firewall and the makeshift medical station of
the van. Perhaps twenty minutes passed. She had no
grasp of them, but only of the heat and noise—which
grew more intense by the second, as did the sense of
alarm at the wildfire's sweeping approach.

And then it was upon them. There was a suspended
moment of stillness as all eyes turned to the trench. For
as far as it stretched, the fire stopped moving. But no one
had a chance to rejoice as the corraled line of flame blos-
somed to the south. The water trucks lurched into motion, circling to gang up on the south-spreading blaze as
hand-to-hand combat began anew.

Sam didn't want to think about how the battle might
end as volunteer after volunteer began to show up at the
van—some dizzied by heat, others choking from the
smoke, a few with burns. The oldest Ingram boy was
struck in the eye by a smoldering cinder. After cleaning
and bandaging the injury, Sam hurried back outside and
saw with relief that—finally—the tide had turned. The

flames at the boundary of the trench were dying; and
those at the south, clearly on their way to defeat.

When the flames were finally quelled, Matt, Drew,
and George took the water trucks on a tour of the area—
searching out and hosing down smoldering pockets that
continued to glow like evil eyes across the blackened
fields. Sam couldn't begin to estimate how many acres
had succumbed. For as far as she could see, a smoking
swath marked the fire's fiendish path.

As the trucks labored in the distance, their headlights
marking their positions, Sam ministered to a collection of
abrasions and burns. Considering the numbers of inexpe-
rienced townspeople who'd been in close contact with
the blaze, there were relatively few who had been in-
jured, and none severely. She'd just finished checking
once more on the Ingram boy when the water trucks returned, and the three vineyard bosses rejoined the lingering crowd.

Sam stepped away from the van, her gaze fastening on
Matt as he walked forward—scanning him from head to
toe for signs of injury. But all she could see in the meager beam of headlights was that his shirtless body was
streaked with soot, as was his face.

"Thank you," he said to the exhausted folk he faced. "I
want to thank you all . . ." Trailing off, he peered at the
lot of them for a few seconds before he turned and
stalked back toward the idling truck. Drew fell in beside
him, and as they gained several yards of distance, Sam
saw him plant a hand on Matt's slumping shoulder.

"We're mighty beholdin' to ya," George announced. As
he turned to follow Matt and Drew's path, Larry walked
along with him.

"It's a damn shame, George," Sam heard him say. "I'll
be back at first light to see if I can tell how the damn
thing got started."

As the three trucks moved off in the direction of the
winery, the crowd broke up and drifted in solemn groups
toward the vineyard road. Sam gave Edwin, the Ingram

boy, and a few others a ride back to their cars, then drove up to the chateau.

"Well, I made a big pot of coffee," Nadine exclaimed with tearful eyes as Sam walked inside. "But nobody wants none. George went home, and Drew's in the dining room getting ready to drink himself silly, and Matt's acting like he's been struck deaf, dumb, and blind. Lord, I don't know what to do."

Sam put an arm around her shoulders and walked her down the hall. "There's nothing you *can* do, Nadine. You're here if they need you. They know that. But they're going to have to work through this in their own ways. I'm going to check on both Drew and Matt. So, don't worry."

"Damn drought!" the elderly woman muttered as Sam opened the door to her room. "I always despised a damn drought. Look at what kind of misery it brings."

Sam ushered her over to the bed. "Lie down, Nadine. And try to stop thinking about droughts and misery."

Closing Nadine's door behind her, Sam proceeded to the dining room, where Drew was parked in a chair by the window. As she walked in, he tossed down the contents of a shot glass.

"Are you hurt, Drew?"

"On the outside, no," he replied woodenly.

Sam strolled closer. Like all those who had fought the fire, he was wearing its blackening marks. "Is there anything I can do for you?" she added.

"Yeah. Go upstairs, and take care of Matt. He's been burned in more ways than one."

With that, Drew pushed up from the chair and strode to the liquor cabinet. Sam climbed the stairs to find the door to Matt's bedroom open. The light of the hall lamp spilling through the doorway was the only illumination in the room, where he sat in the shadows on the foot of the bed. Sam walked in and set her bag down beside him.

"What time is it?" he said without looking up.

"I don't know. Four o'clock, maybe. Are you all right?"

"I guess so."

Sam knelt between his sprawling knees and put a lifting hand beneath his chin. Matt slowly looked up, his skin so dark from the fire that the whites of his eyes seemed to jump at her from the shadows. "I don't see any serious injuries," she said with a small smile. "Although it's hard to tell beneath all that soot. Let me see your hands."

He mutely offered his bearlike paws. Sam turned them in gentle hands and examined the palms. Even in the dim light she could detect several blistering welts. A lump rose to her throat as she remembered the way he'd snatched Clara from the flames.

"You have a few blisters here," she murmured. "But considering the way you spent the past couple of hours, I'd say you got away lucky."

"Sam," he uttered, his deep voice filling the room. She looked from his hands to his eyes and found them glistening.

"Help me," he said.

"Of course I will, Matt." She started to reach for her bag. He caught her wrist.

"I don't mean that. Help me get away," he mumbled with a wince as his blistered fingers seemed to clench spasmodically.

Sam knew instantly what he was saying. Suddenly the clock seemed to spin back six months, and it was *she* begging *him* to drown out the reality of Crystal Waters's tragic death. The hurt Sam felt for him swelled inside her until she thought she might burst.

"They were kind of like children," Matt rumbled. "My vines—"

Shifting forward, Sam stopped his lips with her own, and proceeded to kiss him with a desperate passion that strove to sweep away the pain. Matt embraced her and would have fallen back with her across the covers. Planting her hands on his shoulders, she pushed firmly away and rose to her feet. He looked at her questioningly but said nothing as she walked away from the bed.

Sam closed the door and locked it, plunging the room

into darkness but for the silvery moonlight streaming through the west window. Never before had she experienced the intensity of emotion that overwhelmed her at that moment. She felt the power of Matt's need for her, the hunger of hers for him. But her fingers were surprisingly steady as Sam unzipped her jeans and shed them, along with her panties, to the bedroom floor.

She walked back to the bed, unbuttoning her shirt in the process. As she stood before Matt, she shifted it off her shoulders and let it fall. His gaze roamed her nakedness before lifting to her face. In the darkness his eyes caught the sheen of the moonlight. There was no doubt that the glittering look within them had changed from agony to desire.

Sam extended a hand. He silently took it and followed her lead into the bath. As Sam started the water, Matt stripped off his boots and jeans. She stepped into the roomy stall, moved beneath the showering jets, and allowed the cleansing water to drench her. When she wiped her eyes and turned, she found Matt watching her, already in a full state of arousal.

Once again Sam offered a hand. As he joined her in the shower, she turned him beneath the water. He planted his palms on the wall of the stall as she soaped her hands and began washing him from the back—her palms trailing along the muscular arms, over the shoulders, across the incredible back. As the soot was washed away, she discovered several abrasions and pressed a kiss to each.

The water spiraled over Matt in a crystal veil, shimmering on his body with heart-stopping beauty. Unable to resist the urge to take him in her arms, Sam moved full-length against his back, reached around his stomach, and felt his sharp intake of breath. Seconds later Matt spun in her embrace and gathered her up as he had that day in the swimming hole. Her arms were locked about his neck; her legs, around his waist; her body poised above his formidable manhood. He kissed her with the same furious passion that was racing through her veins, and as he entered her, Sam vaulted to a plane of sensation that left her oblivious to all but the man possessing her.

The love they made blazed like the fire they'd fought together, and was just as consuming. During the midst of it Matt maneuvered a trip from shower to bed, somehow managing to remain inside her along the way. The climax that eventually claimed Sam shook her to the core, and apparently had the same effect on Matt. When she surfaced from a state of dozing ecstasy, he was soundly asleep in the circle of her arms.

Sam's mind came acutely awake. Suddenly, she was aware of all kinds of things—the euphoric fulfillment of lying next to Matt; the creeping dread that it would never happen again; the glaring fact that although she'd never put the feeling in such words, she was in love with the man. She, Sam Kelly—supposedly a bright woman— had fallen desperately in love with a man who'd be out of her life within a month. Lifting a hand, she ran her fingers over his silky hair.

"Sam?" he mumbled.

"Hmmm?" She shifted back to see his face. Matt's eyes remained closed as he bestowed a sleepy smile and turned on his side. Sam nestled against his back, and stared at the eastern window as the gray square gradually brightened with the approaching dawn.

When she finally climbed from bed, the sun was fully up, its light outlining Matt's sun-bronzed body with a golden glow. Having kicked off the covers, he lay before her in all his naked glory. Sam couldn't take her eyes off him as she noiselessly pulled on her sooty clothes.

He was magnificent, and she loved him. What would it be like to wake up every morning in that bed with Matt beside her? The idea shocked her with a rush of feeling; the stark thought of what she'd have to give up struck her with terror. Everything she'd worked for, every dream she'd ever had for the future . . . home, family, the only kind of life she'd ever imagined living. And yet Matt would settle for nothing less.

Bending over the bed, Sam trailed loving fingers along the side of his beard-stubbled face. He didn't move a muscle, and she left him sleeping with the peace of one exhausted beyond remembrance while she crept from his chamber with stinging eyes.

Scarcely more than an hour after Sam returned to the clinic, she received a call from Edwin Pettigrew, whom Larry had contacted by radio.

"He needs you out at the vineyards," Edwin said.

"What's wrong now?" Sam questioned with a flash of alarm.

"Two things. First of all, Larry and the boys he rounded up to help him have found evidence that the fire was deliberately set with kerosene. Second . . . well, they found Paw Greenfield. He's dead, Sam."

In the clear light of a Sunday morning, the decimated acres glared a blasphemous black. Adding to the morbidity of the scene was the motionless figure of Paw Greenfield, who lay mere yards from the edge of the fire's path—still holding onto a charred blanket he'd apparently used against the blaze. As Larry and a half-dozen "deputies" hovered, Sam knelt by the body. It didn't take long to determine the cause of death.

"Smoke inhalation," she pronounced. Rising to her feet, Sam continued to look down on the old man. "I don't recall seeing him at all last night. I suppose there was too much happening for anyone to notice when he got in trouble."

"So, now it's not just arson," Larry observed. "It's manslaughter."

Sam lifted tired eyes that felt as though they'd burn forever. "Have you found anything that might suggest who did this?"

"Not who, but we did find the path we think he used—an old animal trail leading into the woods. It comes to mind that Red Carter disappeared in those woods not much more than two weeks ago, and it was after a violent confrontation with Matt."

"Red Carter," Sam mused, the familiar shudder of disgust sweeping over her.

"It also comes to mind that when the Simons' place was broken into, part of what the crook made off with was a supply of kerosene. It wouldn't have taken much to start a wildfire—not with the drought we've had. I think I'd better take this posse of mine on a fresh hunt."

"But if Red did this horrible thing," Sam said, "don't you think he'd finally leave the area?"

Larry tipped his hat back on his head. "I doubt it. Just like before, I reckon Red's got his best chance of surviving right here on his home ground. The man's a damn good woodsman, and a damn good hunter. He probably figures he could hide out around here indefinitely. And he might be right."

"Don't let him get away with this, Larry," Sam said in a deadly tone. "I never thought I'd say this about a human being, but I'd love to see Red Carter fry."

As Larry and the others began discussing plans for the search, Sam returned to the clinic. When Celie and Hannah arrived at midday, she retired to her room and tried to take a nap, but found herself besieged by thoughts of Red Carter, Paw Greenfield, and—of course—Matt. Although Sam instinctively sensed that he wouldn't call or come by, her ears pricked at every noise. Finally, she gave up on the notion of resting and went downstairs, where she contented herself with the company of friends, and the entertainment of Jason's lighthearted play.

Celie, Hannah, and the boy left at sundown. Shortly after that, a Pettigrew Mercantile truck stopped in front of the clinic, and Edwin and Larry appeared at her door.

"Guess who we've got in the flatbed?" Larry said.

Sam stepped out on the porch and peered across the yard. In the dusky light, the white sheet covering a form in the back of the truck glowed with eerie portent.

"Who?" she questioned, curiosity mixing with alarm.

"Red Carter," Edwin said.

"The first time around we didn't think of looking out at Ezra's Swamp," Larry said. "We didn't figure anybody would be fool enough to try hiding out there. Guess Red figured that, too, and was cocky enough to think he could pull it off. He didn't."

Stepping forward, Sam moved with the two men to the edge of the porch. "How did he die?" she asked.

"We found him halfway in the shallows," Larry answered. "The best I can figure, he was cutting across and stumbled into a mess of moccasins."

"Moccasins?" Sam repeated with a quick look.

"Maybe two dozen or more," Edwin commented. "Sometimes they congregate in the water during the heat of the day. And everybody knows moccasins would just as soon strike as look at you."

"It looks like they made quick work of him," Larry added. "But we figured we should let you verify that before we take him on out to Hal. By the way, have you stayed in touch with Ida?"

"I've had a couple of letters, yes. She's in a shelter in Savannah. They don't give out the address."

"I'll have to notify her somehow," Larry said. "Regardless of their split up, she's still Red's legal wife. I guess she stands to inherit half the sawmill unless he left it to his brother."

Sam nodded. "She can be reached through Candler Memorial Hospital. I'll give you the phone number. But for now, I suppose I should examine the corpse."

"It's not pretty," Larry warned as she started down the steps.

"I'm sure it isn't," Sam replied.

There were twenty or so purplish swellings marking the sites of bites. As Sam examined the body, she formed a theory of what must have happened. The first half dozen or so strikes to the legs had brought the man down, at which point the snakes had closed in on hands and arms, and even the neck. There were two bites near the jugular, one almost directly into the artery. Sam covered the body and backed away from the truck.

"Considering the massive amount of venom that entered his body at one time," she began, "I'd say Red

Carter went into immediate shock, stopped breathing, and was dead within minutes."

Looking up, Sam met Larry's eyes. "I can't help but note a certain poetic justice in this," she added quietly. "I never met a man I considered more fit to live with snakes, and he turns up dead from their poison."

"So, that's it, then," Edwin murmured. "Crystal, Celie, Matt . . . all three are avenged."

Sam looked around as a revelation suddenly dawned. "Red was most certainly responsible for the unspeakable things that happened to Crystal and Celie. But he didn't set the fire at the vineyards."

"How do you know?" the two men demanded in unison.

"Judging from the condition of the corpse and the extent of rigor mortis, I estimate he's been dead forty-eight hours. Maybe longer. One thing is certain—he wasn't walking around the vineyards last night. He was lying dead at Ezra's Swamp."

"Who the hell did it, then?" Larry muttered.

Sam lifted her shoulders. "I don't know."

"I've had my fill of mysteries for one day."

"At least you found Red," she replied. "That's one mystery we no longer have to worry about." But as the men drove away, Larry's question rang in Sam's mind—*Who the hell did it, then?*

The more she thought about it, the more an ugly suspicion congealed. Images tumbled through her mind— Drew digging the firewall beside his best friend, their shovels moving in uncanny rhythm . . . Drew gazing at Lucy with helpless hunger in his eyes.

Once again Sam heard the echo of their cloistered voices behind the study door of the chateau: *This kind of thing harms everyone, Lucy. . . . There's no other way, Drew.*

Once again Sam saw his tortured look after the fire. *Take care of Matt. He's been burned in more ways than one.*

Was Drew's torment attributable purely to sorrow? Or

was it *guilt* that he'd been seeking to drown in a bottle of whiskey?

God, she didn't want to think it. But as the night wore on, and fragments of memories fell together in an increasingly clear picture, Sam couldn't think of anything else. Despite her weariness, she hardly slept. It was barely breakfastime the next morning when she drove out to the chateau.

Without ringing the bell, she walked in, and found Matt and Drew having coffee at the dining table. With typical, gentlemanly aplomb they rose from their chairs as she entered the room—both wearing lightweight shirts and jeans suggesting they were ready for a day's work, both sporting Band-Aids here and there testifying to the night of the fire.

"Sam, honey!" Nadine greeted from the kitchen doorway. "Will you have some breakfast?"

"No, thanks," she answered with a brief smile that faded as she looked back to the table, her gaze drawn ungovernably to Matt. The last time she looked upon him, he'd been sprawled on the king-size bed upstairs—his body caressed with the soft light of dawn. Looking swiftly to the other side of the table, Sam made herself concentrate on the issue at hand.

"Could I speak with you privately, Drew?"

"About what?"

"I'm not sure you want me to announce what it's about."

Both men drilled her with their eyes—Drew's, puzzled and questioning; Matt's, growing narrower by the second.

"There's not anything you could say to me that you can't say in front of Matt," Drew suggested. "Is there?"

"Maybe not," Sam answered. "Maybe it's best just to go ahead and get it out in the open. Why don't you both sit down?" As they complied, Sam moved to the head of the table but found herself unable to voice the accusation.

"What's on your mind?" Drew asked, breaking her paralysis.

"The question of who set the fire."

"Larry's leaning toward the idea of Red—" Drew started to say.

"They found Red late yesterday," Sam interrupted.

"We heard." Matt muttered.

"Well, did you hear how long he'd been dead? It was at least a couple of days. He couldn't have set the fire."

"Carter didn't do it," Matt acknowledged. "What do you want with Drew?"

Drawing a sharp breath, Sam looked steadfastly in Drew's direction. "I'd like to ask him about his involvement with Lucy Tyler."

"You don't know what you're talking about," Matt muttered.

"I hope you're right," Sam replied, her eyes remaining on Drew.

"What about my involvement with Lucy?" he asked.

"She was in Riverbend the day of the fire. And a few months ago when Matt was out of town, Lucy was here at the chateau. I overheard the two of you, Drew. Do you deny that you agreed to sabotage the vineyards on her behalf?" She was gambling a little, stretching what she'd heard to try and force an admission.

Drew looked at Matt, then back at her. "No," he answered after a few tense seconds of silence. "I don't deny it."

Sam's wide eyes swerved to Matt. "Did you hear that?"

"I heard," he replied.

"Is that all you can say?"

Matt rubbed his hand across his brow before folding his hands on the table and giving her a stony look. "I insist that you keep this confidential. The fact is Drew was only carrying out a plan."

"What plan?" Sam demanded.

"When Lucy approached Drew with a shady proposition, he told me about it, and we've been stringing her along ever since. The afternoon of the fire, we got enough to make it conclusive."

"I don't understand," Sam mumbled.

"I've been recording her," Drew said. "There's enough on tape to charge Lucy with conspiracy to commit a federal offense. We're betting that rather than have the tapes turned over to the authorities, she'll opt to give Matt a long-overdue divorce."

"It was Drew's plan," Matt put in. "Now, it's his play. He's going to Savannah in a few days to spring the trap."

"I'm ... sorry," Sam stumbled.

"That I'm about to become a free man?" Matt snapped.

"Of course not. I mean for what I was thinking about Drew. I feel like a fool."

Matt's eyes glittered beneath scowling brows. "Welcome to the club. By the way, thanks for the *TLC* after the fire. That's a helluva bedside manner you've got there. Unfortunately, you slipped away before I could tip you for a job well done."

"Damn, man!" Drew exclaimed with a frown.

"That's low, Matt," Sam said, her sparkling eyes leveled on his.

Once again he rose to his feet. "I know," his deep voice rumbled. "I'm sorry."

They stared at each other for a long moment.

"Well, if Drew had nothing to do with it," Sam eventually said. "And Red Carter didn't set the fire, then who—"

"Sam," Matt broke in, seemingly restraining himself as though he longed to bellow at her. He ran a frustrated hand over his hair. "I don't really give a damn about that right now, okay?"

Stalking away from the table, he presented his back as he slouched against the wall by the window. Sam's gaze darted to Drew, who released a heavy breath and shrugged as if to say he had no control over his friend.

"I apologize for what I was thinking, Drew."

"Apology accepted," he replied. "Standing in your shoes, I'd have thought the same thing."

"Goodbye, then," Sam said, her gaze flickering to Matt, who didn't turn. Spinning away from the table, she strode out of the chateau, her heart thundering and aching with equal measure.

Sam started up the van with a quick hand, and sped onto the vineyard road. On each side of her, the vines were like green walls. Soon it would be time for harvest. She'd be gone before then. Up ahead and to the left, the leafy green came to an abrupt halt where the scarred acres began. The impulse to return to the origin of all this destruction struck out of the blue, and for the second morning in a row, she found herself turning between columns of grapevines and driving in that direction.

Reaching the edge of the charred fields where the fire had started, she got out of the van and headed toward the woods where the perpetrator supposedly had fled. She spotted the animal trail Larry had mentioned and followed it beyond the line of trees. Sam stopped just inside the screen of pines. If the arsonist had wanted a concealed vantage point from which to survey the vineyards, he couldn't have done much better than this.

She turned in a slow circle, her eyes scanning the patchwork of trees and underbrush, meadow grass and pine needles. She didn't know what she was looking for—why she should think she might spot anything of significance when a half-dozen men had combed the area. She was turning to go when a flash of yellow caught her eye.

Stepping off the path, Sam crouched to her knees and retrieved the delicate chain of dandelions. Her heart plummeted to her feet as Rae's voice rang in her memory—*It's just something I do to pass the time.* . . .

When Sam walked in, the place was empty except for Rae, who was putting away fresh glasses in the overhead racks behind the bar.

"Hello, Sam," she said, but as had been typical for the past few weeks, the greeting was bereft of the remembered, cheery smile. "You're up and around early this morning," she added. "I don't open till ten, but I can put on a pot of coffee if you like."

"I don't want any coffee," Sam replied dismally.

"No? What can I do for you, then?"

Walking up to the bar, Sam held out her palm. "Please tell me this doesn't mean what I think it does, Rae."

Rae's arms drifted to her sides. "Where did you find that?"

"In the woods by the burned-out vineyards."

"Well, well."

"Tell me you didn't do it, Rae."

Rae slowly shook her head. Like a sprung trap, Sam's hand clenched about the damning wildflowers.

"Why?" she whispered. "You love Matt." Rae laughed, and the sound was horrifying, like the mad keen of a banshee.

"You say the word *love* as though only good and holy things can come of it. Don't you know by now that's a fairy tale?" The haunted look that dropped over Rae's face was even more terrifying than the eerie laugh.

"Yes, I love Matt," she continued in a hollow tone. "I've loved him so hard that it's eaten me up day after day, year after year, on and on until I thought I couldn't stand it anymore. But I went on standing it, just to have him in my life, just to catch the crumbs he tossed my way."

"Oh, Rae," Sam murmured, her voice filled with sympathy. Rae gazed beyond her with a dazed expression, seeming not to have heard as she carried on.

"It nearly killed me when he married Lucy. Then came the comfort of learning he despised her. I could handle the fact that he wasn't free. I could handle him having one affair after another. What I couldn't take," Rae forced in a choking voice, "was watching him fall hopelessly in love right under my nose." Her dark eyes swerved to Sam.

"I knew it," she concluded. "From the moment I met you, I pictured you and Matt, and I just . . . knew."

"Nothing's going to happen between Matt and me," Sam softly replied.

"It's already happened!" Rae cried with painful sharpness. "He's so head-over-heels in love with you he can't see straight! It's like a fever burning him up inside, haunting every minute he draws a breath. Believe me, I know how he feels. Why didn't you just go? You hated the house. You hated Riverbend. And you were being terrorized. Why didn't you just go back to Boston?"

"I . . . guess I'm just not the type to give in, Rae. Not to Riverbend. Not to Red Carter."

"It wasn't Red!" Rae exploded. "Don't you get it?"

The dawning of an idea shocked Sam so that her heart seemed to skip a beat. "No," she said. "I don't get it."

"Yes, you do. You just don't want to believe it."

"The mess on my door . . . the chicken . . . the skull . . ."

"The dummy hanging on your porch," Rae supplied.

"I never told anyone about that."

"I know. Not even your best friend here."

Tears started to Sam's eyes. "You mean all this time you've just been pretending—"

"I never had to pretend to like you, Sam. But I couldn't help feeling other things, too. Old Juda managed to drive Mary Tyler crazy. I thought the least I could do was drive you out of here. You'd be back where you belonged, no worse for the wear, and things could go back to the way they'd always been."

Rae hesitated, her eyes shining with the same pain Sam felt in her own. "It wasn't until the night Matt was shot and I drove him out to his place that I realized things never would have been the same, even if you *had* run. Here, or in Boston, you've got Matt, and it's not going to change. You're the love of his life. There's irony for you—Matt Tyler, the biggest ladykiller in Georgia, turns out to be a one-woman man."

Putting a hand to her brow, Sam started to turn. "I can't take any more of this—"

"Hold it!" In a flash, Rae had reached beneath the bar

and produced the pearl-handled Colt-45. Sam lifted wide
eyes from the barrel of the gun pointed directly at her
heart.

"Just hold on." Circling the bar, Rae kept the pistol
trained in Sam's direction as she came to stand mere feet
away.

"Don't, Rae," Sam whispered. "Don't do this."

"You know what I've learned, Sam?" she replied with
tears spilling down her cheeks. "The journey to hell
starts with a small step that doesn't really seem to matter.
And then the steps grow bigger, the road darker, and one
night you find you've gone so far there's no turning back.
The devil is a tricky son of a bitch. I set fire to the vineyards to make Matt hurt the way I was hurting; instead,
I ended up sealing my own fate."

"It doesn't have to be that way," Sam said in a tone of
desperation. "Please, Rae. Don't make things worse."

"Things can't get any worse. Paw Greenfield is dead
because of me. I can't live with that, and I damn sure
ain't going to jail for it. They call suicide a deadly sin,
don't they?"

As a new shock stunned her, Sam's heart seemed to
stop once more. "What?" she heard herself say as if from
a distance.

"Pray for me, Sam." With that, Rae turned the revolver
and pointed it at her own chest.

"No!" Sam screamed, lunging forward as the gun went
off. Rae's knees buckled. Sam grabbed for her, tried to
support her, and ended up cradling Rae's head in her lap
as the two of them sank to the floor.

In the seconds it took to fall, a red circle of blood had
bloomed on the front of Rae's blouse. Swiftly covering as
much of the stain as she could with her palm, Sam applied pressure to the center of the spot in an instinctive
effort to stem the flow. Blood seeped around her fingers
as she looked desperately into the tear-streaked face of
her friend.

"Shit," Rae muttered, a smile flickering across her lips
as her eyes closed. "Hell can't be any worse than this."

"Rae?!" Sam's bloody hand moved scant inches to her heart and found it still. "Rae?!" she cried again.

The gunshot was like the ring of an alarm. Minutes after it sounded out, Larry Edison and a host of others rushed into Rae's Place, halting in their tracks when they discovered Sam sitting in the floor clutching Rae's bloody body. On one side of them lay a Colt-45; on the other, a chain of dandelions.

Chapter Nineteen

Thursday, July 28

Everyone within miles had loved Rae, and despite the shocking circumstances of her death, most of the countryside turned out for her funeral. It seemed fitting that the day should be the first rainy one in weeks. A fine drizzle fell, not a rain really, but more a melancholy mist that enveloped the cemetery in somber gray.

The Reverend Bishop delivered a touching eulogy that avoided all allusion to the violent way Rae died, until his concluding prayer that she might "find the peace she so desperately sought."

As the crowd broke up and moved away, Sam remained at the gravesite. From the shelter of her umbrella she regarded the flower-laden casket and found it hard to accept the fact that Rae was inside. A few minutes passed, and then Matt stepped up beside her and placed a gardenia among the roses. As Sam looked up with blurring vision, he reached for the umbrella and offered an arm.

"I can't imagine Riverbend without her," he said as they walked away from the monument.

"Neither can I," Sam replied. They didn't speak again until they cleared the iron gate of the cemetery. There,

Matt handed her the umbrella, stepped back, and seated
a black Stetson on his dark head. Framed by the glory of
ancient oak and Spanish moss—wearing a tailored black
suit and dark tie—he was, as usual, so striking that he
took her breath.

"Larry told me Rae confessed to setting the fire," he
said.

"Yes," Sam returned.

"And then she killed herself," Matt brusquely went on.
"You were with her when she died. Why did she do it,
Sam? Why did she do *any* of it?"

"Don't you know?"

"No. I don't." Matt peered down on her from beneath
the dark brim of his hat, his eyes filled with hurt and
confusion. Sam searched for a kind way to say: *It was
you, Matt. She loved you to the point that it killed her.*

"Rae had lived with a great deal of pain for a long
time," she said evasively.

"You mean she was sick?"

"You could call it a sickness. In the end I believe it
drove her a little mad, and she struck out at the one she
loved best. She always loved you, Matt. You must know
that."

"Yeah," he admitted after a moment.

"Then remember that about Rae, and forget the rest."

A faint smile curved his lips. "Thanks, Doc."

"You're welcome," she replied with the beginnings of
an answering smile that quickly died as his disappeared.

"Your time here is getting pretty short," he commented.

Sam glanced aside, momentarily studying a forming
puddle on the sidewalk before lifting her gaze once
more. "Actually, it's shorter than expected," she said. "I
heard from the corps yesterday. They're sending a new
doctor in two weeks."

"Two weeks," Matt repeated curtly. "That cuts into
your year, doesn't it?"

"By a number of days, yes. But it seems my replace-
ment is eager to get his service underway."

"And you're just as eager to have yours finished."

Sam gazed into his eyes. "I have mixed feelings."

"That's nothing new."

"Dammit, Matt. You know I'll miss you."

"Yeah," he said. Taking his hat by the crown, he crammed it low on his brow. "Just like I know Rae loved me. Somehow, I can't seem to draw much comfort from either thought."

He started to step away, then looked around once more. "I'd like to know when you're leaving."

"I wouldn't go without saying goodbye," Sam managed as her throat seemed to constrict. With no more reply than a predictable tug of his hat brim, Matt strode into the mist.

Sam turned in the opposite direction, her sad gaze lifting as she strolled along the walk, which by now was deserted but for a woman standing ahead at the corner of the black iron fence of the cemetery. Fashionably dressed in a navy dress with matching heels and umbrella, she stepped forward, and Sam noted her walking cane.

"Hello, Dr. Sam," she said.

Sam's eyes flew wide as the voice tipped her off; otherwise, she never would have known the woman. The long hair once streaked with gray was clipped to chin length, and a pleasant chestnut brown. The eyes, once downcast so much of the time that one failed to note their color, were a bright cornflower blue. And beneath the stylish hemline of her skirt extended two well-turned calves.

"Ida?" she breathed.

"Reckon I look a mite different," she said with a small smile.

"Reckon so," Sam agreed. Bending beneath their clashing umbrellas, Sam gave her a quick hug. "You must be feeling wonderful to look so marvelous. How's the pain?"

"There ain't no pain *atall*—not compared to what used to be."

"How about your therapy? How's that going?"

"Dr. Brooks released me just yesterday. Said I was doin' so good I didn't need to go back to the hospital no more, just keep on workin' my leg and come to see him in three months."

"Why don't we go to the clinic, have a glass of tea, and you can catch me up on everything?"

"Can't," Ida replied. "Hal's waiting by your place to take me on back to the house. I'll walk up the street with you, though."

And walk, she did—with a barely perceptible limp that made the cane seem more for looks than support.

"I'm absolutely amazed by you," Sam complimented.

"Thanks," Ida replied with another flickering smile.

"When did you return to Riverbend?"

"Just this morning. Hal's been right neighborly. He picked me up at the bus stop, and we buried Red out back with their folks."

Sam glanced ahead, a hard look crossing her face. "I suppose I should offer my condolences on the loss of your husband—only I'm too well aware that it's no loss."

Ida expelled a heavy breath. "That's for sure. I know it ain't Christian to be glad somebody's dead, but I got the feelin' God forgives me for feelin' that way about Red. Sure was sorry to hear about Rae Washburn, though. I had no idea when I was ridin' out from Savannah that I'd end up goin' to *two* funerals today. Rae was always mighty good to me."

"She was good to a lot of people," Sam observed. "It's no wonder such numbers turned out to pay their final respects."

"I'll never forget the way she took me in the night I left Red. And then let me work for room and board until time for the surgery."

Up ahead, a Carter Sawmill pickup was parked in front of the clinic. But as Sam and Ida drew near, both were looking across the street at the morbidly quiet inn with the dark windows and padlocked doors.

"It looks right sad all closed up like that, don't it?"

"Yes," Sam affirmed. "It does."

"Rae don't have no kinfolk. Reckon the place will go back to Matt Tyler."

"*Go back?*" Sam questioned. "What do you mean?"

"Rae's Place used to be the old Tyler Inn. Must be fifteen years since Matt Tyler gave it over to Rae, *and* paid to get it fixed up and going."

"I never knew that story," Sam murmured.

"Maybe he'll need somebody to run the place."

Sam's eyes brightened. "You mean . . . you?"

Ida shrugged. "The mill's half mine now, but I don't want to live there. I was thinkin' I'd go back to Savannah. Maria said she'd help me look for a job. And then this mornin' I saw Rae's Place all shut down, and I thought—shoot, I've spent my whole life cookin' for folks and cleanin' up after 'em. Maybe I could do it for a livin'."

"I think that's a wonderful idea!"

"Good," Ida returned. "Maybe Matt Tyler will, too. I was beholdin' to Rae. It'd do my heart good to think I could carry on for her."

"I'm sure she'd like that," Sam quietly replied, her momentary buoyancy swiftly ebbing. They reached the pickup, and Sam was shocked as Hal climbed out, tipped his hat, and circled around to open the passenger's door.

"See what I mean?" Ida murmured with an arch look. "Right neighborly, wouldn't you say?"

"I'd say," Sam answered smilingly. Her heart lifted anew as she watched Ida walk off with astonishing grace, but then fell once more as the truck pulled away, and her gaze turned again to the building across the street.

Rae's Place. The establishment was appropriately named. Hopefully, Ida Carter would be able to build a new life there, but to Sam—and to many others, she was certain—the place would always carry Rae's indelible mark.

Now, as she peered through the misting rain, Sam could envision the familiar figure waving from the boardwalk as clearly as though she were truly there. Perhaps her spirit was. Turning through the gate, Sam proceeded up the walk to the clinic, and felt Rae's haunting presence with every step.

Friday, July 30
Savannah

The sun was going down as Drew took the familiar turns through the Historic District. As soon as he pulled over in front of the Tyler house, he spotted her. She was in the garden clipping roses—wearing a dress the color of her eyes, and a basket of fresh-cut blooms on her arm. Her hair was down, the light of sunset firing it to the hue of molten gold. His heart began the familiar tattoo.

Taking a deep breath, Drew tucked the compact recorder in his shirt pocket and walked up to the gate. Having noticed his approach, Lucy strolled between flowering bushes of pink, white, and scarlet, and met him at the walkway. A profusion of summer greenery and flowers provided a picturesque backdrop as she looked up and held forth her basket.

"Care to choose a rose?" she inquired.

Drew gazed down on her. The perfect face was flushed with color, reminding him of the afternoon when her cheeks had burned bright with a passion *he* had put there. If she never spoke to him again after today, at least he'd have that.

"Actually, I suppose I should offer you the entire basket," she added with a dimpling smile that again brought their intimacy hurtling back to the present. Coming from another woman, he wouldn't have questioned she was referring to their lovemaking; coming from Lucy . . .

"I must say I'm impressed with your bravado," she went on. "A fire, Drew? We only discussed tainting a barrel or two of wine."

The beginnings of his cautious smile evaporated. "I didn't set the fire, Lucy," he replied in a tone of disgust.

"You didn't?"

"No."

"Then, who . . ." She trailed off as he pulled the tape player from his pocket. "What's that?" she added.

"A pocket-size tape recorder."

"What's it for?"

"For recording and playing back."

Lucy gave him a miffed look. "I understand that, but—"

He switched on the machine, and her live voice broke off as her recorded words sounded out with admirable clarity: *"I tried the lawful way, and it got me nowhere. The time for this discussion is past, Drew. I've already made a bid on that Riverfront club you like in Savannah. There's nothing more for us to talk about, except the question of when you're finally going to take action."*

Drew pressed the stop button, and the garden spot dissolved in silence—but for the shriek of Lucy's blue eyes.

"I don't want to take this to the authorities," he said quietly. "But I will if you force my hand."

"What does this mean?" she breathed on a note of horror.

"It means I want you to give Matt a divorce—a *sensible* divorce that will put an end to the bloodsucking way you've been living your life for the past twelve years."

The shrieking eyes blinked. "And if I don't?"

"Like I said, I don't want to turn you in. But don't make the mistake of thinking you can twist me around your finger. It's over, Lucy. It's high time you stopped living like a witch, and started acting like a woman. I know you can. Remember?"

Her face had drained of color. Now, suddenly, it rushed back in a rosy flood.

"So, that was really all you wanted," she rasped as though she couldn't breathe. "To screw Lucy Beauregard. I'll bet you and Matt have shared some good laughs over that one."

Drew frowned down on her. "I haven't told Matt about that, or anyone for that matter."

"After this chicanery, how can you expect me to believe you?"

"I don't know," he replied solemnly. "But it's the truth."

"How could you do this to me? I thought I could trust you, depend on you. All these years I actually thought you—" She halted, her eyes glittering with a surprising sheen of tears.

"Go ahead. Say it."

"All right, then," Lucy spat. "I thought you loved me."

"I *do*," Drew admitted, his heart knocking as though it would ram through his chest. "At least I'd like to try."

"Go away, Drew!"

"No."

"Then I will!" Tossing the basket of roses to the ground, she whirled out of the gate, and ran down the sidewalk.

"Lucy!" he cried.

But Lucy paid no heed, the heels of her sandals clicking ever more swiftly as her legs churned in a way they hadn't in years. Her chest began to heave, her breaths burning down her throat as tears ran down her cheeks. With a quick swipe at her face, Lucy planted her palm at her aching side, and carried on—oblivious to the stares of the evening strollers she dashed past.

Finally, at the Riverfront, she ran out of room to run. Grasping the handrail, she peered unseeingly across the water as she gasped for breath.

"Lucy?" She looked around with a start to see Robert Larkin hurrying toward her, a look of concern on his face. The tears welled up again.

"Are you all right?" he anxiously asked as he came to her side.

"Oh, Uncle Bob!" She collapsed against his shoulder, and the abysmal story tumbled out in a sobbing torrent.

"There, there," he consoled when she finished. "Everything will be all right. You'll see."

Wiping the fresh tears from her cheeks, Lucy backed

away a step and met his eyes. "Everything will *not* be all right," she replied. "How could Drew do this to me?"

"Maybe because, with you, there's no other way. You drive people to desperate measures, Lucy. I'd say he beat you fair and square."

"I'd hardly call it fair. He tricked me. He used me."

"He outsmarted you," Robert put in.

"He *betrayed* me!" Lucy cried. "And now I stand to lose everything!"

"Maybe you have everything to gain."

"Like what?!"

"Like the freedom to begin a life worth living. Matt isn't the only one who's going to be free, you know. *You* will be, too. Did you stop to think maybe that's the reason Drew did this?"

She shook her head. "I don't—"

"Drew loves you, Lucy," Robert broke in. "Give him a chance, and I wager you'll find you can love him back."

She stared for a moment, then buried her forehead in a graceful hand. Robert put an arm around her shoulders.

"Come on," he said. "I'll walk you home."

They arrived at the Tyler gate to discover Drew sitting on the front steps. As he spotted them, he rose to his feet and peered in their direction, but made no move to approach.

"Go to him, Lucy," Robert urged.

"And say what?" she mumbled, her wet eyes shining in the fading light.

"In the old days you'd have marched up to him and ordered him off your property and out of your sight. Is that what you want to do now?"

"No," she answered after a moment.

"Then go to him, Lucy. He'll take it from there." She moved hesitantly to the gate and looked over her shoulder.

"Go on," Robert prodded, and flourished a hand as though shooing a fly.

Lucy turned to look up the walkway once more. Drew

tucked his hands in his trouser pockets, and returned her look. She began walking toward him, and experienced the sensation that the pavement came to life and carried her speeding to his feet. Suddenly she stood before him, and had no more idea of what to say or do than when she was outside the gate.

"You're still here," she murmured.

"Do you want me to go?" Drew replied in a deep voice.

Lucy gazed up at him, and was besieged once again by strange sensations. She'd known the man for years, but somehow felt as though she were seeing Drew for the first time. His handsomeness was nearly blinding; the provocative stir in her blood . . . dizzying.

"No," she admitted finally.

Withdrawing a hand from his pocket, he lifted it to her face, his thumb reaching to stroke a cheek. "Real tears," he noted quietly. "I've never seen you cry before."

"I've never felt this way before. All of a sudden, I don't know who I am."

"Want some help finding out?" Drew asked.

Lucy gazed into his searching eyes. "I think so," she mumbled, and saw the breaking of his white smile just before he stepped forward and took her in his arms.

Having watched from the gate until Lucy reached around Drew in an answering embrace, Robert gave his walking cane a lighthearted twirl and moved away. He smiled as he proceeded down the dusky street—breathing in the scent of roses on the river . . . savoring the flavor of romance in the air.

There was no place like Savannah.

Sunday, August 14

Sunday afternoon Sam drove to the airport to pick up Dr. Aaron Stein, who was slight and dark and sporting a sparsely filled-in beard that only made his boyish face look younger. She almost could have laughed. A Jewish whippersnapper from New York—almost as bad as a Catholic woman from Boston.

But he was undeniably enthusiastic, unquestionably bright ... and Sam couldn't get past a feeling of resentment. Tomorrow, after another trip to Savannah International, it would be *Aaron* in the driver's seat, *Aaron* returning to Riverbend while she left it behind. Now she knew how veteran executives must feel when abandoning their offices to bright-eyed newcomers.

On the way to Riverbend she tried to sketch a picture of the town and its way of life, but could see by the rather blank look on Aaron's face that he had no true comprehension of what she was saying. How could he? Like herself, he was a product of the city. Of the North. Tall buildings and busy streets did little to prepare one for the harsh grandeur of the rural South.

"You'll see," she said finally, and restricted the rest of her conversation to medical matters.

The sun was low when they crossed the town limits— its golden light shimmering on the oaks and bathing Main Street with a glow of charm. "This is it," Sam announced and pulled over in front of the clinic.

"It's very pretty," Aaron commented with a note of surprise.

Sam looked past the trim fence and immaculate lawn to the house, which—thanks to a vote by the town council—wore a fresh coat of white paint.

"Yes, it is," she confirmed proudly. "The proprietress of the inn across the street is a friend of mine, Ida Carter. She's expecting you for the night. Why don't we stop there first, and then I'll show you around the clinic?"

Aaron retrieved an overnight case from the back of the van, and they crossed the street, which was quiet as usual. Leading the way, Sam pushed through the saloon doors, and then leaped back as an explosion of voices shook the hall. There must have been fifty or sixty people crowded into Rae's Place—all of them shouting.

Sam's wide-eyed gaze darted to the ceiling, where a banner announced: WE'LL MISS DR. SAM ... then flew

across the sea of faces—Hannah, Celie, Ida, Nadine . . .
George, Justine, and their children . . . Drew and
Larry . . . the Ingrams, the Simons, the Pettigrews, the
Bishops . . . Sam put a hand to her mouth, and was
drawn into the noisy group by George Waters.

The bar was set with a Southern-style spread that
would have made Rae proud. Music played, tea and beer
flowed, and Sam spent the ensuing hour introducing
Aaron through the crowd. Everyone she would have expected was there . . . except for the glaring exception of
Matt.

"He said you'd understand why he couldn't make it tonight," Nadine explained when they found themselves
with a moment of privacy.

Sam released a heavy breath. "Knowing Matt, I guess
I do."

"He said to ask if you could stop by the vineyards tomorrow before you go."

"I'll stop by."

"He'll be out where the fire was."

"In the burned-out acres?" Sam questioned. "I'd have
thought he'd be busy getting the crop ready for harvest."

"Everybody else is," Nadine replied with a look of
concern. "But the past few days, Matt's been going at
those black fields like the devil himself was cracking the
whip."

Before Sam could learn more, Eloise Pettigrew
stepped forward and began tapping a spoon noisily
against a glass. When the crowd stilled to an expectant
hum, she walked over to Sam and offered a small package.

"As first lady of Riverbend," she announced, "it is my
pleasure to present you with this token of our best
wishes."

All eyes were on Sam as she tore the paper from the
box and lifted the lid. It was a beautiful lapel brooch,
gold with tiny amethysts set in the shape of a grape cluster.

"It's lovely," she whispered.

"Drew found it in Savannah, but we all chipped in," Eloise announced, and matter-of-factly proceeded to remove the ornament from the box and pin it to the collar of Sam's shirt. There was a wave of applause, and calls for a speech.

"I don't know what to say," Sam mumbled.

"That's a first," Drew hooted, and triggered a round of laughter through the crowd.

"I suppose that's true," Sam said, her smiling gaze traveling across the faces turned her way. "But right now, the only thing I can think to say is very simple. Thank you. The brooch is lovely, and I'll treasure it always—just as I'll treasure memories of all of you." There was a moment of solemn quiet.

"And she claimed she didn't know what to say," Drew challenged, once again eliciting laughter and putting the festive mood back in the air. The summer sun was down, and children beginning to nod, when the party broke up. Drew was the first to take his leave.

"I've got a hot date with Lucy," he said.

"I'm really happy things are working out for you, Drew."

"Thanks," he replied with a rare look of solemnity. "I wish they could have worked out for you and Matt as well."

"Me, too," Sam quietly agreed. Opening his arms, Drew moved close and gave her a hearty embrace.

"You take care of yourself up there in the big city, now," he teased as he walked away, the rakish grin back in place.

Sam made it through the goodbyes that followed with what she considered to be admirable composure.

Even Celie . . . "I'm gonna miss you, Dr. Sam," she said, her dark eyes shining.

"You've got my address," Sam murmured as she hugged the girl. "You'd better write."

Even Nadine . . . "I sure do hate to see you go, honey. I can feel it in my bones that you're taking a wrong turn."

"This is hard enough as it is," Sam replied as she

stretched a fond arm around the plump shoulders. "Let's not bring your bones into it, okay?"

Ironically enough, it was Edwin Pettigrew who nearly made her crumble.

"I'll certainly strive to serve you well," Aaron was saying. "In time I hope you'll come to trust and depend on me."

"Don't worry, son," the mayor replied, his gaze turning to Sam. "We've been broke in by the best." When the old codger slipped her a wink, Sam was forced to spin around as the tears she'd been holding back sprang to the surface.

That night, as she sought sleep in the old house for the last time, memories turned relentlessly through her mind. She tried to stop the carousel with thoughts of home. Tomorrow night Mother and Father would pick her up at the airport. The following evening she was having dinner with John Thomason. In a week she'd be back at St. Elizabeth's. But all of it seemed foreign and unreal, and did nothing to bring on a restful state.

She rose early the next morning, treated herself to a long shower, and took her time dressing in the light beige travel suit she'd selected. Pinning the amethyst brooch to the lapel, Sam packed the last of her things, Aaron arrived, and the hours began to fly. His bags came in, hers went out. They toured the clinic, reviewed the records, discussed patients. It was midafternoon when the two of them reached a mutually comfortable stopping point.

"It's a good thing you booked an evening flight," Aaron observed. "When do you think we should leave for the airport?"

For the past few hours Sam had managed to keep the sense of dread at bay. Now it bloomed through her mind, and went spiraling down her spine.

"Soon, Aaron," she replied. "There's one last house call I have to make."

Summer sunlight flooded the vineyards, which were as green and lush and breathtaking as the first time she saw them. Sam had the feeling of having come full circle, particularly when the boom of a propane cannon split the air. "Damn birds," she muttered.

Once again, she turned through the banks of vines and made the drive toward the charred acres. As she approached, her gaze drifted to the forest, she recalled the day she found the condemning dandelions, and she looked swiftly in the opposite direction. It was then that she spotted Matt some distance to the west. Shirtless as usual, he was wearing the familiar getup of jeans and cowboy hat as he shoveled rubble into the bed of a pickup.

Turning at the perimeter of the fire site, Sam drove to a point parallel to where he was working. As she pulled into his line of vision, he straightened from his task. She got out of the van and moved to the edge of the scarred ground. The stretch of earth before her was rough and black, like a lava field spewed forth from a vanished volcano. And there was Matt, smack in the middle of it, pitting his bare back against the desolation. Tossing the shovel aside, he walked to meet her—big as a mountain, dark as night, his chest and arms streaked with soot.

"Beautiful savage," Sam murmured before he came within earshot.

"So, this is it," he said as he arrived.

She barely lifted her shoulders. "This is it."

"You're free and clear, and on your way to a glorious future in Boston." His gaze swept the length of her. "And you certainly look the part."

"I'm not sure whether to say thank you to that, or not."

Matt offered a small smile. "You look damn good, Sam. But then you always did."

"You always did, too."

Spreading his work-gloved hands, he glanced down the front of himself. "Even now?" he challenged.

"*Especially* now," Sam replied, her eyes reaching for his across the few feet of ground that separated them.

Matt's arms fell to his side as he took a slow step closer. "Is that the pin they gave you last night?"

She lifted a hand to her lapel. "Yes. I love it."

"Grapes, huh?"

"Yes," she affirmed with a slight smile. "Grapes."

His gaze rose from the brooch to her face. "I figured you'd know why I didn't show at your party. Saying goodbye is going to be tough enough without doing it in front of the whole town."

"I know," Sam agreed quietly. "I've been dreading this moment for a long time, and now it's here."

Matt shifted his weight to one leg in the familiar way, and studied her from beneath the shadowing brim of his hat. "*This moment* doesn't have to be happening at all. No one's forcing you to go back to Boston. You're going because you want to."

The accusation in his voice cut like a knife. Sam met his perusal with a steady gaze.

"Is wanting to fulfill a life's ambition such a travesty?" she questioned.

"I'm the wrong one to ask."

"I wonder if you've ever considered the years I worked and trained toward one goal, Matt. And I finally made it. I'm a surgeon. At Saint Elizabeth's I used to perform on the average of twelve to eighteen procedures a week. Do you know how many I've done this year in Riverbend? None. Not one."

He folded his massive arms. "I thought the point of being a doctor was helping people—like you did with Nadine and Ida and Celie and who knows how many others. Don't they count for anything?"

"Of *course*, they count for something," Sam snapped. "You're being deliberately obtuse."

A smile flickered over Matt's lips. "And you're losing your temper. You always start throwing around the big words when you lose your temper."

"One thing is certain," she returned. "You can make me lose it faster than anyone I've ever met."

Matt laughed at that, and it was like a sweet echo ringing from the past. But the sound faded quickly away, as did the brightness of his passing smile. His gaze locked with hers, and an odd feeling of expectancy gripped the pit of Sam's stomach. Then he swept off his hat, and sunlight showered his hair and eyes.

"Sam," he began in a husky tone. "In two weeks I'll be free—finally, legally free to build a life that matters. Along with that gift, God has let me find the woman I want to build it with. I'm asking you to marry me, and have children with me. I'm asking you please ... don't go."

Sam's heart was pounding at such a pitch that for a moment she couldn't speak. She reached up to cup his cheek in her palm.

"Matt," she said finally. "You know I have to go." Wrenching away from her touch, he pierced her with a glaring look. "But that doesn't mean I don't care—"

"So, old Juda wins after all," he cut in.

"What does Juda have to do with anything?"

"You might be right about Mary being poisoned by lead, but *she* was right about the future of the Tylers. She cursed us to wither, and we have. When I cash in, the family will be no more."

"Wait a minute," Sam objected heatedly. "Let me get this straight. Are you blaming *me* for Juda's curse?"

"I spent my whole life searching," Matt stated. "And I know this feeling will never come again."

Sam regarded him with flashing eyes. "It isn't fair to heap *old Juda's* victory on my head, Matt. You've traveled to Boston before, and you could travel there again. Plenty of people stay in touch from miles apart. *You're* the one putting an end to this."

"And *you're* the one still trying to make me ride a fence I damn well ain't gonna ride," he boomed. "I told you months ago, and I'm telling you now. I want the real thing, Sam—not another long-distance affair."

"Sometimes people can't have everything exactly the way they want it," she replied, her voice rising shrilly. "Sometimes people actually have to compromise."

"You tell me how to compromise raising a family between Boston and Riverbend! Tell me that!"

"Well, maybe you could give up your beloved vineyards and move up north!"

Matt shook his head. "You're right. I love the vineyards. They've been the only thing I *could* love for a long time. But that's not the bottom-line reason I won't leave. There are too many people counting on me here. I couldn't walk out on them even if I wanted to. It has to be you, Sam. *You* have to make the move."

Sam's breast heaved with thrashing emotion. Tension-wrought seconds ticked by as she stared wordlessly into his eyes. They were filled with sunlight, glittering like pieces of gold.

"But you won't," Matt supplied finally. With a vicious slap of his hat against his pants leg, he crammed it low on his brow and began backing away. "Hey, thanks a lot for stopping by," he added with sarcastic lightness. "Have a nice life, huh?"

With that, he turned on his booted heel and started back toward the truck. Sam stood there and watched—seething and aching—as he picked up the shovel and jammed it into a pile of debris. So, this was how it would end. Part of her longed to run after Matt and swat him with his damn shovel; the larger part was drugged with a sadness that sought to root her feet to the ground as she stalked back to the van.

Scant hours later the jet was in the air and on its way to Boston. Sam peered out the window, immune to the showcase of the starry night sky. In her mind the sun continued to shine, blazing across the Georgia countryside, gleaming on Matt's broad shoulders as he faced up to the seemingly endless stretch of blackened acres.

Chapter Twenty

Saturday, September 17

It was barely nine o'clock on a Saturday night. Harvest was proceeding so smoothly that a rare day of rest had been declared for Sunday. In the old days Matt would have settled with Drew, Larry, and Edwin at the front table in Rae's Place—a night of cards and drink in store. But things were different now.

Drew was in Savannah, escorting Lucy to one of her high-society affairs. And although Larry and Edwin provided their usual camaraderie, the ebullient spirit Matt had always found in Rae's Place was gone. Pushing back from the table, he rose to his feet.

"See ya later, boys," he said, and calling a good evening to Ida, pushed through the saloon doors. Ida was doing an excellent job, but each time Matt went inside his old haunt, he sensed a giant hole where Rae used to be. He paused on the boardwalk and looked across the street. Similarly, every time he saw the clinic, he couldn't help but picture Sam inside it.

A shadow crossed the lighted parlor window, and Matt's heart did a ridiculous leap. The realization that he was getting excited over the image of Aaron Stein prodded him off the boardwalk and into his Jeep.

Stein seemed to be an adequate doctor, and a nice enough guy, but it had turned out he couldn't make it in the Georgia countryside. According to Celie, he'd proved allergic to every pollen in the area, and spent most of his time sneezing his head off. The upshot was he'd negotiated a transfer with the corps. Soon, the clinic would be empty once more; though of course to Matt's thinking, it had been empty since the day Sam left.

The night was warm and sultry, the wind coursing past his ears with the songs of crickets as he drove back to the chateau. Thoughts of Sam closed in on him once more, and the image of green eyes danced beyond the headlights.

She'd been gone a month, and each day—despite the absorbing work of harvest—Matt had only felt the loss more sharply. This was what he'd tried to avoid by steering clear of her all those months. But it hadn't made any difference. Maybe Drew was right. Maybe he should have taken what he could get while he had the chance. At this point, he didn't see how it could have made things any worse.

Parking the Jeep by the front entrance, Matt noted the chateau's dark windows and remembered that Nadine was at George and Justine's for the night. The deserted house was depressingly silent. He climbed the stairs to his bedroom and switched on the stereo. The notes of a moody sax filtered from the speakers, and he was reminded of the rainy afternoon Sam had come to him wearing nothing but his bathrobe. The same kind of sexy jazz had been playing that day.

Stalwartly burying the thought, Matt decided to take a shower, and stripped off his clothes. But when he walked into the bath, the image of Sam returned once more, this time standing naked in the shower and extending an inviting hand.

"Dammit," he muttered, and plowing through the memory, stepped into the stall and turned the water icy cold.

But on this night, nothing could chase Sam away for

long. As soon as Matt stretched out on the bed, thoughts
of her returned, and he found his eyes turning to the
phone on the bedside table. He knew the number of her
parents' house by heart . . . assuming she was still staying
there.

He could call to say he was sorry for the way they
parted—which he was. But hell, Sam knew that. He
would be calling purely to hear her voice. She'd know
that, too. And it would solve nothing.

God, what was he going to do in another week when
harvest was over and he had nothing to fill his time but
gnawing memories? Maybe he'd fly to Boston and haul
her back, kicking and screaming. Maybe he'd buckle
under and crawl, agreeing to see her on whatever terms
she'd allow. Maybe he'd just lose his mind, like an addict
forced to go without a fix.

As the night wore on, Matt dialed the Boston number
in his mind a dozen times, but never reached for the
phone.

Tuesday, September 27
Boston

Standing by the doctors' lounge window with a cup of
coffee, Sam gazed pensively across the city, which was
veiled with a cool, gray, autumn drizzle. In Riverbend
the sun was probably pouring from a clear sky, showering
the landscape with the shimmer of Indian summer. The
thought of it continued to hang in the shadows of her
mind as though she'd left it only yesterday.

Taking a sip of coffee, Sam continued to peer out the
window. The city was the same. St. Elizabeth's was the
same. And when she was in surgery, she felt the same
vibrant urgency she'd always felt. But there was no denying that everything seemed different, nor that the difference lay entirely in herself.

She never would have believed it. Boston was boring.

Comparing it to the daily challenge of Riverbend was like putting a bland bagel next to Georgia pecan pie.

"How did the appendectomy go?"

Sam glanced around to meet John Thomason's eyes. "Everything according to expectations," she answered absently.

"Made any progress finding an apartment?"

"Not yet."

"Do you *want* to find an apartment, Sam?"

Finally giving him her full attention, Sam found John studying her the same way she'd seen him size up a hundred patients. "What does that look mean?" she asked.

"Frankly, you haven't been the same since you came back. Oh, I don't mean your work has suffered any. You're brilliant as always in the O.R. But to anyone who knows you, it's obvious that your mind is somewhere else. I can only guess it's in Riverbend."

"I was there for a year, John. Don't you think it's natural for me to think of it now and then?"

"Now and then, yes. Every moment you're not working, no."

Stepping away from the window, Sam gave him a fleeting smile. "I'll get over it," she said.

But as she took the rail back to Dorcester that afternoon, she wondered—*would* she get over it? Would she stop seeing Matt in every tall stranger she happened to pass? Would she stop dreaming about him and thinking about him through every idle minute? One night last week she'd stared at the phone for nearly an hour—prickling with the sensation that he was going to call. He hadn't. And although she'd fabricated the whole thing, she'd felt the letdown for days.

If she didn't put Riverbend behind her, she was going to drive herself crazy. She'd been replaced, and the town was in good hands with Aaron Stein. Then why did she keep feeling as though she'd deserted her true purpose when she'd thought she was returning to it? Surely, if that were the case, there would have been some kind of sign besides her private, emotional turmoil.

Preoccupied and moody, Sam walked into the town house only to have her mother hurry over and whisper: "Chad's in the parlor."

"Etheridge?" Sam questioned, and received a look that said—*Of course, Etheridge! What other Chad is there?*

She stepped to the parlor threshold. He was seated in Father's chair, and as usual, was elegantly groomed and dressed. But since last Christmas, the thought of Chad had stirred nothing more than a mild sense of distaste. As she walked in, he sent her a lazy smile.

"So, you stuck it out the whole year," he said.

"There was never any doubt," Sam lied.

"I imagine that stud I met at Christmas helped to make it cozy."

"What do you want, Chad?" she demanded. "I don't feel like sparring with you. There's no point."

Finally, he rose to his feet and swaggered up to her. "There's a point." His blue eyes sought hers as he reached up to brush a lock of hair behind her shoulder. "And you *know* what I want."

Sam was spared the oncoming overture by her mother's timely intrusion. "This came for you today, Sam," she said, offering a letter as she directed a cool look to Chad. "From Riverbend."

"It's from Celie," Sam announced excitedly. Turning her back to Chad, she tore into the envelope.

Dear Dr. Sam,

It seems like a long time since you left. A lot has happened. Ida's doing great at Rae's Place. Hannah has started helping her out most days. Grape harvest is in.

Mr. Matt's throwing a street dance Saturday night. His divorce is over, but he still doesn't seem happy like he used to be. And I know why.

Dr. Stein is a real nice man, but it turned out he's allergic to most everything that grows around here. He left yesterday for what he called "an urban post." So,

*now we're out of a doctor again. I guess they'll send
somebody else one of these days.*

   *I'll bet you love being back at St. Elizabeth's, but I
can't help wishing you were here. I miss you.*

   Love, Celie

By the time Sam finished the note, her face had taken on
a vibrant warmth. "This is it," she murmured. "This is
the sign. If I had the sense God gave a mule . . ."

   "If you had *what*?" Chad questioned.

   Sam looked around to find such a look of horror on his
perfect face that she broke into a merry laugh.

   "You'll have to excuse me," she said. "I've got a phone
call to make to the National Health Service Corps."

   "What's happening, Sam?" her mother anxiously asked.

   "Remember when you said you wanted fair warning if
your daughter was moving? Well, I'm giving you fair
warning."

   "Oh, my heavens," her mother murmured.

   "Moving where?" Chad bellowed. "Why are you calling the corps?"

   "To tell them they've just placed a permanent doctor
in Riverbend."

   "You must be joking."

   With a beaming smile, Sam shook her head and
backed away. "Goodbye, Chad," she said when she
reached the threshold. "And I *do* mean good*bye*, honey,"
she drawled, and laughed for pure joy as she hurried
down the hall.

Two weeks later Sam drove the old van through the
countryside with clashing feelings of excitement and
trepidation—like a player with everything riding on a
single roll of the dice. She'd surrendered her post, her
life, and her future in Boston to return to Riverbend.
What if it had changed? What if Matt had changed?

   She kept telling herself that *now* was not the time to
worry about such things, but couldn't seem to stop.
Maybe she should have notified them she was coming in-

stead of keeping it a surprise. Maybe not. What the hell . . . it was too late now.

Evening was closing in as Sam crossed the town limits. She slowed the van, her heart swelling at the familiar sights, the remembered quiet, even the smell of the air. Parking in front of the clinic, she got out and looked across the street. Lights were blazing at Rae's Place, and there appeared to be a fair-sized supper crowd within.

Proceeding to the rear of the van, Sam started unloading her bags. Hannah was the first to emerge from the inn. Running out of Rae's Place with Jason on her hip, she was swiftly followed by Celie and Ida—who was moving at a startling pace—and apparently everyone inside the place.

Sam laughed as the crowd enfolded her, pelting her with questions at such a rate that she couldn't possibly answer any of them. As Larry, Edwin, and several of the men grabbed her luggage and took the lead to the house, she failed to notice Drew's car scratching off toward the square.

Fifteen minutes later the parlor was filled with chattering folk when the door burst open and Matt strode in. Sam's heart flew to her throat. He was wearing the customary close-fitting jeans, open-front shirt, and cowboy hat. She didn't know how he could be bigger and more handsome than she remembered, but he seemed so.

"Hello, stranger," he said, and swept off his hat.

"Hello, Matt," she replied.

As her eyes locked with the amber ones of her memories, Sam was dimly conscious of Celie and Hannah hustling the crowd out the door, and completely unaware of the knowing smiles of the folk who made a hasty exit.

"What does this mean?" Matt asked when they were alone.

"It means I'm back."

"For how long?"

"I was thinking fairly long-term."

Shifting to one leg, he attained the old, sexy stance as he studied her. But he didn't say anything—just peered at her as though she'd spoken in a foreign language. Sam strolled up to him.

"I thought a lot about Juda when I was in Boston," she said.

"You thought about Juda," he repeated in a tone suggesting she'd lost her mind.

"I really don't like the idea of a voodoo witch winning out in the end—I mean, particularly when I have the means to thwart her curse once and for all."

"*You* have the means?" Matt said.

"If I say so myself, I come from a long line of very productive people. Look at Mother—eight children, and twins run in the family. If I put my mind to it, there's no telling how many little Tylers I could turn out before I was done."

"Did you say, *Tylers?*"

"I'm not interested in any other kind," Sam replied. The silence grew heavy. God, had she waited too long? "I guess I had to go back to discover the truth, Matt. I found out I can live without Boston, but I'm not too sure about doing without you."

"You mean you're still not sure?" he returned in a deep voice.

Sam trembled with conviction. "I've never been more sure of anything in my life."

The smile that broke across Matt's face came slowly, but it spread until it seemed to light the room. "Are you, by any chance, asking me to marry you, Doc?"

"Well, I didn't come back from Boston to pick grapes."

Matt grabbed her and twirled her around. "God, I love you, Sam."

"I love you, too."

"I know. I've known it from the start."

"You have not."

"I have, too. You haven't been able to get me off your mind since we first met."

Drawing back, Sam stared into his twinkling eyes. "You truly are the most arrogant man, you know that?"

"And boorish," Matt mumbled as he bent to her mouth. "Don't forget boorish."

He kissed her, and once again Sam caught fire—only this time she clasped him to her with no reservations, no questions, no shadows creeping into the light. They were both free—he, of a shackling marriage; she, of a long-cherished dream.

She would always love Boston—but from a distance. And she would always love practicing medicine—but as part of her life, not the sum of it. Like the man she adored had told her from the start, she was a woman as well as a doctor. And as a woman, Sam had everything she needed right there in her arms.